I0738405

THE
GLOAMING

J.R. SCHUYLER

Lucid Prose Publishing

First edition: October 2019

Cover design by Adriatica Creations
Formatting by Polgarus Studio
Editing by Dominion Editorial

ISBN: 978-0-473-49145-1 (paperback)
ISBN: 978-0-473-49146-8 (kindle ebook)
ISBN: 978-0-473-49147-5 (epub ebook)

Published by Lucid Prose Publishing

Contents

PART ONE

August 11, 2013

Chapter One

IT CAME WITH a strong wind on All Hallows' Eve and again for a thousand moons thereafter. The lesser-educated among Morton's citizens spun frightful tales of a shadow monster with crimson eyes and claws more than two feet in length. The scholars spurned their words, publicly declaring them to be nothing more than the fanciful imaginings of youth. But in the privacy of their homes, even the scholars tossed and turned and whimpered in their sleep, haunted by phantasms of a creature they knew was all too real.

Billy Porter shivered and burrowed deeper under his blankets as raindrops beat against the tin roof. He was ten years old today—quite old enough for his own room, thank you very much. After months of whining, his parents had finally, if reluctantly, granted his request. The small space only allowed for a wire-frame bed and a moth-eaten dresser, but he treasured it nonetheless.

"*Don't open the curtains after dusk,*" his mother had warned, handing him a brass candelabra. "*Light the candles if you need to, but don't turn on the lights or go near the window under any circumstances.*"

The candelabra stood on his dresser now, casting ghostly shadows across the bedroom. He'd lit the candles at nightfall, but the sullen flames were no match for the howling wind that seeped through the tiny gaps in the window sash. The light had flickered and died, but the faint odor of smoke lingered on.

I've got to be brave, Billy told himself firmly. He pulled the covers up to his eyes and peered into the all-encompassing darkness. *I can't go crying to Mom every time I hear a scary noise. I'm not a baby anymore.*

If Mother Nature heard his thoughts, she interpreted them as a challenge. Wind whipped the house with increased intensity, lifting garden furniture and hurling it against the weatherboards. A child living in any other part of Kansas would assume a tornado was on its way and make haste for the storm cellar. Things were different in Morton. Here, the raging gales were a sign that something far worse was coming.

A faint *snick* met Billy's ear, and he jumped out of his skin. Dark shapes flitted behind the curtain, performing an unnatural puppet show. He squeezed his eyes shut. *I can't do this. The monster's right outside. It's going to eat me, I just know it. I've got to get out!*

The pressure in his chest grew until he realized he'd forgotten to keep breathing. The resulting inrush of air came as a bittersweet relief. Sweet because he was no longer on the verge of fainting; bitter because he still had to deal with whatever lay in wait.

Two minutes passed before Billy dared to make his move. He peeked out from under the blankets, wide eyes fixed on the silhouette at the window. Its jerky movements reminded him of the skydancer at Foley's Gas Station. The accompanying squeal of claws on glass sounded like something out of a horror movie. He threw off the blankets and made a blind dash for the door. The metal handle struck the center of his palm, and he wrenched it open. He risked a glance over his shoulder, heart thudding. *It's gone. It must be looking for another way in.*

Spurred into action, Billy tiptoed past the room he used to share with his two younger brothers. James and Hamish could sleep through anything, be it a thunderstorm or a rock concert, but he didn't want to risk being the exception to the rule. As long as they stayed put, their boarded-up windows would keep them safe. In theory, anyway.

Billy shuffled into the kitchen without turning on the lights. His mother's warnings echoed through his brain. *The monster's attracted to electric lights. It senses these things. It knows...*

He shivered, rubbing his arms with both hands. Nightfall sent local temperatures plummeting by at least eighty degrees Fahrenheit, even at the height of summer. Mr. Graham, Morton Elementary's science teacher, claimed it was due to climate change. Billy wanted to believe him, but his father insisted the whole thing was a load of rot. The real cause, he insisted, was "those demons from out East." Confused, but too afraid to question him, Billy accepted the explanation and let the words rattle around his head when he couldn't sleep.

"Where are the matches?" Billy whispered. *Mom usually keeps them in the top drawer, but we used the last box to light my candles. There's got to be spares somewhere.*

He fumbled with the cupboard doors one by one and reached inside. Unable to see in the dark, he let his hands do the work. A stack of porcelain plates and a glass mixing bowl met his fingertips. He explored a bit farther, feeling along the shelf until he found a rectangular object. *A mousetrap?* He pulled back in alarm. Even with his quick reflexes, it nearly flayed the skin off his hand.

No matches here, he thought, wincing. *Is it even worth finding them? If I relight the candles, the wind will just blow them out again.*

Theoretically, he could block the gap in the window with an old T-shirt, but that would require going near the window in the first place—an action that, aside from being expressly forbidden, was too terrifying to even consider.

I'll have to sleep on the sofa tonight, Billy decided, abandoning his search. *I don't want to go back to my room with that monster creeping around, and I'm too old to crawl into my parents' bed. I'll sneak back at dawn. Before my brothers get up.*

The more he thought about it, the more confident he felt. He closed the cupboard doors and padded down the hallway, carefully avoiding the creaky floorboards outside his parents' room. The lounge door was ajar, which gave Billy pause. His mother always closed it before she retired to bed. He tiptoed toward the door, fear creeping back into his chest. His parents' hushed voices emanated from inside.

"I used to think Bowers was a respectable fella," Mr. Porter rasped, his Texan drawl more pronounced than usual. Billy froze, not wanting to miss a word. "'Course, now we know he's one of them. Why else would he let those two devil spawn join the police? Answer me that one, eh?"

"You're letting your imagination get away with you, Jerry," Mrs. Porter replied. "If Chief Bowers thinks they can help, then maybe it's for the best."

"'Course they can help! They're in on it, aren't they? We didn't have no monsters before the wraiths came, and after they showed up, boom! Monsters. Their little pet is tearing this town apart. We oughta do something about it."

"The monster?"

"The wraiths! If we kill 'em all, maybe their pet will go away too."

A coughing, spluttering fit came over Mr. Porter, followed by short, breathy wheezing. He'd developed a bad case of bronchitis the previous winter, and it never went away. Every time he got worked up about something, he coughed until his eyes watered, and his face grew redder than a tomato.

"You need to calm down," Mrs. Porter said. "You'll wake the children with the way you're carrying on."

"There's too much excitement in this town," he said between gasps. "I've got a rifle and a night vision scope in the gun safe. A couple hours' hunting and we can live in peace again."

Mrs. Porter's voice hardened. "You want to murder innocent children?"

"Nothing innocent about 'em. They'd do the same to us if we gave 'em half a chance. Let me guess. You want to get a government man in to do everything nice and proper. Well, sweetheart, we've already tried that. Ol' Winston sent a petition to the White House and you know what they gave us? A bunch of white coats. Head shrinks. To them, we're nothing more than a bunch of superstitious backcountry hicks in league with the UFO nuts. They ain't gonna do nothing to help us. Meanwhile, those *things* are terrorizing our neighborhood."

"Jerry…"

"I mean, they're not even *human*, are they?"

Another coughing fit seized his body, and this time, he kept spluttering for several minutes.

"You really need to get that cough checked out," Mrs. Porter said, the frown evident in her voice. "What will happen to us if you come down with pneumonia?"

"It's just… just bronchitis. Don't you fuss over me."

"If you say so. Where's your inhaler?"

"I must have left it in the study. I don't need it… I don't want…"

"I'll get it for you. If you keep this up, no one in this house will be able to sleep tonight."

The sound of muted footsteps brought Billy rushing back to the present. *She's coming! I've got to hide! But where?*

The clothes tree at the end of the hall looked promising. He dove behind his mother's faux-fur coat mere seconds before the lady herself opened the lounge door. She passed him in a blur of pink, unlocked the study, and went in. Before he could so much as think about moving, she exited with the inhaler and returned to the lounge. Billy sighed in relief. She'd been too focused on her ailing husband to notice her eldest son's presence.

Billy freed himself from the coat and crept over to the study. He'd been forbidden from entering without supervision, but a wild new idea took hold of him and he ignored the rule.

The gun safe…

Mrs. Porter had left the keys on the desk, right next to the keyboard. Easy pickings, as long as he didn't get caught. Without hesitation, Billy unlocked the safe. LED strips lined the interior, illuminating the plethora of firearms crammed inside. Billy reached for a gleaming revolver, then paused, listening for any hint of danger. Other than his parents' muted voices, he heard nothing.

Sucking in a deep breath, Billy took the revolver and hid it in the waistband of his pajama pants. His father wouldn't miss it. He had two more exactly like it, and he preferred to use a rifle anyway. *Now I just need some ammo. Dad usually keeps it in the other safe, but I don't know the combination for the lock. Maybe I can find some lying around his office instead.*

A few minutes of quiet searching turned up a handful of suitable bullets. Billy took them and crept down the hallway. His parents still occupied the lounge, but the gun gave him the courage to return to his room. If the monster dared to show its face, he'd take it down. *I'll be a hero! And Dad might give up on his plan to shoot the wraith kids!*

None of the adults seemed to like the wraiths, but Billy couldn't understand why. Sure, they looked a little strange, and they had funny names, but most of them minded their own business. If he could take out this monster, whatever it was, then things might settle down for a while. Life might return to a semblance of normalcy.

Taking a deep breath, Billy inched the door open to his room. He half-expected the monster to jump out at him, but the attack never came. He shuffled inside and shut the door with a quiet click. The bullets were heavy in his hands. *I should have loaded the gun before I came in here.* Heart racing, he found the courage to look at the window. The monster hadn't returned.

It's probably moved on to another house, Billy thought. *That's what it always does. I could turn on the light to bring it back, but Mom and Dad would have a fit if they noticed. I'll lie down and see what happens. If it doesn't come back, there's always tomorrow.*

He bundled himself into bed, grateful for the warmth his blankets provided. The chamber of the revolver popped open, and he placed the bullets inside. For a moment, he thought about cradling it in his arms as he slept so he'd be ready if the monster came back. Even through his drowsy fear, though, his father's lecture on gun safety came back to him.

"You'll blow your own head open if you keep it under your pillow," he'd said. *"Better to keep it on your nightstand with the safety on."*

Billy hadn't expected to need the advice, but he was grateful for it now. He placed the gun on the dresser, keeping his eyes fixed on the curtains. Anxious seconds dragged into uneventful minutes, and as the minutes stretched into hours, he drifted into an uneasy sleep.

Chapter Two

A DISTANT CRASH roused Billy from his slumber. He leapt out of bed, fumbling for the revolver. After a couple of heart-stopping moments, his gaze fell on the beige curtains and the golden sunbeams splayed across them. The blessed unexpectedness of dawn brought him back to the present, sucking the night's terror out of him like poison from a wound.

Mrs. Porter's sing-song voice echoed down the hallway. "Wakey, wakey, boys! Time to get up!"

All thoughts of the shadow monster vanished in the face of a more imminent danger. Billy yanked open the top drawer of his dresser and shoved the revolver inside, burying it amidst the rumpled T-shirts, holey socks, and patched-up jeans. He shuddered to think what would happen if his mother saw the gun. *It'll be worse than a grounding, that's for sure.*

Mrs. Porter rapped her knuckles against his bedroom door and entered without waiting for a response. "Billy, time to... Oh! You're already up. Breakfast in ten minutes? I'm making pancakes."

"Sounds great, Mom," Billy said. His heart hammered when she gave the dresser a cursory glance.

"Well, it *is* the first day of school. You deserve something special."

She left the room, shutting the door behind her, and Billy fell flat on his bed. *That was close. I need to get the gun out of here as soon as I can. If the monster doesn't show up tonight, I'll put it back in Dad's safe.*

That or try to find a better hiding spot.

When his heart stopped racing, Billy grabbed some clothes and went to the bathroom for a quick shower. He hated showers. The tepid water dribbling from the nozzle did nothing to warm him up in winter or cool him off in summer. It didn't even get all the shampoo out of his hair. The only benefit of showering, as far as he could tell, was that it kept his mother happy.

He returned to his room with two minutes to spare—long enough to get his things ready for school. His books, decorated with cut-outs of action heroes, sat in a neat pile beside his brand-new satchel.

"Backpacks are lame," he'd informed his mother when they went shopping for school supplies. *"Everyone else wears a satchel."*

"They're bad for your back," she'd retorted.

"But Mom—"

"If the kid wants a satchel, let him have a satchel," Mr. Porter cut in. *"They last longer than backpacks anyway."*

In the end, his mother gave in, and he became the proud owner of a plain black messenger bag. It might not be as fancy as the ones he'd seen at school, but it would help him to fit in.

And that's all that really matters, Billy mused.

He shoved his books inside, along with his new pencil case and a shoebox of toy soldiers. Several soldiers escaped the loose-lidded box, but he made no move to put them back inside. He'd bought them specifically for his summer project on the civil war, intending to glue them to a hand-drawn map of the battlefield. Unfortunately, his brothers had wanted to play with them first, and he wouldn't be able to put the finishing touches on his project until he got to school.

Billy carried his satchel to the front door, then backtracked to the lounge. Mr. Porter leaned forward in his chair, pawing at the laces of his work boots. His hawk-like eyes locked on to Billy's face.

"Finished your breakfast already?" he asked.

"Not yet. I need to get my poster for class presentations."

"Well, you'd better be quick about it. The foreman needs me on-site at eight-thirty sharp. If you ain't ready, you'll have to walk."

"Okay, Dad."

Billy walked to the bookcase and stretched as high as he could. With the tips of his fingers, he grabbed a sheet of A3 paper from the top shelf. Green pencil lines covered most of the map section, showing the borders of Morton as they existed today. Black circles showed where major historical battles took place. He'd spent hours poring over old newspapers to make it as accurate as possible.

I bet even Ms. Clemmons doesn't know about the Battle of Turnpike Hill, he thought.

Mr. Porter cleared his throat, and all thoughts of self-congratulation faded from Billy's mind. He carried the poster to his satchel, rolling it up as he walked, and tucked it into the side pocket.

"Billy! James! Hamish! Pancakes are ready."

The smell of fresh batter and maple syrup wafted into Billy's nostrils, and he hurried to his seat at the kitchen counter. His younger brothers raced into the room soon after, clad in their pajamas.

"What am I going to do with you two?" Mrs. Porter shook her head at their disheveled appearance. "You can't go to school like that."

"I guess we'll have to stay home instead," James teased, taking a bite of his pancakes. "Mmm, these are really good. Thanks, Mom."

Mrs. Porter refused to be distracted from her crusade. "I'll dress you myself if I have to."

James grimaced. "I'll do it, I'll do it. Soon as I finish eating. Promise."

"Do we have to go to school, Mommy?" Hamish asked.

Billy leaned over and ruffled the boy's hair in sympathy. "'Course we do. How else are we supposed to get a good job when we grow up?"

"But what if the monster catches us?"

Mrs. Porter crossed the kitchen in four short strides and wrapped her arms around him. "Sweetie, I've told you before. The monster only comes out at night."

"What if it makes the sun go down early?"

"The monster doesn't have any control over the sun, darling." She released Hamish and pointed at the window above the sink. "Look, isn't it a beautiful day outside? Lots of sun, no wind, and no monsters."

In spite of himself, Billy looked too. It *was* a beautiful day—far too nice to waste sitting indoors for hours on end. "Hey, tell you what, Hamish. How about we go to the park after school and get some ice cream?"

The sniffling stopped. "You mean it?"

"Sure!" Billy said. He'd learned early on that ice cream was the cure to all ills where Hamish was involved. "I got some birthday money from Gran. You can have any flavor you like."

"Can I have ice cream too?" James asked.

Billy shrugged. "If you want."

James whooped excitedly and tore off down the hallway to get dressed. Flashing Billy a thankful smile, Mrs. Porter collected their empty plates and rinsed them in the sink. Playing the big brother role exhausted Billy sometimes, but he loved it all the same. Taking responsibility made him feel grown-up—like he could deal with anything. In a town like Morton, that kind of confidence couldn't be taken for granted.

"You boys ready yet?" Mr. Porter barked, striding in from the lounge.

Billy gave him a mock salute. "Yes, sir."

"At least *someone* is. Hamish, you ain't even dressed yet. Chop, chop. And tell James to get a move on while you're at it."

The clock read 8:28 a.m. by the time they were ready to go. They piled into the back of the pickup, with Billy taking the middle seat to prevent the younger boys from fighting.

Mr. Porter started the engine, grumbling all the while. "I'm gonna be late for work again. The foreman'll just have to deal with it, won't he? Serves him right for being late with my paycheck."

Billy never knew what to say when his father started ranting, so he chose to stay quiet. Realizing he'd lost his audience, Mr. Porter lapsed into silence too, save for the rattling breaths that signaled an impending coughing fit. Billy hoped the episode wouldn't be severe enough to send them into the path of oncoming traffic.

Luckily, the rest of the drive passed without incident. They pulled up at the school, and the boys scrambled out of the pickup. Billy slung his new satchel over his shoulder and leaned toward the open passenger window.

"Thanks for the ri—" he began, but the pickup tore off in a hail of gravel before he could finish his sentence.

The boys went their separate ways at the school gate: Hamish to the kindergarten classroom, James to the third-grade classroom, and Billy to the fifth-grade classroom. Walking to the other side of the school took time, but Billy didn't mind. It gave him a chance to soak up the community atmosphere. To remember that real life existed outside the walls of his home. Although the school wasn't perfect, it was the one place in Morton where humans and wraiths coexisted in widespread, if tentative, peace.

His father hated the wraiths, but as far as Billy was concerned, they were just kids like him. Classmates. Playmates, even. They'd been around as long as he could remember. According to Ms. Clemmons, they'd arrived in Morton one hundred years ago and didn't exist anywhere else on the planet. *I bet she made that up. They had to immigrate from* somewhere, *didn't they? It's not like they appeared out of thin air.*

He crossed the courtyard in the middle of the school, surprised by the bustle of activity there. Men dressed in white coveralls marched back and forth between a rusted van and the science center, unloading supplies for the semester ahead. A pack of teachers herded bright-eyed children toward their new classrooms. And then there were the wraiths. As always, they took Billy's breath away.

Darker than any human, their skin resembled a void cut from a starless patch of sky—a black hole, tearing apart the fabric of reality. Insubstantial violet threads rippled through them, forming strange, shimmering runes that glissaded across their skin in a fashion so fleeting it made Billy doubt they existed at all. Most of Morton's human residents believed they were symbols of the occult, but he wasn't so sure about that either. The wraiths had never performed any rituals or sacrifices when he was around.

A rough shove brought him back to the present. He fell to the ground, hissing when his bare arms scraped the concrete.

"What are you staring at?" a harsh voice said.

"N-nothing." He squinted up at his attacker, stomach sinking. "Leave me alone, Corvus."

The wraith boy paused as if to think, then grabbed the unguarded satchel from Billy's side. His violet eyes blazed with a mixture of mischief and malevolence.

"Well, well, well. What have we got here?" Corvus asked. He opened the bag and picked out a plastic soldier. "Wittle Billy can't go to school without his dolls."

"They're not dolls. They're figurines. It's for my summer project."

"Oh, you mean this?" Corvus grabbed the rolled-up poster and unfurled it. "Looks like a lame map to me."

Billy jumped to his feet and tried to snatch it, but Corvus pushed him back to the ground. With a smug grin, the wraith boy tore the paper in half and Billy's heart along with it.

"Stop it," Billy said, his voice dangerously close to a whine.

"Aw, don't worry. Maybe you can stick it back together," Corvus cooed. He threw the ripped paper on the ground and pulled out a small bottle. "Tell you what. I'll even give you some superglue to do it."

Toy soldiers flew in all directions as he yanked the box out of Billy's satchel. Smirking, he tossed the broken lid aside and squeezed glue over the box's contents. All Billy could do was watch in numb horror while his summer project went up in figurative flames.

"Back off, Corvus!" someone shouted.

Billy looked up, his eyes swimming with tears. Two of his friends approached from the school gates, their expressions indignant. Zane was the tallest boy in their grade, and despite his lankiness, he presented a terrifying figure when he lost his cool. Murdock jogged after him, holding his glasses on his nose with one hand.

"Or what?" Corvus taunted.

"Or… or I'll beat you up," Zane stammered.

Corvus craned his neck to scrutinize the boy's towering form, then dropped the box and glue. "Whatever, dude. I could take you on any day."

He sauntered off toward the other wraiths, most of whom were watching the scene unfold with interest. The few who chose to turn away erupted into gales of laughter. *It's the first day of school, and I've already been humiliated. Just having a new satchel isn't good enough. I'll never be cool! If I hadn't drawn attention to myself, Corvus would have left me alone.*

The wraith group's mirth gave way to disgust when Corvus came within six feet of them, and they formed a tight circle with their backs to him. Apparently defeated, he slunk off, his head drooping in glum contemplation. *Even his own kind don't like him.*

"You okay?" Murdock asked, crouching next to Billy.

"I guess so." He tried to inject some enthusiasm into his voice, but his attempts fell flat. "My project's ruined."

"That's too bad. Maybe we can help you fix it?"

"How?"

Billy wanted to be optimistic, but he'd labored over the map for hours. Besides, superglue didn't come off easily. He'd learned that the hard way when he glued his fingers together in second grade.

"Ms. Clemmons has Scotch tape in her classroom, doesn't she?" Murdock cocked his head to one side. "We could stick it together with that. I'm not sure what to do about your soldiers, though."

"You can peel the glue off when it dries," Zane said. "It doesn't take long if you've got scissors. I can help with that."

The bell behind Billy emitted a shrieking tone to announce the start of the school day. He winced, staring at the tattered remains of his summer project.

"Thanks, guys."

They worked in silence, picking up the ruined map pieces and freeing the congealed mass of glue and plastic from the concrete. Billy wrinkled his nose and deposited the filthy amalgamation in his brand new satchel. It pained him to risk ruining the leather, but he couldn't see an alternative. He surveyed the crime scene a final time before they departed for their first day of the new term. His bully was nowhere to be seen.

I may be a loser, Corvus, but at least I'm a loser with friends.

Chapter Three

"SHAUNA, YOU'RE UP next," Ms. Clemmons said.

The girl in front of Billy stood up and shuffled to the front, scuffing the carpet with her shoes. He shot her a sympathetic look before returning his attention to the poster on his desk.

"I did my summer project on Oilskin Lake," Shauna said. "My dad's an environmental scientist, and he helped me to take samples of the water and test it for contaminants. My results showed…"

As interesting as her speech was, Billy found himself unable to concentrate. His mind kept returning to his own plight. Shiny adhesive tape ran down the middle of his poster, giving it the illusion of wholeness. Splotches of dirt clung to the paper, ruining the illusion. Even with his friends' help, he'd been unable to remove them. Most of the toy soldiers were too damaged to add to the map, so he'd created mini formations out of the few that survived Corvus's ambush. Speaking of Corvus…

Billy risked a glance over his shoulder. The wraith bully sat at the desk behind him, his body slumped against the wall. He passed a note to the wraith girl behind him, who smiled and scribbled a hasty reply. When she passed it back, Corvus's lips curved into a smile of his own.

"That was very interesting, Shauna. Thank you for sharing with us," Ms. Clemmons said. "Billy? You're up next."

Heart racing, Billy carried his project to the front of the class. Public speaking didn't scare him, but Corvus's mocking face turned his stomach inside out.

"I did my summer project on the Battle of Turnpike Hill," he began, proud when his voice barely trembled. "Not many people know it, but the hill is right next to the library. During the civil war, Morton didn't exist. The area was just a big open field for everyone to fight in. Over two hundred people died there. I made this map to show where it happened."

He raised the poster, not daring to make eye contact with his classmates. Before anyone could tease him for its marred appearance, he handed it off to Ms. Clemmons and retreated to his desk.

Corvus kicked the back of his chair when he sat down. "Nice going, *Billy.*"

"Hmmm, okay." Ms. Clemmons eyed Billy's project with obvious disappointment. "Who's next? Corvus?"

"I didn't do a summer project, Miss," Corvus piped up.

"Why not?"

"I forgot."

Ms. Clemmons tutted at him. "You kids are getting more irresponsible every year. Expect a detention on Saturday, Corvus."

"But Miss—"

"You had three months to remember," Ms. Clemmons interrupted, her tone icy. "Another word out of you and there'll be two detentions."

Corvus rolled his eyes and muttered something Billy couldn't make out.

Ms. Clemmons cleared her throat. "Rem? You're up next, dear."

The wraith girl sitting behind Corvus skipped to the front of the room, still smiling from whatever they'd been talking about. Halfway along, she tripped over her own feet, eliciting giggles from the other kids. Her cheeks blushed lilac.

Rem... So that's her name.

Billy had spoken with her in passing, and she seemed like a sweet girl. As far as he could tell, she only hung out with a bully like Corvus because the other wraiths shunned her.

"I did my summer project on the Monster of Morton," Rem began, sending a shiver down Billy's spine. "As you know, it's been haunting the town for nearly three years now. Rumors say it's a giant beast with giant claws to rip people apart. Everyone's scared of it, but no one's ever gotten close enough to get a good look at it. We're all assuming it wants to hurt us, but what if it's lonely? What if it just wants a friend? Most of the houses in Morton are made of wood, which should be easy for it to destroy. If it really wanted to hurt us, you'd think it would have done it by now. Furthermore—"

"That's quite enough, thank you," Ms. Clemmons interrupted. "I'm sure you worked hard on your speech, but the topic is inappropriate for the classroom. The monster is dangerous. I don't want anyone to get the idea it's safe to try and make friends with it."

"But—"

"Enough," Ms. Clemmons repeated firmly. The bell rang, signaling the end of school. No one dared to leave their seats. "We'll finish the presentations tomorrow morning, starting with Zane. Billy, stay behind. I want to talk to you."

"Good luck, *Billy*," Corvus sneered. He gave the seat another savage kick before sauntering out the door.

Billy winced as the action jolted his spine, but he didn't say anything. Fighting back would get him suspended, and then his father would be on his case. He stayed seated while the other students filed out, accepting the sympathetic looks they gave him. When the door finally swung shut, he joined Ms. Clemmons at her desk.

"Billy Porter," she intoned.

"Yes, Miss?"

"Do you want to tell me what's going on between you and Corvus?"

"There's nothing going on."

"Really?"

"Yeah. He kicked my chair a few times by accident."

"It didn't look like an accident to me," Ms. Clemmons prompted. When no response was forthcoming, she continued. "There's also the matter of your summer project."

Billy cringed when she fished it out of the pile. Dried glue crumbled off the paper in small chunks, and one of the toy soldiers lay abandoned on the desk.

"I dropped it on the way to school," he lied.

"Dropping a piece of paper doesn't make it tear down the middle. Billy, I *know* something happened, but I can't help you if you don't talk to me. Did Corvus do this?"

"Yeah, but I don't need your help. I can handle him."

"I'm sure you can, but sometimes it's better to get an adult involved. You're not the only person he's bullied. Corvus's dad is a policeman, and I can guarantee he'll take a hard line with him. He's done it before, and it straightened Corvus out for a few months."

"He went back to being mean, though."

"Unfortunately, yes. It takes time for people to change. A long time, in some cases."

Billy thought about it. "What do I have to do?"

"You don't have to do anything. I'll call his dad and have a chat with him. If things stay the same, you might have to make a formal statement."

A formal statement? Billy's heart sank.

"It's very unlikely it would come to that," Ms. Clemmons added upon seeing his petrified expression. "Seisan is a strict man. If there's one good thing to say about the wraiths, it's that they take these things seriously. It's an insult to their honor or something like that."

"Oh."

"Anyway, I've taken up enough of your time." Ms. Clemmons stood and wiped her hands on her dress. "Go on home and enjoy your afternoon."

"Thanks, Ms. Clemmons. I will."

Billy all but sprinted out of the classroom, desperate to escape the stifling atmosphere. James and Hamish sat on the stairs outside, drumming their heels against the concrete.

"What did Ms. Lemons want?" Hamish asked.

"Clemmons, not Lemons," Billy corrected. "She just wanted to talk to me about my summer project. No big deal. Come on, let's go get some ice cream."

"Now you're talking!" James said. He skipped ahead of them, eager to reach Morton Park and its ever-present ice cream truck.

The park was less than half a mile away, but the scenery in between made Billy uneasy. Distracted by the promise of food, his brothers didn't notice the problem. It was probably just as well. Strips of wood had been sloughed off the houses, leaving gouges in the shape of giant claws.

The giant claws of a monster, Billy thought. *Whatever Rem was talking about in class, she was wrong. The monster doesn't want a friend. Friends don't try to break into each other's houses.*

Chapter Four

AN HOUR BEFORE the town-wide curfew, Billy stumbled through the front door with his brothers in tow. Heaving gasps rocked his chest, and he leaned over, hands on his knees, in a vain attempt to regain control of his breathing.

Mrs. Porter rushed over, her face pale with fright. "What's the matter?"

When he didn't immediately respond, she gave him a once-over for signs of injury. Finding none, she straightened and held his gaze in anxious anticipation.

"Nothing," Billy said between gasps. "It was starting to get dark, and Hamish thought the monster might come out. He made us run all the way home, just in case."

Hamish nodded, eyes wide. "I thought I saw it behind a tree."

"Oh, don't be silly, love. It was probably just a dog," Mrs. Porter said. "Go and get washed up for dinner, okay? Your father will be home any minute."

"Okay, Mom," the boys chorused.

While the younger two fought over the bathroom, Billy retreated to his room and dumped his satchel on the floor. The sight of his moth-eaten dresser reminded him of the previous night's events, and he instinctively slid open the top drawer. *The gun's still there. They haven't noticed yet.*

Giddy, he lowered himself onto his bed. The final dregs of daylight filtered through the windows, creating dusky silhouettes on the wall—a harbinger of the darkness to come and the monster's impending return. His whole body ached from running, which wasn't ideal for what he had planned. Fortunately, the worst of the pain confined itself to his calf muscles. It wouldn't prevent him from wielding the revolver with deadly force. Of course, if the monster decided to chase him...

No. I'm not going to think about that, Billy told himself. *I'll enjoy my dinner and watch* MacGyver *reruns with Mom and Dad. I won't start worrying until the monster actually gets here.*

"Billy! Dinner!"

Groaning, he stood up again. His feet protested the action, sending waves of discomfort up his legs. His father said that people felt the effects of exercise more keenly as they got older, but he'd assumed that was for really old people, not ten-year-old kids. He shuffled to the dining table and took the unoccupied seat between his brothers.

"I'm starving," Mr. Porter declared. He'd mashed his food together during Billy's absence and loaded his fork with the resulting mixture. "It's your turn to say grace, James."

The middle sibling folded his hands on the table and closed his eyes in fierce concentration. "Thank you, God, for the food on our table. We pray that you will bless it and also protect us from the monster. Amen."

"Amen," Billy repeated. Never before had his brother's candid prayer seemed more appropriate. His mother's exasperated expression told him she didn't agree.

"Did you have to mention the monster, James? Why can't we have a nice family meal without thinking about horrible things like that?"

James shrugged, his cheeks already bulging with food. Shaking her head, Mrs. Porter picked up her fork and stabbed a chunk of potato.

The food was plain and unseasoned, but it was hot and there was plenty of it. Billy demolished his first plate load in less than ten minutes. Halfway through his second helping, the doorbell buzzed in an urgent, staccato pattern.

"That better be Phillip with my paycheck," Mr. Porter grumbled, wiping his mouth with a napkin.

The front door squealed when he opened it, and Billy strained to see who stood outside. The position of the table stopped him from seeing anything beyond the scowl on his father's face.

"*You*," Mr. Porter said, his tone dripping with revulsion.

"Me," the stranger agreed. The deep, unaccented voice provided a stark contrast to his father's Texan drawl. "I've come to talk to your son, Billy. If that would be agreeable to you, of course."

"Well, it's not," Mr. Porter spat. "Your kind ain't welcome in my house. I don't care what Chief Bowers says. And you're not talking to my son neither. The last thing I need is for you to poison his mind with your wraith apologist nonsense."

Wraiths? Billy perked up and lowered his fork. *Maybe it's Corvus's dad.*

He swallowed the last of his food and went to the door, curious to see what an adult wraith looked like up close. He never saw them walking around town, except for the two who worked as honorary police officers. He'd thought about approaching them before, but he always chickened out. Policemen unnerved him at the best of times.

"It's okay, Dad. I'll talk to him," Billy offered.

"You'll do no such thing," Mr. Porter said. "Get back to the table, boy. Unless you want to be sacrificed to their little *pet*."

"I'll take the risk," Billy said, wincing when an angry vein popped out of his father's forehead. He gave the visitor an apologetic smile. "We can talk on the porch."

Mr. Porter stomped inside, a murderous glint in his eye. His wife guided him back to the dining table, but he kept gazing at his office, no doubt wondering if he could get away with shooting the man outside.

Billy stepped into the cool evening air, keeping the door wide open in case his father's dire warnings came true.

"So, you're Billy," the wraith said, peering down at him. "My name is Seisan. I'm Corvus's father. How do you do?"

Billy gazed up at him, disoriented. Seisan's height mirrored the average human male's, but the scale of him seemed wrong. Compared to the younger wraiths, he looked like he'd been stretched too thin for his body.

"I'm fine, thanks," Billy answered.

"I'm glad to hear it." Seisan smiled, baring a set of violet teeth that glowed under the porch security lights. "I wanted to apologize to you personally for my son's behavior. It was completely uncalled for, and I've taken steps to prevent it from happening again."

"Oh. Um… thanks."

"Corvus will apologize to you tomorrow, and that should be the end of the matter. If he forgets his place again, please let me know. A school should be a place of learning, not of misanthropy."

Mis-what? Billy thought. *This guy talks like he's reading an essay.*

He nodded in spite of his confusion, unconsciously backing toward the doorway. "I should go before my dad gets any angrier. Thanks for coming all this way to apologize."

"You're most welcome," Seisan said. "I was already patrolling the area, so it was no trouble."

Billy tried to step inside, but his mother blocked the way. Her grease-stained apron billowed in the fledgling wind.

"You're patrolling out here?" she asked Seisan, resting one hand on the door jamb.

"Yes, ma'am." Seisan dipped his head in a little bow. "We've had reports that the monster frequents this area more than any other. We hope to catch it tonight."

"Hah!" was Mr. Porter's contribution from the kitchen.

"I wish you the best of luck with that, Officer," Mrs. Porter said, offering the wraith a tight-lipped smile. "I'm sorry about my husband."

"Not to worry. I've gotten used to it over the years."

Mr. Porter stomped over, his eyes blazing. "Don't apologize, Marge. He deserves everything coming to him. How many months have you freaks been trying and failing to catch that monster? I know you're in on it."

The corner of Seisan's mouth quirked upward in apparent amusement. "Us 'freaks,' as you so eloquently put it, are stretched thin with more serious cases. As for catching the monster, you would do well to remember that the team in charge is predominantly comprised of your own species. That is to say, humans."

"I know what my own species is!" Mr. Porter shouted. "And you! You call yourself a wraith, but I know what you are: a demon from the deepest depths of hell. Get off my land or I'll call the real cops!"

"No need, sir," Seisan said, bowing. "I know when I've overstayed my welcome. Billy, Mrs. Porter… Good evening to you both."

The wraith turned on his heel and glided like a shadow into the cover of darkness. Billy stared after him, trying to convince himself his visitor hadn't vanished into thin air.

"If I ever see that freak on my property again, I'll make him wish he never left the stinking pit he crawled out of," Mr. Porter growled.

He yanked Billy inside by the collar of his shirt and slammed the door. Billy yelped in surprise, hands scrabbling at the taut fabric around his neck.

"There's no need to talk like that," Mrs. Porter said. "What if he heard you?"

"Who cares if he did?" Mr. Porter scoffed. "He's not even a real cop. There ain't a single person in this town who would convict me if he wound up dead."

"I would," Mrs. Porter said, crossing her arms. "I didn't marry a murderer. And let go of Billy. You're hurting him."

Blinking, Mr. Porter noticed his hand was still bunched in his son's shirt. He released his grip, and Billy rubbed his neck. It hadn't been physically painful. Not really. The unexpectedness of it upset him more than anything else.

"I don't want you to hurt him either," Billy murmured. He shrank back when his father laughed—a great booming chuckle that grated on his ears.

"'Course you don't. You're only a kid." Mr. Porter mussed his hair playfully. "You'll understand when you grow up."

"The only one who needs to grow up around here is you," Mrs. Porter cut in, glaring daggers at her husband. "I've had enough of this unpleasantness. Billy, go and see if *MacGyver* is on yet."

Billy glanced back and forth between them, sensing the rising tide of enmity but powerless to stop it.

One more reason to kill the monster tonight, he thought as he scampered off to obey his mother. *I can save the wraith kids. I can save Seisan. And if I'm lucky, I can stop Mom and Dad from fighting too.*

Chapter Five

MIDNIGHT CAME AND went with a silence only the dead can understand. The monster-driven wind remained absent for so long that Billy wondered if Seisan's plan, by some miracle, had actually worked. His eyelids drifted shut, but the quiet outside was anything but peaceful. After dealing with Morton's strange weather phenomena for so long, normality no longer felt normal or safe. He lay awake for hours, unable to move or do anything except listen to his family's rattling snores.

A little after 2:00 a.m., a whistle and an almighty crash jolted him out of bed, and the stillness of the night shattered into frantic, whirling gusts of air. *It's here. The monster's here.*

Trembling with fear and excitement, Billy grabbed the revolver from his dresser. It felt light in his hands, as though the bullets had spontaneously disappeared. He released the cylinder to check. Six openings. Six bullets.

He breathed a sigh of relief and closed the cylinder. He *knew* he'd loaded it the previous night, but as his old man always said, it was better to be paranoid and alive than overconfident and dead.

The advice had been passed on during one of their many hunting trips, right before they forded a river for the first time. Billy almost smiled at the memory but caught himself and grimaced. His current venture was nothing like a hunting trip. For one thing, deer never fought back. The chances of the monster extending the same courtesy were slim to none.

Realizing his feet were still glued to the spot, Billy forced himself to inch closer to the forbidden window. The silky curtains billowed out as if they were struggling to contain an unseen force, and he would have ground to a petrified halt if not for the revolver. *It's not a ghost. It's just the wind. You know that. The monster is the only thing you need to worry about. Focus on the monster.*

He crept to the window and drew back the curtain. Flying objects flashed across his field of vision before he could identify them, propelled by the raging winds. No monster revealed itself amidst the chaos. He backed toward the door of his room, unsure whether to summon his foe or flee to the safety of the hallway. His fingers hovered over the light switch for an indeterminate length of time before he committed to turning it on. The accompanying click made him shudder. *I just signed my own death warrant.*

His heart raced, nausea running laps up and down his throat. Any minute, the monster would beat its snarling, needle-toothed maw against the window. He pictured the horrible crimson claws reaching toward him, unzipping his guts with a single blow. His family wouldn't hear the commotion over the howling wind. They wouldn't find him until the next morning—no longer a boy but a smear of red across the threadbare carpet. The first casualty of Morton's great monster hauntings.

The revolver trembled in Billy's grasp. His arms froze at a ninety-degree angle from his body, his shoulders stiff with effort. *The waiting is the worst part. The not knowing.*

He didn't know how long he'd been standing there when fear lost its grip on him. In his mind, it had been an eternity, but his watch—had he bothered to glance at it—would have told him it was twelve minutes. Twelve minutes of waiting and zero monsters.

I have to go out there, he realized with a sinking feeling in the pit of his stomach. Unbidden, his thoughts returned to Seisan, and a burst of hope shone through the darkness. *I talked to an adult wraith and survived. I stood outside at night and survived. It* can *be done. I'm going to take that monster down, mark my words.*

The thought comforted him more than it should have. A little voice in his head told him his fighting words were nothing but false bravado. He promptly told the little voice to shut up.

Billy switched off the light and lowered himself onto the edge of his bed, gun pointed at the window. He wanted to leave immediately, but he'd get himself killed if he didn't let his night vision kick in first. He used the first few minutes to put on the darkest clothes he owned—a pair of black jeans and an Iron Maiden T-shirt. The rest of the time he spent lacing and re-lacing his shoes.

After ten minutes, he could make out both the trees on the horizon and the lawn furniture outside his window. He opened the sash and peered outside. *The coast's clear. Now for the tricky part.*

Billy sat on the windowsill with his back to the garden. The hair on the back of his neck prickled, but he did his best to ignore it. Carefully, he spun around on his rear, tucking his knees in as tight as he could. When he had enough room, he dangled his feet outside.

A bed of gardenias rested underneath him, surprisingly undamaged by the rogue winds. His mother prized them above all the other flowers, no doubt due to the miracle of their continued survival. Billy set the soles of his feet against the wall, adjusting his weight as he did so. If he got his positioning right, he could use the wall to launch himself over the gardenias and onto the grass.

Easier said than done, Billy thought as the wind tried to buffet him back inside. *Especially if you're holding a revolver.*

He supposed he could tuck it into his jeans, but the idea of leaving himself defenseless, even for a moment, was a risk he wasn't prepared to take. A half-second of calm in the storm gave him the courage to move. Concentrating his weight in his feet, Billy pushed himself out the window. Instead of clearing the flowers, he fell into them, knees first. He leapt to his feet, swinging the gun around in case the monster lay in wait. When no attack came, he returned his attention to the fallen gardenias.

Oops. I guess I should crush all of them. Otherwise, the only damaged ones will be right outside my window, and Mom will know I snuck out. That or she'll think the monster hangs around my window all night. I'll lose my room! He hesitated, letting the thoughts run their course, then shook his head. *I can deal with the flowers later. Right now, I need to keep moving.*

Choosing a direction at random, Billy jogged into the night. Claw marks furrowed the surrounding soil, their paths too criss-crossed for him to read. When he reached the nearest intersection, a flash of violet caught his eye. He hit the deck without thinking and army-crawled into a bush. The leaves swayed around him, scratching his bare arms.

Wraiths! he observed from his hiding spot. *Two of them. One of them looks like Seisan, but who's the other guy? Another cop?*

He knew there was a second wraith officer in Morton, but he had no idea what the man looked like. What if the guy next to Seisan was a suspect? What if he was the one controlling the monster? Billy waited until the wraiths strode out of sight before he emerged from the bush. If Seisan saw him wandering the neighborhood after curfew, it would be a straight ticket home and a grounding to boot.

A second, more potent thought entered his head, too terrible to ignore. *What if they catch me walking around with a revolver? I'll be arrested on the spot! I can't get rid of it, though. I'll be easy pickings for the monster without it. Besides, I've come too far to stop now.*

He dog-trotted in the opposite direction of the wraiths, hoping the darkness would keep him hidden. As he ran, heaven's floodgates ruptured and released a deluge the likes of which he'd never experienced before. Silver bursts of rain struck his body like thousands of tiny needles, soaking him to the core. *I should have brought my jacket.* When he thought about it, though, he was glad he hadn't. Thin and fluorescent yellow, his jacket would offer better mileage as a dinner beacon for monsters than a safeguard against the wild weather.

Nets of lightning descended from the sky, singeing the tops of the trees and casting serrated shadows over the land. The brief flashes showed him his inevitable destination: Oilskin Lake.

The water, if it could be described as water, lay stagnant under the night sky. No rain touched its surface; rather, it evaporated milliseconds before impact. The lake evinced a deep midnight-purple that the unwary traveler would write off as a trick of the moonlight. Billy had visited often enough to know this was its natural hue. The council had spent hundreds of thousands of dollars trying to drain it, believing it to be poisoned. For all their efforts, though, the water level never dwindled.

Billy approached the lake warily. A series of *Danger: Keep Out* signs surrounded the perimeter at strategic intervals. He'd seen them before and usually obeyed them. Tonight, he couldn't afford to follow the rules.

I'll be fine, Billy reassured himself. He wiggled his frozen fingers a few times before returning them to the revolver. His index finger cupped the trigger. *The wraith kids come here all the time, and they're fine. No reason to think I won't be.*

The little voice in his head pointed out the wraith kids didn't have a monster to deal with, but he did his best to ignore it. Worrying about what *might* happen created more problems than it solved. That's what his mother always said.

Steeling himself, Billy stepped over the post-and-chain fence and approached the water. What lay within the murky depths of this abominable pool? He'd never entertained the idea that a monster might live in such a foul and inhospitable place. The more he thought about it, though, the more sense it made. *This must be where it lives. When it comes home, I'll kill it. I swear I'll kill it.*

The first thing he needed to do was find a defensible position. A hill on the other side of the lake looked promising, so he resumed his dog-trot, careful to give the discolored water a wide berth. The storm waned as he got closer to the hill, and he redoubled his speed. Soon, the wind and rain stopped altogether, and a feeling of foreboding inched up his spine. He checked over his shoulder to make sure the monster wasn't sneaking up on him.

It's too early, Billy thought. *The wind stops with the sunrise... doesn't it?*

He turned around, heart hammering against his rib cage. He wanted to believe he'd scared the monster enough to provoke a change in pattern. He wanted to believe the knots in his stomach came from eating too much at dinner. But most of all, he wanted to believe he'd imagined it when the hill sat up and winked at him with a glowing red eye.

A strangled exclamation escaped Billy's mouth, and he raised the gun. Tears of fright clouded his vision, and his hands shook so badly he could hardly squeeze the trigger. A bullet coughed out of the barrel and lodged itself in a tree. The monster reared up, snarling, and slammed its grotesque paws into the ground. He wiped his eyes and took aim again.

The beast lurched forward, saliva dripping from its maw. Holding his breath, Billy pulled the trigger. The monster howled as the metal slug pierced its flesh. *Keep going. Just keep going. Just—*

"Stop it!"

The words cut through Billy's stampeding thoughts. For a moment, he wondered if the whole experience had driven him mad—mad enough to believe monsters could talk. Belatedly, he spotted the purple outline of a wraith child standing next to the creature. *It's Corvus! Looks like Dad was right; the monster* is *their pet.*

The wraith boy strode forward and batted the revolver out of Billy's hands. Another bullet hurtled into the night. "You're hurting her!"

"That's the idea," Billy retorted, making a move for the gun.

Corvus kicked it into the lake, where it sank into the gangrenous depths.

"Why are you doing this?" Billy whispered. Helpless tears streamed down his cheeks. "The monster's going to *kill* me."

A sneer crossed Corvus's face. He opened his mouth to reply, but a cracking sound filled the air, and he clamped it shut. *The sound of a branch underfoot.* Halogen lights flooded the clearing, as blinding as the sun.

"This is the police! We have the lake surrounded. Put down your weapons and get on the ground."

Billy dropped to his knees in a daze. *It's over. I failed. Dad's going to kill the wraith kids. He's probably going to kill* me. *And Mom's going to…*

He didn't finish the thought, cursing himself instead for following through on such a foolish plan. Whatever happened next was his own stupid fault.

"It's time," Corvus proclaimed.

The monster bowed its head and writhed into the contaminated water. Corvus waded in after it up to his ankles. The wraith boy made eye contact with Billy for a split second before a miasmatic fog swept the clearing. The air crackled and hummed with electricity that seemed to radiate from the lake itself. Despite the chaos of the situation, Billy felt an overwhelming urge to get closer, as though magnets were drawing him in. The glare of the searchlights vanished in the thick fog surrounding him, obscuring his actions from the police.

I'm not going to run, Billy insisted. *I just want to touch the water.*

The appearance of a new and contradictory urge didn't strike him as odd until much later. He crawled forward on his hands and knees, submerging a hand in the mysterious pool. If he'd listened to Shauna's presentation earlier that day, he might have known which chemicals made up the elbow-deep sludge. A high-pitched whine filled the air, reminiscent of a dentist's drill, and Billy's teeth vibrated in his skull. The echo of Corvus's voice was the last thing he heard before his vision swirled and he faded out of reality.

Chapter Six

BILLY WOKE WITH his face half caked in mud. A tingling sensation formed at the base of his skull and rocketed down to his toes when he tried to move. He blinked once, allowing his eyes to adjust to the spectral lights overhead. Then he rolled onto his back and wiped his face clean with the hem of his T-shirt. Oilskin Lake looked the same as before, but the surrounding environment did not. It was as if the entire thing had been uprooted and transplanted into another forest.

What happened back there? Where am I? And why is the sky purple?

Deadwood spires towered over the edges of the clearing, curving like a dinosaur's rib cage to form a makeshift prison. A single dusty path cut a hole through the trees, but Billy sensed it would be a bad idea to follow it. Out of the corner of his eye, he saw Corvus standing over the monster. It lay on its side, whimpering like a kicked puppy. Violet-tinted blood trickled from its shoulder and soaked into the cracked skin of its belly.

Memories flooded back into Billy's mind. *I shot the monster! And then… I don't know. The police showed up and everything went weird.*

He scrambled up the bank, eager to get away from the lake and whatever strange properties it possessed. His father's gun lay under a deadwood tree ten feet to his left, and he hurried to pick it up. Part of him realized something was wrong—that the gun shouldn't be there—but he shrugged it off. How the gun made it back to dry land didn't matter. What mattered was that he could use it to defend himself.

"Where am I?" he demanded.

Corvus spun around, shock written all over his face. "What are *you* doing here? Don't tell me you touched the portal."

"Portal?"

"The lake! Did you touch the lake?"

"I… yeah." Billy frowned. "You're saying Oilskin Lake's a portal? To where?"

"Here, obviously." Corvus rolled his eyes and stuck his hands on his hips. "The Gloaming. Also known as the Wereforest, if you want to get technical. Heathens like you probably call it Wraithland."

"Your home country?"

Corvus snorted. "Home dimension, more like. But who cares about that? My best friend is dying because you had to go and shoot her."

"She's dangerous," Billy protested. His mind swam from the unexpected influx of information.

"She didn't do a thing to you. All she wanted was a friend. Why couldn't you follow curfew like everyone else?"

He opened his mouth to make a sharp retort, but no words came out. No matter how cruel the kid had been, Billy didn't have the heart to give him a taste of his own medicine.

"I don't think I can heal her," Corvus murmured, tears brimming in his eyes. "If she doesn't stop moving, there's no way my spells will hold. I won't be able to get the bullet out."

A lump formed in Billy's throat, and he lowered the gun. *I don't know what he means by "spells," but Corvus was right about one thing: the monster had every chance to hurt me and it never did.*

Corvus knelt in the dirt, palms glowing, while the monster groaned and beat its limbs against the ground. Billy edged closer, hoping to get a better look at his bully's so-called best friend. Its head and torso boasted a pale complexion similar to his own, while its lower half comprised a midnight-purple carapace. Vibrant red talons extended from its paws—two inches long, not two feet like the rumors claimed. The red of its eyes had faded to a milky pink, as if the light behind them were moments away from being snuffed out forever.

"Is there anything I can do to help?" Billy asked, unsure what else to say. The words left a sour taste in his mouth, but he didn't want to give Corvus any more reasons to hate him.

The wraith boy looked up at him with hopeful eyes. "Could you hold her head for me? It might help if you say something soothing to her as well. She won't hurt you, I promise."

"I guess I can do that," Billy agreed, approaching the monster's head. "Fair warning, though, I'm going to shoot her again if she attacks me."

"She won't attack you."

"How do you know?" Billy asked. He sat on his heels and touched the monster's scalp with a cautious hand. The skin there was slick with water from the lake, and a shimmer of white light pulsated beneath it. He tightened his grip when Corvus reached for the bullet wound.

"Because Rem told me."

"The girl who always sits behind you in class? No offense, but she's wrong. I've seen what the monster can do, and it's not pretty. Are you sure this thing is really your friend? What if it's just using you? What if it wants to eat—"

"You know who Rem is?" Corvus interrupted, surprise coloring his voice. "I didn't know humans bothered to learn our names except to torment us."

A thoughtful look came over his face as he struggled to pry the bullet free. It popped out in a flash of bright purple, covered in threads of torn sinew. The monster whimpered, and Billy found himself stroking its bony forehead without knowing why.

"Got it!" Corvus crowed, holding the bullet above his head like a trophy. "Now I've just got to stitch up the wound. It shouldn't take long."

"Was that magic?" Billy asked in awe.

Corvus placed a hand over the hole he'd carved. "Yup."

"You can use *magic*?"

"That's literally what I just said."

A cool glow emanated from the wraith's hands, and the monster's torn skin rippled outward, joining together to form a seamless whole. Questions raced through Billy's mind, but he got the sense Corvus wouldn't welcome the interruption.

"Right. You can let go now." The wraith sat back on his heels to observe his handiwork. "The bleeding's stopped, so her life isn't in danger anymore."

Billy jumped to his feet and backed away in case the monster wanted to stand up. Corvus pulled a glass vial and a small marble bowl from his pocket.

"What are you doing?" Billy asked.

Corvus scooped some water from Oilskin Lake into the bowl, then added the contents of the vial. The resulting mixture curdled into a dull amber sludge, which he swirled liberally.

"Do you promise not to tell anyone?" he asked.

The question sounded like a threat, but Billy nodded anyway. The curiosity was killing him. "I promise."

"You did help me, so I guess you deserve to know," Corvus said. He continued swirling the mixture, his eyes downcast. "How much do you know about wraith culture?"

"Not much," Billy admitted.

"Anything about blood oaths?"

"Nope, sorry."

Corvus sighed. "When we turn thirteen, we have to go back to the Gloaming for a coming-of-age ceremony. The king cuts our palms and binds us to his service with a powerful piece of blood magic. Some wraiths try to fight against it, but the king always wins. Some wraiths manage to break the spell later on, but they're shunned for the rest of their lives. We call them oathbreakers." He paused, sucking in a breath. "There are only two oathbreakers alive today, as far as I know. My father... and Rem's. All the others were killed."

Billy sucked in a breath of his own. *What do I even say to something like that?* Fortunately, Corvus kept talking without expecting a response.

"As soon as the other kids found out, they starting shunning *us* too. They think we'll grow up to be deviants like our parents. I've never had any trouble standing up for myself, but Rem… she couldn't handle the bullying. She found a potion recipe in one of her dad's books. A potion to turn her into a human. I tried to talk her out of it, but she wouldn't listen. So I helped. We gathered all the ingredients and mixed them together. We didn't know what we were doing, though, and it backfired badly."

He gazed at the monster, whose ruby eyes glistened up at him in melancholic solidarity.

"Every night, the moonlight turns her into the creature you shot," Corvus finished with a helpless shrug. "A hybrid gone wrong."

Billy looked into the monster's eyes himself. He couldn't see any trace of Rem inside them, but he recognized the gentleness of her movements. *I can't blame her for freaking out earlier. I'm the one who had a gun.* The implications of the memory stung him like a hot brand. *I shot a wraith! I shot* Rem*! I'm no better than my dad.*

Bile burned his throat, and he bent over to steady himself. "I'm so sorry."

"What's done is done," Corvus said. "In any case, I've got a way to fix it now. Lothaire—I mean, Rem's dad—helped me brew a potion to get rid of the effects. He's really good at magic."

The wraith waved his hand over the bowl, drawing Billy's gaze back to its contents. A faint sheen formed over the liquid, its glow strengthening with every passing second. The light drew Billy's eyes to a puckered knot of scar tissue skirting Corvus's collarbone.

"How did you get that scar?" he asked.

"You wouldn't believe me if I told you," Corvus deadpanned. His eyes brightened when the potion turned a sickly green. "Hey, look! It's time to add the elemis root."

He grabbed something thin and white that resembled a vanilla pod and dropped it in whole. The potion turned a dazzling, translucent gold. Lips pursed in concentration, he tipped the concoction into Rem's mouth. A thick fog rolled over them, and for a moment, Billy feared it would transport them to another new world. Relief filled him when the smoke cleared. They hadn't moved after all, but a wraith now stood in place of the monster.

"Rem! You're okay," Corvus exclaimed. He swept her up in a fierce hug, which Rem returned with a grin.

"You did it!" she said. "I *knew* you could."

Their celebrations made Billy all too aware of his status as the third wheel, but he stayed quiet and let them enjoy the moment that was obviously a long time coming for both of them. Several minutes passed before Corvus remembered his uninvited guest.

"Rem, this is Billy," Corvus explained. "He came through the portal by accident."

"I know. I was there."

"I'm sorry I shot you!" Billy blurted out. Wide-eyed surprise met his outburst, compelling him to continue. "I didn't know it was you. All I knew was that you scared me to death. I thought you were going to eat me or something."

Rem stared at him for a couple of tense seconds before bursting into musical laughter. "It's okay, Billy. I did look pretty horrifying as a hybrid, so I don't blame you. Besides, you helped in the end, and that's what matters."

"Weren't you afraid I would shoot you again?"

"Of course not. Guns don't work here. Technology doesn't either."

Now it was Billy's turn to stare. "What do you mean?"

"Try to shoot something right now," Corvus instructed.

Frowning, Billy pulled out the revolver and aimed at one of the deadwood trees. He squeezed the trigger and... *nothing? Why isn't it firing?* He twisted the cylinder open to check. Three bullets sat in their chambers, unblocked and ready to go. He closed the cylinder and aimed at a different tree. No matter how many times he pulled the trigger, nothing happened.

"How is this possible?" he demanded.

"Magic," Corvus said, spreading his arms wide. "Welcome to the Gloaming."

"I don't understand."

"That's okay. I'm not sure I do either. Not fully, anyway. I can't officially start magic training for another three years."

"When you do, can you teach me?" Billy asked. *Imagine all the neat stuff I could do. I'd never have to clean my room again!*

"I'm not sure if humans can use magic."

"They can," Rem said. "I read it in one of Dad's books."

"Well, there you go. You learn something new every day." Corvus clasped his hands together and favored her with a brief smile. "We should really get back to Morton now. It's not exactly safe here."

"I agree," Rem said, returning to the lake. "Do you want to do the spell, Corvus, or shall I?"

"I'll do it," Corvus decided. "You need to save your strength. Come on, Billy. You need to touch the portal for this to work."

Billy picked his way to the water's edge. "What happens after this?"

"We go back to get arrested by the police," Corvus replied, as if it were the most obvious thing in the world. "That reminds me. You should throw your gun away before we leave. You'll get in a lot of trouble if they find it on you."

"But it's my dad's."

"I can get it back for you later, when the heat's off."

Billy grimaced. The revolver had been a constant, if treacherous, companion throughout his adventure. The idea of letting it go upset him more than he thought it would. *I don't want to do this, but what choice do I have? It's not like Dad will miss the gun anyway. Come to think of it, he'd probably raise my allowance if he found out I shot a wraith. But never mind that. This is one story I'm never going to tell him.*

He lifted the revolver above his head and hurled it across the clearing with every ounce of strength he could muster. It sailed through the air in a perfect arc and landed in the dust, bouncing a few times before sliding to a halt.

"Nice throw," Corvus acknowledged.

"Thanks," Billy said, stepping into the water. "There's just one more thing I want to ask before we go."

"Which is?"

"What happens at school tomorrow? Between the three of us, I mean."

Corvus's brow knitted in a frown. "Nothing."

"So everything goes back to normal? You'll go back to kicking my chair and destroying my stuff?"

Corvus's gaze dropped, and he shifted his weight from foot to foot in obvious discomfort. Tiny ripples spread across the pool, disappearing within inches of their origin. "I honestly don't know. I'll do my best to tone it down, but I have to keep up appearances with the other wraiths. I can't promise anything, Billy. I'm sorry."

Rem punched Corvus's shoulder. "For a brave guy, he can be a real coward sometimes."

"I know it'd be hard for you to hang out with someone like me, but at least I'd be a true friend," Billy said. "The other wraiths are already shunning you, so it's not like things can get much worse, right?"

"Wrong." Corvus loosed a bitter laugh. "If they see me hanging out with humans, they'll report it to the king. He doesn't trust the children of oathbreakers. He'll torture me during the blood oath ceremony if he finds out we're friends."

"The other wraiths hang out with humans all the time," Billy pointed out.

"Yeah. Apparently, it's all right for them to do it, but not me and Rem. The whole thing's so stupid, but I can't do anything about it. Not if I want to escape with my life."

Billy inclined his head solemnly. "I understand. Do you want to hang out after school instead? My parents work until five-thirty, so my house would be free for a few hours. The other wraiths wouldn't see you."

Corvus mulled it over. "That would make things a lot easier for me.

I really am sorry, by the way. You didn't deserve any of the things I did to you."

"It's okay. I forgive you," Billy reassured him. *After everything he told me tonight, how could I not?* "We both made mistakes today, but I think it's fair to call it even and start again," he continued, sticking out his hand. "Hello, my name is Billy."

The wraith boy reached out and shook it firmly. "Nice to meet you, Billy. I'm Corvus."

Chapter Seven

THE AIR THRUMMED with electricity as the portal returned Billy and his newfound friends to Morton. He managed to stay conscious this time, but everything passed by in a blur of sepia. The world spun in crazy circles when they landed on the muddy banks of Oilskin Lake.

"Looks like the police are gone," Corvus said, surveying the clearing with a practiced eye. "The human ones, anyway. Dad and Lothaire must be around here somewhere."

"How long were we away?" Billy asked, squinting into the sunlight. "It didn't feel like that long."

"Hard to say. Maybe five hours?" Corvus tilted his head to one side. "Time passes differently between the two realms."

"What if we've been away for months? What if we've been away for *years*? I saw it happen on *Doctor Who* once. The girl's mom put missing person posters up all over town."

Corvus rolled his eyes. "Stop freaking out. This is real life, not one of your stupid TV shows."

"*Doctor Who* isn't stupid," Billy retorted. "Besides, how am I supposed to know these things? I didn't believe in magic before last night, let alone portals to other dimensions. You can't blame me for not knowing everything."

Corvus thought for a minute. "You're right. I'll try to remember you're new to all this."

They walked to the edge of the clearing and climbed over the post-

and-chain fence. Rem's leg caught on the drooping metal links, and she staggered forward, tumbling to the ground. Both boys hurried to her aid, but she shooed them off.

"Don't worry about me. I'm fine," she insisted, standing up and brushing the dirt from her clothes. "I always get a bit wobbly after changing forms. It's not easy to control a completely different body every twelve hours. The arms and legs don't always move the way I want them to, and my hands itch like crazy. It makes me want to break things."

I guess that explains why the houses were all scratched up.

"Rem! Corvus!"

Billy's head snapped in the direction of the unfamiliar voice. Two dark figures raced toward them, the first of whom he identified as Seisan. The second, taller figure reached them first, sweeping Rem into a bear hug.

That must be Lothaire, Billy thought.

Seisan approached at a more sedate pace, staring at his son instead of displaying open affection. Corvus averted his gaze.

"Did the potion work?" Lothaire asked. He released his daughter and scooped the other wraith child into a hug.

"Yup, just as you said it would," Corvus replied, struggling to free himself from the stifling embrace. After a few vain attempts, he gave up and patted Lothaire awkwardly on the back.

"I'm so glad." Lothaire beamed. The dark indigo tint of his teeth unnerved Billy, but he swallowed his apprehension in case the wraiths could sense it. "You're not going to experiment with magic again, are you?"

"Not until I'm in a supervised classroom," Rem promised.

"That's my girl."

Having ensured the safety of their children, the adult wraiths zeroed in on Billy, whose stomach lurched. They might as well have been staring into his soul.

"What are you doing here, Billy?" Seisan asked calmly.

Too calmly.

"I… I just… uh…"

"He wanted to help," Corvus finished, flashing Billy a warning look to keep quiet. "Is that a crime?"

"As a matter of fact, it is," Seisan said. "The curfew is not optional. We instituted it to keep people safe. Anyone found outside after seven p.m. can be fined or imprisoned. Including you, Corvus. Why didn't you tell me you were involved in this whole debacle?"

Billy's eyes widened. *Seisan didn't know?*

"I knew you'd react like this," Corvus complained. He jammed his hands into his jean pockets, resentment simmering in his gaze. "Lothaire and Rem needed my help. You can't expect me to ignore them."

"I've already had words with Lothaire," Seisan retorted, making Rem's father blush. "This conversation isn't over. Come along, Corvus. We're going home."

The wraith boy bowed his head and trailed after Seisan, shoes scuffing the ground as he walked. A lump formed in Billy's throat. *I never thought I'd feel sorry for Corvus, but he can't catch a break. No wonder he's so mean all the time.*

Lothaire strode over to Billy and wrapped a meaty arm around his shoulders. "I don't know who you are, kid, but any friend of Rem's is a friend of mine. Thanks for helping my daughter."

"Uh… that's okay, Mr. Lothaire," Billy said, shrinking back.

It felt wrong to accept the man's praise after shooting Rem, but he didn't have a choice. If Lothaire found out, the arm around Billy's shoulder would migrate to his neck and choke him to death, broad daylight or not.

"You two should hurry along home," Lothaire said. "I've got to report back to the police station and tell them I 'killed' the Monster of Morton. You've got some time left before school starts. You might want to clean up a bit before you go."

Billy looked down at his filthy clothes. *Good idea.*

"Okay, Dad," Rem agreed. "Did you take down the weather charms?"

"Already done," Lothaire said, patting his jacket pocket. "Have a good day, kids."

The older wraith departed, whistling a cheery tune. Confused, Billy turned to Rem. "Weather charms?"

"That's right. Dad set them up so no one would come out at night and try to hurt me. Now that everything's back to normal, there's no need for the charms to stay."

"Huh. Why was I able to get close to you, then?"

"Dad weakened the charms last night so Corvus and I could reach the portal unharmed. If you'd tried to get near me on any other day, the wind would have blown you all the way to Oklahoma."

I'm even luckier than I thought, Billy reflected. *Imagine if I'd ended up in another state. Mom would have had a fit!*

They set off down the street in companionable silence, broken only by a sparrow's trilling. The sound harkened the arrival of a new dawn— not just the dawn of a new day, but of a whole new era where the future looked brighter and a tiny bit less hostile. Billy glanced at Rem, admiring the way her ebony hair flowed down her back.

"You're very quiet. Are you sure you're okay?" he asked.

"Give me a break, will you?" Rem teased. "In the past twenty-four hours, I've switched forms three times and had a disgusting potion poured down my throat. It tasted like earwax and used dishwater." Her face contorted into a grimace, and Billy gagged in sympathy. "I'm a little tired from all the craziness, but I'll be fine after a good night's sleep."

"I'm sure you will be," Billy said. "I'm pretty tired too, to be honest. I don't know how I'm going to make it through school today."

As soon as the words left his mouth, he felt the truth of them. The last time he'd stayed up all night was New Year's Eve with James. They'd loaded themselves up on sugar and watched movies through the night, only to crash an hour before sunrise.

"Maybe your parents will let you stay home," Rem suggested.

Billy groaned and slapped his forehead, stopping dead in his tracks.

"My parents are gonna kill me if they find out I left the house. What time is it?"

"Nearly eight, I think. Would they really kill you? I know humans love their guns, but I didn't think they'd shoot their own kids."

"No, they won't shoot me. It's just a saying, Rem," Billy explained as they resumed walking. "It means I'm going to be in a whole lot of trouble. They'll probably make me move out of my bedroom and go back to sharing with my brothers."

Rem cocked her head to one side. "That doesn't sound too bad."

When you compare it to being tortured for talking to the wrong kids at school... "Yeah, I suppose you're right. I don't want to upset my parents, though."

"If you're worried about their reaction, maybe you can tell them you shot the monster. They'd be happy about that, right?"

"My dad would love that, but it won't do any good. They'll only get mad at your dad when he claims credit for it. Besides, I already got rid of the gun."

"Oh yeah." Rem's face fell. "Maybe you can tell them the monster kidnapped you from your room and that my dad helped you to get away."

"That's a good idea," Billy mused. "My dad might stop being so suspicious of wraiths if he hears I was saved by one."

"I wouldn't count on it," Rem said. She stumbled and caught herself at the last moment, cursing her potion-induced balance problems. "It's a nice thought, but one good deed isn't going to change anyone's opinions about us. Dad's been trying to convince people that he's a good man since he moved here. He makes cookies for bake sales. He donates money to fundraisers. He works as a police officer to keep Morton safe. He does all kinds of things, but everyone still hates us."

"I don't hate you," Billy told her honestly. "I think you're really cool, Rem. I'm sure there are lots of people who feel the same way."

The wraith girl smiled, her teeth a soft, radiant pink. It was a nice smile, Billy thought. A kind smile. The sight of it jolted his memory back to the previous day. He hadn't been the only one to draw Ms. Clemmons's attention with a failed project.

"You told us the monster wanted a friend," he blurted out. The unexpectedness of his outburst caught Rem by surprise, and she raised an eyebrow in his direction. "In your presentation, I mean. You were talking about yourself."

She nodded. "I've never had any friends besides Corvus. Everything he told you was true, by the way. The bullying... all of it. The monster thing was an accident, but people hated it more than they hated the real me. Now that I'm back to normal... I don't know. I'll have to try harder to be brave."

"You won't be alone this time," Billy promised. "I'll stand up for you."

"You're really sweet, Billy," Rem said, her smile faltering. "I'm not sure that's a good idea, though. I don't want you to get bullied too."

"I can take care of myself. It's you I'm worried about."

"I'll be okay. I know it's not going to be easy, but I'll manage. This isn't your fight. You shouldn't have to suffer for me."

"You shouldn't have to suffer either," Billy pointed out. "Why don't you want me to help you? Are you afraid the wraiths might report it? Corvus said something about torture earlier, but I wasn't sure if he was making it up or not."

"He wasn't," Rem said. "He thinks he can still prove himself to the king, but I think we're going to be tortured no matter what we do. So yeah. I'm scared. But I don't mind if the other wraiths find out we're friends. I just don't want to cause trouble for you with the other humans."

How can she be so calm about this?

Billy wanted to ask her about it—to insist her well-being mattered more than human approval—but he couldn't find the words before the two of them parted ways at his mailbox.

"Thanks for walking with me," he told her past the lump in his throat. "I'll see you at school, okay?"

Rem nodded and kept walking, her steps clunky and uneven. For a fleeting moment, he considered volunteering to accompany her, but he thought better of it. Rem knew how to take care of herself. More than that, she might view his offer as an insult.

He glanced up at the wind-battered exterior of his house and swallowed hard. *No sense in worrying about Rem. As soon as I walk through that front door, I'm going to have enough problems of my own.*

Chapter Eight

"WE THOUGHT YOU were dead!"

Billy's mother sobbed into his shoulder, her tears coalescing with the dried mud on his T-shirt. The floral aroma of her perfume tangled with the noisome odor of Oilskin Lake, forcing him to hold his breath to avoid inhaling it. He patted her on the back with the same awkwardness as Corvus had Lothaire, shooting his father a beseeching glance.

The man stood a few feet away, leaning against the wall with his arms crossed. An air of stony authority replaced his initial relief, and he stared back at Billy without blinking.

You scared your mother, his eyes said. *You will stand there and do whatever it takes to make things right again.*

"I'm okay, Mom," Billy reiterated.

She drew back, studying him as though she couldn't believe he was really there. "Why would the monster take you? You never caused trouble for anyone."

"I don't know. I'm just glad I'm home safe."

As expected, his parents had taken to Rem's lie like a duck to water. Mr. Porter balked at the idea of a wraith saving his son, but Lothaire's testimony would convince him soon enough. *All in all, it was a good plan.*

"I'm glad you're safe too," Mrs. Porter said. "Now go and have a shower before your brothers see what a state you're in. And don't tell

Hamish what happened. He'll never sleep again."

"Okay. I promise I won't."

Billy hurried down the hallway, all too aware of the eyes boring holes in his back. As he entered the bathroom, he caught a glimpse of his parents embracing. *I guess they're not fighting anymore.* Happiness wriggled through him, dislodging the terrible weight of anxiety from his chest. He shut the door and ran a bath with both taps on full blast.

Baths were frowned upon in his household for being wasteful, but he couldn't handle another lukewarm shower after the stress and terror he'd endured. His parents would understand. Dirt flaking from his body, he undressed and kicked his filthy clothes under the sink.

Mom's probably going to burn these.

She'd never approved of his fondness for band T-shirts, much less the music said bands produced. His jeans, on the other hand, would be mourned and replaced by Christmas.

A faint gurgle prompted him to glance at the bath, and he hurriedly shut off the taps. Water lapped at the rim of the tub, warm and inviting. He dipped a toe in the water, hissing when it burned his skin. He tried again, easing his body into the water this time. He sat there for half an hour, soaking in the warmth and scrubbing himself clean with a bright green loofah.

The water darkened to a murky brown by the time he got out, and chunks of mud remained stuck fast to the ceramic. After pulling the plug, he attempted to scrub away the worst of it, but his efforts only smeared it around the tub. Conceding defeat, Billy wrapped a towel around himself and walked to his bedroom to get dressed.

According to his Batman watch, the time had ticked over to 8:45 a.m. Too late for his father to offer him a ride, which suited him just fine. The fewer questions he had to answer, the better. He rifled through his dresser and picked out a white polo shirt and his tidiest pair of black slacks.

The shirt was a relic from his stint on the school baseball team. At the time, it'd been miles too big for him. Two years after quitting, he'd finally grown into the vast swathes of cloth. He'd intended to throw the shirt out, but his mother liked it enough to veto the idea. Her preference for seeing him in tidy clothes inspired him to wear it now.

He emerged from his room and headed for the lounge. Mrs. Porter sat on the sofa, paging through a photo album. Her handbag and coat sat next to her, apparently forgotten. Tears glimmered in her eyes.

"There you are, dear," she said, flashing him a shaky smile. "You should really go back to bed and rest. You had an awful night."

She snapped the album shut, hugging it to her chest. Worry lines creased her forehead, and Billy got the sense he'd walked in on something he wasn't meant to see. He sat down anyway, squinting to make out the embossed lettering on the album cover.

"Are those Heather's old photos?" he asked.

She recoiled at the suggestion, her brown eyes searching his. After a moment, her arm snaked around his shoulders and gave him a gentle squeeze.

"Yes. There are photos of…" She faltered and bit her lip. "Photos of your sister in here."

She dropped the album into her lap, and the leather cover bounced open. Billy leaned forward, eager to catch a glimpse of the infant who should have been his eldest sibling. An unfamiliar ache lanced his heart when he saw the first photo. Heather lay screaming in her mother's arms, her face wrinkled and pinkish-red from the stress of birth. She clenched the ear of a terry cloth rabbit in one fist and her mother's nightgown in the other.

You were a fighter, Billy thought, brushing the photo with reverent fingers. *I wish I could have met you.*

"This one was taken when she was four days old," Mrs. Porter said. "Two days before…"

Her voice cracked, and she fell silent.

Billy swallowed. "I know."

He turned the page, the images searing themselves into his brain. They never talked about Heather anymore. Not as a family. Apart from their annual visit to her grave, it was like she never existed.

"Do you miss her?" Billy asked.

Mrs. Porter squeezed him tighter. "Every day."

The sincerity in her words made him feel a little better. Heather may not have survived her first week on Earth, but she hadn't been forgotten. It comforted him to know that if he died in a freak accident one day, his parents wouldn't relegate his memory to a dusty corner of the basement.

"What happened?" he asked, looking up at his mother.

"We never did tell you, did we? I suppose you're old enough to know the truth. Especially after last night." She paused to gather her thoughts. "Your sister was born twelve years ago, one week before something called the Halloween Massacre. Have you heard of it?"

"No."

"I'm not surprised. Very few young people have these days." Mrs. Porter paused, tracing her late daughter's face with her index finger. "Your father and I never celebrated Halloween, but the wraith children were holding a festival in town. A fundraiser. They needed new clothes for the winter, so we decided to make an exception. It was our first outing as a family. Out of nowhere, an adult wraith started killing people with his bare hands. He took Heather..."

A lump formed in Billy's throat when her voice broke again. Hot tears spilled down her cheeks and dripped onto his shirt. "Mom..."

"A policeman showed up and shot him, but it was too late. She was gone. We'd only been living in Morton for a few months. Your dad wanted to leave, but no one would buy the house. That's when he started stockpiling guns. He didn't want anything like that to happen again, and neither do I. Do you understand what I'm saying, Billy?"

He shook his head mutely.

"Your dad isn't a bad man. He goes too far sometimes, but he only does it because he wants to protect our family. We talked things over, and we're both certain the monster took you because you talked to that wraith last night."

"No! A wraith *saved* me. The monster had nothing to do with them."

"All the same, things are going to change around here. Our job as parents is to keep you safe. You need to stop talking to the wraiths, okay?"

"But—"

"We won't lose another child to them. You *will* do as you're told, won't you, Billy?"

One look at her distraught face sent his head bobbing in agreement. "Yes, Mom."

"I'm glad to hear it. Now, I think it's time you went back to bed. You look like you're going to pass out."

Billy went without arguing.

Chapter Nine

THE CRUNCH OF tires on gravel confirmed Mrs. Porter's departure at half-past nine. Billy rolled out of bed fully dressed and shouldered his satchel. Despite his outward acceptance of the new rules, he had no intentions of following them.

It doesn't make any difference if a wraith killed Heather, he thought. *Whoever that guy was, he's either dead or in prison now. Corvus and Rem were nice to me. They're nothing like him.*

But deep down, he worried his parents were right. What if the wraiths' niceness was all an act—a deliberate ploy to lower his guard so they could attack him at his most vulnerable? To find out their true motives, he'd have to dive into the friendship headfirst and hope for the best.

Billy shuffled into the kitchen and tore a page from his mother's shopping pad. On it, he penned himself a late note, complete with forged signature. Satisfied with his efforts, he tucked the note into his satchel and jogged outside. The simple act of moving around got his blood pumping, and his earlier exhaustion receded. Feeling the sun on his back helped too.

Reptiles gain energy in sunlight, Billy thought, his brain still muddled. *I wonder what kind of reptile I would be?*

He liked Komodo dragons the best because they were huge and could spit venom, but he felt like more of a gecko—small, fast, and good at climbing. In his mind's eye, the bumpy footpath became a sand dune in a faraway desert. Imaginary lizards raced past him, and he kicked his legs out to the side in an effort to imitate them. *Being an animal would be so much easier than being a human.*

When he reached the school gates, he resumed walking normally. Everyone his age said that ten was too old for make-believe, and he didn't want to be ridiculed for it.

The school grounds were empty, save for a handful of staff loitering outside the science center. A van with tinted windows idled next to the building, enticing Billy to slow down and get a better look. Scientists in white coats unloaded equipment from the back and carried it inside, casting furtive glances in every direction. A row of men in black suits stood nearby, their arms crossed. One looked down at his watch and tapped his foot impatiently.

Weren't they here yesterday? Billy thought. *And what are those metal things? I hope we get to use them this year and they aren't just for the teenagers next door. We never get to play with the cool stuff.*

He crossed the courtyard to his classroom, ready as he'd ever be to face the day. A loud, indignant shout tore through the air, and he whipped around, frozen in place. Mr. Graham stood next to the van, gesticulating at its contents. His voice resonated with suppressed rage, but Billy was too far away to hear what he said. One of the suit-clad men pulled out a wallet and handed it to Mr. Graham, whose face paled. He stumbled back, shrinking into himself, and scurried away as fast as his legs would carry him.

Grownups sure are weird, Billy thought.

Ms. Clemmons's class was buzzing with activity when he arrived. He slipped the forged late note onto her desk, but she merely glanced at it before handing him a math textbook and shooing him away. The other kids had split into groups away from their usual desks, maintaining a steady stream of chatter as they worked.

As expected, neither Corvus nor Rem acknowledged Billy's presence, so he joined his human friends instead.

"Hey, guys. Did I miss anything?"

Murdock spun a yellow pencil around his finger, his face sagging with boredom. "Nothing important. Where have you been?"

A million possible answers raced through Billy's mind, but he settled on Corvus's words from the night before. "You wouldn't believe me if I told you. What are we supposed to be doing?"

The vague response must have satisfied their curiosity because they didn't push him further. Instead, Zane launched into a detailed explanation of how to add and subtract fractions. The boys had solved most of the problems already, so Billy copied from their books. *I'm too tired to do basic math right now, let alone fractions. Who cares about fractions anyway?*

They worked steadily until Ms. Clemmons sent them back to their seats to go over the answers. Murdock returned their textbooks to the front of the classroom while the other two boys retreated to their desks. Billy's legs wobbled as he sat down, his muscles aching from his late-night adventure.

"Swap books with someone near you," Ms. Clemmons instructed the class. "I don't want anyone changing their answers at the last minute."

Noticing Shauna's absence, Billy turned in his seat to face Corvus. The wraith lobbed a pitch-black notebook at his face, and he barely caught it in time. No trace of compassion lurked beneath the boy's stolid features. Behind Corvus, Rem held up an identical notebook and flashed him a small but encouraging smile. Unsure what to make of it, Billy handed over his own book.

"All right, let's look at the first question," Ms. Clemmons said. "You walk seven-eighths of a mile to the store to buy some milk…"

Billy opened the notebook, red pen at the ready. Blank, wrinkled pages stared up at him. He flipped through them, hoping to find Corvus's work, but came up short. *What's he playing at?* On the verge of giving up, he spied a message scrawled across the inside cover.

B—

Lothaire gave me a pair of charmed notebooks as a reward for helping R. We can use them to talk to each other. Just write what you want to say, and I'll see it in my notebook. To everyone else, it'll look like math equations.

Talk to you soon,

—C

Billy's eyebrows shot up. *This is incredible! It's like texting but better.*

His parents refused to let him have a cell phone, claiming he was far too young to need one. But this… this could make all the difference in his burgeoning friendship with the wraiths. If Corvus's claims were true, they could talk all they wanted without fear of being caught. He chewed the end of his pen, then lowered it to the paper.

Hey, he wrote.

Hi.

Is this Rem or Corvus?

It's Rem. How do you like the notebook?

It's great! Your dad's really clever.

Awww, you're too kind 😊

How does it work?

I don't know. There are a lot of complicated charms involved.

Magic?

Of course.

Billy tapped the end of the pen against his lips, gathering his thoughts. *Is Corvus in a lot of trouble with Seisan?*

Not really. He'll get over it.

I hope so. Seisan's scary when he's angry.

My dad's much scarier, believe me.

I believe you. I think my dad's scarier than both of your dads combined, though.

That's for sure.

Billy paused. *So, do you want to come over this afternoon? My brothers have after-school activities, and my parents won't be home until late.*

Sure! We can hang out for an hour or so. I'll try to bring Corvus along too.

"All right, class," Ms. Clemmons said, clapping her hands together. "That's all of the answers. Swap books again and see how you did."

Billy reluctantly handed the notebook back to Corvus. The other boy slapped it out of his hand, and the notebook cartwheeled to the floor, its pages splayed and bent. Rem gasped at her friend's cavalier attitude toward such a valuable possession.

Corvus smirked. "Keep it, *Billy*. How else could you do my homework for me?"

The spiteful words rolled off his tongue so easily that Billy's stomach flip-flopped with dread. Hands shaking, he picked up the book and shoved it into his satchel. *He has to do this. It's the only way he can protect himself from being tortured during his ceremony thing.* Billy glanced around the classroom, expecting glares of disapproval from the other wraiths. None of them showed the slightest hint of interest. Tears blurred his vision, but he refused to let them fall.

I bet you made it all up, he fumed. *They wouldn't report you. Why would they? You just like being a bully.*

Part of him realized this new, irrational thought was nothing more than a by-product of his exhaustion. He wished he'd listened to his mother's advice and stayed home rather than braving the classroom. If he had, he'd be drifting through the land of Nod instead of struggling to hold back a tidal wave of ridiculous emotions.

The recess bell brought an end to his misery. All around him, children fled from the classroom, eager for a respite from fractions and overbearing teachers. Corvus strolled after them, with Rem close behind. Her gait seemed much steadier than before, and Billy was struck by a sense of unreality. A sense that the previous night had been a figment of his imagination.

But it happened. I know it did, he thought, gazing down at the notebook. *Corvus might be acting mean again, but he did give me a present. And Rem agreed to come over later.*

"Are you really going to do his homework?" Zane asked, frowning. He'd approached silently, which was an impressive achievement for someone of his build. "Enough is enough, Billy. If you don't tell Ms. Clemmons, he's never going to stop harassing you."

"She already knows," Billy said. "And don't worry, I'm not going to do his homework. I'm just going to hold on to it and let him get a detention when he doesn't turn it in."

Murdock chuckled. "That's a good plan. It serves him right too."

Billy nodded, relieved they'd bought his excuse. "I'm not worried about Corvus. Do you guys want to hang out in the library or something? I heard they got some new comic books."

"Sounds good to me," Murdock said. "Zane?"

"Sure, why not?"

The path to the library took them past the science center, which reminded Billy of the strange things he'd seen earlier. Seeing Mr. Graham change from a ball of anger to a timid mouse had been the strangest thing of all—stranger than the van and all the men in suits. He'd borne the brunt of the teacher's ire a few times, usually for playing with Bunsen burners or leaving unwashed test tubes in the sink. Mr. Graham didn't suffer fools gladly, nor did he give in to external pressure. If the men in suits could change that aspect of his personality, they were bad news.

By unspoken agreement, the boys slowed to a halt outside the lab. Zane cupped his eyes against the window.

"Looks like there's no one in there," he reported.

"All the science people must have left," Billy said, bouncing on the balls of his feet. "Come on. The comic books are waiting."

The excitement of new comics aside, being around the lab gave him a bad feeling in the pit of his stomach. The smell of sulfur burned his throat, inciting a coughing fit to rival his father's. The scientists must have broken some of their chemical bottles when they unloaded the van.

"Wait! I see someone all the way at the back," Murdock said. He, too, stood with his nose pressed against the glass. "No—not just one person, there's a group of them! They must be the guys my dad told me about."

Billy tiptoed to the window and peered inside. The shadowed outline of a man stood near the back wall, facing away from them. "What guys?"

"You know, the government scientists," Murdock explained. "They asked my dad for a permit to study the wraiths, but he said no. Someone else on the council went over his head and gave them one anyway. He was mad about it for days."

"What do you mean, 'study the wraiths'?" Billy asked.

"I don't know what they're doing exactly. Dad wouldn't tell me. I think they're giving them health checks and IQ tests and stuff like that."

"Oh."

"They were here a couple of years ago too," Zane commented. "You were away on a hunting trip, and Murdock was home sick with pneumonia. They called the wraiths out of class, and some of them didn't come back for ages."

A shiver went down Billy's spine. "What do *you* think they're doing?"

Zane pulled back from the window. "I don't know, and I don't care. As long as they stay away from me, they can study anything they want."

Chapter Ten

BILLY PASSED THROUGH the morning in a haze of exhaustion. When he succumbed to the sweet embrace of sleep at 1:00 p.m., drooling over his desk and snoring loud enough to wake the dead, Ms. Clemmons sent him home. Her face expressed both irritation at being interrupted and concern for his well-being. Fortunately, she hadn't seen fit to call his mother—or worse, his father—to complain about his "blatant disregard" for her instruction.

He arrived home half an hour later, unable to walk faster than a slow shuffle. Fatigue steamrolled his body, and he collapsed onto the sofa. *Rem and Corvus are coming over in a few hours. I need to stay awake.* With that thought, he immediately dozed off into a deep and dreamless sleep, clutching the magic notebook like a teddy bear.

At 3:45 p.m., a loud knock jolted him awake. In his groggy state, he interpreted the sound as a monster attack and fell off the sofa, arms flailing. The short, sharp shock of hitting the floor restored his senses, and he raced over to let his friends in.

"About time you opened up," Corvus groused. "Anyone could have seen us. I'm wearing a hoodie next time. I don't care if it's the middle of summer."

"Nice to see you too," Billy retorted. The tears he'd been fighting all day came back with a vengeance, but he blinked them away before the wraiths could see.

"I'm sorry we're so late," Rem said, shutting the door behind them.

"We were going to come straight over, but Corvus wanted to get your dad's gun first."

She pulled a familiar revolver out of her backpack and handed it to him, grip first. A few dings and scratches marred the barrel, none large enough to cause concern. If Mr. Porter noticed, he'd write them off as normal wear and tear.

"Thanks," Billy said, flashing them a relieved smile. "I'll put this back in the safe and then we can hang out. Wait here a minute."

He jogged off, leaving them alone in the lounge. The keys to the gun safe weren't where he left them, but a quick search of the desk drawers turned up a spare.

Rem was studying a black-and-white family portrait when he rejoined them. "I like your house, Billy. It's way bigger than mine."

"Cleaner too," Corvus added, earning himself a playful swat from Rem.

"You're one to talk. Your room is a pigsty."

While the wraiths squabbled back and forth, Billy led the way to his room and waved them inside. Rem perched on the dresser, while Billy sat on the bed. Corvus's gaze flickered between the bed and the floor before he settled on the latter.

"So, what do you guys want to do?" Billy asked. "I've got a ton of Lego if you want to play with that."

"We don't really play with toys," Corvus said

"Oh. Okay. What do you want to do, then? Play video games? Watch TV?"

"We don't do that stuff either."

Billy paused, dumbfounded. "What *do* you do?"

"Most of the time, we just talk and study magic prep."

"Magic prep?"

"Yeah," Rem said. "We have to learn the fundamentals before we turn thirteen. Otherwise, we might not get into the Academy."

"There's an academy for magic?" Billy asked, his eyes widening. "Is it like Hogwarts?"

Corvus frowned. "Hog-what?"

"Hogwarts. It's a school for young witches and wizards to learn magic. It's in *Harry Potter.*"

"Oh. One of your human books," Corvus said, his voice condescending. "I've never read it, but I guess it's similar."

"And the Academy is in the Gloaming?" Billy guessed.

"That's right," Rem said. "If you don't get in, you don't get a second chance. They put you in hard labor if you fail the entrance exam."

"Well, that sucks," Billy said. "What if you get the flu the day before and your head's so full of snot that you can't think straight?"

"We can't catch human illnesses, so I don't think that will be a problem," Rem replied.

"Okay, but what if you catch a wraith illness? What happens if you fail the exam but you're too sick to work?"

"You die."

"Wait, *what?* Really?"

"That's what my dad told us," Corvus said. "There's a famine in the Gloaming. If King Grigoth decides the laborers have done enough work for the day, he gives them food. If he's annoyed at them, they starve."

"Grigoth sounds like a big jerk."

"He is," the wraiths replied in unison, and all three children erupted into gales of laughter. When their mirth subsided, Corvus hugged his knees to his chest.

"That jerk is our king," he said, looking tired all of a sudden. "We're not bound to him yet, but we will be. One way or another, we're going to be serving him. All we can hope for is to get into the Academy and graduate at the top of our class. If we can do that, he'll make sure we get food to eat and a roof over our heads."

"I guess you'd better study hard, then," Billy said.

"I always study hard."

"You didn't finish your math problems today."

Corvus pouted. "That doesn't mean I don't study. I do. Just not at school. Who cares about numbers and grammar when you could be learning magic? Who cares about adding water to acids in science class when you could be mixing potions?"

"Um… you're not supposed to add water to acid," Rem reminded him. "It has to be the other way around. Otherwise, it splashes up and burns you."

"Really?" Corvus tilted his head to one side. "Couldn't you have told me that last semester? I might have passed my test if I'd known that."

"I *did* tell you," Rem said, shaking her head in exaggerated disgust. "You just didn't listen."

"Never mind that," Billy interrupted. "Tell me more about the magic. I thought you guys weren't supposed to be practicing yet."

"We aren't, but we can still test things out if one of our parents is supervising," Rem explained. "The other wraith kids won't learn anything until they enter the Academy, so we'll have a big advantage over them. It's not exactly fair, but—"

"The world isn't fair," Corvus finished. "I'll do whatever it takes to get to the top. We both will."

"Why not stay here in Morton?" Billy asked. The other kids shot him puzzled looks, compelling him to continue. "I mean, if things are as bad as you say they are, wouldn't that be better?"

"We can't *stay*," Corvus spluttered. "That would be *blasphemous*. No one in their right mind would consider it."

"Besides, things aren't so great here either," Rem added. "The townsfolk hate us. The teachers hate us. And now the scientists are back—"

"The scientists!" Billy sat bolt upright, suddenly wide awake. "I forgot all about them. Murdock told me they're studying your health or something."

"I wouldn't call it that," Corvus said, his lip curling in disgust. "You saw them call Volner out of class. Didn't that seem odd to you? A random stranger from out of town walks in and forces this kid to go with him, and Ms. Clemmons doesn't even question it?"

Billy blinked. "Volner?"

"Yeah, the kid who sits in the back corner."

"I must have missed it."

"Now that I think about it, you *were* snoring pretty loudly," Corvus conceded. "And to think you made fun of *my* study habits. At least *I* stay awake in class."

"I was tired," Billy protested. He shifted into a more comfortable position, his eyebrows knitted together. "You're right about Volner, though. Those scientists are super shady. My friend said they've been to the school before and wraiths started disappearing."

Corvus made a noise in the back of his throat that could have been a chuckle but sounded more like a dying walrus. His left hand moved to the scar on his neck, rubbing it as though it pained him.

"Your friend's right about that," he said. Bitterness laced every word. "Things are going exactly the same way as before. The scientists show up. We get called out of class one by one. We come back worse for wear a few days later. It's the in-between where my memory gets hazy."

Fear gripped Billy's heart. "They called you out too?"

"Not recently," Corvus clarified. "Last time. It was a couple of years ago. I only remember bits and pieces of it."

He dug his fingers deeper into the scar, kneading it until the surrounding skin lightened to a reddish-purple. Rem hopped down from the dresser and joined her friend on the floor, resting a supportive hand on his shoulder.

"All of the scientists had different theories about us," Corvus explained when his voice returned. "All of them were equally stupid. The scientist who chose me for her experiments was one of the tamer ones. She thought we were diseased humans who spent too long hanging around the 'chemicals' in Oilskin Lake. She got a bunch of samples from me and then let me go. I've still got a scar from one of her needles."

He stopped rubbing his collarbone and pointed at it with a shaking finger.

"The needle they used was way too big, and it hit a major vein," Rem explained on his behalf. "He would have bled out if he hadn't put pressure on it straight away and gotten my dad to heal it. Believe it or not, he actually had it easy compared to the other kids."

"What happened to them?" Billy asked.

"Most of the scientists wanted to prove how 'inferior' we are compared to humans," Corvus said, averting his gaze. "Some of the kids weren't fed for days. Some were electrocuted for hours at a time. Some were dissected while they were still alive."

"That's horrible! Why don't their parents do something?" Billy exclaimed. "My dad would be down there like a shot if some random scientist was experimenting on me. My mom would too."

"The other wraiths aren't like us. They don't have parents on Earth," Rem said. "Grown-up wraiths never come here unless they're oathbreakers or under direct orders from the king himself."

"They don't live with their parents?" Billy repeated numbly. Both wraiths shook their heads.

"There's an old homestead a few minutes' walk from the portal. Most of them live there," Rem said. "Even if their parents *were* here, I doubt they'd do anything. There are government agents with the scientists. They'd probably get themselves shot and killed if they tried to interfere."

"None of the humans would stand for this," Billy asserted. It felt strange to mention his own species as though he were no longer a part of it. "I know they wouldn't. Remember the unit we did on World War Two? The Nazis did experiments like that, and everyone hated them for it. It wouldn't even matter that you're wraiths. We just have to tell someone what's going on."

"Yeah, because we haven't tried that already," Corvus said, rolling his eyes. "The scientists can do whatever they want until they're given a formal order to leave. It takes weeks for that kind of paperwork to go through. Months, even. Most people think we're lower than animals. That we're evil and deserve to suffer. They're not going to do anything to speed it up."

"If we can't get rid of them fast, maybe we can slow them down instead," Billy said. He climbed off his bed and knelt in front of the wraiths. "They brought a bunch of equipment with them, right? Equipment they need for the experiments."

"Right," Corvus said.

"So, what if we destroy that equipment?"

"You'd have to be crazy to even try. If their setup is anything like last time, they've got government agents guarding the whole building."

"We can distract them. If we do something big enough, they'll have to leave. We can get in and out before they know what hit them."

"How on earth are we going to do that?"

"I don't know yet, but I'll work it out. Zane and Murdock would probably help us."

Corvus's face scrunched up in displeasure. "You'd have to tell them about our friendship."

"I know. It's not going to be easy for either of us, but I don't think we can do it without them. Everyone knows you've threatened Zane before, so no one would be surprised if you two started a fight in the courtyard or something. I reckon that would distract the scientists."

"You want me to fight him?" Corvus squeaked.

"You said you could 'take him on any day.'"

"Yeah, but I didn't mean it. He scares the living daylights out of me!"

"It won't be a real fight," Billy reassured him. "I've seen how good you are at acting. If you can sell it to me, you can sell it to the grownups. You just have to make it look bad enough that they won't go back into the lab. Me, Rem, and Murdock will handle the destruction."

"Why Murdock?" Corvus asked.

"His dad works for the council. If he sees what's happening, he might be able to get his dad to speed up the paperwork," Billy replied. "Plus, when Zane and Murdock see what a good guy you are, you'll have two more people on your side."

"Human people," Corvus groaned. "It's too risky. If the other wraiths find out—"

"They won't care. If anything, they'll love you for saving their skins. Honor is important to wraiths, right? Wouldn't it be honorable to save them?"

Corvus pondered his words for a long moment.

"Billy's right. It *would* be honorable," Rem said, elbowing him gently.

Corvus blew a stream of frustrated air through his lips. "Fine. We'll try it. Just don't expect me to get all buddy-buddy with the humans when this is over."

"I wouldn't dream of it," Billy said, biting back a grin.

Something metallic rattled down the hallway, putting an abrupt end to their conversation. Anxiety flickered in the wraiths' eyes. *Is someone unlocking the front door?* Billy held his breath and listened for the telltale clunk of work boots. If Mr. Porter was home early, it meant nothing but trouble—both for himself and for the guests he harbored in his room. The man's plodding footsteps didn't come, but the clack of high heels did.

"That's my mom," he hissed, rushing to open the window. "You'd better go before she comes in."

"You said she wouldn't be back until later," Corvus retorted, climbing outside. He held out his hands to help Rem, but she ignored him and landed blithely on the grass.

"Yeah, well, I was wrong," Billy said. "How was I supposed to know she would come home early?"

The wraiths glided out of sight without wasting their breath on goodbyes. Biting back a frustrated growl, Billy closed the window. The frame squealed as the two panes aligned. His gaze flitted across the room, checking that no evidence of his illicit visitors remained. Seeing nothing, he dove into bed. The door opened seconds later, and his mother peeked in.

"Billy? Are you asleep?"

He lay motionless beneath the sheets, shallow breaths tickling his nostrils. Mrs. Porter came into the room, her soft footsteps slowing in front of him. Through the tiniest slit between his eyelids, he saw the tortoiseshell buttons of her coat. She coaxed the magic notebook from his fingers, her expression tender. *I should have put it down earlier.* Corvus claimed the notebook would encrypt their discussions, but he didn't know how trustworthy Lothaire's charms were.

"Never mind homework. You need your rest," Mrs. Porter murmured, sliding the notebook onto the dresser.

The bed dipped next to him, and a cool hand pressed against his forehead. It took all of his willpower not to lean into the touch. His mother stayed for several minutes, stroking his hair and humming a lullaby under her breath. Then the hand disappeared, and she slipped out of the room as quickly as she'd entered.

All the tension seeped out of Billy's body, loosening his knotted airways so he could breathe again. Her arrival had put him in a difficult position with the wraiths, but with a bit of luck, they wouldn't be too mad at him. *I should write to them and apologize.*

He tried to wiggle himself into a sitting position, but the softness of his pillow made it impossible. His sleep-deprived brain dragged him down into the world of dreams and refused to let him go. He didn't wake up for dinner.

Chapter Eleven

"You're home late."

Rem met Seisan's probing gaze for three whole seconds before she looked away and let Corvus handle the situation. Three seconds—that was two seconds longer than her previous record. Enough time to study his expressionless face and assess the level of threat. His mild tone of voice told her the statement had been one of intellectual curiosity rather than an accusation, but she preferred not to take any chances.

"Yeah, something came up," Corvus said, grabbing a candy bar from the pantry on his way past. "So, what are we studying today?"

A mewling whine escaped his lips when Seisan plucked the snack from his hand and replaced it with an apple.

"I had planned to teach you some basic cloaking magic this evening," Seisan said, ignoring his son's displeasure. "However, given your less-than-satisfactory behavior last night, I've decided that neither of you are mature enough to learn them. In light of this, you will be brewing healing potions instead."

Rem looked down at her shoes, blushing furiously. *This is my fault. I shouldn't have tried to turn myself into a human with that stupid cloaking potion. Seisan must think I'm an idiot.*

"Is this a punishment?" Corvus asked. He bounced the apple in his palm a few times, contemplating whether to eat it, then returned it to the fruit bowl.

"No, it's not a punishment," Seisan said. "You atoned for your actions this morning, and I forgave you. That's the end of the matter."

"Why are we making potions, then? You know I suck at them."

"The only way to get better at something is through practice. As for the reason..." Seisan hesitated. "It has come to my attention that certain unscrupulous individuals have returned to the area. Lothaire and I suspect they may cause harm to your classmates."

"You mean the scientists?" Rem asked, breaking her silence.

"Yes. If they do cause harm, whether by accident or design, it is vitally important that we have enough healing potions on hand."

"Or we could just get rid of the scientists," Corvus suggested, shooting a flinty glare at Seisan.

"We've talked about this before, Corvus. You know it isn't that simple." A hint of regret flickered under Seisan's otherwise aloof expression. "We may live on Earth, but this isn't our home. If we want to stay, we cannot afford to rock the boat. If we oust the scientists, we'll be clearing the way for a group with less virtuous motives to take their place."

"Less virtuous motives?" Corvus snorted in disbelief. "They're already *torturing* us. It can't get any worse than that."

"Perhaps, but at least they do it for the sake of knowledge rather than sadistic pleasure. If we ended up with scientists in the latter category, things would be much worse. There's a good chance your classmates would be abducted and transported to their private laboratory in Nevada. If that happened, Lothaire and I would no longer be able to heal them. A little poking and prodding in the local laboratory is a small price to pay in exchange for our lives."

"A little poking and prodding? More like a whole lot of stabbing and jabbing. You know what happened last time. You can't just sit here and do nothing."

"I understand your frustration, Corvus. Believe me, I do. The last thing I want is for you to get the impression I approve of what the scientists are doing. But would you rather suffer for two days in Morton or a lifetime in Nevada? Two days under the knife or two months starving to death in the Gloaming?"

The questions hung in the air like a thick fog, and Rem shivered. Neither option appealed to her, but short-term suffering was the logical choice, especially if healing took place afterward. No such hope existed for an unbound wraith outside of Morton. Seisan's doom-and-gloom theories about abduction, on the other hand, could be safely ignored. They'd never come true in the past, and she saw no reason to start believing them now.

"Anyway, I've done enough talking," Seisan said, clapping his hands together. "Let's get started on the potions so we can help your classmates."

Rem and Corvus accompanied him to his private storeroom, where he handed each of them a cauldron and some bottled ingredients. Rem staggered back to the dining room and placed hers on the table. Corvus followed suit.

"Right," Seisan said as he rejoined them. "I know you're already familiar with this potion, but feel free to ask for help if you need it."

Rem rolled up her sleeves, mentally reviewing the recipe. The first step called for two ounces of pulverized lavender and half an ounce of koerak scales. She unscrewed the lids of the appropriate bottles and tipped the contents into her mortar, using the pestle to grind them into a fine powder.

Corvus cleared his throat. "Dad?"

"Yes?"

"Why do we need to make potions? Wouldn't it be easier to cast a healing spell?"

"Excellent question. You are correct that a healing spell would be easier. However, some situations are better handled with a potion. Why do you think that is?"

"If I knew, I wouldn't be asking you."

Seisan turned a deaf ear to his son's snarky comment and turned to Rem. "What about you? Why do you think potions are important in this day and age?"

Rem's cheeks heated up. "I don't know. Maybe they can heal things that spells can't?"

"An excellent guess," Seisan said, favoring her with a smile. "There *are* some illnesses that can only be cured by potions. But there's another very important benefit that potions have. Do you have any idea what it might be?"

He actually smiled! *Maybe he doesn't think I'm stupid after all.*

"I can't think of anything," she admitted, emptying the contents of her mortar into the cauldron. "Is it something to do with energy?"

"Yes, that's exactly right. Casting spells is easy in the Gloaming because the entire dimension is built on a wellspring of magical energy. Accessing that wellspring from Earth is much more difficult. Because we can't draw enough energy from the Gloaming to fuel our spells, we have to supplement it with energy from our bodies. Do you know why that might be dangerous?"

"Because our bodies have a limited amount of energy?" Rem guessed.

"Right again," Seisan said. "It's a matter of simple arithmetic. If someone tries to cast a spell that requires more energy than their body can spare, the overdraft will either drain them to a husk or kill them outright. Healing spells are all-or-nothing, so they possess a unique risk. Potions offer a much safer alternative because they store their own energy. Charmed objects work in a similar way."

Rem added a splash of ricrawth bile to the cauldron and stirred it around. "Charmed objects? You mean like the notebooks?"

Seisan's brow furrowed. "Notebooks?"

"Dad gave me and Corvus a charmed pair so we can talk to each other."

For a fleeting moment, Rem thought Seisan would be angry, but he merely raised his eyebrows.

"A valuable gift," he said. "As I was saying, charmed objects can also be useful when energy consumption is a concern. They have other benefits too, of course. You can imbue them with special properties, like your notebooks. You can charm a sword to be as light as a feather in your hand and heavier than an anvil when someone tries to take it from you. You can even charm the hilt of your sword to jump back into your hand if you drop it during a duel. Speaking of which, have you practiced with your swords today?"

Rem and Corvus shook their heads.

"I suppose that can't be helped. You'll have to make up for lost time tomorrow."

"But I hate sword fighting! It's too hard," Corvus groused.

"Nothing worth doing is easy," Seisan reminded him. "With the way things are in the Gloaming, developing skill with the blade is more important than ever. Grigoth has been taking full advantage of his kingship to alter not only the laws of magic but its underlying essence. If he carries on like this—and I have reason to believe he will—the spells you've learned may very well fail you in battle. When that happens, you'll be glad of your sword."

"But we're not going back to the Gloaming for three years," Corvus said, rolling his eyes. "Do we really have to practice already?"

"Yes, you do," Seisan replied. "I know you don't like it, but it's a necessary evil. Out of interest, is that why you didn't practice today? Because you hate sword fighting?"

Corvus shook his head.

"Then why?"

"Billy invited us to his house."

Genuine surprise etched itself into Seisan's features. "Billy Porter invited you over? Of his own free will?"

Uh oh, Rem thought. *Meltdown in three, two, one…*

"Obviously! What kind of thug do you take me for?" Corvus snapped.

"I never said—"

"You think I *enjoy* pushing humans around? If you ever spent time with me, you'd know better. Billy's my friend now, but I have to treat him like dirt at school because of the stupid blood oath ceremony. It's not fair!"

With that final declaration, Corvus spun on his heel and ran to the safety of his room.

The suddenness of his departure didn't surprise Rem. Although she was no telepath, their bond meant she could follow the color of his emotions as easily as her own. He ran when he was afraid—when he was hurting and too embarrassed to show it. He never ran from simple anger. She resisted the temptation to rush after him, knowing it would do more harm than good. Instead, she glanced at Seisan, who stared after his son like a lost puppy.

"I've never seen him like this before," he murmured.

"He'll be okay," Rem reassured him. "He's just under a lot of pressure."

"Yes, of course he is." Seisan blinked distractedly. "You're welcome to go home whenever you like, Rem. We'll resume the potions tomorrow."

"I understand." She hung her head and peeked up at him through her lashes. "If it's all right with you, I'd like to stick around a little longer. I want to check on Corvus before I go."

"Are you sure that's a good idea?"

Rem thought about it. "We're Promised to each other. He'll talk to me."

"Well, if you insist, I won't stop you. Just don't forget to keep an eye on the time."

"I won't."

She left the shell-shocked wraith behind and traversed the dark hallway to Corvus's room. No sobs or screams of rage met her ears, so she pushed the door open. Her friend sat in the corner of the room, hugging his knees. He looked up at her with the hopeless eyes of a condemned man. *So far, so good.*

Corvus needed time alone after a blow-up, but "time" for him varied between thirty seconds and one minute. Any shorter and his emotions would explode in intensity; any longer and he'd interpret her absence as siding with his father. Both outcomes resulted in a cold shoulder for days afterward.

Rem didn't say anything as she approached Corvus, nor when she slid down the wall to sit next to him. His cheeks were flushed violet and streaked with frustrated tears, but he wasn't crying anymore. She placed an arm around his shoulders, and he melted into her.

"I won't take the blood oath. I won't! It's not fair," he mumbled.

"I know it's not fair," Rem said. "I don't want to take it either. But what choice do we have? We can't stay in Morton."

"We could run away."

"Do you really think we can survive on our own?"

"I don't know, but the other wraith kids do. Why not us?"

Rem studied Corvus. *Is he serious about this or just upset?*

"Where do you want to go?" she asked.

"I don't know. Anywhere but here. Somewhere Grigoth won't send his goons after us."

"If we go that far away, the scientists will look for us instead."

Corvus's eyes darkened. "And we'll dissect *them* for a change." He paused for a long moment, lips pursed, then shook his head. "I didn't mean that. I don't know what came over me."

His voice cracked on the last word, and Rem hugged him tighter.

"You've had a stressful day. Anyone in your position would react the same way. How long has it been since you last slept?"

"A couple of days. Why?"

"Even wraiths have to sleep sometime."

Corvus's lower lip curled petulantly. "Not me."

"*Especially* you. Come on. You'll feel better after a good night's rest."

She sensed his resolve weakening and struggled to her feet, hauling him up with her. His arms draped around her middle, and he gazed at her with hooded eyes.

"How am I supposed to sleep?" he protested. "You got shot today. I almost *lost* you. Dad hates me. The scientists are back. My mind won't shut up."

"I'm right here. You didn't lose me," Rem soothed. She readjusted her grip on Corvus and half-led, half-carried him to his bed, feeling more like his mother than his friend and future bondmate. "Your dad doesn't hate you either. I know it might feel that way sometimes, but

I've seen how much he cares about you. He's just worried, Corvus."

The boy harrumphed but didn't otherwise challenge her statement. Balancing him against her hip, Rem pulled back the covers and deposited him on the bed. He rolled onto his back, allowing her to tuck him in.

"What about the scientists?" he asked. "They could grab us any day, you know. They've already taken at least one kid."

Rem crouched in front of him and rocked back on her heels. "I know. But Billy's got a plan to stop them, remember? Things will work out."

"You trust him."

"Don't you?"

Corvus hesitated. "I don't know. It might come back to bite me, but I think I do. He's not like the other humans."

"No, he's not," Rem agreed. "So what are you worried about?"

Corvus turned to face her, propping himself up on one elbow. "Everything! I want to help Volner, but we could get in a lot of trouble. I can't believe I agreed to fight Billy's friend. What if I hit him too hard and he dies? I could get the death penalty."

"You can't get the death penalty if it's an accident."

"Yeah, but I'm a wraith. The judge will take one look at me and assume the worst."

"You worry too much," Rem said, guiding his head back to the pillow. "Corvus, listen. I know you. You won't hurt him. Everything's going to be fine. But if it makes you feel better, we can talk to my dad about the scientists instead. Maybe he can help us to come up with a different plan."

"It's no use. Your dad will side with mine and tell us to stop 'rocking the boat.' Parents are all the same."

Corvus's fist clenched in helpless frustration, and Rem took it as a sign to backtrack. "All right, all right. If you don't want to tell him, we won't. It was just an idea."

"A bad idea," Corvus retorted. "So, no, we're not telling him."

"Okay."

"Good."

Neither of them spoke for a long while. Rem sat on the floor, hedged by a stack of books on one side and a giant pile of clothes on the other. She chose a book at random, hoping to read her friend to sleep, but his amethyst eyes remained stubbornly alert. He tolerated several chapters before his gaze flickered to his alarm clock.

"It's nearly midnight. You'd better go, Rem."

"Yeah, I know. I wouldn't want to turn into a pumpkin."

Corvus's brow knitted in confusion. "Why would you turn into a pumpkin?"

"I don't know. It happened in a human fairytale I read."

"Humans are so weird."

"Not weird, just different," Rem quipped. Mirth bubbled up in her chest when she saw his bewildered expression. "Anyway, you're right. I really should be going. Have a good sleep, Corvus."

"I'll try."

Rem switched off the light and tiptoed out of her friend's room. Come morning, he'd deny their conversation ever took place, and she'd go along with it because it proved he was back to normal. Besides, she didn't want to indulge his cut-and-run fantasies any more than she had to.

Rem passed through the empty lounge and headed for the front door. Soft light spilled under the door of Seisan's bedroom, and she heard his shoes scuff the cedar floorboards. She nearly called out to say goodbye but thought better of it. It would be cruel to disturb him for the sake of a pointless social custom. With a final glance at the dark house, she stepped out into the night.

Chapter Twelve

"PARTNER UP, PARTNER up!" Mr. Graham's wheezy voice carried across the science lab. "We're going to be doing something a little special today. Teams of three, everyone. Teams of three."

Billy stifled a groan and shuffled to his usual work station. *Which is it, then, sir? Partners or teams of three?* He didn't dare to say it out loud. The man was half deaf and should have retired ten years ago, but his ability to hear and punish insolence was second to none. His advanced age also earned him a great deal of respect, which explained why he'd stayed in a hole like Morton for so long.

"Aiden, you're going to be my assistant today," Mr. Graham announced. He patted a supply trolley laden with black, vacuum-sealed bags. "I need you to hand these out. One to every group. Quick as you like."

The moon-faced boy turned a curious shade of green, but he obeyed without complaint.

"We'll be studying the art of dissection today," Mr. Graham continued, his voice inappropriately cheerful. "When you get your package, I want you to open it *very* carefully. You'll find a scalpel in the plastic container on your workbench. Any tomfoolery and I'll keep you in detention until your hair turns gray. Understood?"

While the children mumbled their agreement, Aiden approached Billy's workbench. The greenish tinge to his skin faded to a ghostly milk-white, as though all the life were being drained out of him. He picked one of the bags off the trolley with his thumb and index finger and dropped it on their workbench. It hit the laminated surface with a squelch, making all four boys grimace. Having completed his duty, Aiden shambled on to the next table.

Billy's forehead crinkled in concern. "Do you think Aiden will be okay? He looks terrible."

"I heard he's a *vegan*," Murdock whispered conspiratorially.

"What does that mean?"

"I don't know exactly what it means, but I do know there's a lot of things he can't eat. He went to Luke's birthday party last weekend, and he couldn't have any of the food. Maybe he ate something he wasn't supposed to at lunch."

"So it's like an allergy?" Billy tilted his head to the side. "My brother can't eat shellfish or he swells up like a balloon and pukes everywhere. Do you think we should call the nurse?"

"You two need to calm down," Zane said, rolling his eyes. "'Vegan' just means he doesn't eat meat or anything that comes from animals. It's a choice, not an allergy. He'll be fine."

"Huh." Murdock furrowed his eyebrows. "But why would anyone give up meat if they weren't allergic to it? It's delicious."

"Beats me," Zane said. He returned his attention to the package on the table. "Anyway, one of us has to open this thing. Shotgun, not me."

"Shotgun, not me," Murdock echoed.

"Fine, I'll do it," Billy grumbled. He ripped open the plastic, sending slimy preservative oil all over the table. The other boys leapt back to avoid the resulting splatter.

"Carefully, boys! I said *carefully*!" Mr. Graham barked.

Murdock grabbed a roll of paper towels from the front desk and tried to mop up the excess goop. Mr. Graham shook his head in dispirited silence and moved on to the next workbench. With the surface clear, Billy built up the courage to peek inside the bag. After Corvus's story yesterday, the idea of dissecting *anything* sickened him. What if they had to chop up a wraith heart? A brain? A piece of Volner? Hands trembling, he peeled open the bag.

Inside was a frog.

A frog!

A titter of relieved laughter flew out of him before he could stop it, and he clamped a hand to his mouth. Zane gave him a sideways glance but didn't otherwise question his abnormal reaction. Billy donned a pair of latex gloves, took a few deep breaths, and manhandled the frog out of its wrappings. A twinge of guilt pierced his heart.

He didn't mind hunting animals for meat. After all, a fully grown deer would feed his family for two weeks when mixed into a casserole. Dissection was a different story. He got the sense it was something serial killers did—carving small animals apart to see what their insides looked like.

He glanced at Corvus and Rem, who stood with their backs to an unopened packet. Unmitigated disgust marred their features. *This must be too close to home for them. How can the school force the wraiths to do this, knowing what they went through a couple of years ago?*

Murdock grabbed a scalpel from the plastic container on their bench. "So, how do we do this?"

"You have to pin the legs first," Zane said, pointing at Mr. Graham's demonstration table. "If you don't, it'll jump all over the place, and you might cut the internal organs by accident."

Billy's stomach lurched. *Dissectiondissectiondissectiondissection—*

"Guys, we need to talk," he said, averting his gaze.

Murdock looked up from the frog. "What about?"

"Do you remember the scientists we saw at recess yesterday?" Billy asked. The question elicited nods from both boys. "You were right that something fishy is going on. I found out what they're doing, and we need to do something to stop them."

"What do you mean?" Zane asked.

"What I mean"—Billy lowered his voice—"is that those scientists are torturing students."

Zane snorted. "I'd believe that."

"You would?"

"Sure. Look at Mr. Graham. He's torturing our whole class with these stupid dissections. No one wants to do them."

"Zane, I'm being serious," Billy said, leaning closer to his friends. "Those creepy people in lab coats are taking the wraiths away and experimenting on them. It's just like Murdock said, except they're not giving them health checks. They're dissecting them while they're still alive."

Zane loosed another uneasy laugh. "Are the formaldehyde fumes getting to your head? If you want to go outside for a minute, I'm sure Mr. Graham wouldn't mind."

"He said he was serious." Murdock leaned forward like Billy. "How did you find out?"

"You have to swear not to tell anyone."

"Okay, I swear I won't."

"Same here," Zane agreed.

"It's a long story, and I don't have time to go into all the details, but I was hanging out with Corvus and Rem last night, and they told me."

Silence reigned for an uncomfortably long time as the boys digested Billy's words. Their expressions betrayed the shock they felt, and it didn't take long for anger to surface too.

"Why would you hang out with *Corvus* after everything he's done to you?" Zane asked. "He doesn't have a single redeeming quality. He's a jerk, plain and simple."

"I thought so too, until I got to know him. Like I said, I can't tell you everything. But they experimented on him and some of his friends a few years ago, and not all of them came back. He's got a scar and everything."

"So what? He could have gotten it in a fight," Murdock pointed out. "How do you know we can trust him?"

"I just do," Billy said. "I know I'm asking too much for you to trust him, so trust me instead. Help me get to the bottom of this. Wraith or not, no one deserves to be tortured."

His friends exchanged glances.

"Okay, okay. I'm in," Zane said. "Murdock?"

The shorter boy put down the scalpel and shoved his hands in his pockets. "I guess I'm in too. What's the plan, chief?"

Billy relayed the idea he'd come up with, trying not to feel hurt by his friends' incredulous expressions.

"You want me to fight Corvus?" Zane hissed. "You're completely nuts."

"No, it's brilliant," Murdock said, rubbing his hands together with fiendish glee. "I wish I could do it instead. I'd love to punch him in the face."

"The fight is to distract the scientists, not to hurt Corvus," Billy reminded him.

"That whole idea is stupid, if you ask me," Zane said. "The scientists won't come out of the lab to break up a schoolboy fight. We need to come up with a better distraction."

"Like what?"

"How about a fire?" Murdock suggested.

"We can't light the school on fire," Billy spluttered. "We'll be suspended. Probably expelled. People could get hurt."

"What if they just *thought* there was a fire?" Zane asked. "We could set off a smoke bomb in the lab. The scientists would have to evacuate."

"And they'd have to bring Volner with them," Billy said, catching on to his friend's plan. "Everyone would be able to see what they put him through."

Zane nodded. "From there, the teachers will put a stop to it."

"Meanwhile, we'll have free access to their equipment," Murdock finished, eyes glittering. "We can make sure they never hurt anyone again."

Billy listened to their excited whispers, basking in the ray of hope they created. Corvus and Rem might be resigned to their fate. They might believe their teachers wouldn't lift a finger to help them. But his friends' optimism lent him courage. *We can do this. I know we can.*

Mr. Graham's wizened visage popped up behind Murdock, and all three boys jumped.

"What are you up to?" Mr. Graham asked, his eyes narrowing. "I've been hearing an awful lot of whispering and not a lot of working."

Billy looked down at the frog, torn between guilt for slacking off in class and pride for not taking part in the dissection.

"Not squeamish, are you?" the teacher persisted.

The boys refused to make eye contact with him, and Mr. Graham tutted. "If you're not going to participate, you'd better sit down and start copying notes from the textbook. *Silently.* I thought you'd be glad to get out from behind the desk. Kids these days…"

He moved on to the wraiths' table, and Billy exhaled heavily. He'd expected a detention at the very least. The boys returned to their desks, and Murdock and Zane got to work on their note-taking. Billy tried to follow their example, but he couldn't bring himself to care about biology when someone's life could be at stake. He waited until Corvus and Rem slunk back to their seats, then grabbed the magic notebook. Hiding it in his science book, he penned a quick message.

Hey. Are you there?

Yeah.

I talked to Zane and Murdock, and they're on our side. Just wondering… do you know how to make a smoke bomb?

Why would I know that?

Wait, is this Corvus or Rem?

Corvus, obviously.

Well, can you ask Rem?

After a long pause, Rem confirmed she could make the bomb if he provided her with titanium tetrachloride.

It's dangerous stuff, she warned. *It can burn you pretty badly if you get it on your skin. You'd better get some safety goggles and respirators for the smoke as well.*

It won't kill anyone, will it?

No, I don't think so. It'll give them a sore throat, though, and they might feel a bit sick.

I guess that's okay. Thanks, Rem! I'll do my best to find some.

Billy closed the notebook and leaned back in his chair, relieved. His friends had pulled through for him. Now he just needed to find a bottle of titanium tetrachloride—whatever that was. Not for the first time, he thanked his lucky stars that the visiting scientists chose to store their supplies at the school. If the chemical was as dangerous as Rem claimed, he'd be hard-pressed to find it otherwise. He ripped a small piece of paper out of his science book and copied down the list she'd given him.

"Hey, Murdock," Billy whispered. The boy looked up from his notes and gave him a questioning glance. "Rem can make the smoke bomb, but she needs supplies. Can you sneak into the storage room and get them?"

Murdock's eyes bugged out beneath his glasses. "Why me?"

"You're a better ninja than I am."

"Yeah, but I'm not a ninja *master*. What if Mr. Graham catches me?"

"It's a risk we'll have to take."

Murdock stared at him, wheels spinning behind his eyes. Asking him to stick his neck out for a wraith kid he'd never spoken to was a stretch, and Billy knew it. He prayed he hadn't overstepped his bounds.

Finally, Murdock sighed. "All right. I'll go. But you better cover for me."

"I will. I promise."

Several minutes passed before they got their chance. Mr. Graham zeroed in on a group of students who had diced their frog to smithereens instead of dissecting it. A stream of harsh words leapt from his tongue, distracting everyone, including himself, from Murdock's actions. The bespectacled boy tiptoed to the front of the classroom and disappeared into the vast, open storage room.

"What on earth are you two up to now?" Zane whispered.

"Getting stuff for the smoke bomb."

Zane lowered his head into his hands as if he couldn't believe what he'd heard. "Why would you steal chemicals from the school? We could have bought a kitset from the store."

I should have thought of that. Billy shrugged. "It's too late to turn back now."

His gaze shifted back and forth between Mr. Graham and the storage room as though he were watching a tennis match. The teacher yelled at the boy in charge of the errant group, ranting that he'd never pass a biology exam at this rate. At any other time, Billy would have felt a pang of sympathy for the teary-eyed victim. With Murdock's well-being on the line, every emotion but anxiety disappeared.

Having said his piece, Mr. Graham flounced back to the demonstration table and threw his used equipment in the trash. Murdock's head poked around the door and immediately pulled back. Billy's heart jumped into his throat. In the split second their eyes met, Billy read an unspoken plea for help.

He glanced at the clock. *Class ends in two minutes. If Mr. Graham doesn't move, Murdock won't be able to get out before the bell. He'll get caught for sure. What should I do? There has to be a way to fix this.*

"That'll do for today's lesson," Mr. Graham said. "Clean up your workbenches and head back to your usual classroom."

The students bustled about with cleaning supplies, foisting their dissected frogs into a large rubbish bag. Billy packed up his books and joined in. He'd promised to stay and help Murdock, and he refused to go back on his word. He scrubbed his workbench with a damp rag, keeping a wary eye on his science teacher in case the older man tried to enter the storage room.

"That's enough cleaning, Billy," Mr. Graham told him. "As much as I appreciate your help, you need to run along to class."

Billy swallowed hard. "Yes, sir."

He made eye contact with Corvus, the only other kid left in the room. The wraith boy responded with a grim nod, as if to say, *leave this to me.* Corvus marched over to the biological safety cabinet and punched the glass as hard as he could. It didn't shatter, but the resulting thud made Billy jump.

"What do you think you're doing, boy?" Mr. Graham roared, striding toward Corvus. "Do you have any idea how much that cabinet's worth? Do you know how many years I scrimped and saved pennies out of my own pocket to buy equipment for ungrateful brats like you?"

With the teacher distracted, Billy waved Murdock outside to safety. His friend's satchel bulged with evidence of his ill-gotten gains. Mr. Graham's face hovered inches above Corvus's, too close for comfort. The wraith ducked under his teacher's flailing arms and sprinted for the door.

"I'll have you expelled, you little devil!" Mr. Graham yelled, spittle flying from his cracked lips.

Corvus fled past Billy and out of the classroom, stumbling down the stairs in his desperation to escape. Billy jogged after him, leaving Mr. Graham's outraged cries behind.

"I've never seen him turn psycho like that," Billy said, studying his friend. "Are you okay?"

Breathing hard, Corvus nodded. "I've had worse."

They hurried to catch up to Rem, who was chatting with Zane and Murdock. A wraith Billy didn't recognize walked beside them.

"Are you sure the smoke bomb will work?" the unfamiliar wraith asked. A wisp of black hair fell across his nose, making it appear crooked.

"I'm sure," Rem replied. "I made one for fun last year, and it filled the room in seconds."

"I remember that," Corvus said. "It was really cool to watch."

Zane and Murdock noticed the former bully's presence for the first time and gawked at him, as if unsure how to interpret his civil tone. Billy understood their confusion; gaining Corvus's friendship still seemed surreal to him.

"Thanks," Murdock said, stifling a cough. "You know. For helping me out."

Corvus shrugged. "No problem."

"So we're all a team now?" the unfamiliar wraith asked. "My name's Almwin, by the way. I'm Volner's friend. Rem invited me to come along. What are your names?"

"Murdock, Zane, and Billy," Billy said, pointing to each of the humans in turn.

Almwin inclined his head. "Nice to meet you. I think this whole plan is crazy, but I'm glad we're doing it. There's no time to waste, really."

Billy's stomach flip-flopped. He wanted to help end the torture, but it all seemed so sudden.

"Wouldn't it be better to wait until tomorrow?" he asked. "I mean, we need to make sure we're prepared."

"We *are* prepared," Rem said, regarding him with a puzzled expression.

"Yeah, but shouldn't we think this through a bit more? What if we forgot something and it goes wrong?"

"We'll cross that bridge when we get to it. You're not chickening out, are you?"

"No! Of course not. I just want to make sure we get Volner out safely. There's no point in doing this if we get caught straight away."

"We won't get caught," Almwin said. "Rem knows her stuff when it comes to chemistry."

"That's right," Corvus agreed. "You've got nothing to worry about. If anyone should be worrying here, it's me. Your buddy's probably going to break me in half."

A sheepish smile flitted across Zane's face. "You don't have to worry about that. There's been a change of plan. We're not fighting anymore."

Corvus's eyes narrowed. "We aren't?"

"Nope," Zane said. "The smoke bomb will be enough of a distraction. All we have to do is keep watch outside and make sure no one tries to go in."

The tension in Corvus's body evaporated. "Oh. Okay. Sounds good to me."

"Now we've got that cleared up, we should get moving," Billy said. "We need to sneak into the heart of the science center. How long will it take to make the smoke bomb, Rem?"

"Not very long. I could smoke the scientists out in less than two minutes."

"All right. Murdock, Rem, Almwin… you're with me. Zane, Corvus… you know what to do. Good luck."

The two groups went their separate ways, and Billy sucked in a deep breath. *This is it. This is really happening.* His knees knocked together as he led the way back to the science center, past the airy classrooms and into the doldrums that housed the private labs. The dim lights alone set Billy's nerves on edge. He could only imagine how terrified Volner must be. *What if we go in there and Volner's being cut to pieces? What if we see him being electrocuted?*

Billy's stomach twisted, and he came dangerously close to losing his lunch. Up until this point, he hadn't considered what condition he might find Volner in. Judging by his friends' gung-ho attitudes, they hadn't either.

"Okay, this is it," Billy whispered as they approached the main lab.

Fighting a wave of apprehension, he peeked through the window. Scientists bustled around, scribbling notes on clipboards and frowning at oversized machines. In the far corner, he glimpsed a flash of black and purple.

He's in there, Billy thought, swallowing hard. *Now's the time to be brave. Not just for Volner, but for Corvus and Rem and every other wraith they've hurt.*

Chapter Thirteen

"OKAY, SO HOW *do* you make a smoke bomb?"

The question came from Murdock, but Billy and Almwin leaned forward too, eager to hear Rem's response.

"It's pretty simple," she said. "Titanium tetrachloride is volatile in water. Add them together and you get titanium dioxide plus hydrochloric acid."

Murdock gave her a blank look. "I understood some of those words."

"You don't need to worry about the scientific side of things," Rem said. "I've got them under control. The only thing you need to know is that it's going to make a *lot* of smoke."

"I think I get it," Billy said. "That titanium stuff is like an instant smoke screen. Just add water, right?"

"Well, since titanium tetrachloride is *technically* an acid, we need to add it to the water and not the other way around. You see, if you add water to an acid—"

"It splashes up and burns you," Billy finished.

Rem blinked. "That's right. You actually remembered."

Billy grinned, basking in the warm glow of her approval. Murdock placed his satchel on the ground and eyed them suspiciously.

"How do you know so much about chemistry?" he asked.

Rem shrugged. "I read a lot. My dad says chemistry and potions have a lot in common and that I should learn both if I want to reach my full potential."

Potions? Murdock mouthed, his eyes widening.

"I hate to rush you guys, but we don't have a lot of time here," Billy reminded them. He crouched next to Murdock's bag and donned a pair of goggles. "We should gear up and move out."

"Good point," Rem said. She grabbed another pair of goggles and a respirator from the open pocket. "Did you get any hazmat suits for us?"

"I couldn't find them," Murdock admitted.

"Oh." Rem's face fell. After a few seconds, her lips quirked into a fake smile. "Don't worry about it. I *think* we'll be okay without them. We'll just have to be extra careful not to let it touch our skin. Almwin, can you get us some water when you're done?"

"How much?"

"As much as you can get."

"I'll need something to carry it in."

Billy's gaze alighted on a plastic barrel next to the exit. It looked like a chemical barrel, but the open top suggested the scientists were using it as a trash can.

"What about that?" he suggested, pointing at it.

Almwin went to look. "There's broken glass in here."

"Then tip it out. Murdock, can you help him with the water?"

Almwin and Murdock grimaced and trudged off to obey. Billy didn't like ordering them around, but they couldn't afford to waste time negotiating. They'd already wasted enough time with idle chatter.

The muggy heat of the corridor assailed Billy's senses, making it feel more like a sauna than a school. He eased a respirator past his goggles and down to his chest, where it dangled from a nylon neck strap. He didn't want to wear the claustrophobic mask any longer than he needed to. Rem didn't share his reservations. She stood there like a googly-eyed Darth Vader, her breath whistling down the corridor.

Bored of waiting, Billy peeked into the lab again, hoping to catch a glimpse of something incriminating. The scientists hovered around Volner, but he couldn't make out what they were doing. Keeping his gaze fixed on the proceedings, he pressed an ear to the door.

"Pin his arms," a gruff voice ordered.

The words sent shivers down Billy's spine. *Dissectiondissectiondissectiondissection—*

"It's just a blood sample, dear," a feminine voice cooed. "You'll feel a little prick, that's all."

"I don't *want* my blood taken," Volner whined. Billy couldn't see his face, but he could tell by the heavy, snuffling quality of his voice that the boy had been crying. "Why can't you leave me alone? Why ca—*let go of me!*"

A suit-clad agent smothered Volner's mouth with his arm, muffling his screams. The boy screamed louder, his strangled cries reverberating through the lab. He sounded more like a wounded animal than a wraith, and Billy stepped back, sick to his stomach.

"What is it?" Rem asked.

He shook his head, unable to explain what he'd seen. "Murdock and Almwin need to hurry up."

Fortunately, he didn't have to wait long. The boys re-entered the corridor, struggling with the weight of the full barrel.

"All right, you two," Rem said. "Pour the water so it goes under the door."

"Easier said than done," Almwin grunted. "This thing's heavy, you know."

"I'll help," Billy volunteered.

Between them, they managed to tip the barrel onto its side. Water sloshed onto the linoleum, surging under the door and splashing against the frame.

"Gently! They might hear you," Rem said.

Not over all that screaming, they won't.

"Okay, that's all of it," Murdock said. He handed the empty barrel to Almwin, who returned it to the corner. "Does that mean it's time for the titanium tickle-whatsit?"

"Yes. It's time."

Rem rummaged through Murdock's bag and pulled out one of the stolen bottles. The moment she unscrewed the lid, a corrosive stench invaded Billy's nostrils. He recoiled, fighting back the urge to cough and vomit at the same time. He fumbled with his respirator, nearly dropped it, and then pulled it snugly over his face. After a few panicked breaths, the burning sensation subsided. Even so, his mouth and throat remained unbearably dry, as if he hadn't drunk anything in days. *Rem wasn't kidding. That's some powerful stuff.*

"I'll do the hallway first," Rem said, stepping back from the puddle. "That way, they'll leave the whole building instead of just the lab. We won't have to worry about them sneaking up on us."

"Good plan," Billy said.

Rem held the open bottle at arm's length, tilting it back and forth as if working up the courage to go through with it. Another step back. Another deep breath. Then she upended the bottle.

It was upside down for a split second, but that was long enough for the chemical inside to work its magic. Colorless liquid splashed down to meet colorless liquid, and tangled threads of dense, white smoke erupted from the floor. As Rem predicted, the noxious cloud choked the length of the corridor within minutes.

Murdock squeezed Billy's left shoulder; Rem crushed his right hand. Both were invisible to him. If they hadn't been in physical contact, he would have assumed they left without him.

"This way," Rem's disembodied voice said. He followed her lead without question. "Almwin, I need you to open the door for us. Not all the way. Just enough to throw this stuff in. Billy, you're good at throwing things, right?"

"I guess so."

"Good. You can do that part." Rem let go of his hand and pressed the glass bottle into it. "You should have a couple of seconds before the smoke blocks your view. Aim for the water and smash it down as hard as you can. Got it?"

"Got it."

"Okay. On my count. Three, two, one, go!"

The door creaked open a few inches, revealing the main lab. Unhindered by physical barriers, Volner's screams pierced their eardrums. The true intensity of his distress stunned Billy into inaction. He stared in horror as a blonde scientist removed a seven-inch needle from Volner's arm. Purple blood spurted out of the hole it left behind. Another scientist applied a hasty pressure bandage. Everyone in the lab had their backs to the door, but it was only a matter of time before they turned around and saw him.

Murdock dug his fingers into Billy's shoulder, snapping him out of his paralysis. He fixed his gaze on the center of the puddle and threw the bottle as hard as he could. The glass shattered on impact, eliciting startled exclamations from the scientists. Smoke engulfed the lab, hiding the children from view. Almwin slammed the door shut.

"You did it! Come on," Rem said, leading Billy away from the lab and into a hidden alcove.

A split second later, the fire alarm screamed to life. Billy flinched and clamped his hands over his ears, vaguely aware of his friends doing the same. The scientists stumbled for the exit, coughing and spluttering into their elbows. The crunch of broken glass accompanied their retreat.

"They're gone," Murdock said in a stage whisper. "We actually scared them off."

"Yeah, but they left Volner behind. That wasn't part of the plan. We've got to help him." Billy staggered back into the corridor. "How long is that smoke supposed to last, Rem?"

"I don't know. I've never tried letting off smoke bombs in a building this big before."

Billy opened the door to the main lab. "We'd better work fast, then."

"Watch out for broken glass."

"I'll try to."

The hazardous pool blocked Billy's path, so he kept to the edges as much as possible. A thick blanket of smoke filled the lab. He couldn't see Volner anymore, but he could hear him. Retching replaced the boy's earlier screams, and he gasped as though he were drowning.

The smoke! Billy despaired. *We should have brought him a mask!*

He rushed toward the sound, bumping into tables and machines along the way. Volner lay motionless in his chair, his arms restrained by tight leather straps. Billy wrestled with them, then gave up and used a shard of glass to do the job instead. The shard dug a notch into the leather, creating a hairline cut across his palm at the same time. He hissed in pain.

"Let me," Rem said, pushing him aside. Her hands closed around the straps, and a purple glow snapped the leather clean in two.

You used magic, Billy wanted to say. *You promised your dad you wouldn't.*

He supposed promises went out the window when dealing with emergency situations.

"Almwin and I will take him outside," Rem told Billy. "Meet us at the oak tree when you're done."

"Gotcha."

The wraiths maneuvered Volner into the corridor, leaving the two humans behind.

"Now that they're gone, is it time for destruction?" Murdock asked.

"Yup," Billy said. "Grab any papers you can find, but feel free to break everything else."

"Awesome!"

While his friend got down to business, Billy focused on the desk next to Volner's chair. Several stacks of paperwork lay on top of it, and he swept all of them into his satchel. The sudden movement unbalanced a rack of test tubes, and they toppled to the floor. Luminous purple liquid—*wraith blood?*—splashed onto his shoes.

A second terrible crash rang out behind him, and he whirled around. Murdock stood over the wreckage of a stainless steel frame. A metal bar rolled across the linoleum, dislodged by the ferocity of his attack. With a savage grin, Murdock scooped it up and bashed the remaining bars out of shape.

Not to be outdone, Billy picked up a metal chair and rammed its legs through an LCD screen. A shower of sparks and broken glass rained down on the desk. With a grim smile, he repeated the action on the entire row of machines. It felt good to break them, but it felt even better knowing the scientists would never use them again.

"I found another wraith!" Murdock shouted.

Billy dropped the chair and rushed to join him. His friend knelt next to a wraith boy who looked no older than Hamish. The boy sat with his knees curled into his chest, trying to make himself as small as possible. Tears leaked from his eyes, though Billy couldn't tell if it was from the smoke or the trauma of what he'd experienced.

"Get him out of here," Billy ordered. "Go meet up with the others."

Murdock scooped the younger child into his arms without arguing and carried him out of the room. Billy stood rooted to the spot, his fists clenched. *What if Hamish had been in his place?* A wild, hot anger seared through his chest, and he grabbed the metal pole Murdock abandoned. *If they can torture little kids, there are no limits to how evil these scientists are. They'd kill Hamish if he'd been born a wraith. They'd kill Hamish!*

The thought consumed him, and drunk on its potency, he resumed his rampage. By the time he was finished, nothing remained on the benches or shelves. He stood amidst the wreckage, trembling. *Did I go too far?*

The wheezing wail of a fire engine prevented further self-reflection. He bolted for the door, glass fragments popping under his sneakers. Five steps to the exit. Four. Three. He slipped on a small plastic rectangle and scrambled to regain his footing. Somehow, his fingers closed around the object, and he shoved it into his pocket. Two steps. One. He burst into the corridor and ran as fast as his legs would carry him.

Chapter Fourteen

ON A NORMAL day, Billy wouldn't be caught dead on a sports field. Today, crossing one looked like his only option. The tree Rem chose as a rendezvous point straddled the school's boundary line at the far end of the field. Its isolation from the main school ensured they wouldn't be disturbed. Unfortunately, it also meant they had to traverse a wide-open area without being seen. Billy didn't know if his friends had been successful, but he took the lack of teachers as an encouraging sign.

He launched into a headlong sprint, glancing over his shoulder every few seconds. He half-expected to see a fireman hot on his heels—not a real fireman, but a sooty-faced amalgamation of his worst nightmares rolled into one. His imaginary pursuer wore glasses like Ms. Clemmons, a white lab coat like the scientists, and screamed at him to stop in the name of the law. In reality, no such fate befell him. He made it to the oak tree without a hitch.

"Hey, Billy," Murdock greeted him. "Did you get out okay?"

His friend sat several feet away from the wraiths, who clustered together in a tight semi-circle. The small boy they'd rescued sat on Rem's lap, his eyes fixed on Volner's slumped form. Almwin sat between his peers, ripping a blade of grass into increasingly smaller pieces. Zane and Corvus were nowhere to be seen. *I hope they're okay.*

"Yeah, I'm fine," Billy answered, sinking to his knees. "What about you?"

"I'm all right," Murdock said. "Jarsha is too."

"Jarsha? You mean the kid?"

"Yeah. Rem said she's going to take him home when Volner recovers enough to move."

Billy studied the injured wraith. Volner was, quite literally, a shadow of his former self. The purple runes decorating his skin had faded to black, and with his eyes closed, he no longer resembled a wraith, let alone any kind of three-dimensional being. The only thing giving definition to his shapeless form was the bandage wrapped around his left arm.

"Is Volner going to be okay?" Billy asked.

"Of course he is," Rem said, flashing him a small, uncertain smile. "I sealed the wound and gave him some of my energy. He just needs to rest a bit before I take him home. Then my dad will heal him, and it'll be like it never happened."

"Are you sure?"

"She's right. I'll be fine," Volner rasped. He opened a bleary eye and squinted up at Billy. "Thanks for saving me, by the way. I don't think I would have survived much longer in that place."

"You don't have to thank me," Billy said, relieved the wraith still had the strength to talk. "I'm glad I could help."

Volner nodded and looked away. "I hate needles, but at least I didn't get cut open like last time. Dr. Crane would have done it again if that blonde woman hadn't taken over."

Billy shifted his weight, uneasy, and something rigid pressed into his thigh. He reached into his pocket and pulled out the plastic card he'd taken from the lab. A woman's name and image covered the front side, her steel-gray eyes staring him down in obvious contempt for the photographer. Dull blonde hair framed her face.

"Amelia Stanford," Billy read.

"Dr. Stanford, yeah." Volner pushed himself into a sitting position. "How did you know?"

Billy showed him the card, and the boy winced in recognition.

"Yeah. That's her, all right. She took a blood sample from me right before you guys showed up."

"I've heard of Dr. Stanford," Rem said. "I think she's the one who gave Corvus his scar."

"She was," Corvus confirmed.

Billy jerked back and hit his head on the tree trunk. Corvus stood several feet away, his arms folded as if he'd been there all along.

"Don't *do* that," Billy complained.

"Do what?"

"Sneak up behind us!"

"I didn't sneak. I walked normally."

"A likely story."

Corvus rolled his eyes. "How did the invasion go?"

"It went well," Rem said, casting a meaningful glance at Billy. "We rescued Volner and Jarsha, and the whole place is kaput. Are you okay, Corvus? You look awful."

Billy turned to study him, his heart sinking. Bright purple blotches marred the boy's face, and his knuckles dripped blood to the grass below.

"I'm fantastic," Corvus deadpanned.

There's only one way to get injuries like that.

"You fought Zane, didn't you?" Billy said, frowning. "Why? I told you the smoke bomb would be enough of a distraction."

"I know you did," Corvus said. "But a couple of scientists found gas masks and wanted to go back into the lab. Starting a fight was the only thing I could think of that might distract them."

"And it worked?"

"You didn't get caught, did you?"

"No, we didn't," Billy conceded. "Where *is* Zane, anyway?"

"I have no idea. He said he didn't want to come with me. I think he's upset he got sent to the principal's office, but I don't know why. I'm the one who got suspended, not him."

"You got *suspended?*"

"That's usually what happens when you start a fight at school. Don't worry, I didn't tell Mr. Matlin anything about your rescue mission."

"Did you hurt Zane?" Murdock asked. A sharp edge entered his voice, one Billy hadn't heard before.

"Are you *kidding*?" Corvus gestured at his own battered body. "He walloped the living daylights out of me. I don't think I landed a single punch after the first one."

Almwin cackled. "How does it feel to be beaten up by a human?"

"Oh, shut up," Corvus groaned.

"Guys, this isn't helping," Billy said, holding his hand up for silence. "We're here to stop the scientists, not to make fun of each other."

"He's right," Volner croaked, capturing everyone's attention. "You destroyed their equipment, but that won't stop them from getting more. Rem said you stole their paperwork. We need to decide who to give it to. Who can help us? Who do we trust?"

"The police?" Murdock suggested.

Corvus shook his head. "Bad idea. My dad works for them. Rem's dad does too."

"So what? Wouldn't they be proud of you for stopping the scientists?" Billy asked.

"Yeah," Murdock piped up. "What if it was *you* in that chair? Wouldn't they want you to be saved?"

"The only thing my dad cares about is making sure we don't rock the boat too much," Corvus said in measured tones. "He's a coward."

"What parent would rather have their kid lay down and die than fight back?" Murdock exclaimed. "Almwin, Volner, what about your parents? Why don't we tell them?"

Almwin's posture stiffened. "We don't have contact with our parents."

"Your caregivers, then."

"We don't have those either. It's not normal for wraith kids to live with adults."

"So you live all by yourselves?"

"With each other. But yeah, pretty much."

"Rem and Corvus live with their parents."

Corvus turned away, annoyance flashing across his face. "Yes, we do. We're the freaks of the wraith family. Welcome to the freak show, blah-de-blah. Old news. No one cares."

"It's a sensitive issue," Rem said, patting Corvus's shoulder.

"Okay, so wraith parents and the police are out," Billy said. "Murdock, your dad works on the council. Is there any chance he could help?"

"I doubt it," Murdock said. "It's like I told you yesterday. His boss loves what the scientists are doing. There's no way he'd be able to file a complaint."

"So Murdock's dad is out as well. That leaves the principal."

Corvus raised an eyebrow. "You really think that's a good idea?"

"Well, he *is* in charge of the school," Billy pointed out. "He'd kick the scientists out if he knew what they were doing."

"I wish he'd kick the wraiths out instead," someone muttered.

Billy gasped as Zane limped over to join them. The boy's cheek had ballooned out to double its normal size, pushing his left eye shut. With his good eye, he shot Corvus a hateful glare.

Billy stared in disbelief. "Zane! What happened? Are you all right?"

Even as he said it, he regretted the stupidity of the last question. Of course his friend wasn't all right. He looked like he'd been thrown in a tumble dryer with a bag of bricks.

Murdock raced over to check the severity of Zane's wounds. Incensed, he turned on Corvus. "You said you didn't hurt him!"

"I didn't know!" Corvus yelped as a fist struck him in the stomach. "I swear I didn't. He gave back as good as he got. You can't blame it all on me."

"But it's *your* fault," Murdock said, landing another punch. "None of this would have happened if we didn't help you!"

"Murdock, stop!" Billy darted forward and pulled him off Corvus.

Murdock struggled against him, his fists hitting thin air. Corvus stumbled a few steps away and collapsed, clutching his stomach.

"I'm done with wraiths." Murdock spat, breaking free of Billy's grasp. "They're weird, and they hurt Zane. I'm not going to stand around and take it anymore."

"Neither am I," Zane said. "We didn't have to help them, but we did, and I got beaten up for it. Let's get out of here, Billy. We don't owe them anything."

"You're wrong," Billy blurted out. His human friends glared daggers at him, but he carried on regardless. "I'm sorry you got hurt, Zane, but Volner and Jarsha had it much worse in the lab. I want to make the scientists pay for what they did, and that means sticking with the wraiths. We can't leave them to deal with this on their own."

"Maybe you can't, but I can," Zane said. He spun on his heel and stalked off. "Let's go, Murdock."

The remaining kids watched them go in tense silence. Tears pricked Billy's eyes. He'd been through rough patches with his friends before, but their disagreements rarely escalated this far.

"I thought Murdock was on our side. Why did he freak out like that?" Volner asked.

"You know what humans are like," Almwin said. "Emotional and unstable. No offense, Billy."

"None taken," Billy muttered.

"We wraiths aren't much better," Rem pointed out. She offered Billy a sympathetic smile. "You didn't have to stick up for us, you know. You could have gone with your friends."

"I know. But you're my friends too," Billy said. "Murdock and Zane will come around. You'll see."

"If you're sure…"

"I'm sure. They always do."

They sat in silence, unsure what to say next.

Finally, Volner cleared his throat. "So, what now? Do we go to the principal?"

Rem shook her head. "The only place you're going is home. Same with Jarsha."

"I don't think I can walk."

"That's okay. Almwin and I will carry you. Billy, would you be okay with going to the principal by yourself?"

Billy swallowed hard. *Not really. But if it keeps you safe...* "Sure. No problem."

Chapter Fifteen

BILLY SAT OUTSIDE the principal's office, clutching the strap of his satchel. Sweat beaded his brow, and he dabbed it away with the corner of his sleeve. The AC had been broken for weeks, but he suspected he would be sweating regardless of the temperature. Less than five feet away, Volner's tormentor—the woman he now knew to be Dr. Amelia Stanford—wheedled the receptionist for information.

"Look, I'm not asking you to name names," she said. "All I want to know is if Mr. Matlin has identified the culprits. He told me he would look at the security footage."

Security footage? Billy's stomach dropped to his feet. The thick smoke would have concealed their identities during the actual rescue mission, but what about before that? What about when they were skulking through the corridors? If he'd known the cameras existed, he would have worn a mask from the get-go.

"I'm afraid I don't know much about it," the receptionist said, "but if Mr. Matlin said he would look into it, then he'll look into it. If you want, I can ask him to give you a call when he finds out more."

"Can't you buzz me in now?" Dr. Stanford pleaded. "I don't mean to be pushy, but we lost everything we have. Our machines. Our supplies. Our test subjects. Our data. We were promised a secure lab. I don't understand how something like this could happen."

"You'll have to take that up with Mr. Matlin when he calls you. He's busy at the moment, but I'm sure you'll hear from him sometime within the next few hours."

"*Hours?*" Dr. Stanford blanched. "What am I supposed to do in the meantime? I only came to Morton because I wanted to help the afflicted children in your care. Do you expect me to twiddle my thumbs while they run wild?"

"I didn't say that. Perhaps you can get a nice cup of coffee in the teacher's lounge while you wait. How does that sound?"

Dr. Stanford grimaced but took a step back from the reception desk. "I suppose I could suffer a short rest for the sake of coffee. Thank you."

"No problem. I'll notify you when Mr. Matlin is free."

The scientist left without a backward glance, and the knot in Billy's gut loosened. He wasn't out of the woods yet, but at least he didn't have to worry about Dr. Stanford for the next few minutes. The receptionist resumed typing, the pitter-patter of her keyboard counting down to Billy's moment of reckoning.

He squirmed in his seat. Under normal circumstances, he would never admit to his involvement in the break-in. Experience taught him it was better to deny, deny, deny, because being honest led to angry teachers and disappointed parents. This, in turn, led to detentions, groundings, and lost dessert.

However, armed with conclusive evidence of the wraiths' plight, today would be different. Mr. Matlin would understand why he'd resorted to destructive action and see fit to forgive him. He might still get an earful from his parents when he got home, but his heart told him it was worth the risk.

He waited in sweaty silence for half an hour before the principal emerged from his office.

"Billy Porter! I haven't seen you in a while. Keeping out of trouble, I hope?"

"Mostly, sir."

"I'm glad to hear it. Come right in. You can sit anywhere you like."

Mr. Matlin gestured at the door, and Billy shuffled inside. He felt like he was five years old again, being called in for throwing a Barbie doll off the tallest tower in the playground. He'd improvised a parachute from a plastic bag and hooked it under her arms, hoping it would slow her descent. To the horror of the doll's owner, the chute failed to open, and Barbie ended up with a mild case of decapitation. Fortunately, the damage was reversible. His actions weren't. In addition to a sincere apology, Mr. Matlin ordered him to write one hundred lines to drive the point home.

Swallowing his nerves, Billy chose a seat at random and plopped into it, hugging his satchel. A bronze statuette bearing an uncanny resemblance to Mr. Matlin perched on the desk in front of him.

It must have cost a mint, Billy thought. He looked away, perturbed by the intensity of its sightless eyes.

The real Mr. Matlin shut the door and returned to his desk, his leather chair creaking when he sat down. "What can I do for you today, Billy?"

Now or never. The wraiths are counting on me. "I want to make a formal complaint against the visiting scientists."

"Oh?"

"They've been hurting students."

"That's a very serious accusation," Mr. Matlin said, rubbing his chin. He leaned forward to better observe his young charge. "Did the scientists hurt you personally, or did you see them hurting someone else?"

"Someone else," Billy clarified. "Volner from my class and a younger kid called Jarsha."

"Hmmm," Mr. Matlin said. His expression didn't change, but he kept rubbing his chin. "What exactly did you see?"

"They had Volner strapped to a chair in their lab. This one lady, Dr. Stanford, was taking blood from him. He was screaming his head off the whole time, and he could barely walk afterward."

"You're the one who broke into the lab?"

"Yes, but I only did it to save Volner. After I found out what they were doing to him, I couldn't leave him there."

Mr. Matlin nodded thoughtfully. "Where is Volner now?"

"He went home."

"And the other boy you mentioned. Jarsha. What about him?"

"He went home too. I don't know what they did to him. He was too scared to talk."

Mr. Matlin clasped his hands in front of his chin and dropped his gaze in silent contemplation. After a few beats, he inclined his head and took a deep breath. "While I can't say I approve of your actions, I'm very glad you brought this matter to my attention. As principal of this school, it's my duty to ensure the well-being of every student who walks through the front gates. I'll investigate your complaint as soon as possible and let you know the outcome."

Emboldened by his success, Billy pulled out the documents he'd found in the lab.

"I have some papers that might help your investigation," he said, sliding them across the desk. "They talk about all the experiments the scientists want to do and what they've already done."

The principal's face darkened as he examined the papers. The silence between them grew heavy enough to crush Billy's heart.

"Blood tests, tissue samples, x-rays… it all looks perfectly normal to me," Mr. Matlin said. He tore his gaze from the papers and looked up at Billy. "I know it must have been hard to see your friend so upset, but the scientists know what they're doing. The government wouldn't have approved their research otherwise."

"But they *hurt* him," Billy cried. "You've got to believe me!"

"I *do* believe you, Billy. Blood tests are always a little painful, so it's not surprising Volner reacted the way he did. You need to understand that the scientists wouldn't do these tests if they weren't absolutely necessary. The whole reason they're here is to help wraithkind and develop medicines for them."

They don't need your medicines, Billy wanted to scream. *They've got magic. They can heal themselves!*

The statuette caught his eye again, and for a brief moment, he considered throwing the stupid thing out the window. That would show the principal what he thought of his regurgitated lies. Only the heaviness in his chest held him back.

"Can't you *do* something?" he pleaded.

"Like I said, I'm going to investigate the situation," Mr. Matlin said, tucking the papers into a tray under his desk. "You've given me a lot of information to go through, and I want to give it the consideration it deserves. If I find anything, I'll report it to the people in charge. Okay?"

"Okay," Billy replied, fighting back tears. *He's not going to kick them out?*

"Good." Mr. Matlin folded his hands and shifted his gaze to the door. "You can go back to class, Billy. I have a meeting in two minutes."

"Yes, sir."

He fled from the stifling atmosphere of the office and into the open air of the schoolyard. Something was wrong with Mr. Matlin. Five years ago, he would have dropped everything to make sure his students were healthy and happy. Now, he cared more about the timeliness of his meeting schedule.

I bet he won't investigate the scientists at all, Billy seethed. *He probably knows all about their pet projects already. They might even be paying him to keep quiet. How else could he afford to buy a statue of himself?*

He entered Ms. Clemmons's class feeling like he'd been beaten to a pulp. The teacher didn't notice his late entrance, so he sat down and pulled out the magic notebook. Math problems covered the whiteboard, so he figured he could get away with writing in it.

Hey, Corvus, he wrote. *The meeting with the principal sucked. I don't think he's going to help us. What are we going to do?*

He waited a few minutes, but no response came. Giving up, Billy grabbed his real math book and tried to solve the whiteboard problems. After relying on his friends so often, he struggled to figure out the answers by himself. Every now and then, he glanced at the notebook, hoping to hear something from the wraiths. A whole hour passed before they rewarded his patience.

I'm sorry it didn't go well, the message read. *Thanks for trying, though. It means a lot to us. Do you want to come over after school so we can talk about it?*

Of course, Billy wrote back. *Are you doing okay?*

Another worrying pause stretched between them before Corvus responded. *Yeah, but the fight took a lot more out of me than I thought it did. I hurt all over.*

Billy cringed at the memory of his friend's battered body. *I'm sorry you had to fight.*

It's too late to be sorry about it now.

Yeah, I guess you're right. Is Rem with you?

Yup. She's looking after me. Why? Do you want to talk to her?

No, it's okay. I can wait until this afternoon. I was just checking.

Suit yourself. I need to go and lie down for a while. I'll see you when you get here.

All right. Take care of yourself, Corvus.

Chapter Sixteen

SEISAN CROUCHED IN an empty field, next to a mangled red convertible. He knew the driver was a white male, early- to mid-twenties, and that he'd brought his violent, fiery death upon himself by fleeing from the police. He didn't know what spurred the car chase to begin with, but then again, it wasn't his job to know. His role involved nothing more strenuous than cleaning up the mess left behind.

A breadcrumb trail of blood spiraled away from the vehicle, ending in a larger puddle next to the fence where the female passenger had been apprehended. Seisan's lip curled at the sight of it. He was no farmer, but it still pained him to see the earth blighted by such wanton recklessness.

He sifted the soil through his fingers, focusing on the individual grains to calm his mind. Every particle shared a uniform shade of dark brown, indicating an abundance of minerals and other nutrients. This was good soil, he thought. Fertile soil. Completely different from the barren wasteland he once called home.

He wasn't old enough to remember when the Gloaming had grass and crops instead of dead, dusty plains. The land had fallen into disrepair one hundred years ago, shortly after Grigoth murdered King Vaeril and took the throne for himself. Seisan was not a paranoid man by nature, but it didn't take a conspiracy theorist to link the two events together.

He bounced on his heels and stood up, wiping his hands on his trousers. Lothaire walked over to him, eyeing the blood warily.

"How's it going?" he asked.

"Slowly."

Lothaire fished a piece of paper out of his pocket. "I've got something that might cheer you up. The chief wants us to investigate a possible wraith sighting around Oilskin Lake."

Seisan scanned the paper. "It could be one of the children."

"Impossible. None of them are six feet tall."

"They could be experimenting with magic."

"And where would they learn to do that?"

Seisan mulled it over. His son would sooner hack his own arm off with a butter knife than talk to his peers, much less teach them the finer points of magic. Rem was more of a wildcard. The other children gave her a hard time, and her strong desire to fit in could prove a liability. He opened his mouth to say as much but changed his mind at the last minute. Lothaire wouldn't appreciate a scathing review of his daughter.

"You're right. They couldn't have learned it anywhere," Seisan conceded. "How do you want to proceed? Shall we leave now and resume our other duties later?"

"That would be the best idea," Lothaire agreed. "Unless you *want* to spend the afternoon scraping melted flesh from the driver's seat?"

Seisan grimaced but didn't otherwise dignify the man with an answer.

The lake was a short walk from the crime scene, which was fortunate because neither of them could drive. They didn't have anything against cars in principle, but using them felt too unnatural. Seisan's legs worked perfectly well. Why should he rely on motorized transport the way humans did?

Upon entering Morton Park, though, his perfect legs weakened. The deep purple lake drew him in like a magnet, tempting him almost as much as it terrified him. One small step, one tiny spark of magic, and he'd be careening back to the land of his adolescence. Squaring his shoulders, Seisan strode along the banks, searching for any sign of the reported wraith. The acrid scent of recently cast magic permeated the air, and he followed it like a bloodhound.

"Be careful," Lothaire warned. "Whoever came through the portal was either under Grigoth's orders or smart enough to find a way around the oath. They're not going to come quietly."

Seisan nodded without listening. He already knew how dangerous their hunt could be. Decades of experience had taught him to keep a stunning spell cupped in his hand, ready to fly free at the slightest hint of trouble.

The rustle of leaves caught his attention, and he froze in place. His purple tongue darted out to taste the air, confirming his suspicions. An invisible presence stood less than ten feet in front of him. He signaled to Lothaire, who responded with a curt nod. If this unknown entity was the wraith they'd been searching for, they were in trouble.

Invisibility spells took a lot of energy to maintain. Even an accomplished mage like himself struggled to hold one for more than a minute. Most wraiths were too weak to cross the barrier at all, much less perform magic within hours of arrival. That left two options: a powerful emissary or King Grigoth himself.

Steeling himself, Seisan released the palmed spell and dove to the ground. A bolt of pale violet light sizzled through the air and exploded on impact. The blast stripped away the entity's defenses, revealing the brawny outline of a male wraith. The wraith's body slammed into the ground, flopping and writhing like a fish out of water. Cursing, Seisan scrambled over to finish the job. His stunning spell had hit the wraith off-center, preventing it from immobilizing him. The wraith tried to sit up, but a foot to the chest put an end to that.

Seisan peered at the squirming wretch. This man wasn't Grigoth, but he looked familiar. Lothaire joined them, his hands glowing in anticipation of further violence. He stared at the vagrant wraith for a long moment before allowing the magic to subside.

"Darthan?" he asked.

Hearing the name out loud sent alarm bells ringing through Seisan's mind.

"That's right," the wraith said. He leaned his head back against the grass in a gesture of submission. "Good to see you again, Lothaire. Can't say I think much of the welcoming committee, though."

Seisan's eyes narrowed, but he removed his foot from Darthan's chest and helped him up. "You shouldn't be here. We had an agreement."

"Yeah, yeah, yeah," Darthan said, waving a dismissive hand. "Watch the king and make sure he doesn't do anything murder-y. That's easier said than done, you know. The least you could do is show a little gratitude."

"Don't mind Seisan. He's just disappointed he didn't get to blow anyone up today," Lothaire joked.

Seisan resisted the urge to roll his eyes. Just because he excelled at magical combat didn't mean he reveled in it. "I take it you have news from home?"

"As a matter of fact, I do," Darthan said, his expression sobering. "Is it safe to talk here?"

"As safe as anywhere these days," Seisan said.

"All right." Darthan leaned in and lowered his voice to a whisper. "I have reason to believe Grigoth is building his army. A regiment of two thousand was seen in Calzarn Creek a few days ago, and a smaller battalion has been patrolling in the east."

"Two *thousand?*" Lothaire's eyebrows shot up.

Seisan overrode his own incredulity to seek the facts. "What were they doing? Has there been any fighting? Casualties? And where are they getting food from?"

"I think it would be easier to show you than explain," Darthan said. "Will you come back to the Gloaming with me?"

Seisan glanced at Lothaire. His friend's eyes burned with a determination he hadn't seen since they were children. When Lothaire got into a state like this, he charged into things with no regard for the consequences. Seisan placed a restraining hand on his shoulder.

"This concerns all of us. We'll both go."

The Gloaming looked the same in real life as it did in Seisan's memory. The wraiths walked through the dead air in the same formation they'd favored twenty years ago. Darthan looked older under the dreary glow of the werelights. Older and more worn. His reconnaissance duties must have exacted a heavy toll from him.

"This way," Darthan muttered.

Seisan didn't need the verbal guidance, but he took comfort in it nonetheless. After spending the better part of his life on the noisy blue-and-green ball called Earth, the stillness of the forest unnerved him. He gazed up at the deadwood trees, trying to picture what they must have looked like one hundred years ago. Had they resembled Earth trees? Or were they purple-tinged, like so many other things in the Gloaming? He didn't know, and he supposed it didn't matter. Dead was dead, and the only thing still worth worrying about was the fate of wraithkind.

"How much farther?" he asked, jogging to catch up with their guide. "I promised Corvus I would be home in time for dinner."

"Not far," Darthan said. "Is Corvus your son?"

"He is."

Darthan shook his head. "Fancy that. I never pictured you as the paternal type. No offense."

"None taken. What of your children? Did you find out what happened to them?"

"I never thought to look."

Their conversation petered out, and Seisan dropped back to walk with Lothaire. Estrangement from one's progeny was par for the course in his homeland. Parents couldn't afford to feed themselves, let alone their children, so they left them in the care of the Hatchery. The nurses there sustained the hatchlings on a diet of pure energy—a substance too rich for older wraiths to digest. It wasn't a bad life, but it wasn't a good one either.

Ten years ago, Lothaire tried to convince him they should adopt their genetic offspring and raise them on Earth. Seisan had fought tooth and nail against the idea, but to no avail. He remembered carrying a small bundle out of the Hatchery, wondering what in the world his friend had gotten him into. But when the boy inside gazed up at him with huge violet eyes, his heart melted. Sure, Corvus's attitude drove him up the wall sometimes, but he didn't regret bringing him home for a minute.

Darthan cleared his throat, drawing Seisan out of his thoughts. The man stood in the middle of the path, his hands clasped.

"The thing I wanted to show you is over the crest of this hill," he said. "I should warn you, it might come as a shock."

"Thank you, Darthan. I think we've already established that," Seisan said.

Their guide rolled his eyes and got down on his belly. Seisan and Lothaire did the same, and all three of them crawled up the hill. Seisan arrived first. The lack of vegetation—and hence the lack of cover—worried him, but their target was so far away that it didn't matter.

"What are they *doing*?" Lothaire breathed.

A disorganized crowd of wraiths stood in the middle of an open field. Their bone-thin arms stretched toward the soldiers encircling them, their desperate hands clawing the air for an unseen prize.

Food, Seisan thought with a sinking feeling in the pit of his stomach. *The soldiers took their food.*

His eyes raked the scene with mounting disgust. A larger group of soldiers sat off to the side, helping themselves to a supply wagon.

"The soldiers were supposed to deliver food to the laborers," Darthan explained. "Apparently, they decided to taunt them with it instead."

"Is this a common occurrence?" Seisan asked.

One of the laborers ducked under the soldiers' arms and made a dash for the wagon, only to be struck down by three different death spells. The wraith's mouth opened in an unvoiced scream as the rest of his body disintegrated beneath him.

"Common? No. But it's getting worse," Darthan said. "I'd show you the actual labor camps, but a brief visit doesn't give you a true picture of how bad things are. The laborers work eighteen-hour days with strict targets to meet. If they fail, they don't get fed. I suspect that's what happened with our friends down there."

Lothaire cut in with some questions of his own, but Seisan tuned him out. Conditions in the Gloaming were far worse than he'd imagined. He knew all about the injustices in theory, and he'd frequently warned Corvus about them. But to see them firsthand…

I've been fortunate, he thought. *If I hadn't made a clean break from my blood oath, I would be down there with them.*

"I hate to ask favors of you two, but I'm afraid I have no choice," Darthan said. "The soldiers are bad news, but there's something else that neither of you have noticed yet."

Seisan frowned. "What?"

"Of all the places to set up a labor camp, they chose to do it here. Not next to a supply depot, like the others. Not even close to one. In fact, the closest feature for miles around is the portal. Combine that information with the appearance of a full battalion, and you've got to ask yourself what Grigoth is planning."

"You think he might attempt an invasion of Earth?" Lothaire asked.

"I think that's a definite possibility."

"But why would he do that?" Seisan asked. "Swords don't stand a chance against guns. He'd be leading his soldiers to their deaths."

"Starvation can do strange things to people," Lothaire pointed out. "If Grigoth was desperate, there's no telling what he'd be willing to try."

"He isn't desperate yet," Darthan said. "If he really wanted to, he could reverse the damage he's done to the land and allow crops to grow again. Failing that, he's got a whole storehouse packed to the rafters with provisions, all protected by his royal seal."

Seisan's frown deepened. During his time at the Academy, he'd heard whispers of the so-called royal seal. According to his classmates, Grigoth used his dominion over magic to ban the import and cultivation of foodstuffs. Any food he did not manually bless disintegrated into ash—

or so the story said. He hadn't believed it. Not at first. Shortly after breaking his blood oath and fleeing to Earth, he learned the truth of it.

Unable to work regular jobs, he and Lothaire had resorted to dumpster-diving in the hopes of finding their next meal. About a week in, they stumbled on the jackpot: an unopened forty-pound bag of chicken wings. It was only a day past the sell-by date, so they hauled it back to the homestead and divvied it up amongst the wraith children.

After their feast, Seisan brought the leftovers to Oilskin Lake, intending to give them to his famine-affected friends. As soon as he arrived in the Gloaming, every chicken wing combusted into a light gray powder.

Since then, he and Lothaire had tried to bypass the spell in any number of clever ways, but Grigoth always seemed to be one step ahead. The whole process was like trying to fill a leaky bucket. In theory, you could plug the holes, but why bother when someone kept making new ones?

"Why invade Earth?" Seisan asked. "If he's not desperate, why would he risk it?"

"Because sooner or later, things *will* be desperate, and he doesn't want to be forced into a corner," Darthan said. He drew his finger across the horizon. "See that?"

Seisan squinted and followed his finger. A smudge of black marked the place where the sky met the hills.

"The darkness is rolling in," Darthan continued. "The Oncoming Abyss, we call it. It's like a giant black wall, a void that eats everything in its path. Everything it touches, it wipes out of existence. From what I've seen, it completely surrounds the Gloaming. The seas and outer regions are already gone. Our land is shrinking."

Part of Seisan wanted to tell him the idea was preposterous. Dimensions didn't *shrink*. Countries on Earth sometimes shrank due to wars or rising sea levels. But dimensions? He shook his head, clearing his thoughts and allowing counterarguments to rise to the surface. Just because he hadn't heard of something before didn't mean it didn't exist.

And if Darthan was right—if that conniving backstabber was telling the truth—then the Oncoming Abyss would destroy his beloved homeland whether he believed in it or not.

"How fast is it shrinking?" Lothaire asked.

"Not very fast. Maybe a few square inches a day," Darthan replied. "It seems to speed up when Grigoth messes with the laws of magic."

"That makes sense," Seisan said. "The Gloaming is inherently magical. If Grigoth corrupts the essence of magic, it stands to reason that our land will become corrupted too. Do you truly believe he would invade Earth just so he can start over in another dimension?"

"I'm saying it's a possibility," Darthan said. "I mean, there's a chance he'll realize the consequences of his meddling and put things right, but I seriously doubt that will happen. If he allows the land to flourish again, the famine will end, and he'll have a harder time trying to control his servants. Control the food, control the people, right? If he leaves things as they are and stays here, he'll die to the Oncoming Abyss. Logically, invading Earth is the best option for him."

Seisan scratched his chin. "I don't know. It seems a little farfetched to me. If the Oncoming Abyss swallows the portal, the connection between Earth and the Gloaming will be severed. He'll lose his ability to use magic. How is he going to control his servants without magic?"

"No idea," Darthan said. "All I know is that we've got less than ten years before the entire dimension is consumed. Ol' Griggles has another two hundred years left in him at least, so it's not like we can sit around and wait for him to die. I'm going to need one of you to come back to the Gloaming full time to help me monitor the situation."

"I'll do it," Lothaire said.

Seisan closed his eyes. *Of course it would come down to this.* "You can't go."

"Oh yeah? Try to stop me."

"Let's look at this logically," Seisan suggested. "We both know I'm better than you at combat magic and concealment. I also have a lot more experience in the field than you. I should be the one to go."

Surprise flitted across Lothaire's face. "What about Corvus? You said—"

"I know what I said," Seisan interrupted, holding up a hand. "Believe me, I do. He's never going to forgive me for leaving, but I can't stand by and let Grigoth threaten our people. I trust you to keep an eye on my son for me."

The idea of leaving Corvus behind made him sick to his stomach, but what choice did he have? If he didn't volunteer, Earth would be no safer than the Gloaming, and that meant his son would be in danger. If Grigoth got his slimy paws on Corvus, he would never forgive himself.

"Very well." Lothaire inclined his head. "If you insist on going, I'll do everything I can to keep our children safe."

"Then it's decided," Darthan said, clasping his hands together. "Come on, Seisan. We've got work to do."

"Whatever it is, it can wait until I've said goodbye to my son," Seisan said.

Darthan wrinkled his nose. "You've gotten soft over the years. But you know what? Fine. I'll give you one hour to get your affairs in order."

That's all I need, Seisan thought, hurrying back to the portal.

Seisan's trouser pocket buzzed when he stepped out of Oilskin Lake, startling him enough to slip in the ooze. A half-formed spell shot out of his fingers and dissipated into the evening air. He stood up cautiously, wiping muddy water from his face. Somewhere in the back of his mind, he remembered the strange silver object Chief Bowers had given him on his first day of work. His fellow officers called it a cell phone; he called it a pointless waste of space.

The buzzing stopped, and Seisan removed the phone from his pocket. He squinted at the backlit screen. *New voicemail.*

"What's up?" Lothaire asked.

"I'm not entirely sure yet."

He'd lived on Earth for most of his life, but he'd never wrapped his head around technology. He fiddled with the colorful icons for a few frustrating minutes before he figured out how to access his voicemail. The robotic voice on the other end added to his irritation, and he held the phone at arms' length until the real message began.

"Hi there, Seisan, this is Mr. Matlin from Morton Elementary School. Your son, Corvus, was involved in an altercation today, and we've had no choice but to suspend him…"

Chapter Seventeen

Ms. Clemmons released the children one minute before the 3:15 p.m. bell. Billy jostled with his peers in the mad rush out of the classroom, eager to escape the stifling atmosphere. Hamish's class emptied soon after, but James's took several minutes to emerge. When it did, Billy grabbed his brothers by the hand and dragged them all the way home.

When they settled in front of the TV, he ran back out, explaining that he needed to visit his friend. Disappointment radiated from their faces, but he ignored it. As much as he loved being a big brother, he wasn't going to sit around playing *Spyro* when Corvus and Rem needed him.

I'll be gone for a few hours at most, Billy reasoned, his sneakers pounding the pavement. *Those two are always glued to the TV after school. They won't have time to get in trouble.*

Armed with Rem's directions, he found Corvus's house without too much difficulty. Even so, the dilapidated exterior froze him in his tracks. The lawn consisted of weeds holding hands rather than grass, and the earth beneath was honeycombed with evidence of burrowing insects. An overgrown willow hid most of the yard from passersby. However, the reigning state of disarray easily earned it the title of "Worst House in the Street."

Does Corvus really live here? Billy wondered.

Steeling himself, he crept down the garden path and knocked on the door. The untreated pinewood felt both spongy and brittle under his knuckles, as though it were rotting from the inside out. Rem answered straight away.

"Hey," she said, offering him a tired smile.

"Hey. How's Corvus doing?"

"Why don't you come and see for yourself?"

Billy trailed her through the hallway into the lounge. No photos or decorations graced the plain white walls, and the black furniture struck Billy as sterile and impersonal. He found Corvus reclining on a leather sofa, entranced by the fireplace. No flames flickered there—the heat of summer was in full swing, after all—but he stared at the grille as though some great ephemeral fire burned in his mind's eye. The trance broke when Billy arrived. Blinking, Corvus swung his legs off the sofa and patted the seat next to him.

Billy sat down. "How are you doing?"

As soon as the words left his mouth, he regretted asking. Corvus looked worse than he had earlier. Dried blood framed the side of his face, brilliantly violet and blotchy. A fresh globule formed on his lip and trickled down his chin. He wiped it away with his sleeve, grimacing at the stain it left behind.

"I've had better days," Corvus said dryly. "Rem, could you get me some water?"

"I'm not your slave. The least you could do is say please."

"But I'm *dying*."

"Would it kill you to be polite?"

"It might. My condition is critical, you know."

Rem held her hands up in mock defeat. "All right, all right. I'll get you some water, you big baby."

A half-delirious, half-pained grin edged onto Corvus's lips as she retreated to the kitchen.

"I know. I'm a terrible patient," he said when he caught Billy staring.

"Are you really dying?" Billy asked.

Corvus sighed. "No, not really. Feels like it, though."

His fever-bright eyes fluttered closed, and he leaned forward, hugging his stomach. He looked younger, Billy thought. Younger and more vulnerable. The boy's hunched posture reminded him of the time Hamish came down with a bad case of food poisoning. Billy had spent hours next to his bed, reading *The Very Hungry Caterpillar* over and over until the worst of his symptoms passed. He wished he could do something similar for Corvus, but he got the sense his friend wouldn't appreciate being babied.

Billy cleared his throat to break the silence. "You're bleeding."

"Yeah. I noticed."

"Can't you heal it or something?"

"There's no point. It'll stop by itself."

"What if it gets infected?"

"It won't. We wraiths can't get sick from Earth germs, remember?"

"Oh yeah. You did say something about that."

Rem walked back into the room and thrust a glass of water into Corvus's waiting hands.

He gulped it down, gasping for air after he drained it. "Thanks, Rem."

She shrugged and flopped backward onto the neighboring sofa. "You're welcome."

"Don't you think you should at least clean yourself up?" Billy persisted, watching Corvus with mounting concern. "I mean, if you're too sore to move, Rem and I could bring you a damp washcloth or something."

"Later," Corvus said, waving him off. "Right now, I want to know what happened with Mr. Matlin. What did he say?"

Billy's gaze dropped to the floor. The gravity of the subject distracted him from the blood, but it also made his nerves go haywire. He didn't want to see his friends' reactions. In a slow monotone, Billy recounted his conversation with the principal.

"I just don't get it," he said afterward. "I gave him proof the scientists are evil, but he acted like it was normal. Why would he do that unless they're paying him to keep quiet?"

"Maybe they *are* paying him," Rem said. "It doesn't matter, though.

Not right now. We beat the scientists today. We should be proud of that."

"And if they come back?" Corvus asked.

"Then we'll stop them again," Billy vowed. He fished Dr. Stanford's keycard from his pocket. "I picked this up on my way out of the lab. We can use it to break into the science center after they've locked it up for the night. As long as we wear masks, they'll never know it was us."

Corvus whistled as he examined the keycard. "Nice going, Billy."

"Thanks." Billy shoved it back into his pocket. "I think we should report them to someone else next time. Someone higher up."

"Like who?"

"The police."

"I've told you before, that won't work. My dad will never go for it."

"What if I convince him for you?"

"You can't."

"Why not?"

Corvus let out an exasperated sigh. "*Because.*"

"Because why?"

Seeing Corvus was dangerously close to losing control, Rem stepped in.

"Because if Seisan openly opposes the scientists, the government will send more of them to control us," she explained. "If that happens, we'll have to leave Morton and risk starvation in the Gloaming."

"You could always hide in the woods," Billy said.

"All of us?"

"Sure, why not?"

"If we're in hiding, we won't be able to go to school. That'll make it harder for us to get into the Academy."

"I don't understand. You'd be close to the portal, so you'd still be able to do magic, right? You could practice tons more if you didn't have to go to school. Wouldn't that make it easier to get in?"

"It's not that simple, Billy," Rem said. "The entrance exams are about more than magical aptitude. We have to prove our Earth education too."

"Really? That's kinda stupid."

Corvus sniggered. "You've got that right."

"I doubt the scientists are coming back any time soon, if ever, so there's no reason for us to hide in the woods," Rem said, bringing the conversation back on track. "Besides, we already know we can beat them. We have no reason to run."

"I guess you're right," Billy conceded.

"She's always right," Corvus mumbled. He used the arm of the sofa to push himself upright. "I'm gonna go wash up. Can you set up the potion ingredients for us, Rem? *Please?*"

"Only because you asked nicely," Rem teased. "Want to help, Billy?"

"I thought you weren't supposed to be doing magic without supervision," he protested.

"Seisan's been supervising us," Rem explained. "We need to have everything set up before he gets home."

"Oh. Of course." Billy kicked himself mentally. *I should have thought of that.* "What can I do to help?"

"Come with me."

Rem led him to a boxy storeroom at the end of the hallway. A naked bulb dangled from the ceiling by a wire, illuminating the mahogany shelves. Mysterious bottles glittered on every surface. She handed him a cauldron filled with a pungent brew that reminded him of freshly milled lavender. He peered into the rheumy liquid with undisguised awe, as though it might hold the secrets of the universe.

"What *is* this stuff?" he asked.

"Portal water. Lavender. Ricrawth bile. Koerak scales." Rem ticked the ingredients off on her fingers. "Lots of stuff."

She selected a bottle from the shelf, examined the label, and placed it in an empty cauldron. She repeated the process with three more bottles.

"I've only heard of one of those things," Billy said. "Did you get them from the Gloaming?"

"Most of our supplies are from the Gloaming, yes. One of Vaeril's mages got really paranoid before Grigoth took the throne and buried a cache of potion supplies near Oilskin Lake. I think he was planning to run away if anything bad happened."

"And he gave them to Seisan?"

"No, the mage died long before that," Rem corrected. "My dad stumbled across the cache when he was on patrol."

"Oh."

"Yeah."

"How long ago did he find it?"

"No idea. Why do you ask?"

"No reason. I'm just surprised you haven't run out of ingredients yet."

Rem stacked her cauldron on top of a second cauldron, which contained the same liquid as Billy's. She picked up the tower with surprising ease and led the way to the dining room.

"We did run out of a few things in the beginning," she said as they walked. "Dad had to find Earth substitutes for them. Fortunately, Seisan worked out how to duplicate ingredients, so we shouldn't have that problem again."

"That's lucky," Billy said. "Imagine if you had to go back into the Gloaming every time you needed more stuff!"

"We couldn't even if we wanted to," Rem said, placing the cauldrons on the table.

Billy copied her move. "Yeah, I know. Too dangerous."

"No, I mean we really *can't*. All the plants that grew there, all the animals… they're extinct. They're gone. There's nothing left to gather."

The weight of her words stunned Billy into silence. He'd seen the desolate wasteland at the heart of the Gloaming, but he couldn't fathom an entirely barren world. If there were no plants or animals, what did the wraiths eat? They couldn't survive on *nothing*, could they? He wanted to ask Rem about it, but one look at her doleful expression told him to wait for a better time.

"So… what does this potion do?" he asked instead.

"It's not done yet," Rem said, "but when it is, it'll stop internal bleeding."

"That's pretty neat. I wish I could make potions like you."

"If you're lucky, Seisan might let you stay and watch."

A deep voice wafted from the front door. "Talking about me?"

Seisan strolled into the room, and Billy's head snapped toward him. The wraith's dark, brooding eyes sank into his haggard face and gave him the appearance of a man twice his age.

"We've been getting the potion stuff ready," Rem told him. "Do you want us to start now or after dinner? I know it's early, but I thought we could make up for the ones we didn't finish yesterday."

"Not now, Rem. I need to talk to my son."

"I'm here." Corvus's muffled voice floated down the hallway.

He emerged wearing new clothes and looking much more alive than before. A network of bruises stretched across his nose and left cheekbone, but the crust of dried blood was gone.

Seisan regarded his son's injuries with distaste. "My office. Now."

He stalked away without waiting for a response. Corvus shot his friends an apologetic look and slunk after his father.

"Is he going to be okay?" Billy asked.

"Yeah, I think so," Rem said. "Seisan doesn't beat him, if that's what you're worried about."

"No, I..." Billy bit his lip, perturbed by the uneasiness swirling through his gut. "I know Seisan's not like that. He looked really serious, though. I think something's wrong."

Rem shrugged. "Maybe it is, maybe it isn't. Corvus will tell us later if it's important."

Chapter Eighteen

CORVUS SAT IN the chair opposite Seisan, staring him down. The only thing separating them was a cedar desk—a strategically placed barrier to protect them in the event of a lost temper. But even though they were in the same room, the distance between them had never felt greater.

A myriad of emotions radiated from Seisan's gaze. Love. Concern. Sadness. Annoyance. *Disappointment.* His own eyes blustered with a contrived defiance he knew was expected of him but which he no longer had the heart to indulge in. The moment Seisan opened his mouth, Corvus lost his nerve and looked away.

"Why?"

The word hung in the air like a storm cloud. *Why did you flunk your summer project? Why did you torment Billy? Why did you punch Mr. Graham's cabinet? Why did you get in a fight with Zane? Why are you like this? Why, why, why, why, why?* The number of possible interpretations made Corvus's head spin. He wasn't perfect—not by a long shot—but he was *trying*, wasn't he? Didn't that count for something?

Seisan exhaled heavily. "Do you have any idea how serious this is? You assaulted a fellow student without provocation. I know you've been under a lot of pressure, but that is no excuse for violence. Did you do it to impress your classmates? Is that what this is about?"

Oh.

"It's not about them," Corvus insisted.

"The blood oath ceremony?"

"No."

"Then what?"

Corvus shrugged. For the first time in his life, he could honestly say he acted out of compassion rather than fear. His fight with Zane may well have saved Volner from a fate worse than death. But explaining the whole elaborate setup would take more energy than he could spare. His father wouldn't understand anyway. He never did.

"You have to promise me you'll do better, Son," Seisan murmured. "You can't keep getting in trouble like this."

"I know, Dad. It was a one-off thing. I *am* going to do better. I promise I will."

Even as he said it, he knew it was a promise he couldn't keep. The world was too big, too dangerous, and too unpredictable. If the scientists came back, he would fight them tooth and nail regardless of the consequences. *Dad had it easy when he was my age. He never suffered like we do. All he cares about is keeping the humans happy. If he cared about wraithkind at all, he would have found a way to get rid of the scientists himself. He's a traitor.*

A stab of guilt accompanied his mutinous thoughts. His father might not have suffered at the hands of an immoral scientist, but he'd endured Grigoth's wrath on countless occasions. When he eventually escaped, he found himself in a strange land filled with strange people. People who preferred to shoot first and ask questions later. The persecution nearly broke him, but he tolerated it in the hopes of creating a brighter future for both sides.

Deep down, Corvus knew their experiences weren't so different and that his resentment came from a place of jealousy. Most humans accepted Seisan these days, albeit grudgingly. But Corvus? It had taken him ten years to find a human who didn't want to kick his face in as soon as he said hello.

"Are you even listening to me?" Seisan demanded, drawing him back to the present.

"More or less," Corvus lied. "My head's a little swimmy."

"I said, I've spoken to the principal and convinced him to give you another chance. Your suspension has been lifted, but you'll be having daily detentions for the next two weeks."

Corvus wrinkled his nose and said nothing.

"What are you going to do?" Seisan asked pointedly.

"Go to school and behave myself and show up for all my detentions."

Seisan regarded him for a long moment. "I hope you mean that, Corvus. I really do. I'm worried about you."

"You don't have to worry about me, Dad. I'm going to be on the straight and narrow from now on. You'll see."

"Hmmm."

Corvus shifted in his seat. *He doesn't believe me.* "Can I go now?"

Seisan laced his fingers together and placed them on the desk. "Actually, there's another matter I'd like to discuss with you first."

The seriousness of his tone sent new shivers down Corvus's spine. Had his father heard about the incident with Mr. Graham's cabinet too? He hoped not. That moment of madness was just as unexplainable as the fight with Zane.

"What is it?" he asked.

"I met an old friend today."

"Who?"

"Darthan."

Corvus's eyes widened, his own worries forgotten. "Didn't he try to kill you when you were in the Academy?"

"Tried and failed. That's all in the past," Seisan reassured him. "Anyway, he's been keeping an eye on things in the Gloaming. He had news for us about Grigoth's movements, and they're concerning, to say the least."

"So Darthan's like a spy?"

"Yes."

"But he's bound to Grigoth! How is that possible?"

"A blood oath isn't absolute, Corvus. There are too many variables in everyday life, and Grigoth can't account for all of them. Take the laws regarding sedition, for example. Grigoth forbids his servants from speaking poorly of him, but the oath only kicks in if the servant uses his real name or pictures his face in their mind. If they refer to him by a false name and imagine someone else, they can badmouth him as much as they want. Finding ways to circumvent certain elements of the oath isn't as difficult as you might think. All it takes is practice and a sharp wit."

I didn't know that, Corvus thought, intrigued. He made a mental note to give the matter further consideration. "So, what did Darthan have to say?"

"He's worried the king is planning military action against Morton. Soldiers have been marching far and wide, stealing food from laborers as they go. Some of them have set up camp near the portal."

"They can't get through, though. They're too weak. You said so yourself."

"That's true for now, at least. There's no telling what will happen if Grigoth builds his army to full strength."

"We can't let him do that."

"No, we can't," Seisan agreed with a rueful smile. "That's why I've decided to return to the Gloaming. Indefinitely."

Corvus froze. The edges of his vision pulsed in and out of focus until all he could see was his father's face, maddeningly calm as it was, staring back at him.

"What?" he choked out.

"I'm returning to the Gloaming," Seisan repeated, this time a little louder.

Sugar-coating things had never been his father's style, but it took a few seconds for Corvus to grasp the reality of the situation. His dad was leaving. His dad was *leaving*, with no indication of when he'd be back. He buried his head in his hands, trying to organize his thoughts.

He can't go! He'll get killed. What'll happen to me? What if I have to live in the homestead? The other wraiths will kill me in my sleep. I can't live with Rem. It'd break the Promising spell—we'd never be able to get married! I can't live by myself. I don't know how. I don't know anything!

"I'm sure it's bit of a shock," Seisan said, which Corvus thought was the understatement of the century. "There's enough food in the house to last a month, if need be, and I've left some money with Lothaire. It's my entire savings since I joined the police force. You can spend it on whatever you need—and I do mean *need*. He'll be the judge of that."

I don't need money, I need you, Corvus thought desperately. *You're my dad. You can't leave. This can't be real. Zane must have knocked me out, and this whole thing is a weird, twisted dream. Or maybe… maybe it is real. Maybe he's fed up with me. Maybe I went too far and he doesn't want me anymore. It's my fault he's leaving.*

"Please don't go!" he blurted out. Tears pricked his eyes, and his throat felt funny. "I'll be the perfect son. I'll get straight A's in all my subjects. I'll make friends with everyone in my class. I'll do whatever you say without arguing. I'll never get in trouble again. I'll… I'll…"

His throat closed up, and he trailed off into miserable silence.

"Oh, Corvus," Seisan murmured. Pain flickered in his eyes. "I'm not leaving because of you. You're my son, and I love you dearly. Perhaps I don't say it as often as I should, but that doesn't diminish my esteem for you. You have a good heart. I'm very proud of you for befriending Billy and moving past your prejudice toward humans. I'm also proud of your dedication toward young Rem. I know that with their help, you will grow into a strong and responsible young man."

Corvus nodded, becoming less and less cognizant of his father's words. A tempest of thoughts whirled through his mind, faster and faster, until he only caught snippets of them. One thought, louder than the others, pushed its way to the surface.

"You'll die in the Gloaming. You'll starve to death."

"Not necessarily," Seisan said. "A wraith my age can survive at least two months without food. Perhaps longer if they're in good physical condition. It won't be pleasant, but I'll survive."

"What if it takes longer than a few months?"

Seisan hesitated. "You know me. I'll find a way to eat. Speaking of which, I brought some pizza home. I ate a few slices on the way here, but the rest is waiting for you on the hall table."

"I'm not hungry," Corvus mumbled. *How does he expect me to eat at a time like this?* "You should take it with you. You need it more than I do."

Seisan shook his head. "You know I can't do that."

Corvus did. On more than one occasion, he'd left a granola bar in his pocket during the portal crossing, only to find a pile of ashes in its place upon arrival. His father wrote it off as a side effect of Grigoth's meddling, but the exact details eluded him.

He sniffed, embarrassed to find hot tears streaking down his face. "Why does it have to be you? Can't someone else go?"

"I truly wish someone were capable of taking my place. Unfortunately, Lothaire and I are the only free adult wraiths in existence. We are the only ones who can stand up to Grigoth. Between us, my magic skills are stronger and more practical for the mission. My involvement is logical."

"You could at least act like you're sorry to go!"

Seisan offered him a sad smile. "I *am* sorry. Perhaps I should take my leave now. Dragging things out never makes them any easier."

"Fine." Corvus folded his arms and tried to ignore the tears on his cheeks. "I'll see you when you come home, then."

"You won't walk with me to the portal?"

Corvus kept his gaze fixed on the carpet. His father waited a few minutes, then heaved a disheartened sigh and walked out the door.

Chapter Nineteen

THE HINGES OF the back door squeaked to mark Seisan's departure, but Billy didn't register the significance of the sound. Bored of waiting for Corvus, he'd made the mistake of teaching Rem how to play charades. She stood in front of him, her cheeks puffed out and her arms swinging from side to side.

"I still say you're terrible at this," Billy said, chuckling. "How am I supposed to guess? Are you a really bad backup dancer?"

"No! I'm a monkey," she explained, waving her arms wildly.

"That's the worst monkey I've ever seen."

Rem's brow creased, and she gave him a playful punch in the shoulder. "I'd like to see you do better."

Billy pulled a face and took up his best monkey stance, with one arm dangling over his head and the other scratching at his armpit. He capered around the room, pretending to grab a banana from the fruit bowl on his way past. Rem guffawed at the sight.

"Hey, that's good," she said when her mirth subsided. "Where'd you learn to do that?"

"My brothers. They love it when I do impressions and stuff. I'm pretty good at animals but not much else."

"Do another one! I'll try to guess what it is."

A loud crash interrupted their antics, and Billy jumped out of his skin.

"What was *that?*" he asked, eyes wide.

All the color drained out of Rem's face, and she raced out of the room. It took Billy a few precious seconds to process the situation before he sprinted after her. By the time he caught up, she stood frozen outside Seisan's study. Muffled sobs emanated from inside, startling Billy. *Surely Corvus isn't...* His mind blanked when Rem pushed the door open. Their friend lay on the floor, curled up in the fetal position as though all the air had been knocked out of him. An overturned swivel chair sat several feet away, its wheels still spinning.

"Corvus, what's wrong?" Rem exclaimed, engulfing him in a hug. When he didn't respond, she added: "I can go and get you some water, if you like. Would that make you feel any better?"

Corvus clung to Rem like a drowning swimmer to a piece of driftwood, mumbling something between hiccupping sobs that Billy couldn't understand. *What did Seisan do to him?* He'd never seen Corvus this upset about anything, not even the scientists. The intensity of his distress scared Billy.

For as long as he'd known him, the boy's emotional range spanned from smug indifference to overt contempt. He almost never strayed into sorrow or regret. Now, grief drained away any trace of his former anger. Even Rem's soothing murmurs seemed to have no effect on him. Billy watched on awkwardly, wondering if he should join the hug or go and fetch some water. In the end, he decided to stay put.

It took a few minutes for Corvus to regain a semblance of control. His shuddering breaths slowed, and he made a half-hearted attempt to dry his face.

"Dad left me," he said, his voice thick with phlegm. "He's going to die, and it's all my fault."

Anguish twisted his face as he tried and failed to hold back a fresh wave of tears. He wept silently this time, but his shoulders trembled with the effort of containing his sobs.

"Deep breaths," Rem coaxed, concern etched into her features. "Where did Seisan go?"

"The Gloaming. He wants to spy on Grigoth and sabotage his army.

He's going to get himself killed, I just know it."

"Seisan's strong. He can take care of himself. I know it's hard, but he'll be back in no time."

"He's not coming back."

"How do you know?"

"Because he said so. He's leaving *indefinitely*."

Billy's chest ached in sympathy. He couldn't imagine how his friend must be feeling. After all, his own dad—biased and ill-tempered though he might be—adored his children more than anything. He wouldn't leave them for the world. What's more, both of his parents insisted work should come second to family. Seisan's inversion of these values came as a shock.

"Let's not jump to conclusions," Rem said. "'Indefinitely' means he doesn't know how long the mission will take. It could be a few weeks, or it could be a few days. We just have to be patient."

Corvus sniffled. "It could be years."

"It could be. But however long it takes, I'll be here for you."

"Me too," Billy said. He stepped forward and wrapped Corvus in a brief hug.

The wraith boy looked up at them with hopeless eyes. "What am I supposed to do? I can't live here on my own. I used to think I could, but I'm not ready. I'm not like the other wraiths. I've never had to look after myself before. Not like this."

"You can come and live with me," Rem said. "You know my dad loves you. There's no way he wouldn't take you in."

"We can't do that. The Promise will break if we live under the same roof before we take the blood oath."

"So what? We'll still be friends, with or without the spell."

"Uh… what spell is this?" Billy asked.

"The Promise? It's kind of like an engagement spell. It's placed over wraiths before they hatch," Rem explained. "Grigoth put restrictions on ours because he doesn't want us to become oathbreakers like our parents. If we break the Promise, we can never get married or have kids.

Not unless the king decides to replace the spell. But pigs will fly before that happens."

Billy scratched his head. "Aren't we a bit young to worry about that stuff?"

"You wouldn't understand," Corvus said, his voice low and watery. "I'm not breaking it, and that's final. I won't risk our future on Grigoth's goodwill."

He crossed his arms in front of his chest, tucking his chin against his collarbone to avoid their eyes. Billy tried to imagine himself in Corvus's shoes but came up short. The thought of getting married and having children had never crossed his mind before. Now that it had, he didn't feel strongly about it either way. Was that abnormal? Or could Corvus's stubborn passion for the subject be chalked up to a peculiarity of wraith culture?

Billy didn't know. All he knew was that he couldn't leave his friend all alone in this ramshackle cottage until Seisan returned. The nucleus of a terrible idea formed in his mind, and his mouth moved before logic could catch up.

"You could live at my house."

All eyes turned to him, and he blushed at the inherent ridiculousness of his own suggestion.

"This isn't the time for jokes," Corvus said. "Look at me. I'm a wraith. Your parents would never go for it."

"What if you make one of those potions that turn you into a human?" Billy asked. "I know it didn't go so well last time, but I bet Lothaire would help you."

Rem's cheeks purpled at the reminder of her failure. "He might. But if we're looking for a long-term solution, it would be better to make a glamour."

"What's a glamour?" Billy asked.

"It's a kind of magical costume. Glamours don't change your body on a physiological level like potions do, so they're a lot safer."

"And I'll be able to take it off for school," Corvus said. The vaguest hint of a smile touched his lips, then faded. "I don't have any idea how to make a glamour, though. Do you?"

"Nope, but it's the next lesson after cloaking spells," Rem said. "I'm sure Dad would help us if we asked nicely."

"These glamours… are they realistic?" Billy asked. "I mean, would they fool my parents?"

"Definitely," Rem said. "You can't tell the difference between a human and a wraith wearing a glamour unless they start acting weird."

Corvus groaned and buried his head in his hands. "I'm doomed."

"I'm sure you could pass as a human if you try," she reassured him. "You're good at acting. All we need to do is give you a new identity and backstory."

"Backstory?"

"Yeah, you know. A different name. A different history. If Billy tells his parents the truth about how you became friends, they're going to flip out. You two need to have your stories straight before you talk to them."

"She's right," Billy said. "My parents always ask my friends a lot of questions when they come over."

"What kind of questions?" Corvus asked.

"What your hobbies are. Your favorite subjects at school. What TV shows you like to watch. What your parents do for work. That kind of stuff."

"I don't have any hobbies outside of magic, though. And I hate school. And TV."

Billy bristled at the final revelation but resisted the urge to argue. If Corvus lived with him, he'd learn the error of his ways soon enough.

"That's why we have to make up a new identity for you," he explained.

Corvus steepled his fingers under his chin, his brow furrowed. "Okay. Let's say my dad's a soldier and my mom's dead. It's pretty much the truth, anyway. My favorite subject is… I don't know. English? Math? What's your favorite subject, Billy?"

"Probably English."

"Okay. We'll say mine is too. What about hobbies? What are some normal things that humans like to do?"

Billy could have slapped his forehead in disbelief. *This is going to be a lot harder than I thought.* "Watching TV, playing video games, hunting, hiking, art…"

"Yawn."

"Corvus, I'm trying to help you."

"I know. I can't help it that I think those things are boring."

"Have you ever used a gun before?"

"Nope."

"Okay, well that rules out hunting. Let's go with hiking."

Corvus wrinkled his nose. "But I hate exercise. Can't I choose something else?"

"You can have as many hobbies as you want. I only suggested hiking because it fits with my dad's hobbies. It's an easy way to get on his good side."

"I wouldn't call it easy," Corvus muttered.

"Billy's trying to help you," Rem reiterated. "It's not like you'll have to go hiking every day."

"Exactly," Billy said. "We're just going to *say* you enjoy it. You probably won't have to go hiking at all."

Corvus studied him, his jaw twitching with unvoiced arguments. Then the moment passed, and his body deflated like a punctured balloon. "Okay."

"Do you want any other hobbies?" Rem asked.

Corvus shook his head mutely.

"Most humans have more than one hobby," Billy said. "My parents don't understand video games, so you could say you like them and they wouldn't know any better. Art would be easy to fake too, as long as you don't show them your drawings."

"I guess so."

"Great." Billy flashed him an encouraging smile. "Now all we have to do is decide on a name."

"What's wrong with Corvus?"

"It sounds Roman."

"That's because it is. The Romans were human, right? What's the problem?"

"No one uses old Roman names anymore. Besides, my dad already knows your name. He'd recognize it straight away and figure out you're a wraith. I think Corey would be a good name for you. Corey Smith."

"Why Corey?"

"It's like a nickname based on your real name."

"Wraiths don't have nicknames. I don't want a nickname."

"But you're going to pose as a *human*. Why do you have a Roman name anyway? Shouldn't you have a wraith name?"

"Exotic cultures have always been fashionable in the Gloaming," Rem explained. "A lot of us have human names."

Billy didn't know what to say to that, so he bit his lip and nodded. An austere grandfather clock in the corner of the room ticked over to 5:00 p.m., counting the hours with a series of discordant chimes.

He glanced at his watch to confirm the time. "I guess I'd better head home. I left my brothers by themselves, and Mom's going to have a fit if she finds out."

"We can't have that," Rem said, rising to escort him to the door. "Are you going to talk to her tonight?"

"Of course."

She nodded solemnly. "Good luck."

"Thanks. Take care of Corvus, won't you?"

"*Corvus* is still in the room," Corvus pointed out, only to be cut off as Billy hugged him again.

"And you look after yourself," Billy insisted. "Try not to worry too much. Things will work out."

The other boy stiffened for a split second, then relaxed into the hug. When Billy pulled back, he detected a hint of warmth in his friend's eyes. *He actually trusts me now. I'd better not let him down.*

Chapter Twenty

"THE GLAMOUR'S READY," Rem sang when Billy met her after school the following day.

His eyebrows shot up. "Really? That was quick."

"We had a lot of help from Dad," she admitted, blushing at his praise. "We're going down to Oilskin Lake to apply it. Do you want to come?"

A grin tugged at Billy's lips. Although they'd spent the day within three feet of each other, his wraith friends hadn't been much for talking. He'd tried to get their attention through the magic notebook, but his attempts fell flat. For once, they were too engrossed in their schoolwork to reply. Billy couldn't wait for things to go back to normal.

"Yeah, I'll come," he said. "I need to take my brothers home first, but I'll be there as soon as I can."

They parted ways at the school gate, with Rem skipping toward the lake and Billy retracing his steps to the classroom. Hamish and James waited for him under the eaves, red-faced and giggling. Billy waved them over, grabbed their wrists, and pulled them down the street.

"Why do we have to run home?" James complained. "It's not like the monster's still around."

"It's good for your health," Billy said. Seeing his brother's raised eyebrow, he added: "And I'm training to be a ballplayer."

"For real?" Hamish asked, his eyes widening.

"Sure," Billy lied. "Maybe you'll see me on TV one day."

"I wish I could be a ballplayer," Hamish said dreamily. "I'd play basketball and softball and baseball and football and…"

Billy let his brother ramble, knowing it would prevent further questions. When they got home, the younger boys dropped their school bags in the lounge and ran into the backyard.

Why aren't they playing video games? Billy wondered.

Regardless of the reason, he didn't have time to stand around and watch them. He dumped his satchel next to the clothes tree and flew out the door.

By the time he arrived at the lake, his friends were already hard at work. He spotted Lothaire first, stooped low over the water, and then Corvus and Rem, who sat cross-legged on the grass. Their palms glowed over a bundle of colorless fabric. A group of wraith children gathered on the other side of the lake, watching on with interest.

"This is so humiliating," Corvus groaned when Billy sat next to him. "First, I have to hang around with an oathbreaker, then *you* show up, and now I have to put on a human glamour with a whole audience watching me."

Lothaire shot him a warning look. "Now, now, Corvus. There's no need to be rude."

Corvus's eyes glazed over, and Billy felt a pang of empathy for him. Lothaire, for all his good qualities, had missed the boat. He failed to see the other wraith kids for what they were. Not silent classmates, not ridiculing bullies, but potential accessories to murder. Everything Corvus did here was practically an invitation to invoke the worst kind of fury on him.

Lothaire dried his hands on the hem of his shirt. "Volner and Jarsha are doing much better today, by the way. They should be back on their feet by tomorrow morning at the latest."

Rem's eyes lit up. "That's great!"

"Yes, it is. We were lucky to heal them when we did. Volner kept passing out from blood loss, and Jarsha showed signs of aconite poisoning. A few more hours without treatment and they might not have survived. You three should be very proud of yourselves for helping them."

Billy frowned. "I thought you didn't wa—"

Corvus elbowed him in the ribs, cutting him off. "We did what any decent person would do."

He offered Lothaire the fabric they'd been toiling over, and the older wraith accepted it with a grateful bow. Folding it into quarters, Lothaire retreated to the edge of the water.

"Why'd you do that?" Billy grumbled, rubbing the place where Corvus struck him.

"Dad doesn't know we broke in," Rem murmured. "He thinks we found them wandering around the school after a freak explosion in the lab."

"An explosion?"

"That's the story Mr. Matlin's sticking to."

"Huh. I guess that's why my parents haven't grounded me. Mr. Matlin never told them the truth."

"It's so unfair," Corvus complained. "How come you can destroy a government-run science lab and gas seven people without getting in trouble, but I get suspended for a minor scuffle? Either you're really lucky or Matlin's a crook."

"Or both," Rem chimed in. "Besides, you're not suspended anymore. You've just got—"

"A million detentions," Corvus finished. "I'd rather be suspended and get a free holiday from school."

I bet you would, Billy thought.

"The glamour's ready, kids!" Lothaire announced.

Billy jumped to his feet, eager to get a closer look. The fabric looked the same as before, except for the opalescent water clinging to it. The droplets shone like gemstones, alternately reflecting the sky, the grass, and the purple-black lake.

Lothaire handed the glamour to Corvus, who wrapped it around himself. The shapeless material morphed in front of Billy's eyes, twisting and growing to fit the body it contained. Within seconds, it enveloped him from head to toe.

"Can he breathe with that thing on?" Billy asked.

"Yup," Lothaire reassured him. "I guess it looks a bit scary if you've never seen this kind of thing before."

The fabric around Corvus's mouth sucked inward, and Billy winced. "You can say that again."

"Why's it taking so long?" Rem asked.

"Newly made glamours conform to the wearer's desires. It's not unusual for the process to take a few minutes," Lothaire explained. "Corvus might be having trouble imagining himself as a human."

"What happens if he can't do it?" Billy asked.

"That's a good question. A glamour is like a mold. Once it's been cast, it holds its shape and transforms whatever's inside it. If the mold is wrong, you have to start again with a new one. In the case of glamours, that may take quite some time. Half a day at least."

Billy bit his lip. "We don't have that much time."

Lothaire's gaze softened. "Ah, yes. You're the one who offered young Corvus a home, aren't you?"

"Yes, sir. I don't know if my parents will go along with it, but they said he can come over for dinner tonight so they can meet him."

"An excellent idea. Rem told you about the Promise, didn't she?"

"She mentioned it, yeah."

"Ah. Then you understand why this is so important." Lothaire paused to study his hands. "You know, for a while, I was afraid I would have to adopt Corvus myself. I love that boy like my own child, and I'd do it in a heartbeat. But if I did, their Promising spell would break. Their future would be much bleaker. You have my utmost gratitude for trying to prevent that."

"It's okay. I *wanted* to help."

"You're a good kid. I'm glad my daughter found a friend like you."

"Da-*ad*," Rem complained.

"Too mushy?" Lothaire teased.

Billy hid a smile. The two obviously had a close relationship—closer, perhaps, than his own family. They shared a comfortable silence before Lothaire spoke again.

"Can I ask you something, Billy?"

"Sure."

"If your parents *do* decide to foster Corvus, are they likely to do it through official channels?"

Billy hesitated. "What do you mean?"

"As I understand it, human children are registered from birth. Corvus doesn't have any of the documents he needs to pass as a human. If your parents try to become his official foster parents, there won't be any record of his existence in the system. That will be a big problem."

I didn't think of that. "What would happen to him?"

"Maybe he'd get taken away. Maybe he'd have to break his cover. I really don't know. So what do you think? Would your parents try to do things by the book?"

Billy sighed and nodded. "Yeah. They probably would."

"I thought so. I'll have to pull a few strings to make everything look legitimate."

"You can do that?" Rem asked. She sounded impressed.

"Of course," Lothaire assured her, then turned back to Billy. "I suppose your parents will want to talk with Corey's father and uncle before fostering him?"

Billy nodded again.

"Yes, I thought they might. It's only natural. Not to worry. I'll take care of that as well."

"How?" Rem asked.

Lothaire tapped the side of his nose. "Corvus isn't the only one with a glamour, you know. I've got a few pre-molded ones in my closet for emergencies. I can modify my voice with magic too, if I have to."

Billy couldn't believe it. Not only was an adult helping them with their plan, but they were willing to break the law to make it work.

"I care about what happens to Corvus," the older wraith continued, as if reading his mind. "If this is the best way to help him, you'd better believe I'm going to do it."

He looked like he wanted to say more, but a series of crackles and pops from Corvus's direction startled him into silence. Billy shrank back even as Rem leapt forward to get a better look at their friend's transformation. Color spread across the fabric like a match to a trail of gunpowder, zigzagging outward to reveal smooth, pale skin. He watched with bated breath, scarcely daring to move as the glamour turned his friend into a stranger.

The boy standing in front of him was completely new. Sure, he shared some features with Corvus. The scar on his shoulder remained, for example, but the bruises from his fight were gone. Black hair sprouted from his head and curled around his ears—not void-black anymore, but the more subdued shade of a raven's wing. Long eyelashes framed his sapphire eyes, curling toward his bushy new eyebrows. Most surprising of all, his clothes were identical to the ones he'd been wearing before. How they managed to seep through the glamour was anyone's guess.

"You look different," Rem said, studying his new features with awe.

Corvus emitted a nervous laugh. "Is that good or bad?"

"Both," she said. "I liked your old self, but you look nice now too. I think Billy's parents will like you."

"Did anyone bring a mirror?" Corvus asked, looking around eagerly.

Everyone shook their heads, but Lothaire produced a cell phone and turned on the front-facing camera.

"Take a look in this," he said, handing it over.

Corvus's new face erupted into a confusing conglomerate of emotions.

Has he always been this expressive? Billy wondered.

"I look…" Corvus swallowed. "I look *human.*"

"That's the idea of a glamour," Lothaire said. "I think we can call this a complete success."

"But I wanted to be blond!" Corvus cried, flailing his arms.

Billy snickered. "There's always hair dye. I mean, if that's safe to use with glamours? I don't know anything about them."

"It should be safe enough," Lothaire confirmed. "I think the hair suits you, though, Corvus."

"Yeah, I guess," Corvus grumbled. "I just wanted to look different from my old self. I don't like that my hair's almost the same. What if Billy's parents work out I'm a wraith?"

"Plenty of humans have black hair. They won't suspect a thing," Billy told him. "If I hadn't seen you change with my own eyes, I wouldn't believe it was you."

Corvus looked up at him. "Really?"

"Really."

"Well," Lothaire said, clasping his hands together. "Now we've got that sorted out, I think it's time we headed home. We can still fit in an hour of swordplay if you're feeling up to it. What do you say, Corvus? Or would you rather go straight to Billy's house?"

Corvus's gaze dropped to the ground. "No. I'll come with you first."

"Excellent!" Lothaire exclaimed. "What time do you have dinner, Billy? Around six? Seven?"

"Six."

"Excellent. I'll send Corvus over around five-thirty. That should give you plenty of time to prepare."

Chapter Twenty-One

"LET'S GO OVER this again," Billy suggested.

Corvus drummed his heels against the dresser he sat on, his blue eyes peeking down at Billy through a veil of hair. Each movement elicited a groan of protest from his makeshift seat, but he seemed unable to stop himself.

"My name is Corey Smith. I like art and video games and…" He paused to wrinkle his nose. "Hiking. My favorite subject is English. I met you in second grade, and we've been friends ever since. I need a home because my dad deployed unexpectedly to Iran. I'm currently living with my uncle, but he hates kids and doesn't want me living with him."

"Iraq, not Iran," Billy corrected.

Disappointment snuffed out the hope in Corvus's eye. "I can't do this, can I?"

"Sure you can," Billy said, clapping him on the shoulder. "You've got most of it already. And you've got me, remember? I can answer questions for you if you get stuck."

"Won't that be a little suspicious?"

"They know your dad just left. They won't expect you to be very talkative."

Shrieks of laughter echoed down the hallway, drowning out Corvus's response. Billy suppressed the urge to throttle his brothers. Why did they have to act strangely today of all days? He had enough on his plate without their shenanigans. When he arrived home two hours earlier, they'd been lying outside on the grass, panting as if they'd run ten miles. Sure, they'd come inside when prompted, but the laughter that met his request had a peculiar quality he didn't like. A quality that told him trouble was brewing.

"Maybe they're laughing at me," Corvus said. His eyes widened, and he leapt down from the dresser. "Maybe there's something wrong with my glamour."

He frantically examined every inch of himself as though he expected to find a hole where his inner wraith leaked out. His concern provoked Billy to check as well. The boy's sallow skin stretched across his face and neck, offering no clues about his true complexion. A collared white shirt, black slacks, and black socks covered the rest of his body.

He'd been wearing a matching blazer and a white silk cravat when he first walked through the door, but Billy convinced him to take them off. Looking tidy was one thing, but wearing a full suit for a simple pizza night? That would raise a few eyebrows.

"It looks fine to me," Billy said. "And anyway, I don't think they're laughing at you. They've been acting weird all afternoon."

The front door creaked open, startling Corvus into a frenzy of anxious pacing. *This is it. The moment of truth.* Billy opened his bedroom door and peered into the hallway. Mrs. Porter waddled into the house with a cluster of plastic shopping bags in each hand. She dumped them on the counter, then looked back at her husband, who trailed her with a stack of pizza boxes.

"We're home, kids!" she sang. "Time for dinner!"

Billy grabbed Corvus's arm. "Come on. Let's do this."

The other boy squirmed out of his grip but followed him to the dining room. Without warning, Billy's mother wrapped Corvus in a hug.

"Hello, Corey," she said. "It's so good to finally meet you."

"Pleased to meet you too," he squeaked.

"I don't know what kind of pizza you like, so we got a few different ones." She released him and turned to face the lounge. "James! Hamish! You need to turn your game off and come to the dining table."

"We can't! We'll lose all our progress!" James said.

"I'll take the PlayStation away if I have to," Mrs. Porter replied. "Come on, boys. Don't let it get cold."

Hamish dashed to the table without arguing, but James grumbled and dragged his feet. A dark expression settled over his face, but his eyes lit up with mischief when he saw Billy. He whispered something into Hamish's ear, and both brothers erupted into gales of laughter.

"What's so funny?" Billy demanded.

"Nothing," they chorused.

Billy shook his head and blew out a frustrated breath. James opened the first pizza box.

"Oh boy, pepperoni," he said, helping himself to a slice. "My favorite!"

"I don't like pepperoni," Hamish said.

"Then pick the pieces off and eat it without," James suggested around a mouthful of pizza.

Mrs. Porter looked at him, aghast. "*Manners*, James. We have a guest."

"There's a triple cheese pizza for you, Hamish," Mr. Porter said. "Try the second box."

While Hamish wrangled with the box, Corvus took a slice of pepperoni and nibbled the edges. His gaze darted around the room, keeping tabs on the Porter family.

He isn't used to this, Billy thought, grabbing a slice for himself. *Not just being in a family, but being around people who are kind to him.*

The more he thought about it, the more he recognized the truth of it. Given Seisan's aloof nature, Billy doubted his friend had known parental love at all. He always looked like a deer in the headlights when an adult hugged him.

The rest of the town held no affection for him either. Their disgust toward wraithkind boiled over on a daily basis, although they rarely resorted to physical violence. For the most part, they preferred to shout insults from a safe distance. What would it be like, Billy wondered, to spend your whole life rejected by the people who were meant to keep you safe? How would it feel to be shunned and threatened for something you couldn't control—for something that didn't change who you were inside?

It reminded him of a documentary he'd watched several years ago. A wealthy lady had dressed in the oldest, shabbiest outfit she could find and pretended to be homeless on the streets of New York. Most people ignored her altogether. The rest shouted at her, swearing so often the censors had to bleep out every other word they said. It wasn't until she changed back into her regular clothes—until she returned to social norms—that people treated her like a human being again.

Was the same thing happening to Corvus but in reverse?

"So," Mr. Porter said, breaking the silence. "Tell me about yourself, Corey. How long have you been friends with Billy?"

"A few years. We met in second grade."

"Second grade, huh? I don't think Billy's mentioned you before."

"Wouldn't be the only friend he hasn't mentioned," James said. He clasped his hands behind his back and adopted a taunting sing-song voice. "Billy and a wraith girl sittin' in a tree, K-I-S-S-I-N-G!"

Hamish joined in on the next line before dissolving into fitful giggles. Billy's cheeks heated up. *Where on earth did they get that from? Did they see me talking to Rem after school? Is that why they've been laughing so much?*

"You kissed her?" Corvus asked, glaring at Billy. There could be no question whom he referred to.

"Of course not," Billy retorted. "She asked me if we had any homework. I told her the page number and left."

"That's the best way to handle it," Mr. Porter said. He turned and frowned at Hamish and James. "I don't want to hear you two joking about that again. It's disgusting."

The younger boys hung their heads, all trace of mirth gone. "Sorry, Dad."

Mr. Porter leaned forward to select another slice of pizza, and Billy used the opportunity to sneak a glance at Corvus. The boy's earlier anxiety had dissipated, but the displeasure stemming from James's taunt remained. If Mr. Porter noticed, Billy figured he'd interpret it as hatred toward wraiths and respect Corvus more because of it. As if to prove his point, the man looked up at the glamour-clad boy and smiled. *This whole thing is twisted. But so far, so good.*

"I hear your father was deployed last night," Mr. Porter said.

"Yes, sir."

"You don't have to call me 'sir.' Jerry or Mr. Porter is fine."

"Okay, Mr. Porter."

"So, where's your father going?"

"Iraq."

Billy bowed his head in relief. *He got it right. We'll make it through this yet.*

"You must be very proud of him," Mr. Porter said.

Corvus stiffened and lowered his pizza slice. "I guess so."

"Of course, it can't be easy for you either," Mrs. Porter cut in, shooting her husband a warning look. "Is it just you and your mother now? Or do you have siblings?"

"It's just me. My mom died when I was little."

A film of tears formed over Mrs. Porter's nut-brown eyes. "Oh, you poor dear! Where are you living now?"

"With my uncle, but he doesn't like me very much. I'd do anything to get out of that house."

Seeing his cue, Billy jumped in. "Mom, I was thinking. Can Corey come and live with us instead? He can sleep in my room."

Corvus looked up at her with hopeful puppy-dog eyes.

"I... I don't know about that," Mrs. Porter stammered. "What would his dad think? He doesn't even know us. Corey's welcome to visit us as often as he likes, but I think he's better off living with his uncle for the time being."

"My dad said I can move in with a friend if their parents let me,"

Corvus said. "He knows I don't want to live with my uncle. You can call him and ask if you want."

Mr. and Mrs. Porter exchanged glances.

"This isn't a decision we can rush into," she said. "Fostering is a big commitment. We'd have to go through training, set aside extra money..."

"I have money," Corvus piped up. "My dad left me enough to cover my expenses. I can pay you rent."

"Nonsense! You wouldn't have to pay us anything, dear." Mrs. Porter cupped his cheek with her free hand. "I'm just concerned about how sudden this is. That's all. Besides, we'd need to have a chat with your dad and uncle before we decide anything."

Corvus's face fell. "All right."

At least it's a start, Billy thought, gulping down the last of his pizza. *If Lothaire does his job right, it won't take much to convince them.*

Mr. Porter looked at his wife, then back at Corvus. "We can't promise nothing yet, but I want you to feel like part of the family when you're with us. How would you like to come down to the shooting range on Saturday?"

Corvus blanched.

"He's never fired a gun before, Dad," Billy said, covering for him.

Mr. Porter's eyebrows shot up. "Never? Your father didn't teach you?"

"He was going to," Corvus lied. "He just never had time."

"That's a real shame. Everyone should learn how to shoot," Mr. Porter said. "I could teach you if you've still got a mind to learn. What do you say? Are you up for it, kiddo?"

"You bet," Corvus said. "I'm only free in the afternoon, though. I've got tutoring in the morning."

Good thing he didn't admit to having a detention. That'd change Dad's opinion of him pretty quick.

"Most times we head down around two o'clock, so that'd be fine," Mr. Porter told him. "I've got a twenty-two caliber for you to learn on. Great gun. The thing about rifles..."

He launched into a spiel about the attributes of various guns, and Billy relaxed a little. Visits to the shooting range were a family bonding activity in the Porter household, and the children were forbidden from inviting their friends along. Mr. Porter's willingness to make an exception for Corvus was a good sign.

The rest of the meal passed in a flurry of light-hearted conversation. Hamish and James excused themselves to go and salvage whatever they'd been doing on the PlayStation. Billy and Corvus followed soon after, plopping themselves down on the sofa. Mr. and Mrs. Porter stayed in the kitchen to make some phone calls. Rap music blared from the TV as James booted up *NBA 2010*, blocking Billy's ability to eavesdrop.

It's all on you, Lothaire, he pleaded. *Don't let us down. Corvus needs this.*

Ten agonizing minutes passed before his parents wandered into the lounge. Corvus whirled around to face them, his back jerking ramrod straight. He brushed his hair out of his eyes with a gesture resembling a salute.

Mr. Porter squinted at the TV. "Playing that basketball game again, huh?"

"Yup," James replied. "It's way better than *Spyro*."

"Take that back!" Hamish shouted.

"No. It's the truth," James said. "Basketball is awesome. I'm going to play in the NBA when I grow up."

"Well, I'm going to be a dragon when I grow up!"

At any other time, Billy would have found their banter amusing. With Corvus's future on the line, it scraped his nerves raw.

"What did Corey's dad say?" he asked.

Mr. Porter sat down, rubbing his temples with his fingertips. "He okayed everything. Said he trusted Corey's judgment. Even offered to pay us."

"What about my uncle?" Corvus asked. "Did you call him?"

"I sure did. Barely got to telling him why I was calling before he asked me to take you in for the weekend. Apparently, he's going to New York on business."

"Yeah, he does that," Corvus said, rolling his eyes. The unexpected announcement didn't faze him at all. "Can you see why I want to leave now? He hates me."

"He doesn't hate you, Corey. He just doesn't know the first thing about children."

Corvus's jaw tightened. "Yeah. You've got that right."

Billy sensed genuine anger in the boy's words, and a cold wave of realization washed over him. The anger came from the raw, bleeding heart of his emotions regarding Seisan's departure. Corvus wasn't acting anymore. He didn't have to.

Mrs. Porter placed a comforting hand on the boy's shoulder. "Your uncle was in a meeting, so we didn't have time to go over all the details, but we agreed to look after you for the weekend. If it goes well, and you decide you're happy here, we can look at making it more permanent."

"Yes!" Billy crowed, unable to help himself. "Thanks, Mom!"

We actually did it! Corvus won't be alone anymore!

"I had a part in it too," Mr. Porter teased. The air whooshed out of his lungs as his eldest son tackled him in a hug.

"Thanks, Dad!"

Billy pulled back after a couple of seconds and glanced at his friend, whose cheeks dimpled in a stunned smile.

"Thank you so much," Corvus choked out. "Both of you. You don't know how much this means to me."

"I think we have some idea," Mrs. Porter said, returning his smile. "I'm just glad we could help."

Chapter Twenty-Two

"A LITTLE FARTHER to the left," Mr. Porter instructed.

Corvus's brow furrowed in concentration, and the barrel of the rifle twitched sideways. "Like this?"

"A little more," Mr. Porter said, crouching next to the prone boy. "Make sure your shoulders are nice and level—yeah, that's right. And relax a little, eh? Being stiff as a board ain't gonna help nothing."

Billy watched with bated breath, the scene reminiscent of his own debut on the shooting range. He could almost feel the scarred earth under his elbows again. Smell the synthetic fertilizer from neighboring farms. The sun had been high in the sky that day, branding his neck with bright red burns. Marks of pride, his father claimed. His mother didn't agree. She'd lathered him in sunscreen before every subsequent outing, rain, hail or shine.

The same sun beat down on him now, and he adjusted the brim of his hat. With his eyes shielded, the uncertainty in Corvus's face became clearer. An audible rush of air entered the boy's lungs and froze there. His finger closed around the trigger. Then a bullet flew through the air, punching a hole in the center of the target.

"Nice job, Corey," Mr. Porter said. "We'll make a marksman of you yet."

"Good one, Corey!" Billy whooped.

Corvus placed the gun on the ground and stood up, brushing the loose dirt from his stomach. Joy radiated from him when he turned around. "I actually did it."

"You sure did," Mr. Porter said, clapping him on the back.

Whatever doubts Corvus might have had about the gun range vanished in the wake of his success.

Or maybe he's just happy to be outside after his detention, Billy thought as his friend walked over to join him. *Anything is better than being locked in a classroom for hours on end. Especially on a Saturday.*

Billy gestured at the rifle. "You're not giving up already, are you?"

"Nah, but I'm getting kinda thirsty," Corvus said. Wringing his hands, he turned to Mr. Porter. "Is it okay if I go and get a soda?"

"'Course it is. Billy will show you where to go." Mr. Porter dug a few quarters out of his pocket, gave them to Corvus, and then turned to the rest of his family. "You're up, James. Let's see what you've got."

Billy and Corvus jogged away over the browning grass, eager to escape Mr. Porter's watchful eye.

"How are you enjoying the range?" Billy asked.

"I thought I would hate it, but it's actually pretty fun," Corvus said. "Far better than swords, but Dad wanted me to learn them, so…"

Billy bit his lip when his friend trailed off. "I wish I knew how to use a sword. I bet it's a lot of fun."

"You wouldn't think so if you actually had to practice. Guns are way better than swords, but we can't use them in the Gloaming, so there's not much point in learning to shoot. Except for fun, of course."

They reached a stucco building on the edge of the field and circled around to the front. A rickety sign labeled it as the main office. Bells tinkled overhead as Billy pushed the door open.

A matronly woman glanced at them from behind the counter, smoothing down her khaki shirt. "How can I help you, boys?"

The scent of fried chicken wafted toward Billy, provoking a low growl from his stomach, but he did his best to ignore it. "I'd like to buy a Coke, please."

"Me too," Corvus added, handing over his coins. "Please."

The woman fetched two soda cans from the fridge behind her and placed them on the counter. "There you go. You boys have a nice day now, y'hear?"

Clutching their ice-cold drinks, Billy and Corvus made their way to the picnic area. Moss-riddled trees draped over their path, shielding them from the boiling sun. Billy collapsed at a weathered picnic table, the splintered wood piercing his thighs. Corvus opted to sit on the table itself, studying his surroundings with wary eyes. Apart from a young woman and her screaming toddler, they were alone. No one would overhear them.

"Boy, my muscles hurt," Corvus said, popping the tab on his soda.

The scent of carbonation filled the air when Billy did the same. "Mine too."

After their shared meal on Thursday night, Mrs. Porter had dug up some old blankets and allowed Corvus to spend the night on the sofa. On Friday evening, the whole family stayed up late, rearranging Billy's room to accommodate a bunk bed and a few of Corvus's belongings. Anything that might give away the boy's true identity remained at Seisan's house. *I can't believe he's going to live with us. It'll be like a never-ending sleepover.* A smile crept across Billy's lips at the thought.

"You seem to be in a good mood today," Corvus observed.

"Yeah, of course I am," Billy said, struggling to keep his facial expressions in check. "Our plan worked. We can hang out openly now. Plus, Murdock and Zane both called this morning to apologize for blowing up at me. They want us to be friends again."

"Oh." Corvus looked down at his shoes. "I take it that doesn't include me?"

Billy shook his head, his own gaze lowering. "Sorry. They're still pretty mad about what you did. They don't want anything to do with wraiths anymore."

"Oh. Well… I'm happy for you."

"Thanks." Billy paused, biting his lip. "I can talk to them about it if you want. Convince them to give you a second chance. It's not like you hit Zane for no reason. You didn't have a choice."

"Don't bother," Corvus said. "I don't really want to hang out with them. You have your human friends at school, and I have Rem. That's the way it should be."

"Is it?"

Corvus shrugged. "I think so. We're friends after school. That's good enough for me."

They sat in silence for a while, listening to the sharp report of rifle fire.

"Did you hear what Shauna said yesterday?" Corvus asked out of the blue.

"No, what did she say?"

The glamour-clad wraith swirled his soda can, turning its contents into a whirlpool. "She was actually upset the scientists are gone."

"What? Why? Doesn't she know what they were doing?"

"I don't know. Apparently, they hired her dad because he's an expert on Oilskin Lake. They were paying him a lot, and she was upset he lost the contract, I guess."

"It's a money thing, then. I bet she doesn't know what the scientists did. Her dad probably doesn't either."

"I'd like to think that too, but she blamed it on wraithkind. I think it's safe to assume where her loyalties lie."

Billy shook his head. "I can't believe she would say something like that."

"At least she had the sense to look guilty when she saw me. All this time I thought she was nice, but she's really just a backstabbing little—"

"Okay, okay," Billy interrupted. "I get the idea. Maybe she said it in the heat of the moment and she doesn't really mean it. I bet she'll feel horrible about it later and apologize."

"Hopefully," Corvus replied in a flat voice. He obviously didn't share his friend's optimism.

Casting around for another topic, Billy drained his soda and threw the empty can in the trash. "Do you think Rem would like shooting?"

"After you shot her? I seriously doubt it."

"It was an accident," Billy said, heat suffusing his cheeks. "Do you think she's scared of guns now? Because of what I did?"

"I don't know if she's scared of them, but she's never liked them," Corvus said. "She thinks they're dishonorable."

"Why?"

"Any coward can stand a hundred feet away from someone and pull the trigger. It takes real guts to go up against someone in hand-to-hand combat. No sneaky underhanded moves. No shots in the back. Just a good old-fashioned duel."

Billy thought it over. "I kinda get what you're saying, but I think a gun is smarter."

"Why?"

"If you have to get that close to an attacker, you're putting yourself at risk. No matter how good you are at fighting, there's always an element of luck, right? The best swordsman in the world could trip over a rock and fall onto someone else's sword. If they keep their distance, they're safer."

"Unless they get shot."

"Well…"

Corvus tossed his empty soda can in the trash and leaned forward. "I get what you're saying. A gun would be better if you were trying to defend your house or whatever. I would actually prefer to use a gun if I could get one to work in the Gloaming. But since I can't, and since you don't have to reload a sword, that's the better option for me, even though I hate it."

"You don't mind that guns aren't honorable?"

"Not if they help me survive. I think Rem would use a gun if she needed to as well, but she wouldn't be happy about it."

"That makes sense."

"Anyway, there's not much point in talking about this," Corvus said, rising to his feet. "I don't think I'm ever going to use a sword *or* a gun in a real-life situation. I'm not that kind of guy."

"Not even against the scientists?"

"I don't know. Maybe. I'm not going to start carrying weapons just in case they grab me one day. But if I happened to have one on me, I might use it to defend myself."

"Fair enough. How are you going to deal with Grigoth if he attacks you, though?"

"You think I could defend myself against him?" Corvus loosed a self-deprecating chuckle. "I'm flattered, but it's pointless to even try."

"Why?"

"Because his magic is too powerful. He can mind-control anyone he wants to. He can stop people from moving, and I can't defend myself if I can't move."

"Maybe not, but if you strike first, you might have a chance."

"I wish."

Their conversation lapsed into a comfortable silence, punctuated by faint gunshots and the wheezy end of a toddler's tantrum. The frazzled mother behind them departed for the parking lot with her young charge in tow.

"We should get going too," Corvus said. "Your dad's probably wondering where we are."

He climbed down from the table, his hair glistening in the dappled sunlight. Unlike his natural locks, the paler shade of black reflected light as well as absorbing it. The difference was subtle, but large enough to remind Billy of how fast things were changing. Not as fast as he wanted, perhaps, but fast enough to keep Corvus safe. For now, that was enough.

"All right," Billy said, heaving himself upright. "Let's go."

PART TWO

February 28, 2017

Three years and six months later…

Chapter Twenty-Three

Gray-and-white static crackled across the TV, competing with the morning chorus of starlings. Billy sat at the kitchen counter, slouched over a stack of golden pancakes. Hamish slipped into the seat next to him and yawned.

"It's no good," Mr. Porter groused, thumping the top of the TV set. "I can't get this blasted thing working."

"I'm not surprised, with the way you're carrying on," Mrs. Porter said. She flipped the final pancake onto Hamish's plate and joined her husband, hands on her hips. "Go and get the mail. I'll sort this out."

Mr. Porter harrumphed. "We're going to miss the end of the game."

"It's only a replay, Dad," Billy reminded him. He uncapped the maple syrup bottle and drizzled the contents onto his pancakes. The sweet caramel scent mingled with the batter to create a perfume of perfection. "We already saw it yesterday. And the day before."

"Yeah, but it was a good game," Mr. Porter retorted. "Seventy-seven, sixty-seven against the Texas Longhorns. *Seventy-seven!*"

He ambled out the front door, and Mrs. Porter shook her head. "That man and his sport. I thought I'd get a break from basketball with James away at camp."

She fiddled with something at the back of the TV, and Josh Jackson appeared on the screen, lining up a three-point shot. The ball sailed through the air and sank through the basket. Blue-clad Jayhawks fans jumped to their feet, roaring their approval. The players roared back, their voices outnumbered a thousand-to-one in a tidal wave of frenzied euphoria.

"It was a pretty good game," Billy said, shoveling a forkful of pancakes into his mouth. "James would have loved it."

Mr. Porter re-entered the house with a wad of junk mail and a crisp white envelope. He dumped the former on the coffee table and collapsed on the sofa with a grunt.

Mrs. Porter shot Billy a sly smile. "Your grandpa didn't enjoy it very much."

"Yeah, well he wouldn't, would he? Being a Longhorns supporter and all," Mr. Porter said. "It was a home game for them. He thought they had it all sewn up. Crazy old man. They're not *that* great."

"You were a Longhorns supporter back in the day," Mrs. Porter reminded him.

"Yeah, but then I moved to Kansas and learned the error of my ways." Mr. Porter paused, tapping the envelope against the arm of his chair. "Hey, Billy, could you get Corey out here when you're done eating? I've got a letter for him."

Billy froze with the fork halfway to his mouth. "S-sure."

The end-of-game celebrations continued in the background, but he barely heard them. *Who would Corvus be getting mail from? Outside my family, the only people who talk to him are Rem and Lothaire. But they see him every day. They wouldn't risk blowing his cover with a letter. Unless the letter's from his dad...*

Billy washed down his pancakes with a glass of orange juice, wincing as the sour tang clashed with the maple syrup. Thoughts raced through his mind at breakneck speed. Seisan hadn't written once since he left three years ago. Not to wish Corvus a happy birthday. Not even to let them know he was still alive. *Why is he writing now, of all times?*

Billy hopped down from the barstool and wandered back to his bedroom. The door was ajar, so he pushed it open and squinted into the darkness. Corvus lay under a blue duvet on the bottom bunk, his bare arms hugging the fabric like a teddy bear. Sunlight slanted through the curtains, illuminating the milky-white scar tissue on his shoulder. Billy's stomach flip-flopped at the sight of it.

The injury—healed or not—served as a constant reminder of the extent to which Corvus had suffered. A constant reminder of the scientists and their scalpels and needles, and of the adults who failed to keep him safe. Billy couldn't have saved him from that particular scar, but he'd prevented hundreds more from joining it.

Corvus cracked one eye open. "What are you staring at?"

"Nothing," Billy said, averting his gaze. "Dad told me to come get you. He's got a letter for you."

"*What?*" Corvus leapt out of bed and dashed across the room, leaving a trail of blankets in his wake. He scooped the previous day's hoodie off the floor and pulled it over his head.

"I don't know what it's about," Billy said, but the boy's frantic actions seemed to confirm his theory about Seisan. "Do you want me to be with you when you open it, or would you rather—"

Corvus sprinted out of the room, his thudding footsteps muffled against the carpet. Billy chased after him for a few steps, then stopped, conflicted. For the first few weeks following his abandonment, Corvus had been an open book to him. Billy had known when he needed to walk on eggshells and when he needed to smother his friend in hugs. But when the intensity of his grief faded, part of Corvus faded too.

These days, reading his emotions was like trying to assemble a puzzle with half the pieces missing. You could put him together through trial and error, but even then, you only saw what he wanted you to see. Never a complete picture of the boy, but an abstract representation of who he might be. Bits and pieces of a fractured whole.

Shaking his head, Billy walked to the bathroom. The over-sink mirror showed him a bright-eyed boy with clear skin, save for a faint red spot on the bridge of his nose. *That wasn't there yesterday.* Grimacing, he dabbed a small blob of zit cream over it. Most of his human classmates had it much worse than him, but the wraiths seemed to be escaping puberty unscathed. Even Corvus's glamour remained maddeningly clear-skinned.

Lothaire had tried to talk him into taking an acne-generating potion, but his friend refused. Instead, he settled for a glamour modification that grew facial hair. Lothaire's first attempt to apply it had gone a little too well, with hair sprouting at a rate of six feet per hour. Fortunately, they managed to fix the problem before Corvus went home for the evening.

Satisfied with his appearance, Billy headed back to the lounge. Corvus stood in the middle of the room, the opened letter pinched between his thumb and index finger. Mr. Porter stood next to him, sneering at the TV. From the sofa, Mrs. Porter shot her husband a series of warning glances, each one a silent plea to keep his mouth shut. Their unnaturally stiff body language prompted Billy to look at the screen. A reporter stood in the streets of a foreign country, one hand pressed to her ear and the other wrapped around a microphone.

"What's going on?" Billy asked.

"Those wraith things are in Japan," Mr. Porter said. "Imagine that! Spreading all over the globe like a disease."

"Jerry!" Mrs. Porter admonished him.

"The wraiths were on the news?" Billy asked, his eyes widening. *How on earth did they get to Japan? It's not like they can catch a plane, and they're too far away from the portal to have teleported.*

"You bet they were," Mr. Porter said. He raised both his voice and the volume of the TV, drowning out his wife's protests. "The cops found 'em wandering around the streets. Up to no good, I don't doubt it."

On-screen, two dozen wraith children walked down a suburban street with their hands on their heads. Japanese police surrounded them, guns pointed. Billy's stomach roiled. Corvus scrunched his father's letter into a ball and stalked out of the room.

Mr. Porter stared after him. "Want me to talk to him?"

"No, give him some time," Mrs. Porter said. "It's the first time he's heard from his dad in three years. Can you imagine how he must be feeling? I'll talk to him later, once he's calmed down."

But was it the letter that set him off? Billy wondered. *The wraith situation isn't great either, and Dad's comments wouldn't have helped.*

Mr. Porter shot a grateful look at his wife, then ruffled Hamish's hair. "Ready to go, champ?"

The boy grinned. "You bet!"

"That's my boy. Come on, Bill. We'd better get you to school too."

Billy shifted his weight. "Actually, I'd rather wait for Corey, if that's okay."

"You'll be late."

"No, I won't. I just want to be there for him, Dad. I'll still get there before the bell."

"Billy—"

"So you'll let James miss school for basketball camp, but you won't let me help my best friend?"

Mrs. Porter held up a placating hand. "It's not like that, sweetie. Of course you can wait for Corey."

Mr. Porter looked at his wife, then back at Billy.

"All right," he relented, heading out the front door. "Have a good day at school."

"See you later, alligator," Hamish added, bounding after his father.

Billy sank into the recently vacated sofa, staring at the screen. The unsettling images burned their way into his retinas. His teachers said the wraiths came to Morton a century ago and didn't exist anywhere else on the planet—a belief shared by Corvus himself. So where did these ones come from? They were tall enough to be the same age as him, but he didn't recognize a single one.

Mrs. Porter plopped onto the sofa next to him, remote in hand, and flipped to another channel. The terrified wraiths were replaced by a talk-show host who looked far too chipper for the early hour. Billy turned to his mother to protest, but the words died on his tongue when he beheld her serious expression. She muted the TV and fiddled with the remote for a few seconds before speaking.

"Do you think Corey will be all right?"

Good question, Billy thought. "It's like you said, isn't it? He got a letter from his dad for the first time in three years. Maybe it was bad news. Maybe he's not coming back."

"You think he might have been killed?"

"No—no! I didn't mean that." But inside, doubt gnawed at Billy.

The US army sent letters to the families of fallen soldiers, but Seisan had nothing to do with them. He served in a very different world with very different rules of engagement. What if he *was* dead? The idea nearly sent Billy careening after his best friend, but Mrs. Porter's hand found his arm, steadying him.

"If that *is* what happened, or if he wasn't coming back for a few more years… how would you feel if we adopted Corey?" she asked.

Billy's jaw dropped. "You'd do that?"

"Of course we would," Mrs. Porter said. "He's part of our family, and we love him just as much as we love you and James and Hamish. Your father and I want to give him a more stable family life and make him feel more included. Adoption would be one way of doing that. What do you think about it?"

Billy's mouth went dry as he tried to process the enormity of the proposal.

"That… that would be great," he said. Despite the stress and uncertainty he'd endured that morning, a smile tugged his lips. *Anything that helps Corvus is fine by me.*

"I'm glad to hear it," Mrs. Porter said. "We'll talk to him about it on Saturday, once he's had a chance to cool down. You can test the waters if you want, but don't give him the idea we're pushing it on him. If he'd rather keep the foster arrangement, that's fine too. We won't treat him any differently."

Billy murmured his agreement, but he couldn't fathom bringing the topic up any time soon. Not with Seisan's mysterious letter weighing on his mind.

Mrs. Porter patted his cheek. "Good boy."

She unmuted the TV, and they sat, unspeaking, for a few minutes. Corvus stormed in, fully dressed, and left the house without saying goodbye. The front door slammed with enough force to rattle the china in the kitchen cupboards. Billy's pulse jumped.

"I guess that's my signal," he said, rising to his feet. He shoved his hands in his pockets to hide the way they trembled. "See you later, Mom."

"Have a nice day, Billy. Look out for Corey, won't you?"

He shouldered his satchel and dashed out the door without answering. He'd always be there to protect his friends, just like they were always there to protect him.

Chapter Twenty-Four

THERE WAS NO sign of Corvus on the way to school. Billy backtracked to Rem's house, hoping to ask if she'd seen him, but the curtains were drawn, and no one answered when he rang the doorbell.

He must have gone to school after all, Billy thought. Doubt wormed through his gut as a more terrifying possibility presented itself. *What if Seisan really is in trouble and that's why Corvus ran away? What if he went to the Gloaming to try and help his dad?*

For a heart-stopping moment, Billy imagined his best friend lying helpless in a ditch, bleeding to death from a grievous sword wound. Bound wraiths showed no mercy to oathbreakers and their spawn in the Gloaming. If they found him wandering around, looking for Seisan, he wouldn't stand a chance. And what if the letter wasn't from Seisan at all? What if his enemies sent it to lure Corvus into a trap?

The idea turned his knees to jelly, and he leaned against the house to keep from falling flat on his face. *Don't even think about that. Chances are ten-to-one that he's at school and you're panicking over nothing. No need to freak out. He'll be fine.*

Murdock and Zane were lounging on a bench outside Morton Junior High when he arrived. The former leapt up to greet him. "Hey, Billy! Did you talk to your parents about joining the debate club? I've signed—"

"Not now, Murdock," Billy said, waving him off. "Sorry. I, uh... gotta go pee."

Faint stirrings of guilt fluttered in his stomach when he saw the boy's hurt expression, but he refused to entertain them. School clubs were the least of his worries. He dashed into the school building and up the stairs, pushing his way through the sea of teenagers.

The wraiths usually hung out in one big group next to the cafeteria. Even outcasts like Corvus and Rem were welcome there, to an extent. As long as they stuck to the fringes of the group and didn't try to interact with the others, they were left in peace. Corvus liked to complain about the arrangement, but he also admitted he felt safer there than anywhere else in the school.

Billy hooked a right at the end of the corridor. Sure enough, the wraiths clustered in their usual spot. He scanned the crowd, hoping to catch a glimpse of his friend.

He's not there, Billy thought, worrying the hem of his shirt. *What do I do now? It's not like I can go to the Gloaming myself. And where's Rem?*

Before he could entertain any further questions, a pair of purple eyes locked on to him. *Glared* at him. Billy froze to the spot, uncertain how to proceed. He couldn't ask the wraiths where Corvus was. They wouldn't know in the first place, and even if they did, they'd never share that information with a human. Not anymore.

"What are you staring at?" the wraith demanded.

At once, silence descended over the group. Twenty pairs of eyes joined their leader's, each betraying a glimmer of anger. Billy's throat closed up. Corvus had warned him things would change between humans and wraiths by the time they got to junior high, and he'd been right. It was like everything he'd done to help them in fifth grade never happened. They acted just as paranoid and aloof with him as they did with everyone else.

"I said, what are you staring at?" the wraith growled.

"N-nothing." Billy ducked his head and took a step back. "Sorry. I'll just go."

"Oh, leave him alone, Chardein," Volner admonished the angry wraith. "Everything okay, Billy?"

"Yeah. Everything's fine," Billy lied.

Volner nodded and turned back to Chardein. "See? No problem. Now, what were you saying about the Enforcers? You can't stop in the middle of a story."

Billy shot Volner a grateful look and hurried in the opposite direction. *At least I have one wraith on my side. If Corvus doesn't show up, I'll corner Volner after school and beg him to take me to the Gloaming.* His desperation dissipated a moment later when Rem swept past him to join the group. Corvus followed soon after, his head bowed to avoid making eye contact. All of the air whooshed out of Billy's lungs. His friend was all right. He hadn't gone on an insane rescue mission in the Gloaming. He wasn't bleeding or injured. He was *alive.*

Of course he's alive, Billy thought, almost laughing at the absurdity of his earlier worries. *Why wouldn't he be alive? This isn't the first time he's walked out when something's upset him. And even if something* was *wrong with Seisan, he wouldn't run off without telling me first. He's not like that.*

Billy scampered downstairs to his homeroom instead of joining Zane and Murdock outside. He needed some peace and quiet to process everything before they dragged him back to reality.

Apart from Mr. Engelbrecht, the wiry-haired teacher who took attendance, he had the room to himself. As always, the man ignored his arrival and kept his nose buried in a history textbook. Relieved of the obligation to make small talk, Billy took a seat at the back of the room. He fished the magic notebook out of his satchel, flipped it open, and scribbled a quick message.

Hey, Corvus. Are you okay?

He waited for a few minutes.

No response.

He'd expected as much, but it irked him all the same.

I guess you're busy, he continued, pausing to chew the end of his pen. *Anyway, I wanted to let you know that I'm here for you if you need me. Let's talk after school, okay?*

Again, no response.

Billy sighed and slammed the book shut. *He's probably talking to Rem or something.*

The bell rang moments later and students poured into the room. All thoughts of Corvus and the mysterious letter evaporated when his friends walked in. *Time to pretend everything's normal.*

"You took your time," Murdock said.

Billy shoved the notebook into his satchel. "I told you. I really had to pee."

Murdock sniggered and took the seat next to him. "Fair enough. So did you talk to your parents last night?"

"Nah, I didn't get a chance to," Billy said. In truth, he'd hoped his friend would forget the whole thing.

Murdock raised a skeptical eyebrow. "You *promised* to join the debate club so I wouldn't be alone with Jeffrey Bancroft and his cronies. You're not flaking out on me, are you?"

"No! Of course not. I just didn't get a chance to ask."

"If you say so. Crikey, Billy. At this rate, you'll be the only one in our grade who hasn't joined a club."

"What's so bad about that? I spend seven hours a day in this prison. Why should I waste more time here? Besides, it's not like there's a law that says we *have* to be in a club."

"No, but it looks good on college applications," Zane said. "I've already signed up for chess and tennis. The computer club looks pretty good too."

"Yeah, well, we can't all be as perfect as you, Zane," Billy teased, earning himself a playful shove. "Besides, I'm not going to college."

"Oh yeah? What are you going to do, then?"

"I don't know yet. Learn a trade maybe."

"And what if you change your mind later? What if you decide you want to go to college after all and you can't get in because you didn't make the most of the opportunities you were given?"

"Calm down, *Mom*," Billy retorted, earning himself another punch.

"I said I'd join the stupid debate club, and I meant it. I just have to ask my parents first because it finishes kinda late. They'll need to find someone to babysit my brothers."

"James is, like, eleven now, isn't he?" Murdock pointed out. "He'll be fine without you."

"Yeah, but Hamish won't be. He still tries to stick a fork in the toaster sometimes, and James will be too busy playing video games to stop him. Those two wouldn't survive a week if someone wasn't watching them after school."

Murdock groaned and threw his head back. "Okay, but how long is it going to take for your parents to find another babysitter? The first meeting is tomorrow. We can't afford to miss it."

"I'll talk to them about it tonight. Just chill out."

"I *am* chilling out!"

"No, you're not," Zane said. "What's got your boxers in a bunch today?"

Murdock ran a hand through his hair. "Nothing."

"You're joining the club to impress a girl, aren't you?"

"No!"

"I think you might be."

"Zane, shut up!"

"Who is it?" Billy joined in.

"No one."

"Mikayla Dunstan?" Zane guessed.

Murdock's face reddened.

"I knew it!" Zane crowed. "Murdock likes Mi—"

"I said, shut up!" Murdock hissed, thumping Zane's arm.

Mr. Engelbrecht's chair scraped backward. "Boys!"

The raspy warning startled them into silence. The man had spoken nary a word all year, but he towered over them now, pinning them in place with his steel-gray eyes.

"If I hear one more sound out of you, I'll send you to the principal's office."

"Sorry, sir," the boys said in unison.

Glowering, Mr. Engelbrecht sat down, took a deep breath, and resumed reading. He didn't react when the bell rang for first period, so the boys fled with the rest of the class.

"What a psycho," Murdock said when they were out of earshot. "Can you believe that guy?"

"Never mind him," Billy said. "What do we have first?"

"English," Zane replied. He'd memorized their entire schedule within the first day of receiving it, unlike Billy, who had yet to remember a single class by himself after seven months.

"Worst luck," Murdock grumbled.

Together, they navigated the overcrowded corridors to the second floor. Returning to the scene of his confrontation with Chardein sent a shiver down Billy's spine, but he shrugged it off. Most of the wraiths had left, and the mad flurry of activity would hide him from any stragglers.

A handful of students milled around the English classroom when Billy entered. He slipped into his assigned seat at the front, while Zane and Murdock headed for the back. He rifled through his satchel for the book they were studying—*To Kill a Mockingbird*. His hand found the magic notebook first, so he checked for a message from Corvus. *Still nothing.*

The scent of sweet jasmine and French vanilla wafted over Billy, and a little thrill jolted his body when Shauna slipped into the neighboring seat.

"Hey, Billy," she said, flashing him an alabaster smile. "Can I borrow your notes? I was away yesterday."

She could have asked him to move a mountain, and he would have responded with the same enthusiasm as when he handed over his book.

"Were you sick?" Billy asked. He studied the soft flush of her face, the long black lashes framing seafoam eyes, the luscious curve of her lips. His gaze lingered there, then returned to meet hers.

Shauna shook her head, her blonde hair swaying from side to side.

"No, I was in Wichita. Dad needed to go there for a conference, so I convinced him to take me with him."

"So you had a long weekend? Lucky. What did you get up to in Wichita?"

"I spent about half the trip shopping. They've got a whole street of boutique fashion stores where everything is super expensive. I didn't buy anything, but it was fun trying things on. There was this gorgeous dress with little bits of lace on the sleeves..." She paused and bit her lip. "Sorry. I hope I'm not boring you."

"No, it's fine. I don't mind if you talk about it."

Shauna smiled at him again, a radiant smile that made his cheeks grow hot and his tongue grow flustered. "You are too cute."

Shauna thinks I'm cute?

"What did you do for the other half of your trip?" Billy asked in a daze.

"Not much, to be honest," Shauna said. "I went to the zoo to see the new baby gorilla, but it wasn't on exhibit yet."

"That sucks."

"Yeah. At least the tigers were cool."

Waves of idle chatter swelled and crashed behind them as the rest of their classmates arrived. Corvus crossed the room and plunked himself into the seat behind Billy. His presence should have been a relief, but with Shauna around, Corvus was the last person he wanted to see.

The blonde girl prodded Billy with the end of her pen. "So, what did you get up to over the weekend?"

"Nothing much. Hung out at the park with some friends."

"Some *wraith* friends?"

"W-what? No!" Billy spluttered. "I'm not... I mean..."

Shauna laughed. "I'm just teasing. I know you're not like that. Besides, you're too cool to hang out with them."

She thinks I'm cute and *cool?*

Billy's heart yearned to perform somersaults in his chest, but with Corvus around, it could only twitch feebly. Shauna's father had conspired with the wraith-abusing scientists. When he lost his job as a result, Shauna's rosy attitude toward the wraiths grew thorns of hatred. Thorns she liked to display at every opportunity. In Billy's mind, they didn't make her any less beautiful, but they stabbed at him all the same.

Thorns can be pruned away with time and care, his heart insisted. His mind wasn't sure it agreed.

"I used to hang out with wraiths when I was a kid," Billy admitted.

"Yeah, but everyone did," Shauna said, patting his shoulder. "We were dumb back then. What matters is that you know better now."

"He's lying," the boy in front of them interjected.

Billy grimaced as the stench of cheap deodorant overpowered Shauna's perfume. *Jeffrey Bancroft.* The boy sat sideways in his chair, leaning so far back his leather jacket squeaked against the radiator. He wrinkled his nose in Billy's direction before returning his attention to Shauna. Everyone knew about his adoration for her; the two had even dated for a few weeks. The whole thou-shalt-not-hate thing had been drilled into Billy from a young age. Nevertheless, he intensely disliked Jeffrey's guts. With a passion.

"Excuse me?" Billy said.

"You heard me," Jeffrey repeated. "I said, you're lying. I saw you with a whole big group of wraiths this morning."

Despite the tension of the situation, Billy laughed. "I wasn't hanging out with them. I was trying to walk *past* them."

He didn't owe the bully an explanation, but he gave one for Shauna's sake.

"You weren't walking anywhere when I saw you."

"Yeah, because they were blocking the way."

"Whatever," Jeffrey said, turning to face the front.

Billy snuck a glance at Shauna. Green-gray mist clouded her eyes, obscuring her emotions from him. Mrs. Clay, their English teacher, bustled into the room.

"All right, class!" she boomed over the noise. "You should be reading, not blabbering to the person next to you. Get your books out and start on chapter twenty-one."

Billy grabbed *To Kill a Mockingbird* and flipped to the assigned chapter, hoping to drown his worries in Harper Lee's expert prose. Shauna sat stiffly next to him, turning the pages with military precision every few minutes.

What if she believes Jeffrey? he thought, sick to his stomach.

When Mrs. Clay turned around to open a window, he penned a short note and handed it to Shauna.

I don't hang out with wraith freaks.

Simple and to the point. His heart thundered in his chest when she read it. She looked at him sideways, selected a pink gel pen from her pencil case, and wrote something under his messy scrawl.

I hope not. They're all horrible. You're better off without them.
Believe me, I know.

She didn't respond after that, but her rigid posture relaxed. Billy reached for the note, intending to pocket it, but a gust of wind from the open window blew it to the floor behind him. He whirled around, desperate to retrieve it before Corvus did. He failed. The wraith boy picked up the scrap of paper and scanned it, his jaw tightening. Then he slapped it into Billy's waiting palm, refusing to make eye contact. Billy shoved the note deep into his pocket, his ears burning.

Why can't I do anything right today?

Chapter Twenty-Five

WHEN RECESS ARRIVED, Billy, Zane, and Murdock headed straight for the library. Fat raindrops pummeled the roof and clung to the gray windows, further dampening Billy's spirits. After a tension-filled English lesson and a mind-numbing hour of math, he'd had enough of schoolwork. But he couldn't escape it. Recess or not, his world history project was due next period, and he had yet to make a start on it.

"What were you and Shauna talking about in English?" Murdock asked.

Billy held the door open for him, and they all trooped inside. "Nothing much."

"It must have been something with the way Jeffrey was hulking over you," Zane said.

Billy rolled his eyes. "He was just being an idiot. He tried to tell her that I hang out with wraiths."

"That's so stupid," Murdock said. His hand moved to the bridge of his nose as if to push up the glasses he no longer wore. Earlier in the year, he'd switched to contacts, but old habits died hard. "You don't hang out with wraiths. You don't even talk to them."

"I know," Billy lied, leading the way to the computers.

"He must be jealous or something," Murdock said. He thought for a minute, then added: "You like Shauna, don't you?"

"What? No! I mean… I don't know."

"Do you think she's hot?"

"Well, yeah. Obviously."

"Do you think about her all the time?"

"Not all the time."

"But most of the time, right?"

Billy's cheeks burned, and he looked away. "I guess."

"So you *do* like her." Murdock dropped into a swivel chair and leaned back in a self-satisfied manner. "I knew it. What about you, Zane? You've been very quiet. Who do you like?"

"No one," the taller boy mumbled.

"Whatever you say." Murdock winked at him and turned back to Billy. "Let me know if you want me to be your wingman. I'll have her eating out of the palm of your hand."

Billy shook his head and took a seat. He couldn't risk pursuing her. Not if it put his friendship with Corvus at risk. With ten minutes left on the clock, Billy opened Google Translate and pasted an entire Wikipedia article into it. He cycled it through a few languages, switched it to Austrian, and deleted all of the citations.

"What are you doing?" Zane asked as Billy moved the text into a document and pressed Print. "That's plagiarism, you know. You could get a zero for that. You could get *expelled*."

"Oh, come on. How's Mr. Allan going to know?" Murdock countered. "Do you think he can read Austrian?"

"Well, what if he can? Billy, you've got to stop. You can't do that."

"Sure I can," Billy said. "Look, I'm doing it right now."

He grabbed the translated article from the printer and fished a crumpled sheet of A3 paper from the bottom of his satchel.

"It's not even in English!" Zane protested.

"Exactly! That's what makes it so brilliant," Murdock said. "Mr. Allan wanted us to make a period-accurate newspaper, and Billy's giving him a period-accurate newspaper. I mean, come on. Do you really think the Austrians were publishing their newspapers in English back then? His is technically more accurate than ours. Worst case scenario, he gets asked to bring in a translation tomorrow, and if that happens, he's got a whole night to write something better."

"Yup. That's what I'm planning to do," Billy said. He cut the article into columns and glued them to the larger piece of paper.

Zane released a long-suffering sigh. "Don't say I didn't warn you."

He rose to his feet and stalked off to browse the non-fiction shelves. Billy ignored him and looked down at his "masterpiece." The crooked, half-glued text made it hideous, but his work never scored points for visual appeal anyway. He rolled it up as best as he could and tucked it back into his satchel. *Done with five minutes to spare. Nice.*

Murdock elbowed him in the ribs. "Billy, look."

He did. Rem peered back at him over the *Harry Potter* display rack, biting her lip. Her eyes were clouded, conflicted. She averted her gaze and walked over to join him.

What are you doing? he wanted to scream. *You said it was too dangerous for us to be seen together!*

"Hey, Billy," she said.

It took a few seconds for his mouth to catch up to his brain. "Uh… hi."

"I need to talk to you."

"No, you need to go away," Murdock retorted. "We're not interested."

Billy wanted to tell his friend to cool it, but the words died on his tongue. Shauna sauntered into the library, surrounded by a gaggle of girls. *Not again.*

"Billy, it's about Corvus," Rem said. "He—"

"Leave me alone!"

The unexpected intensity of his words stunned her into silence. All heads in the library craned toward Billy. Rem shrank away from him, lower lip quivering, and scurried for the door. The head librarian gave Billy a sharp look for making unnecessary noise, then resumed scanning books.

Billy collapsed into his swivel chair, a sour taste in his mouth. He hadn't meant to yell. Not like that. And at *Rem*, of all people? The person who had changed her very DNA in a futile attempt to avoid being bullied? The person who had only gotten through the situation with the support of her friends? Billy could have kicked himself. *Some friend I am.*

"Dude, she's coming over here," Murdock whispered.

Billy sat up taller, ready to apologize to Rem regardless of the consequences, but it was Shauna who sashayed into focus.

"Was that wraith girl bothering you?" she asked. Sympathy laced her voice, a vague improvement over her earlier vitriol.

"Yeah. Sorry you had to see that."

"Don't worry. I understand." Shauna's gaze drifted back to her friends, and she bit her lip. "Anyway, I should go. I just wanted to make sure you were okay."

"Oh. Okay. Well… thanks."

She strolled off, her floral skirt dancing around her knees. Before she went more than a few steps, Murdock shoved Billy forward. Billy dug his heels in, but Shauna must have heard him stumble because she spun around. He shot a glare at his friend, but Murdock merely winked.

How could you do this to me? Billy despaired. *I can't ask her now. Not like this. Not after what I said to Rem.*

"Are you sure you're okay?" Shauna asked. Her seafoam eyes gleamed with concern, and he felt himself being inexorably drawn into their depths. Immersed in them. Drowning in them. For one shining moment, everything else faded into the background, and he surrendered to the fluttery feeling in his stomach.

"I, uh… I was just wondering if you wanna hang out on Saturday."

"You mean like a date?"

Billy's heart skipped a beat. "Yeah. Like a date."

A soft shade of pink dusted Shauna's cheeks. "Sure. Where did you want to go?"

"Do you like the park? We could go there and get some ice cream. Maybe catch a movie after?"

"Sounds good to me. Listen, I've got to go, but I'll see you tomorrow, okay? We can organize a time and stuff then."

"Okay. See you later."

Happy little stars danced in the corners of Billy's vision. *I don't believe it. This can't be real.* His heart felt like it would explode from pure ecstasy.

"I knew it would work!" Murdock crowed, punching Billy in the shoulder. "I told you I'd be a great wingman, didn't I?"

Billy shook his head, more in disbelief than disagreement. "I don't know what to say."

"You don't have to say anything," Murdock said. "But maybe you could repay the favor by helping me with Mikayla? Preferably with a bit more subtlety, since she doesn't know me."

"Yeah, all right," Billy agreed. He didn't have the slightest clue how to help, but signing up to the debate club seemed like a good start. After all, he did promise.

"Great," Murdock said, clapping him on the back. "Come on. Let's go and tell Zane the good news."

Billy followed him through the rows of books, his apprehension slipping away. Shauna was beautiful and clever, and he'd been mooning over her for ages. Rem would forgive his harsh words when he explained the situation. She had to.

That afternoon, Billy walked home on cloud nine. The sun shone. The birds chirped. All in all, nothing could be wrong with the world. But something *was* wrong, and the first sign of trouble hit him when he walked into his empty house.

Corvus isn't here, he thought, perturbed. *Is he upset about Seisan's letter, or did I push him over the edge with that stupid note?*

He fished the note out of his pocket and traced Shauna's neat, pink writing with his index finger. Although the words were ugly, knowing they were penned by her hand made his heart wriggle with delight. He hugged the scrap of paper to his chest, then tucked it back into his pocket. Regardless of what pushed Corvus over the edge, a simple apology should repair any hurt feelings. The boy had said far worse things over the years in an attempt to keep their friendship secret.

Billy padded into the lounge and turned on the TV. A kids' show with colorful cartoon characters came on, and he let it play in the background. He'd never seen the show before, but it looked like something Hamish might enjoy.

His youngest brother didn't have much time for TV these days. He took piano lessons most afternoons with a little old lady who lived on the corner of Belrose Street and Nehemiah Avenue. Billy had dropped him off a few times but refused to stay and watch. Unlike him, Hamish didn't mind the milky tea or the homemade cookies that looked like chocolate chip but were actually raisin. He didn't mind the fat ragdoll cat that lazed beside the piano and lunged at the shoelaces of unsuspecting guests.

After the cat gave him a wicked scar on his ankle, Billy vowed never to return. When the same thing happened to Hamish, the younger boy shrugged it off. He loved the piano enough to put up with it, or at least that's what he claimed. In truth, Billy suspected he kept going because the old lady lived alone and needed the company. Why else would she give him free lessons?

Billy sighed and reached for his satchel. Despite the noisy TV, the emptiness of the house tugged at him. He grabbed the magic notebook and flipped it open. *It's been a whole day. Corvus must have written back by now.* Sure enough, the other boy's spidery scrawl underlined his own. Relief blinded him, preventing him from comprehending it. When he recovered, the words crashed into him with the force of a tidal wave.

How dare you.

Each letter cut a bright red wound into the page, digging deep enough to leave a miniature inkwell in its wake. *Uh oh.*

Where are you? Billy wrote. The previous message looked several hours old. Maybe his friend's outrage had subsided in the interim.

The response came seconds later. *Don't talk to me.*

Billy's mouth went dry. *I'm sorry.*

Tell that to Rem, not me.

For a brief moment, Billy considered tossing the notebook back into his satchel, but guilt stayed his hand.

I will, he wrote back. *I promise.*

No reply seemed forthcoming, so he tried again. *When are you coming home?*

No response.

You don't have magic lessons today, do you?

He tried several more times, but Corvus was apparently busy with something else. Or ignoring him, which seemed more likely. Billy threw himself onto the sofa, bouncing several times before coming to a rest. A starling alighted on a branch outside, squawking an invitation to its friends.

I can't win, he thought, blowing out a hopeless breath. *Corvus is gonna be furious when he finds out I'm going on a date with Shauna. Shauna's gonna be furious if she finds out I have wraith friends. What am I supposed to do?*

No easy answer came. Maybe, in time, Shauna would change. Maybe Corvus and Rem would come to accept her. After the way Corvus fake-bullied him in elementary school, Billy deserved some leeway.

I'll act neutrally toward them while we're at school, he decided. *That's the safest thing to do. And I'll apologize to Rem in private tomorrow. Everything will go back to normal.*

But it wouldn't go back to normal, and in the back of his mind, he knew that. Yelling at your best friends wasn't the best way to maintain a relationship with them, and betraying them for the sake of a girl didn't help either.

Billy grabbed his iPod and shoved the earbuds in his ears. Loud guitars drowned out the TV, the starlings, and the relentless whirlwind of his own thoughts. When Corvus showed up, he'd try to smooth things out. If that failed... well.

I'll figure it out somehow.

Chapter Twenty-Six

HAMISH PRESSED HIS cheek against the steamed-up bus window. Townhouses lined the street outside, blurring together like an old painting. The bus trundled west along the main road, away from Morton Elementary and toward the older end of town.

He normally hated the bus. The other kids elbowed him without noticing and screamed so loud he thought his eardrums might burst. With special permission from his parents, he'd started taking the public bus instead—the one occupied by elderly couples and their groceries. The worst thing he'd seen since the switch was a spirited debate over the best yarn for baby blankets.

The bus pulled over halfway down Nehemiah Avenue, half a block from his piano lesson. Hamish peeled himself out of his seat and jumped from the top step. His sneakers hit the sidewalk with a muffled thump.

The driver winked at him. "See you tomorrow, kid."

Hamish shrank back and waited for the bus to leave before resuming his journey on foot. Mrs. Price's little brick cottage straddled the street corner, fenced in by a hedge of white roses. He let himself through the gate and skipped down the limestone path. The doorbell remained silent when he pressed it.

On the afternoon of his first piano lesson, Hamish had assumed the batteries died and knocked until his knuckles hurt. When that failed, he waited on the steps for two hours, not knowing what else to do. Mrs.

Price had spotted him through the window and let him in, apologizing profusely. Her new hearing aids were meant to receive signals from the doorbell, but she'd disabled the settings by accident. Fascinated by the technology, Hamish forgot about the long wait and his sore hand.

The door creaked open, and an elderly lady peered out at him. Snowy curls framed her face. "Hamish! Come in, my dear, come in."

"Good afternoon, Mrs. Price," he replied in a sing-song voice. He stepped across the threshold and dropped his school bag in the corner.

"I've just put the kettle on for some tea," Mrs. Price said, guiding him into the lounge. "Would you like some honey in yours?"

"Yes, please."

"All right, then. I won't be a minute."

She left him by the fireplace—in front of the crackling heat that split open dry wood and released a fragrant bouquet of smoke and pine sap. Several feet above the undulating flames, the scorched brickwork gave way to an elegant mantelpiece. The photos resting there always made Hamish's stomach turn.

Most of them featured the same two people—a potbellied man with silver hair and a younger man with a goofy smile. Mrs. Price had identified them as her husband and son, but she refused to talk about them. Curious, Hamish had begged his father for information and got the standard response. *They got caught up in the Halloween Massacre, same as your sister. The wraiths ought to be skinned alive for what they did.*

The idea upset Hamish, but for the first time, he didn't believe his dad's assertions. If the wraiths killed Mrs. Price's family, then why did she adopt a wraith child as her own? His gaze slid to the next photo, a candid shot of said child standing beside a two-tiered birthday cake. *Seven candles. This must have been taken right before we became friends.*

Seeing Jarsha outside of school for the first time had scared Hamish out of his wits. Not because of the boy's species (although Mr. Porter's dire warnings hadn't helped). Rather, he hadn't expected a shadowy figure to pop up in the middle of his piano lesson. After spending time with the other boy, Hamish drew his own conclusions. They both liked music, they both liked dragons, and anyone who loved the same things as him couldn't be all bad.

"Hey, Hamish!"

He whirled around to see the boy from the photo smiling at him.

"Jarsha!" Hamish exclaimed, hugging his friend. "I missed you at school today."

"Gran was worried I might have the flu, so she made me stay home," Jarsha explained.

"Does that mean you're contagious? Mom says you can catch the flu from other people."

Jarsha shrugged and shoved his hands in his pockets. "I don't think I'm actually sick. I only sneezed a couple of times. I feel fine."

"The worst illnesses begin with a single sneeze," Mrs. Price said. She hobbled into the room with a kettle in her right hand and three china mugs looped around the fingers of her left.

Piping hot water tinkled against the mugs as she emptied the kettle. Hamish accepted his with a polite smile and took a sip. He didn't care much for tea, but it made Mrs. Price happy to see him drink it.

"Did I ever tell you how I came to adopt Jarsha?" she asked, lowering herself into a recliner.

She had. Multiple times.

"You found him wandering the streets," Hamish replied, knowing she'd tell the story regardless of his answer.

"Yes, wandering the streets like an urchin. It was such a cold night, and he only had rags to wear. I couldn't leave a child out there." The recliner rocked as she settled into her story. "I knew he had the disease the scientists were talking about. The wraith disease. I read an article about it in the *Gazette*. A nice young lady named Dr. Stanford wrote it. I called her a few times, but she told me they haven't found a cure yet. Such a pity. Such a pity."

Hamish gulped down another mouthful of tea and bobbed his head in sympathy. It had become a daily ritual between them. Mrs. Price talked, Hamish listened, and Jarsha zoned out with his head in his hands. Lessons had to wait until both tea and conversation dried up, but thanks to his frequent visits, Hamish never had to sit around for long.

"I suppose you'd like to play the piano now," Mrs. Price said, setting her mug on the side table.

"Yes, please," Hamish said.

She leaned forward and rose to her feet, huffing with effort. "All right, then. You can go and play through your scales while I tidy up. I really think you should go back to bed, Jarsha dear. You're not well enough to practice today."

"Awww, but I wanted to listen to Hamish play," Jarsha said, his lower lip jutting out. "Can I lie down on the sofa instead? Please?"

Mrs. Price's face melted into an expression of pure love. "All right, sweetheart, but make sure you get a blanket first. I don't want you freezing to death in here."

She rescued the empty mugs from their hands and disappeared into the kitchen. Both boys scurried off in opposite directions—Hamish to the piano and Jarsha to his room. Hamish lifted the maple fallboard and lowered himself onto the stool.

The first time he sat here, he'd been too afraid to touch the bright white ivories. Now, he brushed them with ease, feeling the tension beneath his fingertips and imagining the notes that would ring out if he let them. He'd wanted so desperately to be perfect back then. To hit every note with pinpoint precision. To create beautiful melodies like the ones he heard in church. Then Jarsha came along, tapping out a discordant tune that echoed around his mind for days afterward.

He learned it was okay to make mistakes, and that sometimes mistakes could blossom into something beautiful. Over the following months, Jarsha added more notes to his disjointed tune, creating an unusual rhythm that resonated in Hamish's soul. Each swelling crescendo made him want to drop everything and build sandcastles with wild abandon.

Did you make it up yourself? Hamish asked.

Jarsha merely shook his head and continued playing. Later, when they were lacing up their shoes to go to the park, Jarsha confided that the melody was the only thing he remembered of his younger years. The determination with which he tried to recreate it inspired Hamish.

Jarsha shuffled back into the room and collapsed on the sofa. A polar fleece blanket cocooned his body.

"Where's Fluffy?" Hamish asked, stretching his fingers one final time.

"Dunno. Hiding under my bed, I think."

"Good."

No cat would spoil his surprise. Taking a deep breath, Hamish held his hand above the D-major chord. Slowly, softly, he pressed down. He'd practiced for hours on the toy keyboard his parents bought him. Never within their hearing, of course. He didn't want to risk being ridiculed. But here and now, he imitated Jarsha's smooth movements, letting the music fill him up and flow through his fingertips. Blood suffused his cheeks whenever he hit the wrong key, but he didn't stop. He *couldn't* stop.

Jarsha's song was more than a dissonant piece of instrumentation. It celebrated existence and everything it meant to be simply and completely *alive*. It captured the essence of joy, and the sorrow that sprouted new joy, and the energy that sustained all things. That was why the keys thrummed with life beneath his fingers, the same way they came alive under Jarsha's. That was why his friend refused to play anything else.

When the final note hung in the air, a pair of spindly arms crushed Hamish in a hug.

"You played the song," Jarsha said, his voice jubilant.

"I didn't get it right, though."

"Who cares?" The wraith released him and bounced on the balls of his feet. "I don't have it right yet either. It's still missing something. But you played it, and that means a lot to me. Maybe between the two of us, we can solve this mystery."

"I hope so," Hamish said. "It's so beautiful already, though. I can't imagine how it could get any better."

"It needs a harmony line," Mrs. Price said, re-entering the room.

Jarsha hurried to the sofa, but she summoned him back, apparently forgetting she'd forbidden him from playing. The boys sat on the piano stool, gazing up at her.

"Play the same thing you did before, but higher up on the piano," she instructed. "You started on the D-major chord *here*, so one of you should play off the root note *here*."

She pointed to two different places, and the boys placed their fingers on the keys. Jarsha, who had been playing longer, volunteered to perform the harmony. They played in unison, choppy at first, but gaining in accuracy and confidence. After several run-throughs, Jarsha experimented with trills and mordents that sent chills down Hamish's spine. But they hadn't found the magic ingredient. Not yet. He lost himself in the moment, letting the music flow over him like water until all perception of time faded from awareness.

A stray note from Jarsha's side elicited a spark of *something* inside him. It felt like every cell in his body was cavorting and growing. Like his bloodstream had been infused with an effervescent elixir. Prickles of energy spread across his skin, and the boys stopped playing by unspoken agreement. The music and its accompanying energy dwindled into the ether.

"That was it!" Jarsha exclaimed. "It was only one new note, but we're on the right track. I know we are."

Mrs. Price took her leave from their side, one hand pressed to her mouth. Tears glistened in her cornflower-blue eyes. "I don't know what that was, but it was amazing. I'm so proud I could burst."

She left the room in a hurry, and the boys exchanged glances.

"That was so weird," Hamish said, hugging himself. "You know that feeling you get when you rub polar fleece against itself and touch a metal pole? It was kinda like that. What's that called again? Static electricity?"

"Something like that," Jarsha said. "And yeah, I get what you're saying. I think the music is a kind of magic."

"That's for sure."

"No, I mean it." Jarsha turned to him, his expression serious. "That feeling. It's how the older kids describe using magic."

"What do you mean?"

"Wraiths are supposed to have magic powers or something. The older kids told me about it. It's something to do with the place I come from, but I don't know what. I only lived in the homestead for a few months, and I don't remember anything from before that."

"Maybe it *is* magic," Hamish agreed. He might know less about the subject than Jarsha, but he trusted what he felt.

After Mrs. Price composed herself, the lesson went off without a hitch. Hamish turned down a second cup of tea but agreed to spend another hour with Jarsha so they could pore over his comic books. Upon entering his room, the wraith balled up his blanket and flung it onto the bed. A flash of white and caramel streaked past their ankles and into the hallway.

"There goes Fluffy," Jarsha said. "At least I won't have to deal with him meowing all night."

"You're lucky to have a cat," Hamish said, shutting the door. "Dad's allergic to them. And dogs."

"You're not missing out on much. Cats can be pretty evil. Fluffy's tried to kill me at least ten times." Jarsha scanned the bookshelf with his fingers as well as his eyes and pulled out a Batman comic. "Here it is. *Night of the Monster Men.* I can't believe you haven't read it yet."

Hamish slipped the comic into his backpack. "Mom thought it was too scary for me."

"You better not let her see it, then."

"I won't. Thanks for letting me borrow it."

"No problem." Silence reigned for a long moment. Jarsha perched on the edge of his bed, kneading the hem of his shirt. Then: "I lied."

Hamish's brow crinkled. "About what?"

"Having the flu."

"So you do have it?"

"No. I faked having it in the first place."

"Why?"

Jarsha hesitated. "There are some bad things happening. At school."

Hamish sank onto the bed next to him. The rumpled pile of blankets caved under his weight. "What kind of things?"

Another pause. "You know those scientists who showed up at assembly yesterday?"

"Yeah."

"They tried to kill me in kindergarten."

"Like, for real? Or like with Fluffy?"

"For real," Jarsha said, meeting Hamish's eyes for the first time. "They poisoned me with something, and I nearly died. I think they're going to try again."

Hamish's mind reeled. "Have you told anyone?"

"I'm telling you."

"I mean a grownup."

Jarsha shook his head. "Gran can't do anything about it. She hasn't been well lately. And you know how useless Mr. Sullivan is."

"I bet he'd listen if he knew what was going on. I'll go with you if you want. We can make him do something about it."

"No. We can't trust the grownups. It's their fault it happened in the first place. I spent the whole day trying to figure out what to do, and I think I've got it. I'm going to need your help, though."

Hamish pursed his lips. "Okay, what do you need me to do?"

"Talk to your brother for me."

"My brother?"

"Yeah. Billy. He was the one who saved me and got rid of the scientists last time. I bet he could do it again."

Hamish's head swam. *Billy? But he hates wraiths! He'd never do that.* "What do I say?"

"Tell him that the scientists are back and that Jarsha needs his help. He'll understand."

"And if he says no?"

"I don't know yet," Jarsha admitted. "I was kind of woozy when I met him, but I remember he had this keycard thing to get into the lab. He stole it from one of the scientists. If he still has it, we might be able to use it to get inside and rescue anyone they've kidnapped. I think he might have given it to Mr. Matlin, though."

Hamish thought hard. "He does have a keycard in his dresser. It's got a random woman's name and photo on it."

"That'll be the one," Jarsha said. "Take it if you have to, but ask Billy for help first. I think we're gonna need him."

Chapter Twenty-Seven

"BILLY! DINNER'S READY!"

Mrs. Porter's voice echoed down the hallway. Billy lay on his bed, staring at the ceiling. His family had started trickling into the lounge at 5:00 p.m., and the too-empty house suddenly felt too full. He'd fled to the solitude of his room—the one place he could stew in his thoughts without being interrupted. In theory, anyway.

"*Billy!* How many times... Hamish dear, can you go and get your brother?"

Footsteps thudded up to Billy's room, followed by a knock and the squeak of old hinges. Hamish's presence hovered in the doorway.

"Mom says it's dinner time."

"Yeah, I know. I'm coming in a minute."

"You need to come now. Dad's getting impatient."

"Ugh. Fine."

Before Billy could stand up, Hamish grabbed his wrist. "I need to talk to you about something after dinner."

"Today's not the best day. Can't you talk to Mom and Dad instead?"

"No, not about this. Do you remember—"

Mr. Porter's booming voice cut them off. "Boys! Food's getting cold."

Billy tugged his arm free. "Maybe tomorrow, okay?"

"But Billy—"

"*Boys!*"

"Come on," Billy said, jerking his head toward the hallway. "We'd better go."

They trooped into the kitchen and took their places at the dining table. The two empty chairs where James and Corvus usually sat made the room feel smaller somehow. A sense of disquiet surged through him while Hamish said grace.

"So, Billy, how was your day?" Mr. Porter asked, spearing a chunk of meatloaf.

"It was fine."

"That's it? Fine?"

"Yeah," Billy said, twirling mashed potatoes around his fork. "Oh, I was going to ask. Is it okay if I join the debate club with Murdock? The meetings are on Wednesday afternoons."

"Debating, eh? I don't see why not."

"Really? I thought you'd want me to stay home and babysit."

His parents exchanged glances.

"We always appreciate you looking after your brothers," Mrs. Porter said. "But at the end of the day, you're not their parent. We don't expect you to give up your hobbies to look after them. I'm sure we can arrange for one of the neighbors to pop in when you're not here."

Warmth blossomed in Billy's chest. *That was easier than I expected.* "Thanks, Mom."

"What got you interested in debating?" Mr. Porter asked.

"Nothing in particular. I just thought I'd try it."

"Good for you. It's good to try new things," Mr. Porter said. "How about you, Hamish? How was your day?"

The blond-haired boy shrugged. "It was okay."

Mr. Porter opened his mouth to push further, when the front door swung open. Corvus trudged across the threshold, his glamour-clad cheeks flushed from the chilly air. He paused to study the scene in front of him, then averted his gaze and shut the door.

"Corey, dear," Mrs. Porter exclaimed, rushing over to hug him. "You must be starving! And you're so cold."

"I'm okay. I ate at school. I just want to go to bed."

"Are you coming down with something? Maybe you should have a hot shower first."

"I'll do that," Corvus said, yawning in an exaggerated fashion. "Goodnight, everyone."

He shuffled in the direction of the bathroom, and Mrs. Porter returned to the table, her posture stiff with worry.

"What's eating him?" Mr. Porter asked.

"He's been in a bad mood ever since you gave him that letter this morning," Mrs. Porter said. "Did you get a chance to talk to him today, Billy?"

Little knives of guilt stabbed him in the gut. "Not really. He seemed distracted. I didn't want to push him."

Mr. Porter shook his head. "Poor kid. I should've read the letter before I gave it to him."

"That's no way to build trust," Mrs. Porter said. "We have to be patient with him. Maybe you can take him on a hiking trip this weekend instead of going down to the shooting range. Have some quality bonding time. He likes hiking, doesn't he?"

She turned to Billy, who gave her a mechanical nod. "Yeah, he does."

"Then it's settled. The three of you can go on Saturday."

That's when I'm going out with Shauna!

"Actually, I've already got plans for Saturday," he said, trying and failing to sound casual.

Mrs. Porter gave him a strange look. "What plans?"

"Oh, you know." Billy waved a dismissive hand. "Group project for science."

"Well, we can't disrupt your education. I'm sure Corey will have a wonderful time anyway. Maybe your father can teach him a thing or two about bushcraft while they're out."

Billy gobbled the last of his food while his parents debated where the hiking trip should take place. Nostalgia hit him hard when his father described the forests and canyons littering the Texas Panhandle.

A mere two-hour drive from Morton, the area had formed the backdrop to most of their father-son hunting trips. He'd made some of his happiest memories there, but he didn't mind missing out this time. Going on a date with Shauna was a once-in-a-lifetime opportunity.

Billy pushed back his chair. "I've got some homework to do before bed. Thanks for dinner, Mom. It was delicious."

Both parents smiled and wished him luck, but Hamish kept his head down and pushed the food around his plate without eating it. Billy ruffled his brother's hair as he walked past. The younger boy frowned at him, but he hardly noticed.

Darkness swallowed him when he entered his bedroom. The faint orange-yellow glow of a flashlight glimmered beneath Corvus's blanket nest. The boy himself sat cross-legged on the bottom bunk, wearing a pair of Billy's old pajamas. Tiny cartoon pandas littered the flannelette ensemble, each one sporting a wide grin that clashed with Corvus's stormy expression. A sketchpad rested against his knee, and he penciled short, scratchy strokes onto the paper. The scent of sandalwood wafted from his damp hair.

"Do you mind if I turn on the light?" Billy asked.

"I do, actually."

"Mom says working in a dark room will ruin your eyesight."

"I guess you'd better go to bed instead of working, then."

Billy studied his friend. He hadn't planned to do any real homework, especially since Mr. Allan hadn't asked him to translate his newspaper. He *had* hoped for a simple conversation, but Corvus's intense expression gave him second thoughts.

He hopped onto the dresser. "I really am sorry, you know."

"Hmmm."

"I am! We agreed not to talk to each other at school because it's too dangerous. I didn't want to offend Rem, but she broke the agreement. I thought you, of all people, would understand."

"It's not the same thing," Corvus retorted. His eyebrows formed a thick, angry line above his eyes, like caterpillars on the warpath.

Billy gave him an incredulous look. "How is it not the same thing?"

"I can't believe you're stupid enough that I have to spell this out for you again. It's dangerous for *us*. Me and Rem. Not *you*. If you talk to us, the worst that could happen is you get teased. Me and Rem could get *killed*. So if one of us breaks the agreement to talk to you, you'd better get your head out of your butt long enough to listen. Because if we do, it means something serious is going down."

Billy shivered at the coldness of his friend's delivery. *He hates me. I messed up, and now he hates me. This is all my fault.*

"I'm sorry," he repeated, his voice small. "You've got to believe me. I didn't mean to hurt Rem. I only did it—"

"To impress a girl? You know what, Billy? It's that reasoning that disgusts me more than anything else. What do you even see in Shauna?"

"She's gorgeous. Kind. She loves animals and science, and she thinks I'm cool."

"*Kind?* Really? Don't make me laugh. She spits on us when we walk past. She goes to anti-wraith rallies. And the things she says to us? You're delusional if you think she's a good person."

"I never said she didn't have her faults. I don't like the way she acts toward you, but maybe I can change her. Have you considered that?"

"There's no changing someone like her," Corvus retorted, throwing his pencil at the bed. It bounced off the frame and clattered to the floor. "You're only doing this to boost your popularity. And if that means stabbing us in the back, so be it."

The verbal blow knocked the air out of Billy's lungs. "This isn't about popularity. I thought you knew me better than that. I'm not stabbing you in the back. I'm not that kind of person."

"Sure feels like it to me."

"It's a *date*, Corvus. One date. Not some huge conspiracy to make your life miserable."

"I never said it was. But the things you said to Rem so you could score your 'one date'? There's no excuse for that. And there's no excuse for making her cry."

Billy's mouth snapped shut. He hadn't been expecting that. "I... I made Rem cry?"

"Yeah. You did. No one hurts her and gets away with it."

"That sounds ominous. You're not going to kill me in my sleep, are you?"

Corvus regarded him with narrowed eyes. Then the tension in his face broke. "No. I wouldn't kill you. You're one of my best friends, even if you aren't acting like it right now."

Billy nodded solemnly. "I'll try to be less stupid."

Corvus snorted, and the hint of a smile touched his lips, soothing Billy's fears.

"You're not really stupid," the other boy admitted. "You're actually pretty smart, and I think that's why it annoys me so much when you do dumb things."

"Okay, then I'll try not to do dumb things," Billy corrected himself.

"Does that mean you won't date Shauna?"

Billy hesitated. He didn't want to risk upsetting the newfound peace, but Shauna was *Shauna*. Beautiful. Popular. Clever. No one in their right mind would turn down a date with her.

"Sorry, but no. I've made a decision, and I'm not changing it."

Corvus expelled a frustrated breath. "When I said I wasn't going to kill you, that promise doesn't extend to Rem. She might have something to say about this."

"I know." Billy dropped his gaze. "I'll apologize tomorrow. She'll understand when I explain."

"Yeah, well, I hope you do a better job of explaining it to her than you did to me. I still don't understand."

"I don't think anyone understands love," Billy said, risking a glance at his friend. "It's not like we have any control over it."

"Speak for yourself," Corvus said. "We may not follow the human concept of romantic love in wraith culture, but there's nothing complicated about love itself. It's all about loyalty and selflessness. Helping your bondmate and letting them help you. Being there for them no matter what. Love is a promise. And whatever you feel for Shauna is not a promise. It's a flood of ridiculous hormones that delude you into thinking it is."

Billy balked, a stab of outrage piercing his gut. "You don't know how I feel!"

"Sure I do. I can smell the pheromones from here."

"The what?"

Corvus slammed the sketchbook down on his bed. The motion sent a small white envelope flying, and he shoved it under his pillow before climbing under the rumpled duvet. "You really are hopeless, you know that?"

A lump rose in Billy's throat. "I know."

Agreeing to whatever Corvus said seemed like the wisest course of action. The corner of the envelope peeked out from beneath the satin pillowcase, taunting him. Daring him to tempt fate by asking another question. Curiosity may have killed the cat, but it hadn't killed him yet, so he plowed ahead.

"Is that Seisan's letter?"

No response.

"What did he say?" Billy persisted. "Any word on his travels?"

"None of your business."

The flashlight went out, signaling the end of their conversation. With a heavy heart, Billy slid off the dresser and climbed the ladder to the top bunk. *It wasn't supposed to be like this.*

He changed into his pajamas and crawled under the covers, listening for sniffles, whimpers—anything to hint his friend was crying. No such signs presented themselves. Instead, a deep, eerie silence filled the air, drawing his mind back to all the dark places he wanted to forget. Corvus hated him. Rem hated him. Shauna didn't, but she would if she discovered his association with the wraiths. *What a mess.*

The thing that bothered him the most, though, was Corvus's standoffishness. The two of them had been inseparable for the past three years. They'd shared everything with each other. Was his new reluctance due to simple pettiness? Or did that innocuous white envelope contain something so horrific he felt he *couldn't* share it?

Billy shivered. *I should have asked him if it was bad news. I should have reminded him that I care and that I'm here for him. That's what a good friend would have done.* But broaching the subject *now*, when Corvus clearly didn't want to talk, would be like poking a landmine. The boy might even rescind his vow not to kill him. Billy rolled onto his back and sighed. *Why didn't I just listen?*

Chapter Twenty-Eight

REM'S EYES BURNED two identical holes through Billy's back during math class. The sensation intensified as the minutes ticked by, strong enough to make him wonder if she'd cast a spell to aid her efforts.

Good thing we don't have English today, Billy thought, squirming in his seat. If she saw him cuddling up to Shauna... *well.* His life would be forfeit. Corvus's stare barely registered in comparison to Rem's. Resigned indifference dulled his eyes, as though he'd decided Billy deserved whatever Rem threw at him and that was that.

"Dude, are you even listening?" Murdock whispered.

Billy blinked, taking in his friend's downturned eyebrows and quirked upper lip. "Sorry. I was thinking about something else."

Murdock nudged him. "If I had a girl like Shauna, I'd be daydreaming all the time too. I was asking what kind of gift you're going to get her."

"Gift?"

"Yeah. You know. Something to make your date memorable."

"Do you really think I need to get her something?" Billy asked. "I mean, it's one date. It's not like I'm going to be her boyfriend or anything."

"That's why you have to make an effort. If you show her you care, you'll get another date and another date, and before you know it, she'll be all yours."

Rem's searing gaze shifted to the back of Billy's head, and his skin prickled in response. *Oh, great. Just what I always wanted.* But for all his discomfort, part of him *did* want it. To experience the same carefree fun his friends bragged about. To know what it felt like to be in love. Murdock claimed the fluttery feeling in Billy's chest proved he already knew, but Corvus's harsh words threw a spanner in the works. He didn't know what he *was* feeling anymore, let alone what he *should* be feeling.

"I think a necklace might be a bit much for a first date," Murdock was saying when he tuned back in. "Roses are always a good choice, unless she's allergic to flowers. And chocolate. Everyone loves chocolate."

"Isn't she vegan, though?" Billy asked.

"So?"

"Chocolate has milk in it."

"Then get her some good quality dark chocolate."

Billy pulled a face. "Ew. No one likes that garbage."

"I do," Murdock said in mock affront. "How about roses, then? She's not allergic to them, is she?"

"I don't think so. I don't think she'd want to carry them around all afternoon, though. They'd probably wilt or something. That wouldn't be very romantic."

"I guess not."

Billy breathed a quiet sigh of relief when Murdock copied the next problem from their algebra textbook. *Saved by math. Never thought that would happen.* He squinted at the page. The numbers and letters blended together in a confusing conglomeration of... mathy-ness. In elementary school, he'd relied on Zane to walk him through the equation, but Zane had been fast-tracked into AP Calculus this year, leaving Billy stranded.

"I've got it!" Murdock announced, his voice a little too loud for the quiet classroom.

The teacher gave them a sharp look, forcing them to duck their heads and pretend to work. As soon as her attention moved away, Billy asked his friend what he "got."

"A gift idea," Murdock explained. "You two are going to a movie, right?"

"After we go to the park, yeah."

"The theater downtown has arcade games. Coin-operated claw machines and stuff like that. You could win her a stuffed animal."

Billy raised an eyebrow. "Seriously?"

"Yeah! It's super romantic. I've seen it in the movies."

"You need a lot of luck to win something from those machines, though. I've heard they're rigged."

"Of course they're rigged. But if you go to the manager before your date, you can arrange for them to help you out."

"You mean… cheat?"

"Why not? *They* do."

Billy considered it. *You can't cheat a cheater.* "You think they'd arrange something like that?"

"Sure," Murdock said. "I had them do it when I went on a date with Eleanor."

"You went on a date with Eleanor? When?"

"Over winter break."

"Why didn't you tell me?"

Murdock stuck his tongue out. "You're not my mother."

"Shut up," Billy said, giving him a playful shove. "What happened?"

"She was a bit too weird for my tastes. Apparently, she only agreed to the date to make Brad jealous."

"How did that work out for her?"

"Not too well. But hey, she got a giant purple Care Bear out of the deal. That's a much better prize than a dumb jock, if you ask me."

Billy chuckled, but part of him wondered if Shauna planned to use him the same way. Eleanor and Shauna were friends, so he supposed they might stoop to similar tactics. As far as he'd seen, though, Shauna didn't have any ex-boyfriends hanging around except for Jeffrey, whom she despised. Besides, even if someone else caught her eye, she didn't need to play games. She could click her fingers and every straight male in their grade (and several outside it) would fall at her feet.

"The manager really helped you win?" Billy asked.

Murdock placed a hand over his heart. "Swear on my life. He's a good dude. Slip him a fiver and he'll get it done."

"Thanks for the tip," Billy said. *Probably not a good idea, though, unless it was a platonic present. Corvus would kill me.*

Murdock elbowed him and whispered something inaudible.

"What?" Billy asked, leaning closer.

"I said, that wraith chick is staring at us."

Billy didn't have to ask which wraith chick he meant. "Let her stare. Maybe she'll get in trouble for spacing out in class."

"It's creeping me out," Murdock grumbled.

The bell rang and the whole class fled as though the room were on fire. Murdock headed for Geography, while Billy went downstairs to the library. *Time for World History.*

To his relief, Zane had saved him a seat. He settled into it, all too aware that Rem's gaze had migrated from the back of his head to stab him through the chest. She looked like she wanted to say something—or perhaps give him a judicious slap for his behavior—but she sat down instead. Billy swallowed, his eyes drawn to the envelope in her hand. *That's Corvus's letter. What's she doing with it? Did Seisan write one for her too?*

His mind strayed back to his conversation with Corvus from the previous night. *If one of us breaks the agreement to talk to you, you'd better get your head out of your butt long enough to listen. Because if we do, it means something serious is going down.*

Billy's heart fluttered. Did that mean something serious *was* going down? Had Seisan reported something major? Was Grigoth going to make good on his threats of war? He shook the thought out of his head, digging his elbows into the table in front of him. *Corvus would have told me if things were that bad. He wouldn't put my life at risk by not telling me.* The thought calmed him a little, but the uneasiness didn't go away.

"All right, class, listen up," Mr. Allan said, shaking an upside-down hat.

"I've got a bunch of words relating to World War Two on little slips of paper. You're each going to pick one and research the topic you get. The aim today is to learn something new about the war. Tomorrow, you'll be presenting what you learned to the class. Understood?"

"We don't have World History tomorrow," someone said, eliciting titters from the other students.

"On Friday, then. Come and choose your topics."

Billy stood and grabbed a slip of paper from the hat.

Horses, it read.

Billy groaned. He didn't know anything about horses except that a pony had bitten him as a toddler. Since then, he'd stayed well away from them. He trudged toward the agriculture section of the library to see if he could learn anything there.

"Hey. Billy." Rem's voice sent shivers down his spine.

"We can't talk," he said. The words came out like a plea.

"I know a place we can. No one will see or hear."

Heart hammering, Billy shuffled after her. *Was that a threat? Or was she trying to reassure me?* Rem led him to a door guarded by a keypad and punched in the code. Her fingers moved too fast for his eyes to follow. The lock clicked open, and she dragged him into the room, slamming the door behind them.

Stacks of unsorted books littered the floor, their glossy covers reflecting the harsh lights overhead. Thick foam tiles covered the walls, a throwback to when teachers used the space for music lessons rather than storage. Rem was right; no one would overhear them.

"I'm sorry about—"

SMACK!

Rem's fingers splayed across his face, slapping him with a strength he hadn't thought her capable of possessing. He clutched at the reddening handprint, praying it wouldn't bruise in that pattern. *How would I explain that to Shauna? To Mom and Dad?*

They stared at each other for a span of seconds, then Rem's posture slumped.

"That didn't feel as good as I expected it to," she admitted.

Billy rubbed his cheek. "You hit me *hard*."

"I guess we both have something to be sorry for now. Dad always told me we should never resort to violence, but Corvus suggested I give it a try."

"*Corvus* told you to slap me?"

"In hindsight, I think he might have been joking."

"Oh."

They stood in silence a bit longer.

"I really am sorry about what I said yesterday," Billy said, keeping a wary eye on Rem. "There was this girl…"

"Shauna."

"Yeah. I wanted to impress her."

"Corvus told me. He said you're going on a date with her."

"Yeah, I am. This weekend."

"You love her?"

Unlike Corvus, no trace of disgust altered Rem's tone. Warm curiosity flowed out of her, and he got the sense she wanted to know the truth, no matter how much it hurt.

"I don't know if I'd go that far. I don't like the way she treats you guys, but the rest of the time, she's great. I like her a lot."

Rem shook her head. "You and your human love emotions. I don't think I'll ever understand."

"You can just call it 'love,' you know. 'Human love emotions' sounds weird."

"The whole thing is weird."

"No, it's not."

"It is to me."

Billy bit his lip. "Your future bondmate said the same thing. He's got his own view on what love means. I'm not sure I fully agree with him, though."

"Yeah, well, you're human," Rem said. "It's not fair to hold you to wraith standards."

"You believe the same thing he does?"

"Of course. The bondmate relationship is one of duty and mutual care. We keep each other safe by any means necessary. We provide blood to the Hatchery so new wraiths can be born. And that's it. Nothing more, nothing less."

"Whoa, whoa, whoa," Billy said, holding up a hand. "What was that last part about the Hatchery?"

"You want me to explain…" Rem's eyes widened and her cheeks blushed lilac. "No. No, no, no, no. We are *not* having this conversation."

"What conversation?"

"You were going to ask me where babies come from, weren't you?"

"Of course not," Billy yelped, taking a step back. "I was asking about the blood thing. I already *know* where babies come from."

Rem eyed him suspiciously. "Did Corvus tell you?"

"No! Why would Corvus…" Billy tried to sound indignant, but his voice trailed off into anxious silence. "Are you saying it's… different… for wraiths?"

"Like I said—no comment."

"You're the one who brought it up."

"Yup, and now I'm shutting it down."

Billy grimaced as a host of unpleasant images swept through his mind. "Okay, good. I don't think I want to know."

"If you did, you could always ask Cor—"

"So anyway," Billy interrupted loudly. "My date with Shauna. Does it bother you that I'm going ahead with it?"

Rem blinked at the change in subject, and the flush of lilac drained from her cheeks. "Of course it does. It's like you turn into a different person when you're around her, and not in a good way."

His throat tightened. "I know. The way I spoke to you yesterday… I was a complete jerk. I'm sorry, Rem. It won't happen again. I promise."

The hard lines around her eyes softened. "Good."

Billy maintained a respectful silence for the better part of a minute, then gestured at the envelope. "Corvus hinted to me that something was up, but he wouldn't tell me what. So… *is* something up?"

"I guess you could say that."

"Is it something to do with Seisan? My parents said they'll adopt Corvus if he's not coming back. He won't have to worry about a home or—"

"It's not that," Rem said. "The letters aren't from Seisan."

"They aren't?" Billy's head swam. "Then who are they from?"

"King Grigoth."

An icy hand squeezed the air out of Billy's lungs. "Why would he write to you? Is this to do with that oath thingy?"

"The blood oath ceremony," Rem corrected. "Yes. Everyone in our grade got the call to say it's happening in seven days' time."

Billy froze, unsure of what to say. The wraiths had mentioned the ceremony a lot over the course of their friendship. He knew that Grigoth took their blood and used it to bind them to his power. Thanks to Corvus, he also knew that wraiths in contempt of their cultural heritage were at risk of being tortured by the king. Other than that, the details remained a mystery.

"I'm scared, Billy."

The admission came out in a tiny voice, giving Billy all the encouragement he needed to step forward and hug his friend. He half-expected her to slap him, but her body weakened and melted into his.

"We've been careful," Billy said, swallowing the lump in his throat. "You and Corvus stayed away from me. You've been getting the other wraiths to accept you. There's no way they'd think we're friends, especially after yesterday. They won't report anything. You'll be fine."

"Will we?"

"Of course."

Rem sniffed and took a shaky breath. "We'll probably never see you again. I don't want our last memories together to be fighting."

"We'll hang out before you go," Billy promised. "We'll talk about happy things and play board games together like we did in the old days."

"And charades?"

Billy choked out a laugh. "Yeah. Charades too."

Several quiet minutes passed before Rem broke their embrace. Contrary to his expectations, she hadn't been crying.

"Do you really have to go?" he mumbled, scrubbing the wetness from his own eyes.

"The letters were orders, not invitations," Rem said. She sounded tired—like she'd used all her energy in a single burst. "There's no choice. It's an integral part of our culture. An integral part of *us*. If we resist, Grigoth won't hesitate to kill us. There are no second chances."

"You could wear a glamour," he said, desperation weaving through his voice. "You'd fit right in. Corvus is doing it easily enough. You wouldn't have to risk starvation and murder in the Gloaming."

"I know it's hard for you to understand, Billy, but it's not that simple," Rem said. "The Gloaming is a vital part of who we are. Without it, we're nothing."

"Not to me," Billy retorted, tears filling his eyes again. "Isn't there anything—"

The door opened, cutting him off. The head librarian entered the room carrying an armload of books. She jumped when she saw them but quickly regained her composure.

"You kids shouldn't be here. Get back to your class, or I'll tell Mr. Allan you've been slacking off."

Chastened, they squeezed past her and returned to the library. Rem ran to the foyer, no doubt heading for the girls' bathroom. Billy paused to calm his breathing before walking in the opposite direction. Zane found him five minutes later, staring at a magazine with a tractor on the cover. He'd meant to get back to his research topic, but the conversation with Rem kept replaying in his mind.

"Found anything yet?" Zane asked.

Billy shook his head and resumed searching.

Chapter Twenty-Nine

THE SOUND OF simmering cauldrons filled Lothaire's ears. Purple energy pulsed between his clasped hands, pushing them apart like two magnets bearing the same charge. He'd spoiled three potions today—something he hadn't done since his first year in the Academy. Sure, he'd made mistakes since then, but they'd been confined to his more experimental work. Never something as simple as a healing potion.

Today was different. Today, his mind blew in all directions, tossed this way and that by the storms of fate. Before Seisan left, he'd vowed to find a way to free Rem and Corvus from their obligations to take the blood oath. He'd dedicated every spare moment to fulfilling that vow, but without Seisan around to share the workload, his free time soon dwindled away to nothing.

When he wasn't working, he was teaching Rem and Corvus magic. When he wasn't teaching, he was healing the other wraith children and replenishing his potion stores. His mission fell by the wayside, and now he only had a few days left before he lost his daughter for good.

With a sigh, Lothaire pulled a mouse out of the wire cage he'd built. Its pink feet wrapped around his fingers, tiny claws digging into his skin. He deposited it on an empty table and watched it scamper away, nosing the ground for food.

"No snacks right now, buddy," Lothaire murmured.

He'd found the mouse scurrying through his backyard, mangy and bleeding from a run-in with an alley cat. The most skilled vet on the planet couldn't have saved it, but magic made it easy for Lothaire to succeed where they would have failed. The mouse recovered in a matter of days, and he'd kept it as a test subject ever since.

Lothaire cast a mock compulsion spell on the mouse, replicating the urges young wraiths experienced when their blood oath ceremony drew near. Rather than forcing the mouse to make a perilous trip across the Gloaming, Lothaire's spell enticed it to march around the edges of the table. Keeping a close eye on the mouse's progress, he placed a jellybean next to its path.

No reaction.

Satisfied, Lothaire cast an additional compulsion spell, this time flooding the mouse's body with hunger hormones. *Strong compulsions override weaker ones. If the mouse is hungry enough, the survival instinct should kick in and break the compulsion to walk.*

He watched with bated breath as the mouse got closer and closer to the jellybean. Its tongue strained toward the treat, but its magic-addled legs walked straight past. Lothaire slumped in disappointment.

"Sorry, little guy," he mumbled, releasing both spells. *So close and yet so far.*

The mouse tottered forward and nibbled the jellybean with gusto. Lothaire stroked its head with the tip of his index finger, then returned his attention to the cauldrons. The blue liquid in the first one had overheated and now contained lumps of gray goop. Grimacing, he siphoned them out and cast a quick cooling spell. *That was a close call. One more minute and I'd be mopping up* another *failed potion.*

Lothaire grabbed an empty glass bottle from the shelf, poured the smoky liquid inside, and re-corked it. Several children from the homestead had contracted algidus in the past week, a wraith-specific illness similar to the human cold. Unlike a simple cold, however, algidus did not spread by contact. Rather, it lay dormant in every wraith and activated if they experienced a sudden drop in body temperature. Although benign, the symptoms could only be resolved with the aid of a potion.

The second cauldron contained a bright yellow burn-soothing draught, a potion he'd rarely needed over the past three years. One of the younger wraiths had used up his stocks last week after she bumped a pot of boiling water over her legs. Lothaire flinched at the memory, his mind wandering back to his younger years. He'd experienced searing pain too—not from water or flames, but from his blood oath compulsions. Liquid fire had surged through his veins until he stumbled back to the Gloaming against his will.

It was like nothing I've ever experienced, he thought, tracing a finger over the belly of his forearm. *Something made our bodies turn against us. I wonder what would happen if I blocked the root cause?*

Lothaire strolled back to the mouse. The creature squeaked indignantly when he wrapped his fingers around it. Gritting his teeth, he summoned the courage to cast the first spell—not a mock spell this time but the real thing. A spell to flood the mouse's body with the hormones responsible for pre-ceremony pain.

A halo of energy formed around the mouse's head, but Lothaire didn't let the magic leave his body. To do so would be to put his pet— *test subject*—in severe agony until he invented an effective pain-killing spell. That could take anywhere from a few seconds to a few days. Maybe longer. Given the vast biological differences between wraiths and mice, he might not be able to invent one at all. The mouse gazed up at him with shiny black eyes, and a lump formed in Lothaire's throat.

He crossed the room in two strides and put the mouse back in its cage, throwing another jellybean inside before latching the door. Shaky breaths whistled past his teeth, and his knees buckled beneath him. Rem's life mattered so much more than a mouse's. So did Corvus's, and Volner's, and Almwin's, and…

He swallowed. Hurting a single animal was a lesser evil than leaving hundreds of kids to suffer and die at the hands of a tyrant. So why couldn't he bring himself to do it?

He watched the mouse eat for a few minutes, giving himself a chance to calm down. If he couldn't test the spell on another living being, he only had one option: to test it on himself. Lothaire sucked in a deep breath and glanced at the smooth skin on his forearm. *Better make it fast.*

A deep, biting ache engulfed his arm when the spell hit, shortening his breath and squeezing tears from his eyes. His hands spasmed, leaking tiny clouds of purple light as he tried to remember who he was and what he was doing. He fired off a desperate spell, the first arrangement he'd considered. The pain intensified and an inhuman growl exploded from his lips.

The second spell covered his forearm in a numbing salve, but the fire underneath raged on. His capillaries felt like they were popping in the intense heat, but no bruises formed in the shadows of his skin. Stars swarmed his vision when he tried the final spell. For a terrifying moment, he wondered if he'd gone too far and drained all the energy from his body. A slicing pain shot through his collarbone, and the fire in his veins subsided to a dull ache. He fell to the floor in a sweaty heap. *I actually did it.*

The thought brought him more fear than joy. Searching fingers scrabbled at his neck, sliding down his shirt to inspect the damage. The bony protuberance at the base of his throat had vanished. According to his biology notes from the Academy, that particular lump of bone encased the coactus gland—the organ responsible for regulating their oath-based hormones. Troubled by the unknown consequences of its removal, he tried to reverse the spell. Nothing happened.

So removing the coactus gland does *work, but it's permanent. Not a great solution, but it's better than the alternative.*

The cauldron above Lothaire hissed and spat globs of yellow liquid into the air. He dove out of the way and rolled to safety. A vanishing spell cleaned up both the mess and the disaster brewing inside the cauldron. *Whoops.* Part of him wanted to remake it straight away, but he shut down the idea. The compulsion-escaping spell had worked. Not to plan, perhaps, but that didn't matter.

I should go and tell Rem and Corvus the good news, Lothaire thought.

Imagining the relief on their faces gave him strength, and he pushed himself to his feet. Despite the ruined potions and the experimental self-surgery, today was a good day.

Chapter Thirty

BILLY FOLLOWED MURDOCK down the dimly lit corridor, away from the debate club's noisy antics. The meeting had been a failure before it began—firstly because the teacher in charge failed to show up, and secondly because Mikayla was nowhere to be seen either. The final straw came when a motley group of teenagers took over and insisted Billy and Murdock team up with Jeffrey for a mock debate. Both boys opted to leave rather than face the bully's condescending smirk.

"We'll try again next week," Billy reassured his friend.

Murdock heaved a sigh. "Yeah, I know. It's not the end of the world."

They parted ways at the school gates, and Billy jogged home. Memories of his confrontation with Rem swirled through his mind. Her news about the blood oath ceremony had put a damper over everything, and he couldn't shake it off.

If Corvus randomly disappears one day, Mom and Dad are gonna freak out, he thought. *Maybe Lothaire can use one of his glamours to pose as Corvus's dad. We could say he was honorably discharged and that Corvus is going back to live with him.*

Thinking up creative solutions was Billy's forte, but this time, it brought him no joy. Even if he fooled his parents, he could never fool himself. His friends were leaving, and it seemed no earthly force could stop them. For the first time, the problem might be too big for him to fix.

I have to do something, Billy thought, his feet pounding up the driveway to his house. *I'll go inside, grab Corvus, and bring him straight to Rem's place. We can figure this out together. I know we can.* He crashed through the front door, dumped his satchel, and made a beeline for the sofa. Corvus wasn't the only one sprawled there.

"Rem," Billy said, panic rising in his chest. Neither wraith wore a glamour. "What are you two doing? If my parents see you—"

"I know, I know." Corvus waved off his concerns. "I'll get thrown out. I don't care right now."

"Well, *I* do." Billy crossed his arms. "This is about the blood oath ceremony, isn't it?"

Both wraiths nodded. Billy glanced between them, sighed, and joined them on the sofa.

"Did you think about what I said in the library?" he asked Rem.

"I did."

"And?"

Rem stayed silent.

"Corvus, what do you think?" Billy asked, turning to his other friend. "You've spent the past three years posing as a human around my family. Would it really be that bad to wear a glamour all the time?"

Corvus stared at him, unblinking. "You want me to change everything I am just to please other people? You want me to abandon everything—my magic, my culture, and my country—to fit in with a society that treats outsiders like dirt?"

"You've been doing it around my family."

"That was for survival. I wouldn't have lasted a week on my own when I was ten. Things are different now."

"You wouldn't have to abandon everything," Billy persisted. "You could still do magic if you stayed. You and Rem would still be together. We could all stay friends."

"You really think it's that simple?"

Rem placed a hand on the wraith's knee. "Stop playing with him, Corvus."

A meaningful gaze passed between the two wraiths, and Billy's brow wrinkled in confusion. *Playing with me? What's going on?*

"You know how I told you we can't avoid the oath?" Rem asked. "Well, it turns out I was wrong. Dad's been looking for a workaround for years without luck, but he actually found one this afternoon. It's not exactly elegant, but it should be enough to stop the compulsions."

Hope flitted through Billy's chest. "Are you serious?"

"One hundred percent," Rem said. A nervous smile tugged at the corners of her lips. "Dad's already placed the spell over us, just in case. There's no guarantee it'll work, but we'll see what happens when the time comes."

"I… I don't know what to say," Billy said. His emotional rollercoaster hit a brick wall, shocking him into silence. "I'm glad he figured it out, but… wow. He cut it a bit close, didn't he?"

Corvus snorted. "I'll say."

"Do *you* think it's going to work?" Billy asked.

"Probably," Rem said. "But even if it works perfectly, we're painting some pretty big targets on our backs."

"Not that it matters," Corvus added. "We'd be in danger if we returned to the Gloaming as well. The blood oath never did my dad any good. If there's even the slightest chance I can avoid it, I'm going to take it. I'd rather get stabbed through the heart than become one of Grigoth's mind-controlled slaves."

The vehemence of Corvus's resolve surprised Billy, but his reasoning didn't. *I wouldn't take the oath either. There are some things worse than death, and being mind-controlled by a crazy guy is one of them.*

"What are you going to do if the spell doesn't work?" Billy asked. "Would you still want to stay?"

"Sure, we'd *want* to stay, but we wouldn't be able to," Rem explained. "The compulsion to attend the ceremony is programmed into us. Every second we fight it, it gets stronger and more intense until it consumes everything we are. It's not just a cultural thing. It's literally ingrained in our DNA."

"Magic is a powerful drug," Corvus muttered.

"I didn't know it was that bad," Billy said. "When are you going to tell the other wraiths about the spell? Or is Lothaire taking care of that?"

"We're not going to tell them," Rem said.

Billy glanced between her and Corvus, unable to comprehend what he'd heard. "What if they want to stay behind too? Are you just going to let them suffer?"

"It's not that simple, Billy," Rem said. "They feel the compulsion even more strongly than we do. They want nothing more than to leave Earth and its cruelty behind and return to the one place they feel like they belong."

"The Gloaming."

"Right."

"Why do they feel the compulsion more strongly?"

"Because," Corvus said, wrinkling his nose, "their parents aren't oathbreakers like ours."

Despite Billy's earlier relief that his friends weren't leaving, a twinge of guilt entered his chest. His relationship with the wider wraith group had crumbled in the past few years, but most of them were good people. None of them deserved to suffer.

"You should tell them about it anyway," Billy said. "Even if their compulsions are stronger, there's a chance they can be saved, right? They should have the chance to make up their own minds. We have to do *something*."

"Like what?" Corvus asked. "It's not like there's anything we can say to convince them."

"Why? Because your parents are oathbreakers?"

"It's not just that," Rem said. "Corvus and I have had years to think about this decision. Most of them haven't even considered what they'd do if they had a choice."

"Especially since up until a few hours ago, there was no choice," Corvus added. "Going back to the Gloaming and rejoining wraith society? That's a major milestone to them, kinda like finishing school and getting a job is a milestone for humans. It's so deeply ingrained that no one considers there might be an alternative."

"We can't leave them to Grigoth," Billy argued.

"What do you suggest we do, then?" Corvus threw his hands in the air. "We can't change the entirety of wraith culture overnight. That kind of thing takes years. You'd know that if you paid attention in class instead of drooling over Shauna."

"We can still try to talk to them," Billy said, ignoring the barb. "We might not convince all of them, but we should at least try. If even one of them agrees to stay, that's one life saved."

"I know," Rem said. "I'd like to help them, but if one of them blabs to Grigoth, he'll view it as an act of open defiance and punish us more severely when he catches up with us."

"You really think he'd cross the portal to get you?" Billy asked.

Corvus released a pained chuckle. "Why not? He's gone after other wraiths, and there's nothing to stop him from doing it again. It's just a question of *when*. He doesn't even have to cross the portal if he doesn't want to. He could grab us when we visit the Gloaming instead."

"Maybe you should stop going there, then."

"We don't have much choice," Rem said. "The farther we are from the portal, the harder it is to tap into the flow of magic. If we want to cast powerful spells or make certain potions, we have to go there, and then we'll be sitting ducks."

"Do you have to use magic, though?" Billy asked. He shrank back from the horrified looks they gave him. "I mean, I know it's important to you, but if it would save your life—"

"Not using magic isn't an option," Corvus retorted. "How else are we supposed to get medical treatment if we're sick or hurt? Human medicines don't help us, and most of them make the problem worse. Can you imagine what would happen if we went to a hospital? Glamours are good disguises on the outside, but what if some doctor takes an x-ray and discovers our internal organs are completely different from a human's?"

Billy's stomach weakened. "Dissections?"

"Exactly."

"There's another reason as well," Rem said. "Our bodies are fueled by the same magic that formed the Gloaming. Whether we like it or not, we're part of the land, and the land is a part of us. Telling us not to use magic is like telling someone not to breathe. We don't always have control over our abilities."

"I didn't know that," Billy said. A slight frown twitched onto his face as he contemplated the problem. "That connection would explain the compulsion to return as well."

"Exactly," Corvus repeated. "If we betray Grigoth, all he has to do is plant a couple of his goons at the portal, and they'll catch us sooner or later."

The joyful balloon in Billy's chest deflated, and he slumped on the sofa, sinking into the beige upholstery. *Lothaire will keep them safe. Seisan too, if he's still alive. But if Grigoth is as powerful as they say he is, will it even matter?* Tears pricked his eyes as he imagined his friends being slaughtered in cold blood.

"Maybe you shouldn't tell the other wraiths about the spell, then. Keep a low profile instead. It's not worth risking your lives."

Rem straightened, her expression growing serious. "Actually, your first idea might have been right, Billy. I don't want to put myself in danger by telling them, but we're going to be in danger anyway. Since we can't avoid it, why not try to make things better for our fellow wraiths? That would be the honorable thing to do."

"Okay, but forget 'honorable' for a minute," Billy said. "Are you sure you want to do this? Corvus, what do you think?"

Corvus rocked back on the sofa, his eyes squeezed shut. A steady stream of air whistled free from his lips. "I don't like anything about this situation. I don't think there's anything *to* like about it. But Rem's right. It's better to try something than to do nothing."

Billy nodded, swallowing the lump in his throat. *If that's what they want...* "Is there anything I can do to help?"

"Actually, I think this is something we need to do on our own," Rem said, flashing him a regretful smile. "We appreciate the offer, though."

"What are you going to do?" Billy asked.

"The same thing everyone does when there's a problem to solve," Corvus declared, as if it were the most obvious thing in the world. "We're going to hold a meeting."

Chapter Thirty-One

HAMISH SLUMPED AGAINST Morton Elementary's retaining wall. Ashy dust crumbled from the cinder blocks, mingling with the dirt and blighted leaves below. The toe of his left sneaker tapped an abandoned soccer ball, nudging it forward and catching it when it rolled back down the gentle slope. A few silent minutes passed before Jarsha's dark mane came into view. The other boy favored him with a smile, and Hamish smiled back in spite of himself.

"Sorry I'm late," Jarsha said. "Mr. Sullivan made me redo all my work 'cause my handwriting was too messy."

"That sucks."

"Is Billy here yet?"

Hamish scuffed his shoe against the fallen leaves. "He's not coming. He shrugged me off before I got a chance to talk to him."

Jarsha's amethyst eyes hooded with disappointment. "Did you at least get the keycard?"

"Yeah, I've got it. Do you still want to break in?"

"We don't have much choice. Come on. The guards have gone home for the day."

They strolled across the grounds, past the empty classrooms and school buses. Unlike the surrounding structures, the science center glowed like a beacon. Fluorescent light spilled from every opening, beckoning them in. Jarsha went first, peering through the tinted window for any sign of dawdling scientists. Hamish followed close behind. His heart dropped when he saw the door handle. The locking mechanism required a regular key, not a keycard. One look at Jarsha told him the other boy had noticed the same thing. *The keycard must be for the lab itself.*

"Now what?" Jarsha murmured.

"*Hamish?*"

Hamish whirled around to see James's hazel eyes staring down at him. His brother wore baggy basketball shorts and a sweat-stained jersey, and his hair clung to his forehead in damp strings. A black-and-white duffel bag dangled from his shoulder.

"Hey, James," Hamish said, a hint of guilt creeping into his voice. *I forgot he was coming home today.*

"Why are you still at school?" James asked, turning his attention to the door. "Is there anything interesting in there?"

"Uh…"

Before Hamish could think up a plausible excuse, James spotted Jarsha for the first time. "You're hanging out with a *wraith*?"

"I…" Hamish's gaze shifted to Jarsha's mortified expression, then back to his brother. "Y-yes. He's my friend."

"If Dad knew—"

"I know," Hamish interrupted. "So don't tell him, okay?"

"All right. I won't tell him. But I think you should come home with me now."

James moved to grab Hamish's arm, but the younger boy pushed him away.

"I can't. Jarsha's friends are stuck in the lab, and they need our help."

"What do you mean, 'stuck'?"

"The scientists are holding them hostage," Jarsha explained. "They've been doing experiments on them and hurting them. We can't leave them here."

James sidled away from the wraith. "Is this like… a game?"

Hamish shook his head. "It's happening for real, and it's not the first time. They did the same thing a few years ago, and Billy helped the wraiths escape."

"I don't believe this. It's insane."

"Then help us and see for yourself," Hamish suggested.

James held his gaze, then turned and jostled the handle. The metallic rattle confirmed Hamish's suspicions.

"Looks like you're out of luck unless you know how to pick a lock," James said. "You'll have to try again tomorrow."

"We can't give up yet," Jarsha protested. "Maybe we can climb through a window or something."

James raised a sardonic eyebrow. "You think they're stupid enough to leave a window open?"

"One of the back windows is usually open for ventilation," Jarsha replied with a half-shrug.

He trotted around the corner of the building, and Hamish dashed after him. Sure enough, a boxy window sat ajar on the second story.

"There's no way we can reach that," James said, coming up behind them. "Let's just go home."

"I'm not giving up," Hamish retorted. He scanned the area for something to help them and pointed at a dumpster six feet away. "If we all push, I bet we could move that under the window and climb up."

"You're crazy," James said. "Those things are heavy."

"It's empty."

"That doesn't change the fact it's heavy. Besides, even if we could move it, we still won't be able to reach the window. It's too high."

"Not if you boost me on your shoulders. Come on, James! You're tall. We can do it. Me and Jarsha will go in first, and then we'll let you in through the door."

"What makes you think I want to go in?"

Hamish ignored him and joined Jarsha next to the dumpster. He pushed his palms flush against the cool metal, his biceps straining in anticipation. James sighed and wiped his hands on his shorts before helping them. The dumpster creaked and shuddered as the wheels engaged, allowing it to roll forward with ease.

"All right. That's good," Hamish said, stepping back to admire their handiwork. "I'll go first."

Without waiting for a response, he scrambled onto the dumpster. The plastic lid held his weight, but it sagged when he approached the center. *Please don't break.*

"Help me up, James," he ordered.

The taller boy placed both hands on the lid and swung the rest of his body onto the dumpster with enviable ease. Moving at a snail's pace, he got into position and knelt down. *One foot at a time.* Hamish stepped onto his brother's shoulders, leaning against the wall to keep his balance. James grabbed his ankles to help steady him. When he stood up, Hamish fought the urge to claw at the bricks.

"You're almost there!" Jarsha called from the ground. "Just a little farther."

Taking a deep breath, Hamish stretched his left arm skyward. The slight movement made his ankles wobble, and his feet skidded forward half an inch.

"Are you *trying* to fall off?" James demanded, tightening his grip.

Hamish didn't dignify him with a response. Instead, he resumed his attempt—more carefully this time—to reach the window. His fingertips slid through the gap with ease, and he wrenched the pane open. His shoulder ached from the effort. He risked a glance at the window. If he wanted to get in, he'd have to jump. His mom talked about leaps of faith all the time, but he doubted this was what she had in mind.

James cleared his throat. "Are you going to go inside *today*, or are you just going to kill my shoulders a while longer?"

Hamish shifted his weight, bending his knees as far as he dared. Then he launched himself into the air, scrabbling for purchase as the grooved metal frame dug into his forearms. The fingers on his left hand shot forward, grasping for the windowsill. Blessed relief surged through him when they reached their target.

James yelled something incomprehensible, and Hamish heard him dive out of the way of his flailing legs. He shimmied his way through the tiny gap, wincing as his belly scraped over the frame. Angry welts erupted under his shirt, but he ignored the pain and let himself drop to the floor. *I did it! I didn't die!*

He lay there for a moment, basking in his success. Then he remembered the reason for his unconventional entrance and sat up, rubbing his arms. Apart from the wooden beams festooned with cobwebs and the thin white mattresses of insulation, the crawlspace was empty. He squinted into the dingy light and spied the outline of a trapdoor that ought to lead to the lab below.

Hamish grinned. "Hey, James! Get Jarsha up here!"

Chapter Thirty-Two

THE UNNATURAL SILENCE in the Porter house persisted that afternoon. Billy crunched down a bag of potato chips, the tang of vinegar and rock salt lingering on his tongue. But filling his stomach did little to fill the hole in his heart. He shuffled to his room, his eyes widening when Corvus's glamour-clad form appeared in the doorway. *I thought he was at Rem's house.*

Corvus leaned against the jamb, arms folded across his chest. "We have a problem."

"I know. Things have been weird between us lately."

"I wasn't talking about *that*. I was talking about the scientists. They're back."

The world tilted around Billy. "What?"

"You heard me."

"Yeah, but…" Billy trailed off, trying to wrap his head around the news. "Have they grabbed anyone yet? Are they at our school?"

"Nope. Morton Elementary. Hamish ran in here half an hour ago and grabbed Dr. Stanford's keycard. He told me he needed it to help some people. It didn't take me long to put two and two together."

Billy squeezed past Corvus and yanked open his dresser drawer. The card wasn't where he left it. He pawed through his clothes, desperate to find it, but came up short.

A lump rose in his throat. "You should have stopped him."

He's gonna get caught. The scientists are gonna hurt him. Why didn't I get rid of that stupid card?

"He'll be fine," Corvus said. "Thirty minutes isn't that long. We can catch up to him in no time."

"If they did anything to him…"

Billy didn't dare to finish the thought. That would make it too real. He grabbed Corvus's wrist and plunged into a headlong sprint. His lungs burned cold, and puffs of white air escaped his lips with every breath.

"Why do they always… have to target… elementary kids?" he complained between gasps. "They should pick… on someone… their own size."

"Yeah, but the wraiths all leave during eighth grade," Corvus pointed out, tugging his wrist free. "There aren't as many of us. Plus, the elementary kids are less likely to fight back."

Billy felt like his insides were being turned inside out. The image of Hamish lying hurt in the lab superimposed over his memories of finding wraiths in the same position.

I can't think like that, he berated himself. *Hamish would fight back. I know he would. He wouldn't have taken the keycard otherwise.*

Despite his attempts at self-reassurance, every inch of him trembled with nervous energy. Mom would kill him if anything happened to his brother.

The two boys raced through the school gates, across the concrete courtyard, to the science center. A soft glow flickered in the windows, casting yellow threads against the darkening sky. Billy reached the door first. He flung it open and dashed inside, his shoes slapping the linoleum. Corvus's footsteps echoed after him. A tinted glass dome hovered above the entrance to the lab, emitting a tiny red beam. *Probably a security camera.*

Billy pushed the door open. "Hamish!"

A pale face streaked with dirt poked around the corner of an MRI machine, and then the rest of the boy's body came into view. Billy ran forward and enveloped his brother in a hug, inhaling the scent of sawdust from his clothes.

"You came," Hamish said. Surprise colored his voice.

"Of course I came," Billy replied, releasing him. "You should have told me what you were doing. I would have helped."

"I tried, but—"

"*Billy?*" James's voice cut through Hamish's, his eyes wide and incredulous.

Billy's mouth dropped open. "*James?* You're here too?"

The boy shrank back, shooting a nervous glance in Jarsha's direction. "What are you doing here?"

"Rescuing you, of course," Corvus replied on Billy's behalf. "Where are the wraiths?"

James and Jarsha blanched at his forwardness, but Hamish held no such reservations.

"We got three of them out, but Selby's locked in the boiler room," he said, pointing at a door ten feet in front of them.

Billy examined the plywood frame. *I could probably kick it open.* He closed the gap, calculating the angle of his attack. If TV had taught him anything, he needed to start from a standstill and aim near the lock. Screwing up his face, he lifted his knee as high as it would go and slammed his heel into the wood. The door flew open and hit the wall before swinging back to meet him. A large dent marked the point of contact.

"A little warning would have been nice," Corvus said. "What if Selby had been right behind the door and you kicked it in her face?"

I didn't think of that. "Sorry."

Billy squinted into the darkness. A pair of horizontal cylinders loomed against the back wall, dwarfing him by several feet.

A small body pushed past him. "Selby? Where are you? It's Jarsha. We're here to get you out."

A geyser of white steam erupted from a vent, and the dry air thickened into stifling humidity. Coughing, Billy tried to walk past it, but a second jet of steam blasted the exposed skin on his arm. He yelped and stumbled back, tears pricking his eyes. Someone grabbed his shirt and dragged him out into the lab. He flinched when they moved his injured arm under a faucet and again when cold water splashed onto the raw burn.

"Don't move," Corvus murmured, his breath tickling Billy's ear. His footsteps withdrew to the boiler room. "I'll help Jarsha with Selby. Everyone else—stay here."

Billy blinked and rubbed his eyes dry with his free hand. Even with the soothing balm of cool water, it felt like something wanted to burst out of his skin. He shifted his weight sideways and craned his neck to get a better view of the empty door frame. A strangled scream emanated from inside, and Corvus and Jarsha reappeared. A wraith girl leaned on their shoulders, her skin blistered violet and covered in oozing pustules.

Her pain-dulled eyes fluttered to the door, and she took a few tottering steps toward it. Then she pitched forward and lay still. Hamish darted over to help, but James froze to the spot. His gaze drifted from Billy's face to Selby's prostrate form, as though he couldn't decide where his loyalty ought to lie.

The wraith girl stirred, her labored breaths rattling through the lab.

"I can walk by myself," she slurred. "Please… don't touch me. Hurts."

"Okay," Corvus said, holding his hands up to show he meant no harm. "We won't touch you. But we have to get out of here, okay?"

Selby forced herself into a sitting position. "Okay. Just… give me a minute."

Several minutes passed before she managed to get her legs under her, but no one had the heart to hurry her up.

"Where did you take the other wraiths?" Billy asked when she found her feet.

"They went to the office," Jarsha explained. "We're going to take Selby there as well."

"Don't bother," Corvus said. "She needs potions, not human medicine. I know someone who can help. We should take her there now."

Jarsha hesitated, looking to Billy for reassurance. Billy dipped his head in an almost imperceptible nod, and the young wraith returned the gesture. "Okay. Thanks."

He and Hamish guided Selby outside, their arms hovering above her blistered shoulders.

Corvus cast a sideways glance at Billy. "Are you going to be okay?"

"Of course. It's just a little burn. It's starting to feel better already."

Corvus snorted, unconvinced. "Little or not, you need to stay there for another ten minutes, minimum. James, watch him."

He disappeared around the corner, leaving Billy alone with his middle sibling. James detached himself from the wall and ambled over to join him. Under the bright lights, his limbs seemed ganglier than usual.

"Do you need me to get you anything?" James asked.

"Nah, I'm good."

Silence reigned for a while, then James cleared his throat. "How does Corey know someone who can help the wraiths?"

Billy's spine prickled. *Corvus almost gave himself away.*

"I'm not sure," he stalled. "What made you want to break into this place, anyway? I thought you hated wraiths."

Now it was James's turn to fidget. "I don't hate them. I'd just rather be around humans. Hamish roped me into helping him. He said these wraiths were his friends."

The knowledge that his youngest brother had befriended not one, but multiple wraiths surprised Billy. *He clings to every word Dad says. Who would have guessed* Hamish *would rebel?*

"What are we going to do after this?" James asked.

Billy blinked away his thoughts. "Hmm?"

"Do we report what happened?"

"Yeah, but not to the principal. He's useless."

James nodded and dropped his gaze to the floor. "You've done this before, haven't you?"

"How did you know?"

"Hamish told me."

Billy studied his expression for any trace of anger but found none.

"Yeah. The same scientists were here about three years ago. I gave Mr. Matlin proof of how evil they are, and he did nothing."

"But you helped the wraiths escape?"

"Yes."

The tension in James's shoulders dissipated. "Okay. So going to the principal is out. What *are* we going to do?"

Billy glanced around the lab. "We're going to collect evidence and go to the police. Do you want to help with that?"

"Me?"

"I'm not supposed to move from the sink. It would save us a lot of time if you grabbed all the papers and put them in your bag."

"I guess I could do that."

Billy watched him work with a sense of déjà vu. The last time he set foot in this lab, he'd done more than pilfer paperwork—he'd destroyed everything in sight. Part of him wanted to ask James to do that too, but he held his tongue. Talking his brother into an act of vandalism would do more harm than good. *Especially with all the cameras around.*

"Has it been ten minutes yet?" Billy asked when James returned to him.

The tall boy glanced at his watch. "Close enough. You can take your arm out of the water now."

Billy turned off the tap and toweled himself dry with the hem of his shirt. The worst of the pain had passed, but the pinching, crawling sensation remained.

"How does it look?" James asked.

An image of Selby flashed through Billy's mind. "It could be worse. The skin's just a little pink."

"You'll be all right, then. Mom's got some burn cream at home if you're worried about it."

"I'm not."

Billy's gaze landed on the security camera. A thin black wire ran along the crown moldings, dark enough to blend into the wood. He strolled over, tugged it loose, and followed it to the end.

"What are you doing?" James asked.

"Getting evidence," Billy said. The wire led to a wall-mounted box, which he opened to reveal a hard-drive. *Too easy.* "If the paperwork isn't enough to convict the scientists, the video footage should be. My friend at the police department would be very interested to see this."

He grabbed James's duffel bag and shoved the hard-drive inside. A sliver of guilt passed through him, but he ignored it. Theft was a much smaller crime than torture and murder, especially when said theft had the potential to save multiple lives. The kids who went to school here deserved to feel safe.

"You should go home, James," Billy said, clapping his brother on the shoulder. "Thanks for your help."

"Are you sure you don't want me to come with you?"

If a wraith as tiny as Jarsha had freaked James out, meeting Lothaire would make his head explode. "I'm sure."

"All right. See you at home."

James turned and strolled out the door, whistling a tuneless song. Billy followed suit a few minutes later. He'd never seen Morton Elementary under its twilight veil before, looking more like a ghost town than a school. *If I never see this place again, it will be too soon.* He jogged out of the gates, James's bag slung around his shoulders. It crashed into his thighs with every step, but he didn't mind. Anything to get away from that place.

He reached the police station ten minutes later. To his relief, Lothaire's face popped up behind the counter. The wraith's expression brightened when he saw him.

"Billy Porter! How can I help you today?"

"Do you remember how those scientists were hanging around Morton Elementary a few years ago?" Billy asked in a rush.

"Yeah, I remember."

"Well, they came back and kidnapped four more wraiths."

Lothaire leapt to his feet. "No time to waste, then. Are they still in the science center?"

"They were, but we managed to free them," Billy said. "Corvus implied he was going to bring them to your house, so Rem is probably looking after them right now."

"Right. Of course." Lothaire grabbed his keys and headed for the door. "I'm sure she's doing an excellent job in my absence, but a second pair of eyes wouldn't go amiss."

"You aren't mad at us for breaking in?"

"For the sake of saving their lives? Never."

"Seisan would have been. He said it was important that we didn't rock the boat."

"Perhaps, but Seisan isn't here. Wraiths are walking around Japan in broad daylight. The whole world knows of our existence now. The time for caution has passed."

"I saw those wraiths on the news. Where did they come from, anyway?"

Lothaire frowned and grabbed Billy's wrist, his eyes clouded with concern. "What happened to your arm?"

Billy glanced at the raised patch of skin. "Nothing. It got blasted by steam from the boiler room."

"While you were rescuing the kidnapped wraiths?"

"Yeah."

"Did anyone else get hurt while you were rescuing them?"

"Nah, just me. Everyone else avoided the steam."

"That's something to be thankful for," Lothaire said. He ran a glowing hand over Billy's arm, and the tight sensation disappeared. "There. Basic pain-killing spell. It's too risky for me to heal you with magic, but I can give you a potion when we get back to the house."

"Thanks, Lothaire."

"No problem."

The wraith opened the door, gesturing for him to go first, but Billy held his ground. "I need to give you something before we go."

"Oh? What's that?"

"Evidence of what the scientists have been doing. It should be enough to get rid of them for good if the right people get their hands on it."

Lothaire hesitated. "What kind of evidence?"

"Paperwork for all their experiments and security footage from the lab itself."

Lothaire closed the door and returned to his desk. "Show me."

Billy opened the duffel bag and unloaded the papers. The hard-drive crowned the pile, its black wires dangling out like entrails. Handing it over made him uneasy. He couldn't be sure it contained footage of the atrocities that took place in the lab. For all he knew, the hard-drive wiped itself clean, or the scientists turned it off before they started their experiments. As if reading his mind, Lothaire picked it up and plugged it in. A few minutes passed before his eyes widened and he turned off the monitor.

"You did the right thing in bringing this to me," Lothaire said. He tucked the evidence into his personal safe and locked it with a resounding click. "I've got friends in Washington who can turn the scientists' operation upside down. I'll make sure they get their hands on it as soon as possible."

Palpable relief flooded Billy's body. "Thank you."

"No need to thank me. You're the one who saved those kids." Lothaire stood again and returned to the door. "Come on, buddy. We've got some wraiths to heal."

Chapter Thirty-Three

THE HUBBUB STRETCHED across the entirety of Morton Junior High on Friday morning. Police cars circled the neighboring elementary school like vultures waiting for a dying animal to breathe its last. Whispered rumors in quiet classrooms became vibrating text messages, and sooner or later, everyone in the school became a self-appointed expert on the situation.

Some believed the police had been called to contain a first-grade riot. Others suggested a teacher had lost the plot and started throwing chairs at students. That, of all the explanations, was the closest to being correct.

Billy resisted the urge to join in with his peers' restless chatter, but he couldn't help glancing at Corvus and Rem every now and then. Each time, the wraiths dipped their heads forward to acknowledge him. They were the only ones who knew the true origins of the chaos outside. Mrs. Carter strolled into the room, barking at everyone to get on with their work, but her words were lost on the antsy teenagers.

After ten minutes, two policemen exited Morton Elementary School, escorting a red-faced Mr. Matlin by the sleeves of his sports jacket. Matted hair clung to the principal's scalp, the looser strands flopping back and forth due to the force with which they dragged him. He lost his footing several feet from the waiting patrol car, but the officers didn't slow down. They shoved him into the back seat and drove off in a cloud of smoke, unaware of the spectacle they'd created.

"Who was that?" someone asked.

"Was that Mr. Matlin?"

"It couldn't be!"

"But it looked like him."

Another ripple of excitement passed through the classroom, and Mrs. Carter joined them at the window to get a better look. A righteous smile tugged at Billy's lips. *Justice.*

"So he actually got arrested?" Hamish asked, his eyes as round and shiny as CDs.

Billy nodded, pointing to the spot where Mr. Matlin's unceremonious departure took place. "See those track marks? I reckon they're from his shoes when they dragged him out. It probably ripped the leather right off."

Jarsha whistled. "They must have been pretty mad at him."

"Yeah, and for good reason," Billy said. "He was putting you guys in danger."

He turned away to examine the concrete some more, but not far enough away that he missed Jarsha's shiver of apprehension. Not for the first time, he felt a surge of protectiveness toward the younger wraith. *From the rescued to the rescuer. He's a good kid.*

"I wish I'd seen it happen," Hamish said. "We got locked in our classrooms 'til recess, and they pulled all the blinds down."

Billy glanced at his own school. The second-story windows glinted above the shared science center, overlooking Morton Elementary.

"We saw it, but it wasn't that exciting." *Lie.* "What's really exciting is that the scientists are gone for good."

"Did they get arrested too?" Hamish asked.

The hopeful gleam in his eyes crushed Billy's heart. "Not yet, but they lost their licenses and permits. There's going to be a big investigation too, to make sure nothing like this happens again. They'll probably get arrested later."

"They should get arrested now," Jarsha said. "They're the ones who tortured us, not Mr. Matlin. They should get a worse punishment than him."

"I agree," Billy said, "but at least you guys are safe. That's the main thing."

Jarsha pinched his lips into a thin line, but he didn't argue the point.

The three boys walked to the park by unspoken agreement and headed for the swings. Most kids avoided the playground. The low-hanging trees rained leaves, bugs, and other debris on them, and the slide bowed and buckled under the weight of even the smallest child. Billy didn't mind putting up with those things. The absence of other kids meant they were less likely to be disturbed.

"So… Jarsha," he said, lowering himself onto the nearest swing. "Do you know any magic?"

The wraith boy shrugged and leaned against a wooden climbing frame. It creaked but held firm. "Not really."

"You've got your music magic," Hamish piped up.

Jarsha's cheeks purpled. "Yeah, but that's not much use, is it? I can't use music magic to help anyone."

"You can make people happy with it."

"That's true."

"I've never heard of music magic before," Billy admitted. "It sounds pretty cool, though. Hey—that was a pun. *Sounds* cool. Get it?"

The younger boys giggled and shook their heads in disapproval.

Billy's mirth subsided soon after. "If you want to learn some real magic, I might know someone who can teach you."

He didn't want to divulge his friends' identities, but he had no doubt they'd be willing to help. With an inter-dimensional war on the horizon, neither Corvus nor Rem would turn down a potential ally. Jarsha stood there for a full minute, considering the proposal.

"I don't know," he said at last. "I've been living with Gran for years. I feel more like a human than a wraith most days. I'm not sure I can go back."

"They'll accept you the way you are," Billy said, not understanding Jarsha's reluctance. "One of them acts a bit grumpy sometimes, but he's a big softie on the inside. You'll get on great."

"No," Jarsha said. "I mean, I don't think I *want* to learn other magic. It's too dangerous."

"Not all magic is dangerous," Billy said. "You could stick to healing spells and potions if you wanted to."

"I don't want to learn that either. Not yet."

"If he doesn't want to, then he doesn't want to," Hamish said, shooting Billy a dirty look.

"I know," Billy retorted, then turned to the wraith. "Sorry, Jarsha. I'm not trying to push you into anything. You can do whatever you want."

The wraith boy averted his gaze. "I know. I just don't think I'm cut out for that stuff. Maybe I'll change my mind when I get older, but it's too scary at the moment. I only want to do music magic."

Billy released a pent-up breath and nodded his acceptance. After the boy's dazzling bravery the previous day, he'd forgotten Jarsha was five years younger than him—far too young to be roped into a war. He deserved a chance at a normal childhood.

A light breeze tousled Billy's hair, and he threw his head back to look at the sky. Glimpses of blue confetti poked out amidst the explosion of green foliage.

I'm going to be here with Shauna tomorrow, he thought, allowing his mind to drift from the boys next to him. Of all the things he'd been through that week, the idea of going on a date seemed the most ludicrous. And yet… *it's going to happen. It's finally going to happen.* It amazed him how quickly the day had crept up on him. He hadn't checked ice cream prices. He hadn't booked advance movie tickets. He hadn't even talked to Murdock's buddy about rigging the claw machine.

"Earth to Billy!" Hamish shouted, startling him out of his daydream.

"Huh?"

"Me and Jarsha are going home. Are you coming?"

"Nah. I'm going to hang out here for a bit," Billy said, gesturing for them to go ahead. "See you later."

The two boys wandered off without a backward glance, chatting in muted tones. Billy waited until they disappeared from view before he made his move.

First stop, the ice cream truck.

Chapter Thirty-Four

BILLY RUMMAGED THROUGH his dresser drawer, flinging old band T-shirts left and right over his shoulder. They tumbled to the floor in a series of soft thumps, blocking out the sound of Corvus's pencil. In a matter of minutes, he'd emptied his drawer save for two button-down shirts and a pair of ripped jeans.

White shirt or blue? Wait, would a shirt be too formal? Should I go for a band tee instead? We're going to a park, after all. But what bands does Shauna like? I don't want to scare her off. Maybe I have a plain T-shirt somewhere? No, no, that's no good. I should wear a casual check shirt, like the day she agreed to go out with me. Would wearing the same thing be weird, though? Maybe I should wear a different check shirt. No, that won't work either. They're all sitting at the bottom of the washing pile. I'll never be able to get them ready in time.

"What should I wear?" Billy asked the wall of his room.

Unsurprisingly, the wall didn't respond. He turned to ask Corvus, but a steely glint filled the other boy's eyes.

"I've told you once, and I'll tell you again. *I don't care.*"

"Figures," Billy muttered, crouching down to sift through the discarded shirts.

Despite Rem's reluctant acceptance of the situation, Corvus's views hadn't changed. Billy couldn't count on his help for anything related to Shauna.

He peeled a Guns 'n' Roses muscle tank from the pile and tossed it to the side. A flash of blue surfaced in the sea of black garments, and he scooped it out. It unfurled to reveal a long-sleeved raglan shirt. Mrs. Porter had bought it for him before his first school camp, but Billy had never worn it. He scurried to the bathroom and held the shirt against his torso, trying to determine if it "brought out his eyes" the way his mother claimed it would.

Shauna will probably like this, he decided.

He hurried back to his room and draped the shirt over his bed, along with the jeans from his dresser. Outfit chosen, he set to work cleaning up the disaster zone he'd created on the floor. Corvus never looked in his direction, but the intensity of his expression made Billy uncomfortable nonetheless.

He slammed the dresser drawer shut. "I'm gonna go have a shower."

"You've already had one," Corvus said.

"It couldn't hurt to have another."

"For crying out loud, Billy, you don't need another shower. You spent so long in there that there was no hot water left for me."

Billy considered making a snide remark about the water always being cold but held his tongue.

"I suppose you're right," he conceded. "What are you up to? Still talking to Rem?"

After their argument a few days ago, Billy had left his magic notebook on Corvus's pillow as a gesture of contrition. The other boy accepted his pseudo-apology, but the strain between them persisted. Corvus ignored him as often as possible, choosing instead to write notes to Rem. *Back to being the third wheel, I guess.*

"We're making plans for the meeting," Corvus said, shifting the notebook to a more comfortable position.

"Have you decided when it's going to happen?"

"First thing tomorrow morning. And before you ask, no. You can't come."

"I wasn't going to ask that," Billy said, frowning. "Why tomorrow morning, though? Why not do it today and give them more time to change their minds?"

"Because, Billy, your charming father is dragging me along on a hiking trip in an hour's time. Unless Rem wants to talk to the wraiths alone, which she doesn't, there's no way for us to visit them today."

"Oh."

"I don't see you volunteering to help her either."

"You literally just told me I couldn't."

"I know! But would it kill you to offer?" Fire burned in Corvus's eyes, stronger than Billy had ever seen it. "Go on your stupid date. I hope you get everything you deserve."

Billy fled to the bathroom with the clothes he'd picked out. Corvus's behavior made sense, given the enormity of what he and Rem were trying to accomplish. Even so, Billy wished his old friend would come back. *I hope you get everything you deserve. Is that some kind of threat?*

He got changed quickly, trying to shove the words out of his mind. There was nothing he could say to mollify his best friend. Nothing he could do to repair the situation until evening. With that in mind, he brushed his teeth and combed his hair flat. A generous spray of deodorant completed his routine.

He scurried through the lounge, mumbling goodbyes to his parents, and exited the house. The winter sun beat down on his back as he made his way to the park, warming him in spite of the crisp morning air. *I won't let Corvus get me down. I'm going to enjoy my time with Shauna while it lasts, and that's that.*

"Billy!"

Shauna's mellifluous voice floated toward him as he entered the park. She stood under a lightweight shade umbrella, waving one arm above her head to get his attention. The bodice of an emerald-green sundress hugged her curves, cinched at the waist with a black bow. A roseate blush suffused her cheeks. *She's just as nervous as I am.*

"Have you been waiting long?" he asked when he reached her.

"Only a couple of minutes."

"The ice cream truck should be open by now. Do you want to go and get some?"

She slipped her hand into his. "I'd love to."

Billy's heart raced a mile a minute as they set out for the truck. He'd never had a girlfriend before—never so much as a date. And now here he was, holding hands with the most beautiful girl in their grade. Her fingers were smooth and cool against his, exerting a gentle pressure that made his breakfast somersault in his stomach. He swallowed hard.

"What's your favorite type of ice cream?" Shauna asked as they walked.

Billy thought for a moment. "Probably mint chocolate chip or cookies and cream. What about you?"

"Plain chocolate or vanilla. Cookies and cream is pretty good too, but I can't stand anything mint flavored."

"Fair enough. We have chocolate ice cream all the time at home. It's my little brother's favorite."

Despite the morning heat, no crowds formed around the ice cream truck. Behind the counter, a mustachioed man adjusted the straps of his apron.

"What can I get you kids?" he asked.

Billy ordered for both of them—one chocolate cone for Shauna, one cookies-and-cream cone for himself—and dropped a handful of loose change on the counter. The ice cream man took it and scooped their desired flavors into waffle cones.

"Can I have cherry syrup on mine?" Shauna asked.

Billy dropped her hand and fumbled for his wallet. He'd have to pay with one of the larger bills he'd been saving for their trip to the movie theater, but if he did that, he wouldn't have enough money for tickets. *Why didn't I bring extra? I should have planned for this!*

The ice cream man must have seen the panic on his face because he held up a hand. "Don't worry, kid. The syrup's on the house."

Billy's fear deflated, and he stopped his mad search for money. Twenty cents didn't make much difference to the man, but it meant the world to Billy.

"Thank you, sir," he said, accepting his cone with a bright smile.

"No problem. You two have fun now."

"We should sit down somewhere in the shade," Shauna suggested when they resumed walking. "It's pretty hot out today."

"It sure is. Hard to believe it's winter."

The mention of unseasonable temperatures reminded Billy of his wraith friends and the weather magic Lothaire once wrought to keep them safe. Were they responsible for the sudden change? Or was it global warming, like old Mr. Graham used to say?

"Are we really talking about the weather?" Shauna asked, giving him a disbelieving glance.

They looked at each other for a few seconds, then burst out laughing. In that moment, their awkwardness faded, and they were just Billy and Shauna from eighth-grade English again.

"Come on. I know a spot we can go," Billy said, gesturing toward a copse of trees. "There's a covered playground over there. We could sit on the swings or something."

"Sounds good to me," Shauna said, letting him lead the way.

Water pooled in the rubber swing seats, too thick to be the result of morning dew. They hadn't been wet the previous day, so Billy figured it must have rained overnight.

"I can dry them with my shirt if you want," he offered.

He didn't want to reveal his undefined abs if he could help it, but he'd rather embarrass himself than let her sit on a damp seat.

"It's all right. I can do it with my scarf." She rummaged through her handbag and pulled out the garment in question. "You shouldn't have to walk around with a wet shirt."

"But... but your scarf," Billy stammered.

"It's only water. It'll dry out. Besides, it's not like I'm going to wear it today. It's way too hot for that."

Before he could argue, she bunched the floral fabric into a ball and wiped it across the seat of the swing. To Billy's surprise, it absorbed most of the water in one go. When both seats were clear, she squeezed the excess liquid from her scarf and hung it over the frame to dry. Billy waited for her to sit down before doing so himself.

"So," he said, casting about for a topic of conversation. "What do you like to do for fun?"

"The usual stuff. Shopping, hanging out with friends, watching movies. Sometimes I play board games with my siblings too."

"How many siblings do you have?"

"Three. An older brother and two younger sisters. They turned six last week."

"Twins?"

"Yeah."

"That's cool."

"You said you had a brother earlier," Shauna said. "How old is he?"

"I've got two brothers, actually. The one I told you about earlier, the one who likes chocolate ice cream, is eight. His name's Hamish. Then there's James. He's eleven, but he's taller than me."

"That's really neat. Do you get on well with them?"

"I guess. We don't hang out that often, but we have fun when we do. What about you?"

"Most of the time. Are you fighting with James at the moment, by any chance?"

"No, why?"

"I don't know. I saw you dragging a random guy out of your house the other day. I thought he might be your brother."

She's talking about Corvus! Billy thought, panic rising in his chest. *Calm down, Billy. She doesn't know anything about his glamour. It's an innocent question.*

"Oh, that's not James," he said, clearing his throat. "How do you know where my house is, anyway?"

"It's a small town, Billy. Everyone knows where everyone lives."

"I don't."

"Maybe if you got out more, you would," Shauna teased, giving him a gentle punch with her free hand. "I can help you with that."

Billy smiled at her. "I'd like that."

Having finished their ice creams, they rocked back and forth on the swings, skimming their feet over the dusty leaf litter.

"So who was that guy? A friend of yours?" Shauna asked.

She doesn't know anything. Be cool, Billy.

"It's complicated," he said, doing his best to look noncommittal. "My parents are fostering a teenager from another town. He's been kicked out of a lot of schools, so he has to be homeschooled. I wouldn't say we're friends yet."

"Oh, wow. Okay." Shauna mulled over his words. "Your parents must be pretty cool to help him out. How old is he? I'd like to meet him one day. And the rest of your family too, of course."

Billy nearly choked. *Corvus is going to love that.* "He's about our age. He's been through a lot, though. I don't think he'd be up to having visitors any time soon."

"That's okay," Shauna said, reaching out and squeezing his shoulder. "As long as I get to hang out with you, that's all that matters. Maybe our younger siblings can play together some time."

"Maybe," Billy echoed. *Is she using me to get close to Corvus? Does she suspect something or is she just curious? Wait, she wants to meet my family! Isn't that a bit sudden? Aren't you supposed to date for a few months before doing that?*

His racing thoughts distracted him from the procession approaching the playground. A cluster of wraith children, no older than five or six, raced toward the jungle gym. Their shoes squeaked against the wooden climbing frame, jolting him back to the present.

"Not again," Shauna muttered.

"What's up?"

"What do you *think* is up? Those little freaks are hanging around, that's what's up!"

"Keep your voice down," Billy hissed.

One by one, the wraith children stopped what they were doing to stare at her. Hurt filled their purple eyes.

"Don't tell me you like wraiths after all, Billy," Shauna said. "They're unnatural. They're polluting the playground with their filth. No wonder none of the real children want to play here."

"Shauna, they're just kids," Billy pleaded. "Let them play. It's not a big deal."

"They should go and play in Oilskin Lake, where they belong. Maybe we'll get lucky and they'll drown."

Billy's mouth dropped open. "Can you hear yourself right now? I don't care if you hate the older wraiths"—*lie*—"but you can't take it out on *kids*. I mean, look at them."

"I *am* looking at them, and I see nothing but disgusting, diseased freaks. They're no different than the ones at school."

"How would you feel if someone said that about the twins?" Billy persisted. *I can change her. I'll prove to Corvus that I can change her.*

"That's completely different."

"No, it isn't."

"Well, I guess I'd tell them to visit an optometrist to get their vision checked." Shauna stood up and grabbed her scarf. "Come on, Billy. I don't want to be around those *things* any longer."

She stalked off and Billy trailed after her, shooting the kids sympathetic looks. Their shoulders slumped as though all the joy had been punched out of them. *I don't think I can do this anymore.*

"What movie did you want to watch?" Shauna asked, turning to look at him. "I heard there's a new one about a girl living in a time loop."

"I don't think that one's out in Morton yet," Billy mumbled. *I've got to get away from her.*

"Oh well, I'm sure there'll be something else good," Shauna said. Her fingers snaked through his, and he fought back a shiver of revulsion. "They show those artsy French films sometimes. We could watch one of those and pretend we're really posh."

Shauna pulled Billy after her, chattering a monologue as they walked. Her voice drove nails into his brain. Part of him wanted to drop her hand and sprint to freedom, but something kept his palm glued to hers and his legs wobbling in the right direction.

"Hey, are you okay, Billy?" Shauna asked.

He realized he was all but crushing her hand and relaxed his grip. "Sorry. I was just thinking."

"About what?"

"It doesn't matter."

Shauna's barrage of small talk resumed, but Billy didn't listen. Apart from the occasional "uh-huh" to feign interest, he might as well have been a million miles away. *Corvus was right. Some people don't change, no matter what we do. They have to* want *to change, and Shauna doesn't. Maybe she never will.*

An agonizing ten minutes passed before they arrived at the movie theater. The scent of warm, buttery popcorn wafted over Billy as they entered the concession area. The line of patrons extended ten feet from the ticket stand, and an even longer line formed in front of the slush machine. Parents dug through their wallets for spare change while their children hollered and slammed their tiny fists on arcade cabinets.

"Looks like we're in for a long wait," Shauna said. "Do you want to sit down for a while?"

Billy ignored her and scanned the crowd, hoping to find the worker he'd bribed the previous day. Winning Shauna a stuffed animal wasn't high on his priority list, but he'd already spent five dollars to rig the claw machine. *Maybe I can win something for Hamish instead. Or Corvus.* After a few minutes, he spotted his target at the concession stand. The man's eyes lit up when he saw Billy, and he reached for something under the desk.

"I'm going to try my luck on a game or two," Billy told Shauna.

He pulled his hand free from hers, relieved when she let go, and walked to the theater's main claw machine. LED lights illuminated the glass case, casting yellow orbs over the stuffed animals. Billy dug a quarter out of his pocket and shoved it in the coin slot, where it tinkled down to meet its predecessors. Electronic music chirped from the speakers, and the lights flashed in a dizzying array of colors.

His gaze fell on the largest toy—a russet-brown bear with scruffy fur. He slid the joystick forward, and the claw jerked into motion. *Careful…careful… a little more…* He hit the Grab button, and the claw descended, closing around the bear's leg. He may have paid to win, but watching the bear drop into the prize slot made his heart leap with excitement. *No wonder people get addicted to these things.*

"Billy, you did it!" Shauna exclaimed, clutching his arm. "I've never seen anyone win on this thing before."

He winced at the physical contact and bent down to grab his prize. "Yeah, well. Beginner's luck."

She let go of him and grabbed the bear instead, hugging it to her chest. "It's the cutest thing I've ever seen. Apart from you, of course."

Billy kept his gaze fixed on the ground.

"Do you want to keep it, or can I have it?" Shauna asked.

"I was going to keep it," Billy said. But out of the corner of his eye, he thought he saw her lower lip tremble. *It's only a teddy bear. It doesn't matter.* "You can have it if you really want it, though."

Shauna's face lit up. "Thanks, Billy! I'll hug it every day and think of you."

Please don't.

She set the bear on the floor and wrapped her arms around him. He felt her head tilting toward his before he saw her move. Despite himself, he closed his eyes and prepared for impact. A kiss was a kiss. What did it matter if his first one came from a girl who turned into a metaphorical ogre when wraiths were around? She was pretty and popular. Kissing her would make him a legend at school. But as their lips came within millimeters of brushing each other, the memory of her callous behavior made him jerk back.

"What's the matter?" Shauna asked. "Are you nervous? That's so cute."

She tried to lean in again, but Billy held her at arm's length. Her hurt expression mirrored the wraith children's, but he couldn't bring himself to care.

"I'd rather kiss a rotting cactus than a nutcase like you," he snarled. A hush fell over the other patrons, and a hundred eyes turned to watch the scene unfold. "You're the only freak in this town, Shauna. Okay? It's all you. And that's never going to change."

She took a step back. "*Excuse* me?"

"You heard what I said." Billy bent down and snatched the bear off the ground. "Now get out of my way."

Shauna released him and took a step back, her green eyes swimming with tears. She opened her mouth as if to say something, then turned and fled for the bathroom.

Chapter Thirty-Five

CORVUS TRUDGED ALONG the dirt path, dragging his feet through the leaf litter. His sneaker caught on a twig and snapped it in half. He stumbled forward, cursing his clumsiness, and hurried after Mr. Porter. *Stupid Billy. He promised I wouldn't have to do these walks, and now look. I'm stuck in the wilderness with his dad, wasting what might be my last weekend on Earth. I should be talking to the other wraiths!*

He jogged up the hill, his muscles and tendons straining against the glamour. It was a minor miracle he hadn't ripped the magical garment over the past three years. Unlike his non-magical clothes, he hadn't outgrown it either. Somehow, it always fit him like a glove.

"Are we there yet?" he wheezed, knowing full well they had another mile to cover.

"Not yet," Mr. Porter replied. He looked back at his young charge, his eyebrows quirking upward. "You ain't getting tired *already,* are you?"

"Not really," Corvus lied. "Just hungry."

Mr. Porter's face relaxed. "'Course you are. You're a growing boy. I've got a whole pack of hotdogs with your name on it for when we get up there."

He clapped Corvus on the shoulder, and the boy winced internally. "That sounds great, Mr. Porter."

"Come on, Corey. You've been living with us long enough to call me Jerry, or Uncle Jerry. Maybe even 'Dad'?"

His beady eyes fixed on Corvus, whose chest tightened.

"You're not my dad," he blurted out. *My dad is a million times braver than you'll ever be.*

Mr. Porter's shoulders dropped half an inch. "Yeah. 'Course I'm not. I wasn't trying to offend you. I just thought… you know… if you *wanted* to. I didn't mean nothing by it."

"It's okay. I know you didn't mean it."

He meant it, all right. But he'll never be my dad.

They continued along the path in silence. A young couple skipped past them, holding hands, and he scowled at their doe-eyed adoration for each other. Wraiths never engaged in such vomit-inducing displays of open affection. Seeing the couple reminded him of Billy and Shauna, and his heartbeat skittered to a halt.

When it returned, blood pounded in his ears, blocking out the sounds of the forest. *Why did Billy have to fall in love with a hag like Shauna?* The girl had a decent face—for a human, anyway—but looks weren't everything. He couldn't understand how anyone could be enamored with someone so horrible. Why would Billy choose her over him and Rem? Did they mean nothing to him?

Humans are so stupid, Corvus thought. He considered sharing his observation with Mr. Porter, but he knew he'd get no sympathy there.

They reached the top of the canyon twenty minutes later. A vista of rolling hills and dark valleys swept across his field of vision, watched over by a cloudless sky. Corvus threw his bag to the ground and collapsed on a half-rotted log. Mr. Porter crouched a few feet in front of him.

"Ever started a fire before, Corey?"

Of course I have. "No."

"Well, it's real simple if you've got the right tools. See this piece of flint here? All you need to do is strike the edge…"

Corvus zoned out. If he wanted to start a fire, he'd cast the appropriate spell. No need for friction and heat and all the rest of that nonsense.

A tiny orange flame flared to life, wavering at first, and then growing stronger as it caught hold of the kindling. A rogue breeze reduced the fire to a smoldering nest, and Corvus automatically reached for the flow of magic. He wasn't supposed to cast spells without supervision, but quite frankly, the man's incompetence pained him. Besides, he was hungry, and lunch wasn't going to cook itself.

A flicker of electricity rippled under his skin, but it wriggled away when he tried to grasp it. He'd traveled too far from the portal to use magic. *Alone with a crazy person and no way of defending myself. Great.*

Oblivious to his foster son's predicament, Mr. Porter got the fire going and settled down on the neighboring log. It creaked under his weight and again when he fished out a pack of greasy, pale hotdogs. Corvus's stomach gurgled in either hunger or disgust; he couldn't tell which.

While Mr. Porter ripped open the plastic, Corvus studied the other groups who shared the peak with them. The first group contained five or six British tourists in their early twenties, all of whom were taking photos of the view. One of them carried a thermos with "Tea" stenciled on the side in gold letters. Judging by the way he staggered around, the contents did not match the label.

The other two groups were smaller. A family with two-point-five kids—the point-five being a Bichon Frise in a pink sweater—occupied one of the picnic tables. On the other side of the peak, a young couple sat on the safety barrier, their legs dangling over the edge. *Another accident waiting to happen. I bet they'd get offended if I warned them, though.*

"Grab a hotdog, Corey," Mr. Porter prompted, offering him the open packet and a long greenwood stick.

Corvus took the stick and skewered the nearest hotdog. Pale brown liquid dripped from it as he moved it over the flame. Mr. Porter copied his motion and placed the pack where they could both reach it. After a few minutes, black streaks formed on the meat and clear juices bubbled over the surface. Corvus examined his hotdog, nose wrinkling, and sank his teeth into it.

The bland meat went down easily, but the rubbery skin peeled away and stuck to the roof of his mouth. He poked at it with his tongue until it, too, surfed the oil slick down his throat. His stomach gurgled, louder this time, and he forced himself to take another bite.

"So, how've you been doing lately?" Mr. Porter asked.

"Fine, I guess."

"That's good. And your dad? Did he say anything interesting in his letter?"

Corvus choked on his hotdog. Eyes smarting, he grabbed his bottle and gulped water until the blockage went away. *Why does everyone assume the letter's from Dad?*

"Not really," Corvus lied. "He's just been busy with fighting and stuff."

"Yeah, well, war is like that. I bet he would have written sooner if he could. He probably misses you something fierce—at least as much as you miss him."

Debatable. Corvus kept chewing, avoiding his foster father's eyes. The silence stretched out between them.

Mr. Porter cleared his throat. "So, does he know when he's coming home yet?"

"No."

"I'm sorry to hear that. You're more than welcome to keep living with us, you know. We've loved having you as a s—as a guest. Marge and I both want you to know that."

Corvus nodded without saying anything.

"Have you thought about what you want over the next few years?" Mr. Porter persisted. "I know you're committed to your dad and all, but I was wondering. What would you think about joining our family on a more official basis?"

"What do you mean? Like adoption?" Corvus's mind swam. *How can he even suggest that?*

Mr. Porter shrugged and held up his hands. The hotdog teetered at the end of his stick. "We don't want to pressure you into nothing. It's an option, that's all."

His eyes shone with hope, but his calloused hands trembled as though a sudden chill had swept over them. *He's afraid I'll say no.*

The man in front of him acted nothing like the man he'd seen abusing wraiths. But then again, Corvus *wasn't* a wraith at the moment. He looked like a human, he walked like a human, he talked like a human—he probably even smelled like a human. Poor little near-orphan Corey. No wonder Mr. Porter lavished him with affection.

But if he found out the truth…

The thought echoed through his mind, a constant refrain of fear and doubt. Corvus hid his true nature under a glamour, but Mr. Porter was hiding something too—a deep, dark hatred that sank its gnarled roots into his heart and squeezed until there was no room left for reason or sanity. Reconciling the man with the monster required more strength than Corvus wanted to part with.

"I don't know," he said at last. "It's a lot to think about."

"If you did, we'd be able to give you a more stable home life," Mr. Porter said, obviously relieved Corvus hadn't blown up in his face. "I think the extra security would do you good."

"Yeah. Maybe. I think I'd rather wait for my dad, though, if that's okay with you."

Mr. Porter inclined his head. "Yeah. 'Course it is. I understand."

The rest of their lunch break passed in silence, save for the rowdy tourists, who took turns faking American accents and howling with laughter. As soon as they were done eating, Mr. Porter put out the fire and led Corvus back to the trail.

The dry leaf litter crunched under their boots, drowning out the other hikers. After a few hundred feet, the path widened, and Mr. Porter slowed down to walk alongside Corvus.

"Is everything okay between you and Billy?" he asked.

"Yeah. Why wouldn't it be?"

"I don't know. You two haven't been talking much lately."

He's got a girlfriend, Corvus sneered. He longed to break the news to his foster father, to get Billy in trouble, but he kept his mouth shut.

Mr. Porter would almost certainly approve of the Shauna girl. *Why couldn't Billy go for someone nice?*

"Nah. We're fine. We've been busy with different friends and with schoolwork. That's all."

"Ah, I see. And how is school going for you, Corey?"

"It sucks."

"Even English? You seemed to like that back in elementary."

"Yeah, well, things change."

"There must be something you like."

"Nope. Everything sucks."

"*Everything* is a bit overdramatic, don't you think? What would Trish say?"

Corvus winced. After his first few weeks of moping around the Porter household, they'd brought him to a child psychologist. Trish seemed nice enough, but she insisted on using play therapy. He'd indulged her with a game of Monopoly every week but avoided her probing questions.

No matter how often she told him their sessions were confidential, he couldn't afford to believe her. If he talked about his father, he'd have to reveal his true identity as a wraith. If he did that, Trish would either commit him to a mental ward or ship him straight to the scientists in Nevada.

"Uh… she'd tell me not to talk in absolutes," Corvus said.

"That's right," Mr. Porter said. "It's like the Sith in Star Wars…"

Why do humans always have to relate things to their inane movies? Corvus wondered.

His attention waned, but he kept nodding to feign interest. In a way, he supposed Trish and Mr. Porter were right. If he pushed himself, he could identify a few things that didn't suck. Rem, for example, was the best friend he could hope to have.

Billy was pretty cool too—when he wasn't being a jerk. And for all his friend's current faults, Corvus knew Billy would get over his infatuation in a few weeks. If he didn't, Shauna would kick him to the curb sooner or later, and Billy would come crawling back to them. He'd apologize for his stupidity and everything would go back to normal.

That was the theory, anyway.

Chapter Thirty-Six

BILLY LAY SPRAWLED on the top bunk, earbuds in, when Corvus returned from his trip. He pulled them out in one swift motion and sat up.

"How was your hike?"

Corvus grunted and threw his backpack across the room. It landed at the foot of the bed with a dull thud. "I hate walking. I can't believe you talked me into telling your parents it was my hobby."

"Sorry. Things were kinda last minute back then. It was the best I could come up with on short notice."

Corvus stalked over to the fallen bag and grabbed a clear plastic bottle from the side pocket. He drained it in two gulps, tossed it to the floor, and collapsed on the bottom bunk.

Billy peered at his friend's spread-eagled form. "Do you want me to get you some more water?"

"Nah. I'll be okay."

The resigned tone of his voice worried Billy. *Is he still annoyed at me? Or is he disappointed he couldn't talk to the wraiths today?*

Sweat formed dark patches on Corvus's T-shirt that rose and fell, blooming and withering, with every breath. "You're home early. I thought you'd be out with *Shauna*."

The bitterness with which he spat out her name answered the question for him.

"I thought I would be too," he admitted. "It was going so well, but then these little wraith kids came over, and she… she was horrible to them, Corvus. I tried to talk her around, but she didn't want to hear it. You were right. There's no changing her. I'm sorry I didn't listen to you."

Corvus stared at him, unblinking.

"I broke it off with her as soon as we got to the movie theater," Billy continued, looking at the floor. "I wasn't exactly polite about it, but I couldn't stand being near her anymore. She ran off crying. I walked away."

"Just like that?"

Billy's cheeks flushed. "Yeah. Oh, and I got you this."

He grabbed the bear he'd won at the theater and tossed it down to Corvus. The other boy didn't move when the toy hit his chest. "What is this?"

"A teddy bear."

Corvus rolled his eyes. "I know *that*. I meant, why are you giving it to me?"

Billy bit his lip. "Because I'm sorry. And I want us to be friends again."

Corvus stared at him for a moment longer, then reached for the teddy bear, turning it over in his hands. He didn't speak for several minutes, but his lips moved as though he wanted to.

"Are you okay, Billy?" he asked finally.

"What do you mean?"

"Well…" Corvus hesitated. "I might not understand the whole 'love' thing from your perspective, but Rem told me humans can take breakups pretty hard. I just thought… I don't know."

"I don't know how I feel right now," Billy admitted. "I'm kinda relieved it's over, to be honest. Murdock's gonna think I'm crazy for giving her up, but it was the right decision. To tell you the truth, she reminds me of my dad a bit."

"In what way?"

"They both hate wraiths. The only difference is that Shauna doesn't have a gun collection."

Corvus remained silent. When Billy gained the courage to look at him, a faint smile graced his friend's lips.

"I'm glad you finally came to your senses," Corvus said. "I'm not going to say 'I told you so,' even though you deserve it. It's my fault too. I should have talked to you about it properly instead of taking petty jabs all the time."

"So you accept my apology?"

"Only if you accept mine."

A cheesy grin tugged at Billy's lips. "Of course I do."

"Then it's settled," Corvus replied, mirroring his expression. "And for what it's worth, Billy, you can do a lot better than Shauna."

"Do you have anyone in mind?"

Corvus placed the teddy bear on his pillow and sat up. "Nope. But personality-wise, I think you should look for someone like Rem."

"Aren't *you* dating Rem?" Billy frowned. "Technically, anyway. I thought you were Promised to each other or something."

"I wasn't insinuating *you* can date *her*," Corvus yelped, leaping to his feet. "I said someone *like* her. If you hadn't been drooling over Shauna in English class, you might have learned the meaning of the phrase."

"Okay, okay!" Billy held up his hands in mock surrender. "Sorry for being stupid."

"I guess I can forgive you. Rem's amazing, so I wouldn't blame you if you wanted to date her. Besides, it's not the stupidest thing you've said in the past few weeks."

"I'm not sure if I should take that as a compliment or not."

"Eh, that's your decision. Anyway, now that you're being less stupid, I was thinking that maybe you could come with us to the meeting tomorrow."

"You said it had to be wraiths only," Billy protested. "If I come, they'll be less likely to trust you."

"You won't be inside the actual meeting. You'll just be waiting in the wings, so to speak. We need a third person to help us out if something goes wrong, and we'd rather have you than Lothaire."

"Why me? Won't they want to see proof of the spell? And what do you mean by, 'if something goes wrong'? Wouldn't it be better to have someone more… competent… backing you up? I can't use magic. What am I supposed to do? Why wouldn't you choose Lothaire?"

Corvus gave him The Look, and Billy shrank back. *I didn't say something stupid, did I? I don't think I did. All of those were valid ques— oh.* "Is it because the wraiths hate oathbreakers more than they hate humans?"

Corvus's eyes lit up. "That's right."

"They're going to find out about Lothaire eventually," Billy pointed out. "What happens when it's time to cast the spell and they see him?"

"Hopefully, it won't come to that. Lothaire's been teaching us how to cast it, and we've pretty much got it down."

"Already?"

"Yup. It's not a hard spell to master. Inventing it in the first place was the real difficulty."

"Okay," Billy said, chewing his thumbnail. "So what do you need me to do if something goes wrong?"

Corvus fished the magic notebook out of his backpack. "Catch."

The notebook arced through the air and landed on the duvet beside Billy. Corvus's messy script covered the latest page, interspersed with Rem's neater lettering.

"You should read through our conversation," Corvus said. "Rem and I talked about a few different scenarios that might crop up and how to deal with them. Let me know if there's anything you don't understand."

Billy skimmed the text, doing his best to commit it to memory. Some of the things they discussed were incomprehensible to him, but he understood the gist of their plan.

"How likely is it that something will go wrong?" Billy asked.

"About ninety-nine percent." Corvus broke into a weak smile when his friend blanched. "Honestly, the other wraiths are a complicated bunch to deal with. The best-case scenario is that they all laugh in our faces and walk away."

"And that some will be saved."

"Yeah. Rem's a lot more optimistic on that front than I am."

The door burst open, making Billy jump. Mrs. Porter bustled into the room, a powder-blue handbag draped over her arm.

"How was your hike, Corey?" she asked.

Corvus straightened. "It was great, thanks. I'm pretty tired now, though, and my legs are sore. We walked a long way."

"So I've been told," Mrs. Porter said. Her wry smile suggested her husband hadn't stopped complaining about his legs since he got back. "We won't be going to church tomorrow, so you can sleep in if you want to."

"Thanks, Mrs. Porter. I could use the extra rest."

"I thought as much. Listen, I'm heading out to get some steaks for dinner. Do you want anything special for dessert? Cheesecake? Ice cream? Gelato?"

"I'm all right," Corvus said.

"I'm all right too," Billy added. After the day's events, the idea of eating more ice cream sickened him.

"Are you sure?" Mrs. Porter asked. Both boys nodded. "In that case, I'll just get something for your brothers."

She squinted at the book in Billy's hands. "Goodness, you boys are so responsible. You've been running around all day, and you're still making an effort to do your math homework. On a Saturday, no less."

"We want to get good grades this semester," Billy said. In truth, he verged on failing out of math, but out-of-character studying was easier to explain than a magic notebook.

"I'd better leave you boys to it, then," Mrs. Porter said. "I'm proud of you, Corey. You too, Billy."

She left the room before they could respond.

"That was weird," Billy commented. *Why did she put his name first?*

Corvus wrinkled his nose. "I think she knows about the chat I had with your dad on the canyon."

"Chat? Oh, are you talking about the adoption thing?"

"You *knew* about that? And you never told me?"

"I wanted to. You were angry at me, though. I didn't think you'd want to listen."

Corvus considered his answer. "I guess that makes sense."

"What did you tell him?" Billy asked.

"That I'm not interested, and I'd rather wait for my dad."

The rejection came like a punch to the stomach. "Really?"

"Be fair. I've got a lot of other things to worry about. If I get carried off to my death tomorrow, I won't need a home, will I?"

"There's no need to be so morbid. You'll be fine. I know you will."

"Nice to know one of us thinks so." Corvus shifted into a more comfortable position, his gaze lowering. "You know what you said earlier? About Shauna being like your dad?"

"Yeah."

"I've been in a lot of danger living here, haven't I?"

Billy looked at him, trying to ascertain the reason for his sudden concern. "Well, yeah. I told you that from the start."

"You said before that he was like Shauna but with guns. Were you hinting he might *shoot* me if he found out what I am? Because I don't remember talking about that three years ago."

"I'm sure we talked about it," Billy protested. "We must have. And anyway, you're wearing a glamour, so it's not like he'd ever find out."

"Maybe not, but I'd rather not spend time with people like that if I can avoid it. It's one thing to shout insults at someone. But knowing he might *kill* me..." Corvus shook his head. "There's no way I can let him adopt me."

"I don't blame you one bit," Billy said. "I love my dad, but he's got a lousy attitude when it comes to wraiths."

Corvus snorted. "That's the understatement of the century. Anyway, you'd better get back to reading the notes Rem made for you. I need some quiet time to think."

He reclined on his bed, his brow creased in concentration. Billy wanted to say something to reassure him but figured his friend wouldn't appreciate the distraction. Keeping his mouth shut, he resumed studying the notebook in earnest.

Chapter Thirty-Seven

BILLY FLICKED AN ant from his wrist, watching its tiny form fall to the dried mud below. Up until a few minutes ago, he'd been perched in an oak tree—the one place he could view Oilskin Lake without being seen himself. A conga line of ants had crawled onto his skin, leading to an unmasculine yelp and a short tumble back to earth.

"I don't understand," Corvus said when they regrouped. "The other wraiths *always* hang out here on Sundays. Where are they?"

Billy scrubbed at the dirt-stained elbow of his sweater. "We could check the homestead."

"Go to their base? Are you crazy?"

"They're not soldiers, Corvus. They're kids, like us."

"Billy's right," Rem said. "They won't be expecting us anyway, so we'll have the upper hand."

Corvus's purple eyes narrowed. "I'm telling you, this is a bad idea."

Without waiting for a response, he stalked into the forest, waving for the others to follow.

Looks like we're going after all, Billy thought with a jolt of trepidation.

They trekked into the forest as a group, shunning the well-worn paths in favor of Corvus's memory. The broad tree trunks stood close together, their foliage entwining to form a green ceiling. The deeper they went, the thicker the canopy became. Before long, brambles choked the path ahead, forcing Billy to slow to a crawl to get around them.

I wish I had a machete like Rambo, he thought.

Corvus and Rem navigated the terrain as gracefully as gazelles, pausing every now and then to wait for him to catch up. Blood suffused his cheeks every time they did so, but gratitude welled up inside him all the same. If they'd left him behind, he would have been lost in the sea of trees for hours.

They emerged into another clearing after ten minutes of walking. A homestead with a gambrel roof sat in the center, its dark weatherboards splintering under the winter sun. Half of the windows boasted fist-sized cracks, and the others housed nothing but air. All of them were boarded up with wood from old apple crates and reinforced with a mâché of yellowing newspapers. Unnatural silence sucked the life out of the surrounding area.

Billy loosed a short whistle. "You weren't kidding when you said this place was out of the way."

Rem smiled, but it didn't reach her eyes. "Nope. Welcome to Wraith Central."

Her hand found Corvus's, and their fingers laced together. Corvus's eyes searched hers for a silent moment.

"Let's do this," he said softly.

Rem's head dipped in a curt nod, and the two wraiths marched across the lawn. Billy shrank back, resting a hand on the closest tree. This was their mission, not his. All he had to do was wait. Their grim expressions weren't lost on him, though. As soon as they slipped through the front door and out of sight, a heavy cloak of foreboding settled over him. They were on their own.

Almwin, Corvus noted, was skinnier than he'd been in elementary school. The lanky wraith lay sprawled over a ratty sofa, a bottle of cream soda in his hand. Soft snores rocked his chest. As Corvus got closer, the other boy let out a gasp, and his eyes snapped open. The soda bottle crashed to the floor, spilling its pale amber dregs onto the carpet.

Almwin sprang to his feet. "What are *you* doing here?"

Rem was right. They didn't expect us to come to the homestead.

"We need to talk," Corvus said.

"To me? I don't know what—"

"To all of you."

"Good luck with that. I know we used to be friends, but you're not exactly Mr. Popular at the moment. Especially around here."

"I know."

A pause stretched out between them. Beside Corvus, Rem shifted her weight impatiently.

"All right, all right. I'll hear you out," Almwin said. "I can't promise anything for the others, though."

"Where are they?" Corvus asked.

"Upstairs, probably. I can call them down if you want."

"Please do. We'll meet in the dining hall."

As Almwin scampered off, Corvus edged down the familiar corridor. He brushed his fingers over the peeling wallpaper, pulling back in disgust when he reached a wet patch. Someone had slathered fresh wallpaper paste over the damage in a vain attempt to repair it. Corvus grimaced and wiped his hand on his jeans.

The scent of boiled cabbage permeated the air when they entered the dining hall, reminiscent of his younger years. Due to Seisan's intermittent spying duties, Corvus had spent a few weeks in the homestead before starting school. The other kids hadn't known about his oath-breaking father back then, and he'd made friends straight away.

Unfortunately, they'd learned the truth within a week, and everything unraveled from there. Once warm with the fires of friendship, the homestead became a haven of frosty stares and upturned noses. Leaving was the best thing he'd ever done.

And now I'm back, he thought, fighting back a wave of disgust. *What have you got for me this time, friends?*

Rem's hand ghosted over his shoulder, and he released the breath trapped in his lungs. The past didn't matter. Not anymore. The only thing that mattered was their shared future—or lack of it. Footsteps thundered down the stairs, and he braced himself for the onslaught of wraiths.

They entered the hall as a pack—*just as expected*—and eyed him with something akin to surprise. If Corvus's stomach hadn't been tying itself in knots, he might have derived some satisfaction from their expressions.

He cleared his throat. "Take a seat. We might as well be comfortable."

"What's this about?" someone asked.

If you were capable of shutting up for a minute, I would tell you.

"As you know, the blood oath ceremony is in two days," Corvus said, following the speech he'd memorized. "Everyone who turned thirteen in the past twelve months is going."

Some of the older wraiths nodded their understanding, but nobody spoke.

"Rem and I have been preparing for years. Not just for the ceremony, but what comes after. The Academy. King Grigoth. The invitation told you a lot, but it didn't tell you everything. We're here today because we think you need to know the full story."

"Here we go," one of the younger wraiths muttered.

"We know you have no reason to trust us," Corvus said, his voice rising in volume. "After all, our fathers are oathbreakers, right?"

Someone gasped and a ripple of murmurs erupted in the audience.

"The thing is, we can't control what our ancestors do any more than we can control what our friends do. All the hate you gave us hurt at first, but it made us stronger in the end. It pushed us to learn more about the blood oath ceremony and what it means to be a wraith. It forced us to learn magic you can only dream of.

"Chances are, you're not going to believe a word we say about our king until it's too late. I can't prove the claims I'm going to make about him until you're already under his control. But we *can* prove our magical prowess. Whether that's going to be good enough for you or not, I don't know. It's your funeral. All I know is that we care enough about what happens to you—to all of us—to risk showing our faces here. I hope that counts for something."

Blood pulsed in his ears as he observed the crowd. Chardein shot him a look of pure contempt, and Corvus's gaze dropped to the damaged floorboards. Counting termite holes seemed safer than facing the consequences of his speech.

"*You* know magic?" Chardein scoffed. "As if. You're just an attention-seeking little twerp."

"They *can* use magic! I've seen it!" Volner piped up. "Rem freed me from the scientists back in elementary school. That was magic, right?"

Rem inclined her head. "A simple spell, yes. We're a lot more powerful now."

"For example, if I wanted to disappear, it would be only too easy," Corvus said.

He waved his arm for dramatic effect, rendering himself invisible. Shouts filled the room as the wraiths tried to work out where he went.

"Or we could make the dining table disappear," Rem said.

She screwed her eyes shut for half a second, and the twenty-foot oak table blinked out of existence. The wraiths' eyes widened, their chests heaving for oxygen. Several of them pawed at the air where the table used to be.

Corvus's disembodied voice floated across their heads. "Of course, not everything is about hiding."

He reappeared in his original position, allowing himself a private smile at the chaos he'd created. He nodded to Rem, and she returned the table to its original place.

"If we wanted to, we could create fire from thin air," Corvus continued. "Not silly little sparks, but a real, roaring fireball. The kind a dragon would spit out."

His hands tingled and small flames erupted from his fingertips. He drew them together, then flicked his fingers outward. The flames coalesced into a ball, hovering less than an inch from his open palms.

Subdued heat soaked his skin.

"You'll kill us all!" Almwin shouted. His reedy frame cowered in the corner of the room. "I should never have helped you. I didn't call my friends down for this!"

Corvus let the glow of magic fade from his hands. "I know you didn't. You have my word that I won't hurt any of you. The only reason I'm showing you this at all is because I know you won't listen to me without proof. We really do have insider knowledge on the blood oath ceremony and what comes after. And we know you need our help."

Chardein crossed his arms. "Fine. You've got our attention. What's so important, then? What's the big secret?"

"The blood oath ceremony," Corvus repeated. "You know the basics, but you don't know everything. Yes, they cut our palms for the oath and collect some extra blood for the Hatchery. But the oath isn't like a promise. It's a binding contract between you and King Grigoth. You must submit completely to his every command and whim. You won't be able to do anything except what he allows you to. If you disagree even slightly, he will torture you. If he decides the offense is bad enough, he might even kill you."

"How do you know?" Almwin asked. Uneasiness flitted across his face. "I mean, it's not like you've taken the oath. And your... dad..."

"He took the oath and managed to break it, with great difficulty," Corvus replied. "He knows what it was like because he's been there. If he was still here in Morton, he could tell you the same thing under a truth spell."

Chardein frowned. "He isn't here?"

"He's in the Gloaming, trying to stop the king from waging war on Earth," Corvus said. "You'll be part of that war if you join Grigoth."

"Good! Someone needs to teach the humans a lesson."

"Are you kidding? You've seen how badly humans tolerate us when we're peaceful. Any sign of hostile force and they'll slaughter every single one of us. Is that what you want?"

Chardein slunk back, defeated.

"The blood oath ceremony is a one-way ticket to servitude and death," Rem said, taking over the narrative. "It wasn't always like that. Before Grigoth's reign, everything was pleasant and peaceful. The Gloaming was alive and vibrant and thousands of times bigger than it is now. He's been changing things about magic—changing the very fabric of our reality. If he keeps going, it's all over for us. Wraithkind will die out forever unless we take another path."

"What path?" Volner asked.

"Over the past few years, we've been using our knowledge of magic to invent a new spell," Corvus explained. Mentioning Lothaire's involvement would destroy what little trust he'd built with his audience, so he didn't bring it up. "The spell will circumvent the compulsions to return to the Gloaming. You'll still be able to go if you want to. You just won't be *forced* to."

"The compulsions become painful very quickly," Rem added. "Grigoth doesn't want to risk you meandering along the way."

"I don't understand," Almwin said. "What difference does casting a spell make? You say we can choose a different path, but all roads lead back to the Gloaming eventually. We can't avoid the blood oath forever."

"Yes, we can," Corvus replied. "Without the compulsions, we can stay here in Morton for as long as we want to. Rem and I will make magical disguises for anyone who asks for them."

"Whether or not you want to try is completely up to you," Rem said. "We know how hard it can be to break tradition. But remember what Corvus told you about Grigoth. Do you really want to risk torture and starvation to fulfill an outdated sense of duty?"

Several tense minutes passed as the wraiths processed Rem's words. Corvus wanted to say something—*anything*—to break the silence, but his vocal cords might as well have been paralyzed.

"Don't listen to them," Chardein said. "I've met King Grigoth before, and he's not the tyrant they're making him out to be. You guys aren't taking them seriously, are you?"

Corvus bit back an angry retort. *Stay calm. Don't provoke him any further. You're doing this for them.*

"Why would they be lying?" Volner asked, regarding them thoughtfully. "They didn't have to show up or tell us anything."

"Who cares about their motives?" Chardein said. "The fact you're even considering it means they probably put a spell on you. Are you going to stand for that?"

"They did do magic earlier," someone said.

Almwin slapped a hand to his forehead as though he'd been stung. "That's right! They're trying to stop us from going back to the Gloaming. They're trying to bring us down with them."

"We didn't do anything to you!" Corvus roared over the commotion. "All we're doing is offering you a choice."

"Which I'm rejecting," Chardein retorted. "If the others have any brains at all, they'll do the same. For all we know, this could be a test from Grigoth to prove we're loyal to him."

The other wraiths bobbed their heads in agreement and began filing out of the hall.

"Please listen to me," Corvus begged, but the exodus did not slow down.

Within seconds, the room was empty except for Corvus, Rem, and Volner.

"Volner, please," Corvus said. He hated the servile tone in his voice. "I swear I'm not lying to you. We're not with Grigoth. And even if we were, he doesn't need anyone to prove their loyalty. The oath takes care of that. What Chardein said doesn't make any sense."

"I'm sorry, Corvus," Volner said. "I'm sure you mean well, and I guess I can appreciate why you came here. I'm still grateful that you saved me back in elementary school. But after everything you said… staying here and wearing a disguise… I don't want that. I shouldn't have to hide who I am."

"I know how you feel, believe me," Corvus persisted. "But isn't it better to live free than to be a slave? We can still use magic here. Rem and I will teach you everything we know."

Volner shook his head and backed toward the doorway. "I've been a good wraith. I don't have anything to worry about from King Grigoth."

"What about the famine? What about the upcoming war?" Rem prompted. "You'll die, Volner. We won't be able to help you."

"I'll take my chances," Volner said. "Sorry, guys. You're on your own here."

He disappeared around the corner, and Corvus sank onto the bench seat, head in his hands. After Billy's enthusiasm the other day, he'd deluded himself into thinking they had a chance.

Rem placed a supportive hand on his shoulder. "At least we tried."

"If they die, it'll be Chardein's fault," Corvus spat.

"It'll be Grigoth's fault," Rem corrected, helping him up. "Come on. We shouldn't stay here."

Billy peered around the trunk of a pine tree. He'd been forced to move three times since Corvus and Rem left, thanks to a squirrel that kept trying to bury nuts in his trouser leg. Now, though, something much bigger captured his attention. Corvus and Rem emerged from the homestead and shuffled toward him, hand in hand. Their downturned faces sent his stomach plummeting to his toes. *Something must have gone wrong.*

Halfway across the field, Rem stopped dead, turned, and fixed her gaze on a crop of bushes next to the homestead. Corvus's brow crinkled as her action dragged him to a halt. Rem grabbed him by the shoulders and gesticulated at the weeds. Then a bolt of purple lightning struck her in the back.

It took Billy a few precious seconds to comprehend the situation. Rem pinwheeled her arms and collapsed in a heap, crying out in pain. Corvus flinched, his gaze darting around the clearing. He scooped his friend up as though she weighed nothing and sprinted for the trees. Purple bolts sizzled over his head.

"Billy!" Corvus screamed.

"I'm here!" Billy stepped into the open, helping his friend to orient himself, then leapt back to safety.

Corvus dived behind the same tree, tripped on a rock, and face-planted in the soil. It wasn't the most dignified of arrivals, but at least he'd escaped the line of fire. Beside him, Rem rolled over and groaned.

"How did they learn combat magic?" Corvus demanded. He sat up, breathing hard. "They shouldn't know how to do that. *We* don't even know how to do that."

"I don't think it was the kids," Rem said. "I thought I saw an adult wraith behind the house. An Enforcer."

"What?" Billy's eyes widened. "He must have been under Grigoth's orders, right? Otherwise, he couldn't be here."

"Exactly," Corvus said. "I don't like this. We need to get out of here. Can you run?"

"Of course I can," Rem said, getting to her feet.

"No," a deep voice growled. "You will stay."

Billy's heart skipped a beat. An adult wraith towered over them, his eyes glinting with malice. Corvus and Rem sprinted off in opposite directions, twigs cracking under their heels. Despite her injured back, Rem lost none of her usual agility. Billy covered his face, every muscle tensed in anticipation of a beating. It never came. He risked opening an eye and nearly fainted with relief. The wraith was gone.

"Now what do I do?" he asked the forest.

He couldn't very well saunter into the homestead to ask for directions. If his earlier assumption was wrong and Corvus *had* converted some of the wraith kids, his arrival would besmirch their tenuous alliance. If Corvus hadn't been successful, Billy would be skewered over a bonfire. *It's not like I can go after my friends either. I couldn't catch up to them. And even if I could, what would I do? Rem couldn't have predicted this. She didn't leave me any notes on how to deal with it.*

He didn't know how long he'd been walking when he heard the first tinkle of laughter. He froze in place, listening. The nearby crunch of pine needles and dry soil filled his ears, accompanied by jovial voices. A few minutes later, a girl appeared amidst the bracken.

Shauna.

Dapples of sunlight gilded her hair, and her face bore a self-satisfied smirk. "Billy Porter. Fancy seeing you here."

Billy took a step back. "Uh… yeah."

What is she *doing here? Doesn't she know who lives in this forest?*

"You've been hanging out with those freaks again, haven't you?"

I guess that answers my question. "I don't know what you're talking about."

"You're such a liar. Teach him a lesson, boys!"

Billy's pulse jumped as two more figures emerged from the sea of trees—Jeffrey Bancroft and a thin, older boy he didn't recognize. Jeffrey clenched his fists when he saw Billy, his face contorting into an expression of pure hatred. Adrenaline surged through Billy's veins, and he sprinted in the opposite direction as fast as his legs would carry him.

A bony shoulder collided with the small of his back, and he fell, his forehead bouncing off an exposed tree root. Stars exploded across his vision. Rough hands rolled him onto his back, and the thin boy drove his knee into Billy's stomach, pinning him in place.

"This is for my sister!" he shouted, raining down blow after blow. "How dare you hurt her!"

Billy's arms flew up to protect his face, but the punches showed no sign of stopping. He bucked like a bronco, desperate to escape. The excess movement opened up his guard, and a fist caught him in the nose. Hot, coppery blood trickled down his throat. The thin boy— *Shauna's brother?*—stood up. Billy rolled onto his belly, coughing up scarlet-tinted phlegm. Fat droplets of blood spilled from his nose to the soil below.

"It's my turn," Jeffrey said, cracking his knuckles.

Billy tried to turn around, but it was too late. A sledgehammer-like punch walloped his skull, and everything faded to black.

Chapter Thirty-Eight

BILLY WOKE WITH a throbbing headache. Faint voices wafted over him, but he couldn't make out a word they said. His eyes fluttered open, then snapped shut as a bright light pierced them. He groaned, blinked a few times, and squinted down at his body. He lay on a beige-striped sofa with a coarse wool blanket pulled up to his chest. Dried blood stained the top of his sweater.

Eyes widening, he reached for his face, wincing as his fingertips came into contact with the tender flesh around his nose. Some gentle prodding revealed no changes in the bone structure. *Not broken, then.* He sat up and pushed the blanket to the ground.

One of his wraith classmates perched on a wicker chair next to the sofa, watching him with eagle eyes. "You okay?"

"I... I don't know. I think so," Billy said. He brought a hand to the back of his head, expecting to find more blood there, but his fingers brushed over a cotton bandage instead. "Where am I?"

"The old homestead. I found you lying unconscious in the forest and carried you back here. Do you remember what happened?"

Billy frowned. *I was helping Corvus and Rem, and they got attacked. The wraith hit me and then... no, that's not right. It was—*

"Shauna," he croaked. "She was walking around with these two guys. They probably followed us into the forest."

The wraith's eyebrows knitted together. "And they attacked you? Why?"

"I went on a date with her yesterday and things didn't work out. The way she talked about you guys… I couldn't stand it any longer. So I gave her a piece of my mind."

"What did she say?"

"The usual. That all wraiths are freaks and deserve to die. A bunch of little kids overheard her, and they were so upset about it. I couldn't sit there and do nothing."

"If you ask me, it sounds like Shauna got what she deserved. You're a brave guy, Billy."

"You know my name?"

"Of course. Don't you remember me?"

Billy studied the boy's face through squinted eyes, trying to ignore the tiny jackhammers in his brain. "Volner?"

"That's right," Volner said. "I still appreciate what you did for me in elementary school, by the way. I told Corvus and Rem the same thing, but I figured I should say it to you too. You're helping them, aren't you?"

"Yeah, but some help I've been. An adult wraith went after them, firing magic left and right. I don't know where they went."

"That was an Enforcer." Volner shifted his weight, and the wicker chair squeaked in protest. "Two of them have been hanging around for the past week. They were hiding in the hallway during our meeting so they could find out what was going on. It's safe to say some of us are going to be in trouble later."

"During the blood oath ceremony?"

"Yeah, and before the ceremony starts. I'm surprised you know about that."

"Corvus and Rem have taught me a lot. I care about what happens to you guys."

"I can tell."

Billy thought for a moment. "So what's going to happen to them? And what *is* an Enforcer, anyway?"

"They're basically in charge of everything relating to the ceremony and oath magic. They tell us what we need to know—well, I guess it's more what they *want* us to know—and then they escort us to the castle. That's where the ceremony happens," Volner explained. "As for Corvus and Rem... they will have been taken to the Gloaming and imprisoned so they can't run away from their duties. They made a mistake coming here today."

"Maybe," Billy said, "but at least they did it because they wanted to help you."

Volner sighed and steepled his fingers. "They did show a lot of honor. They always have. Part of me wishes we'd stayed friends after fifth grade."

"Then help me," Billy pleaded. "I'm not expecting you to go all the way to the castle, but I can't get past the portal by myself. I don't have a shred of magic in me."

"I can't. The Enforcers could come back any minute, and they'll be watching us more closely now. Corvus and Rem were brave, but I don't want to meet the same fate."

"What fate? Is Grigoth going to kill them?"

"I don't know. They told us a lot of things today. If they weren't exaggerating, then I guess it's a possibility."

"And you still want to follow Grigoth after all this?"

Volner's expression darkened into an impenetrable mask. "I've already made up my mind. I'm not going to change it, no matter what you say."

In one swift movement, he scooped the fallen blanket from the floor and rose to his feet.

"Wait," Billy said, standing up too. His vision wavered, and he grabbed Volner's shoulder to steady himself. "Can you at least point me in the direction of the portal? I don't think I remember how to get out of here."

Volner hesitated. Sparks of fear and compassion warred in his aubergine eyes. Then something gave way, and he inclined his head in a jerky nod. "Go straight ahead from the front door and you'll reach the main road. You can loop back around to the portal from there."

Billy released his grip on Volner. "Thank you."

As the wraith boy scurried away, Billy's shoulders sagged with disappointment. He didn't know why he'd thought he could succeed where his friends had failed. Now that their defeat was total, his chest felt heavy and constricted, as though it were being crushed by a hydraulic press. *Are humans and wraiths really that different?* No easy answer presented itself, so he shambled out of the house and headed back to the forest. He couldn't help Volner, but he could still save his friends.

After half an hour of walking, the emerald-green expanse gave way to gray tarmac. Hundreds of cars crawled past him, spewing exhaust fumes into the chilly air. Billy ignored them and followed the road back to Oilskin Lake.

I need a plan to reach the Gloaming, he thought. *Preferably something better than jumping in the water and wishing really hard.*

He reached the lakeside ten minutes later, but no inspiration struck him. The midnight-purple water rested like death in the dwindling light. Gritting his teeth, he shuffled ankle-deep into the ooze.

"Let me through!" he shouted.

A flock of birds took to the air, startled by the sudden noise, but no resulting rush of electricity greeted him. *Now what?* He waded farther in until the water touched his chest. Pressure built up around his body, like the lake wanted to suck him down into the depths. If Billy had been thinking straight, he would have removed his shoes and outer clothing, but a wild desperation filled him, and he couldn't bear to waste any more time.

He pressed his palms together and dived, hoping to see something at the bottom that might hint at how the portal worked. Darkness engulfed Billy as he descended, deeper and deeper, into Oilskin Lake. Less than ten seconds passed before his lungs screamed for oxygen, but he ignored them and kept moving.

Twenty seconds. Thirty. Everything looked the same down here.

Worse still, the farther he went, the less certain he felt about which way was up and which way was down. Fifteen long seconds later, his outstretched fingers sank into the muddy lakebed.

I did all this for nothing? he despaired, twisting his body around.

He launched himself off the mud, kicking his way upward. Stars pinpricked his eyes, and his limbs vibrated with exhaustion. His lungs burned like they would burst if he tried to hold his breath any longer. But even as Billy's heart galloped toward the void, his head breached the surface. He gasped for air, chest heaving with effort. Brackish water droplets flew from his lips. Oxygen had never tasted sweeter than it did in that moment. He lay back and spread his limbs like a starfish, relishing the simple joy of being alive.

"Billy?"

The muffled voice caught him off-guard, and he floundered upright.

"*Rem?*"

The wraith girl bounded across the banks of Oilskin Lake and splashed through the water to join him.

"What are you doing here?" Billy asked, dumbfounded. "I thought the Enforcer grabbed you!"

"He did, but I got away."

"Yeah, but *how?* He wasn't exactly a pushover from what I saw."

"Not a pushover, no. But a well-placed kick works wonders," Rem said, grinning. She reached out to Billy and clutched his biceps with both hands. Moments later, her smile quivered and dissolved into anguish. "Billy, I couldn't save Corvus."

The news hit him like a punch to the gut. "What do you mean?"

"They took him back to the Gloaming. He put up a good fight, but…" She shook her head. "The Enforcers can teleport at will when they're on the other side of the portal. He's probably in the castle by now. Under Grigoth's control."

"No," Billy whispered. He refused to believe it. "Maybe he'll get away like you did."

Rem shook her head again, her eyes brimming with tears. "They knocked him unconscious before they crossed over. I saw it happen. He might even be…"

She didn't finish her sentence.

"We'll get him before they get a chance to do anything," Billy asserted. "We already know where they're taking him, right?"

"R-right."

Her fingers dug into his arms as she cast the required spell. Billy braced himself, letting the wash of electricity suck him into the Gloaming.

The clearing in the wraiths' homeland looked the same as it had three years ago. A single dusty path stretched as far as the eye could see, lined with the skeletal remains of dead trees. Rem scrambled out of the lake and started down the lonely path, beckoning for Billy to follow. The effort required to keep up with her brisk jog came close to breaking him.

"How far is it to the castle?" Billy asked.

"Keep your voice down," Rem told him in a stage whisper.

"How far?" he repeated in a quieter voice.

"About two days' travel on foot."

Billy's head throbbed. "Two *days*? We don't have any food or weapons. What are you planning to do?"

"I don't know yet," Rem admitted. "We'll have to stop somewhere for the night. I'll figure it out then."

Another thought occurred to Billy. "We have *school* tomorrow!"

"Yes, and clearly an extra day of education is more important than a friend's life," Rem said, her tone withering. "There are bigger things at stake."

"I know," Billy protested. "But what am I going to tell my parents? They'll report me missing or something."

Rem slowed to a halt and turned to face him, hands on her hips. "We're not going back. We can't leave Corvus at Grigoth's mercy."

"I didn't mean…" Billy began, but a wave of nausea cut him off. Rem grew fuzzy around the edges and then went out of focus altogether. He screwed his eyes shut and doubled over, trembling.

"You're hurt," Rem said, pity raising the pitch of her voice. "I saw the bandage, but I forgot to ask. Was it the Enforcer?"

"No, he didn't want me," Billy mumbled. "Shauna sent Jeffrey and her brother after me."

"Your *girlfriend* sent people after you?"

"I've already told you, she's not my girlfriend. She must have followed us into the woods."

"I'd say 'I told you so,' but given the state you're in, that would be cruel."

"Yes. It would be."

"Are you okay to walk?"

"I guess so."

"I could carry you if you want."

"You? Carry me?" Billy blanched. "No, I can walk. It's the running that's a problem. It makes my head all woozy."

"You should have told me earlier," Rem said, wrapping her fingers around his arm and guiding him to the ground. "I might be able to heal you."

Under her careful ministrations, the bandage unraveled from his head and pooled on the forest floor. She inhaled sharply as the final strand fell away.

"Is it bad?" Billy asked.

"Pretty bad. There's a lot of blood."

"You don't have to—"

"Shhh. Let me do this."

Rem placed a cool palm over the wound, careful not to put too much pressure on it. A strange electrical buzz vibrated in Billy's skull, and he jerked back in surprise. The sound of pop rocks tickled his ears, and his tongue flashed hot-cold-hot-cold. Then the vibrations stopped and everything went back to normal.

"There," Rem said, performing a cleansing spell on his hair. "Good as new."

She stood up and stumbled forward, pressing a hand to her forehead.

Billy scrambled over to her. "Are you okay?"

"Yeah, I'm fine. Healing spells can take a lot of energy. That's all. You must have had a concussion for it to affect me this much." A brief tremor racked her body as she straightened. "Try not to get hurt again, okay?"

"I'll do my best. Thanks for fixing me up, Rem."

"It's the least I could do. We should really keep moving, though. Are you ready?"

Billy bounced on the soles of his feet to make sure his vision didn't falter as it had before. Satisfied, he turned to Rem.

"Ready."

Chapter Thirty-Nine

THEY RAN FOR what felt like hours. Billy staggered to a halt and doubled over, his breath coming in short, labored bursts. Rem continued another twenty feet before she noticed his absence, her body a mere silhouette in the funereal twilight. After a few seconds' hesitation, she doubled back.

"Sorry," Billy wheezed. "I haven't done this much exercise in years."

"It's okay. We should stop and find shelter soon anyway. It's nearly nightfall."

Billy gazed up at the sky. *How does she know it's nearly nightfall? It's not like it's getting any darker.* Nevertheless, the idea of stopping warmed his heart.

"My dad taught me how to build a shelter from wood," he said. "I could have it up in half an hour."

"No need. There's an abandoned keep near here. We'll be a lot safer behind a stone wall than a wooden one."

Billy couldn't argue with that logic, so he gestured at the path. "Lead the way."

The keep came into view within minutes, but it took them another hour to get there. Much like in the wraiths' forest on Earth, a dense network of brambles blocked their path. However, the brambles here were long dead and resembled coils of barbed wire rather than plants. The keep itself looked well-tended, despite the blackened ivy woven around it. *How does Rem know this place is abandoned? Maybe someone decided to use it as a house—or worse, a sentry post.*

Apparently unconcerned, Rem skipped up the steps and slammed her shoulder into the door. The heavy wood rattled out of its frame, scraping over the flagstone floor. She caught it with both hands and jerked her head toward the opening, prompting Billy to go first. He squeezed past her, into the bowels of the unknown. The stench of mold and chalk dust invaded his nostrils, and he fought the desire to gag. Exposed stone bricks lined the walls, crumbling away in places to reveal snatches of the world outside.

"It's cold in here," he said, rubbing his arms to ward off gooseflesh.

"Yeah, the insulation isn't the best." Rem slipped inside and heaved the damaged door back into place. "Rebels destroyed the rest of the castle a hundred years ago, but they couldn't destroy the keep. It was too strong and too heavily guarded. They really did a number on it, though."

"How do you know so much?" Billy asked in awe.

Rem shrugged and led the way to the common area. "Dad took me here for my birthday last year. You know, when I was going through my 'history nerd' phase."

"Nothing wrong with being a history nerd," Billy said. "I loved learning about that stuff in elementary school. I don't know anything about wraith history, though."

"Well, now you do," Rem replied. "Dad says wraithkind have been watching humans for thousands of years, copying all sorts of things from them. The Gloaming was a lot more advanced than Earth back then, but our ancestors were obsessed with exotic cultures, and that's how we ended up with castles."

Billy's eyebrows shot up. "Really?"

"Yup. We're like the great cultural scavengers of the universe, so to speak."

"More like the creepy stalkers of the universe," Billy teased. "You've been *watching* us?"

Rem punched his arm, her eyes sparkling. "Oh, shut up. It's not like that."

Although the blow didn't hurt, Billy screwed up his face in mock agony. "Assault!"

Rem giggled and soon Billy, too, collapsed in a fit of laughter.

"Okay, but seriously," Billy said when their mirth subsided. "How did your ancestors find us in the first place? And how did they know where to put the portals?"

"We didn't make the portals," Rem replied. "They were just… there. A member of the High Council found the first one, and then everyone else started looking too. Of course, most of them are gone now, thanks to the Oncoming Abyss. Oilskin Lake is the only one left. Once that's gone, the link between our worlds will be cut off forever."

A torrent of ice ran down Billy's spine. Corvus had told him all about the Oncoming Abyss over the past few years, likening it to a ravenous beast of unfathomable power. The idea terrified Billy, but the consequences of a portal's destruction scared him more. Without a portal to sustain the flow of magic, any wraiths stranded on Earth would lose their powers. Without the ability to heal themselves, it would only be a matter of time before they succumbed to the tides of fate.

I can't let that happen, Billy thought, biting his lip. "Is that why there were wraiths wandering around Japan last week? Because their portal disappeared? I was going to ask you earlier, but it kept slipping my mind."

"I don't know," Rem said. "I mean, the evidence adds up. Losing portal access would make any Earth-dwelling wraith desperate enough to risk traveling to find a new one. I just wish we'd known about them earlier. We could have helped them before the police got involved. Before they got shot in cold blood."

"They were *shot*? I didn't know that."

"The news stations kept it pretty quiet, but there are videos all over the internet. If Grigoth hadn't been messing with magic, the Japanese portal would still be there. Those kids wouldn't have gone searching for another one. They wouldn't have died."

A trace of venom colored Billy's voice. "This is all Grigoth's fault."

"Yeah, well, that's history for you," Rem said, lowering herself to the floor and crossing her legs. "Crazy rulers pop up from time to time, but someone always knocks them off in the end. Whether or not that will happen to Grigoth before it's too late and our portal is gone too…"

The disheartened droop of her shoulders inspired a fierce surge of protectiveness in Billy, but he couldn't think of anything comforting to say. Rem wouldn't appreciate naive expressions of optimism, nor empty vows to kill the tyrant responsible for destroying her homeland.

"We should light a fire," he said at last.

"We can't. If anyone comes in, they'll know we're here. I can cast a warming spell instead if you're cold."

"Yes, please."

She strode over to him, cupping her hands together to produce a purple glow. Heat rolled over his body, restoring feeling to his frozen joints.

"I've modified the spell to accommodate our individual temperature requirements," Rem explained. "That way, it won't get too hot or cold for you overnight."

"That's brilliant," Billy said. "You're amazing at magic, Rem."

"I wouldn't go that far," she said, blushing. "I'm nowhere near as powerful as Corvus."

"But you use your powers wisely. You don't try to brute force things like Corvus does. I bet he couldn't cast a warming spell the way you did."

"Maybe not. The first time he tried, he singed Dad's eyebrows off."

Billy chuckled at that. After a moment, he sobered and met Rem's eyes. "Could you teach me?"

"To singe someone's eyebrows off? I don't think you need my help with that."

"No, that's not what I meant. I want to learn to cast a warming spell. Or any kind of spell, really."

"I know you do, but we've tried to teach you magic a hundred times, and it didn't work. What makes you think it will this time?"

"You know me. I'm endlessly optimistic. Plus, I've got a real reason to learn this time. If I can use magic, I might be able to help you when we reach Grigoth's castle."

"I don't know about that," Rem said. "I appreciate the thought, but even the most basic spells can fail when you add stress into the equation. Besides, we need to get in and out as stealthily as possible. That means no combat." When Billy's face fell, she scooted closer to him. "Hey. I didn't say I wasn't going to teach you. I'll show you something basic, and we'll see how things go. If nothing else, it'll give you something to practice during your watch."

"We're taking watches? Do you think someone might come in here?"

"Maybe. In any case, it pays to be prepared. I can take the first one if you're tired."

Billy thought about it. "All right. But you have to teach me how to do the spell first. I have a feeling today's gonna be the day."

"If you say so," Rem said. She paused to gather her thoughts. "Cup your hands together like mine and close your eyes. Reach into the flow of energy. Feel it swirling through your body from your core to your fingertips. Now imagine a ball forming between your hands and channel the energy into it."

Billy's brow wrinkled in concentration. *Energy, energy, energy.*

"Nothing's happening," he said after a while, opening his eyes. "How am I supposed to 'reach into the flow of energy' if I can't find it?"

Rem looked up from the orb resting in her palms. "You can't feel anything?"

"Nothing."

"Did you feel anything when we crossed the portal?"

"Like electricity? Yeah. But how do I recreate that feeling myself?"

"I don't know," Rem admitted, dropping her hands. The lavender glow popped out of existence, and the room fell back into darkness.

"What do you mean, you don't know?"

"I mean, it's not something I've ever had to think about," Rem said. "Accessing the flow of magic is easy for me. It's like breathing. But how on earth do you teach someone how to breathe?"

The immense stone structure creaked and settled throughout the night. Billy lay awake, wishing he'd asked Rem to fashion an air pillow or something to keep them off the ground. Every time one of his limbs slipped outside the circle of warmth she'd created, the coldness of the flagstone floor seeped into his bones and froze him to the core.

Rem had "woken" him two hours earlier to take over her watch. Now, her deep, even breathing echoed through the room, accompanied by the occasional snore. Evidently, their sleep arrangements didn't bother her as much as they bothered him. He watched her absentmindedly, taking in the gentle rise and fall of her chest, then shook himself and looked away.

What would Rem think if she woke up and caught him staring? Would she assume he had romantic feelings toward her? He wrinkled his nose at the idea. Rem was pretty, but he thought of her as a sister. And after his date with Shauna, the idea of starting a relationship with anyone made him sick to his stomach.

Hoping to distract himself, Billy sat up and resumed his search for magical energy. He closed his eyes and inhaled, deep and slow. A slight vibration tickled the space between his ear and his jaw. *Is this it?* Excitement mounted in his chest, only to fall flat when the sensation turned into a yawn. *Drat.* He tried for a while longer before accepting the inevitable. Magic was for wraiths, and he was no wraith. No matter how much he wanted to be like his friends, that would never change.

Billy ran a hand through his hair. If the length of a single night correlated to a night on Earth, he had a few hours to kill before dawn. Leaving Rem alone was out of the question, but the common area had plenty of features worth exploring. He rose to his feet and stepped outside the reaches of the warming spell, his breath coming out in frosted puffs. *So far, so good.*

Rubbing his arms for warmth, he tiptoed toward the ornate gold frame he'd seen upon entering the room. He expected to see a painting inside—a sophisticated depiction of the Gloaming as it used to be. Instead, the frame held…

Nothing? Billy stared at the exposed masonry, his face blank. *Why would someone take the painting and leave the frame? If it's made of real gold, it'd be worth a fortune.*

He tore his attention away from it and ambled to a plinth on the other side of the room. Curlicues decorated the veined marble slab, which held nothing but a pile of gray powder.

Maybe it's modern art? Billy thought. It seemed a fitting representation of wraith society.

A dark shape flitted past the window, and he jumped, fear clenching his heart in an icy fist. It was the same cold terror he'd felt when the Monster of Morton cast its shadow on his curtains three years ago. But whoever—or whatever—lurked outside wasn't an ally in disguise. Not this time. Billy leaned as close as he dared to the mildewed window, listening for footsteps. The glint of a lantern caught his eye, and he scurried back to Rem. Her waking confusion melted into fear when he reported what he'd seen.

"That sounds like an Enforcer," she whispered, already halfway to her feet. "I thought it would take them longer to pick up our trail."

Her hands glowed purple for a brief instant, and the warm air dissipated.

"They can do that?" Billy asked. He racked his brains for a movie that showed a similar situation. "How? Do they trace you by your magic or something?"

"No, I just made a stupid mistake. We left footprints on our way here. I should have cast a spell to obscure them, but I was so upset about Corvus…"

"Hey, don't worry about it. Let's just get out of here. There's got to be a back door or something, right?"

"Not exactly," Rem replied, leading him down the corridor.

The passage ended in a solid stone wall with a large crack skirting the foundation. Had he been a few years younger, Billy could have crawled through the gap on his hands and knees. At his current size, he'd have to slither through like a snake.

"You've got to be kidding," he murmured.

"I don't see any other options, do you?" Rem asked, jabbing her finger at the tunnel. "Get in."

"There must be—"

The creak of the front door cut him off, and he dropped to the ground. Chunks of broken stone littered the floor of the tunnel, digging into his belly as he slid through. Once or twice, he lifted his head to get a better look at the terrain ahead, only to be showered with stone dust for his efforts. He wriggled out into the open air and burrowed under a row of lifeless shrubs. Rem scrambled after him, adjusting the brittle foliage to better disguise their presence.

"Now what?" Billy asked.

Pale orange light emanated from the hole they'd left through. Someone had lit a non-magical fire inside.

"We wait," Rem answered, her voice hoarse with exhaustion. "Enforcers and Rangers sometimes use abandoned buildings as resting posts when they're on missions. It's possible he doesn't know anything about us."

Her confidence faltered when the light went out, replaced by a lantern fifteen feet in front of them. The wraith holding it took three long strides toward them and stopped, smirking.

"I see you," he croaked. "Come out and face me like a man."

Billy's heart thumped in his ears, blocking out all other sounds. He tensed his muscles, preparing to obey, but Rem's nails dug into his arm, warning him to stay put. Moments later, a second wraith emerged from the trees behind them. His silhouette passed within three feet of them, marching straight into the open field.

"We meet again, my friend. It's been a long chase, hasn't it?"

The cadence of the newcomer's voice sent slivers of ice through Billy's veins. *That's Seisan! What's he doing here?*

"It's been far too long," the Enforcer growled. "The king wants a word with you."

"I'm sure he does," Seisan said. Sarcasm dripped from his tongue as he strode into the light. "Unfortunately for you, I have no intention of going back to the castle. I'm not interested in what he has to say."

The Enforcer chuckled, a low, horrible sound that resembled choking more than laughing. "I think you'll change your mind when you find out what he's planning to do to your son."

The words hung in the air like a bad odor. Seisan's eyes narrowed. "An empty threat, and an obvious ploy to lure me in. You're insulting my intelligence, sir."

The Enforcer pulled a clutch of black threads from his pocket. "Perhaps it's not such an empty threat after all. Does this look familiar to you?"

Billy leaned forward to get a better look. *Is that… hair? Corvus's hair? No, that's stupid. It could be anyone's. The guy probably ripped it out of his own head.*

Seisan's horrified expression suggested otherwise. "If you hurt my boy—"

"I'm a messenger, nothing more," the Enforcer said. "I wasn't the one that knocked him out and dragged him off to the castle."

Seisan drew his sword with surprising speed, thrusting the tip toward the Enforcer's throat. The other wraith stepped back, whipping out his own sword.

"You'd better hope for your sake he's still alive," Seisan growled, slashing at the Enforcer's legs.

Billy and Rem watched in horror as the duel unfolded. Swords sliced through the air in twin flashes of silver. The deafening clang of steel on steel filled the air, and the Enforcer's lantern crashed to the ground. Pungent oil spilled out of the cracked vessel and into the dead grass, but the flame seemed content to stay put. Billy breathed a sigh of relief. At least they didn't have to worry about a forest fire.

Seisan's body flowed effortlessly through a series of techniques, the likes of which Billy had only seen in the movies. The Enforcer's movements were less fluid, but he made up for it with raw muscle. *Come on, Seisan! You can do this!*

As if responding to his silent cheers, Seisan rained a flurry of blows on his opponent, slicing the Enforcer's sword hand clean off. Purple blood spurted from the stump, and he howled in pain, clutching it with his free hand. Seisan kicked the sword out of reach. The metal blade pinwheeled toward Billy, stopping several inches short of his face. Heart racing, he forced his attention back to Seisan.

The former policeman kicked his opponent in the shins, sending him tumbling to the ground. Then, without any hesitation, he plunged his sword into the Enforcer's throat, turning his screams into frightened gurgles. Billy's eyes widened. *He actually did it. He actually* killed *him.*

The Enforcer's eyes pleaded with Seisan, but no potion or healing spell could help him now. His soul would pass from the world as thousands had before him—cold and alone, in the service of a king who couldn't care less about his suffering.

Chapter Forty

SEISAN WAITED UNTIL the man died before pulling the sword free from his throat. He wiped it clean on the dead grass and slipped it back into its leather sheath. The lantern-light sputtered and went out, plunging the world into darkness. Beside Billy, Rem wriggled out into the open.

"Seisan?" she ventured.

The older wraith whirled around, his hand returning to the hilt of his sword. His posture relaxed when he identified her.

"Rem? What are you doing here?" He glanced guiltily at the corpse, then added: "I suppose you witnessed our little tussle."

"We did," Rem confirmed, pulling Billy out of the bushes after her.

"You're both here?" Seisan asked. "Where's Corvus? The Enforcer said he was taken to the castle."

"He was," Billy replied. "They grabbed him in the forest near Oilskin Lake."

"How did this happen?" Seisan demanded. Hints of hidden panic flitted across his face. "And what are you doing in the Gloaming? It's not safe."

"We know," Rem said. "We went to the homestead to talk to the other wraiths about the blood oath ceremony. We wanted them to know the truth, but they didn't want to listen. A couple of Enforcers were hanging around and grabbed us. I managed to get away, but Corvus… didn't."

Seisan buried his head in his hands, as though he couldn't

comprehend what he'd heard. "Did Lothaire put you up to this?"

The man's accusatory tone rubbed Billy the wrong way, but he took it with a grain of salt. Seisan didn't have anything against Lothaire. He was just grieving the possible loss of his child.

"Dad knew nothing about it," Rem said. "Corvus and I came up with the idea ourselves. We wanted to help the other kids."

"And you didn't think to cast protective enchantments first?"

Rem held his gaze. "It's not our fault. We didn't know the Enforcers would be there."

"You should have anticipated it," Seisan retorted. "If you'd taken the necessary precautions, we wouldn't be in this situation."

He stalked over to the broken lantern and crushed it beneath the heel of his boot, spraying glass fragments in all directions. Billy flinched at the uncharacteristic display of violence.

"Sorry," Seisan sighed. He sounded even more exhausted than Billy felt. "It's been a trying day."

I can imagine.

A purple glow formed between the older wraith's fingers, strengthening in intensity until it formed a globe. With a flick of his wrist, the globe jumped several feet into the air and paled to a milky white. The three of them stared at each other without speaking.

Seisan broke the silence first. "You look older. How long has it been for you?"

"About three years," Rem said.

"Is that so? It's only been a few months from my perspective."

"That's the risk you take when you cross the portal. The timestreams don't always synch up nicely."

"I know, but the differences have never been this significant before." Seisan rubbed the back of his neck, mulling it over. "You mentioned the blood oath ceremony before. I suppose that's right around the corner."

"Yeah. We got our invitations on Tuesday."

"My condolences."

"It could be worse. Dad found a way to stop the compulsions, at least. Corvus and I were going to stay in Morton, but now that Grigoth's goons have him… I don't know. He might not have a choice anymore."

"So you're here to rescue him," Seisan said, scrutinizing them from head to toe. "By yourselves?"

"That's right."

"In that case, I'd better come with you. The Gloaming isn't safe for anyone, let alone children."

A flash of annoyance swept through Billy. They were thirteen years old—teenagers, not little kids. Regardless, having an adult take charge lifted a huge weight off his shoulders. With Seisan on their side, they'd be unstoppable.

"We need to get moving," Rem said. "If I'm calculating things correctly, the blood oath ceremony is due to happen at midnight tomorrow. We'll need to hurry if we want to rescue Corvus in time."

Seisan walked to a nearby tree and leaned against it as though he were attempting a vertical pushup. Violet mist surged between his fingers, and the trunk released a guttural groan. He took several steps back, waving for Billy and Rem to join him, and then the tree crashed to the ground. As Billy watched, Seisan stripped the bark with magic and shaped the wood into something that resembled a long, narrow bathtub.

"It's not my best work, but it'll have to do," Seisan said, stepping inside. "Sleighs are much faster than walking."

Rem jumped in behind him, but Billy checked the interior for splinters first. Finding none, he hunkered down behind his friend.

How does this thing work without snow? Billy wondered.

The answer came when Seisan touched his still-glowing hands to the wood. The sleigh lurched forward and stopped, like a stick-shift car in the hands of a learner driver.

"Apologies. I'm a little out of practice," Seisan said, reapplying the spell. "I haven't driven one of these since I was sixteen."

The sleigh picked up pace, skimming along like a boat over flat water. Blurs of purple and black whipped past them, and the wind howled in their ears like a wounded animal. Billy clutched the sides with both hands, watching the ground rush past. *Seisan was right; this is a lot faster than walking. We'll reach the castle in no time!* Hope filled Billy's heart. *Hold on, Corvus. We're coming for you.*

Rem raised her arms, her hands awash with light. The relentless noise gave way to blissful silence, although the wind continued to tousle Billy's hair.

"What did you do?" Seisan asked without looking back.

"I put a sound filter around the sleigh," Rem explained. "It'll block out anything with the same frequency as the wind."

"But we can hear everything else?"

"That's right."

Seisan fell silent, pondering the idea. "That's clever. Did Lothaire teach you that?"

"Nope. I came up with the idea during science class and refined it during my lessons with Dad."

"I'm impressed. Not many wraiths are able to invent their own spells. It's fortunate for our side that Grigoth didn't get his hands on you. You would have made a valuable asset to him, especially in times of war."

"So there *is* a war coming," Billy said. "Corvus told us there might be, but I don't understand. Why would Grigoth wage war on Earth? We haven't done anything."

"Aside from being racist and violent toward children," Seisan said dryly. "Not to mention the vivisections."

"That's just a few people, though," Billy protested. "We're not all like that. Most of the planet didn't even know you guys existed until a week ago."

"Yes. I know." Seisan's voice gentled. "To tell you the truth, I doubt human actions have any impact on Grigoth's determination to invade. He cares more about the resources Earth has to offer, particularly food and land. Things have been bad here with the famine. Wraithkind work day in, day out for the faint chance they'll be fed. The land is dying, and the Abyss is rolling in, swallowing more and more of the Gloaming into darkness. Grigoth either can't or won't restore the land, so he needs to move the remaining populace somewhere else."

"I don't think he knows how to fix it," Rem interjected. "That or it's too late. The Abyss consumes everything in its path. There's nothing left for him to do but abdicate or turn Earth into the Gloaming two-point-oh."

"And he'll never abdicate," Seisan finished. "If an uncorrupted wraith took the throne, they might be able to reverse the damage. It's unfortunate Grigoth cares more about himself than the welfare of his people."

"I've been thinking about the issue with the time differences as well," Rem said. "If it's only been a few months for you but years for us, maybe Grigoth is distorting things to build his army faster."

"That makes sense. The faster your classmates age, the faster he can amass an army to take over Earth."

"But wouldn't that increase the speed of the Oncoming Abyss as well?" Billy asked. "He would have to be desperate."

"Indeed he would," Seisan said. "I have reason to believe he's growing more desperate with every passing day. Over the past few months, he's attempted to develop some new spells and charms. Magic that will allow weaker wraiths to cross the portal. He's also converted the castle's old armory into a closet for unmolded glamours."

"That's weird. What would he be doing with glamours?" Rem asked.

"I think I have a fairly good idea," Seisan replied. "I disguised myself as a guard and patrolled outside the room for a few days. One of the elite mages went in and transformed into a perfect replica of the president of the United States. Knowing Grigoth, I'd wager he's planning to infiltrate Earth before he attacks. If he controls the world leaders, he controls the planet. He can manipulate foreign policies to allow the mass immigration of wraithkind. Everyone here will jump at the chance to get a nice, new home filled with the basic necessities they've been denied for so long."

"Wait," Billy said, his eyes widening in horror. "You said they can impersonate *real* humans? How would they know how to act? Wraith culture and human culture are totally different."

"Oh," Rem said, paling.

"What?"

"The schools. Grigoth's been sending wraith kids to Earth since his reign began. He said it was to give them a better life, but they've been coming back here when they turn thirteen. They know everything about human culture. They know how to integrate."

"It's like an advance guard," Billy realized, his hand flying to his mouth. "You said wraiths could only get into the Academy if they had magical aptitude *and* knowledge of Earth customs. Grigoth's been planning this from the start."

"Yes. I think it's safe to assume the infiltration began a long time ago," Seisan said. "There's been a lot of conflict on Earth in the past hundred years. It wouldn't surprise me if Grigoth's minions had a hand in that too."

"How are we supposed to stop them?" Billy cried. "It's not like we can go up to random world leaders and order them to remove their glamours. If they *are* wraiths in disguise, it's not like they're going to obey. And if we're wrong, everyone will think we're crazy."

"It's a difficult situation, but there's nothing we can do about it right now," Seisan said. "Let's focus on finding Corvus first. We can worry about everything else once he's safe."

Chapter Forty-One

The dank dungeon air mingled with the coppery stench of congealed blood. Corvus cracked one eye open, tried to sit up, and collapsed back to the cold stone floor. Pale werelights floated above him, not bright enough to illuminate the corners of the room, but bright enough to hurt his sensitive eyes. For a moment, he just stared at them as they winked in and out of existence, flaring and fading like embers in a campfire.

Disjointed images of camping trips with the Porter family swam into his mind. Sitting around a roaring campfire. The taste of melted marshmallows heavy on his tongue. The smoky, woodsy smell of his flannel shirt the next morning. Climbing trees with Billy and pelting his brothers with acorns whenever Mrs. Porter wasn't looking.

Trees, trees, trees.

There was something about them—he could feel it in his bones—but he couldn't remember why they made his stomach churn. He drifted through the sleepy haze of memories a while longer. Listening to Billy ramble on and on about the latest episode of *Doctor Who*. Sleeping on the ground for the first time, a tree root digging into his back, and—hang on, why was he lying on the ground now?

All at once, the flood banks around his mind burst. *The Enforcers!*

He sat bolt upright, adrenaline coursing through his veins. Shaky breaths echoed off the stone walls. He remembered punching his captor with every ounce of magic-augmented strength his body could muster, twisting and writhing in his desperation to flee. But that little act of defiance had been his last. The cell around him was proof of that.

Footsteps thudded outside, and a set of keys rattled in the lock. Corvus backed up against the wall before the door swung open. A hulking wraith stared down at him, piggy eyes narrowed. Corvus reached for the flow of magic but found nothing.

Panic fluttered in his chest. *What did they do to me?* The guard's meaty fingers closed around his wrist, cutting off his circulation. Corvus yelped and tried to pull away, but the guard didn't seem to notice. Instead, he grunted and walked out of the cell, dragging Corvus after him like a ragdoll.

Corvus scrambled to find his feet, succeeding mere moments before they reached the stairs. *One, two, three, four, five…* He counted sixteen steps in total but stumbled on the last one and would have fallen if not for the handrail.

I've got to be more careful, he thought, trotting to keep pace with the guard.

Faded tapestries lined the corridor, each depicting a period of history. Corvus knew all about them in theory—several of Lothaire's books delved into the subject—but seeing them in person gave him a greater appreciation of their design. In the first one, straight lines stretched out from the center, forming a sun-like image that symbolized the birth of magical power.

The second tapestry was a perfect replica of Gethen's *Cliffs of Lamentation*, the most famous painting in wraith history. A castle featured prominently in the third tapestry. A circle with feathered edges surrounded the castle, representing the discovery of the portals. In the fourth and final tapestry, Grigoth held the severed head of King Vaeril.

One of these is not like the others, Corvus thought.

If he'd had any doubts about his whereabouts before, the tapestries dispelled them. He was in Grigoth's lair, and that meant he couldn't bully or sweet-talk anyone into granting his freedom. Unless someone broke in to save him, he'd be dead or enslaved before sunset.

Who am I kidding? No one's coming to save me, Corvus thought. *Billy might try. He's always wanted to be an action hero. But if he does come, he'll only get himself killed. Rem and Lothaire might try too, I suppose. I hope Rem doesn't. I'd never forgive myself if anything happened to her.*

The guard brought him into a large, open chamber at the end of the corridor. Judging by its size and lack of furniture, it must have been a ballroom at some point—not that anyone felt much like dancing these days. A sizeable crowd huddled in the center of the room. Their blank eyes stared straight ahead, their malnourished bodies swaying with fatigue. Corvus didn't recognize anyone until he reached the front of the room.

King Grigoth sat on an ornate throne, his chiseled face sneering down at him. Revulsion squirmed through Corvus's entire being. The king studied him like he would a repulsive insect, one he intended to squash beneath his boot. A crown of obsidian cradled his head, and he clenched a matching scepter in his fist. With his other hand, he leaned on a granite basin filled with an odd, metallic-scented liquid. Corvus's gut roiled in protest.

"The blood oath ceremony begins," Grigoth intoned.

Slotting his scepter into its custom-made socket, he unsheathed his dagger. The blade gleamed a sickly green under the werelights. The designs emblazoned on the side resembled no runes Corvus had ever seen, but their implicit meaning sent shivers of fear and loathing down his spine.

"Corvus," Grigoth purred. "Step forward to the altar."

Fat chance, Corvus thought, but his legs moved without his consent.

"Good. Very good. Do you accept me as the one true ruler of the Gloaming, wise and without error, and do you solemnly swear to obey my every command?"

Corvus bit his tongue, trying to keep it from moving. Blood spilled into his mouth, but he paid it no heed. The sharpness of the pain eroded Grigoth's mind control, and he struggled against the guard who restrained him.

"I will never serve you," he spat. Another presence touched his mind, crushing his consciousness beneath its will.

Get out of my head, Grigoth! he thought-screamed. But it was no use. Rubbery and foreign, his lips gave form to the required words.

His legs lurched forward, his right arm outstretched to take the knife from Grigoth. With his mind subjugated to the king's will, there was no risk of a rebellious stabbing. He fought against Grigoth's oppressive presence, throwing everything he had at the mental prison. Rage, fear, willpower, desperation…

He felt his hand grasp the bone hilt. Felt it pull toward the palm of his other hand. The knife hovered there for a moment, a mere whisper away from slicing through his skin. Then it tilted toward his belly, drawing excited murmurs from the crowd.

Dread filled Corvus. *No…*

The blade plunged into his stomach, tearing the flesh in a jagged line from left to right. A strangled scream tore from his throat, so animalistic he didn't recognize it as his own. Rivulets of hot blood streamed down his torso, soaking into his pants and dripping to the floor. A burning, throbbing sensation pulsed through his entire body, emanating from the epicenter in waves of utter agony.

Seppuku…

He'd learned about the ritualistic form of suicide during history class. Disgraced samurai warriors eviscerated themselves in order to regain their honor. Given the wraith's obsession with honor and exotic cultures, it didn't surprise him they'd adopted such a gruesome tradition.

Black spots filled his vision as Grigoth withdrew from his mind. Corvus sank to his knees, hugging himself, and the knife went clattering to the ground. His organs strained against the pocket of open skin, and for a moment, he feared they would fall out. After all, wasn't that the point? Or had something gone wrong?

If this really was seppuku, I'd be dead, Corvus thought. *Either Grigoth doesn't know what he's doing, or he deliberately made the cuts shallow enough that I wouldn't die right away.*

Of the two options, the first seemed more likely. As a child, he'd had to explain a lot of things about human culture to his father, who struggled to wrap his head around the various traditions and social customs. Being more than a century removed from life on Earth, it made sense that Grigoth would suffer the same deficits. Most of the old order regarded humans as exotic curiosities rather than intellectual equals—an understandable mistake, given how advanced wraithkind were prior to Grigoth's reign.

Corvus jolted back to reality when the guard dragged him down from the altar, painting the stairs with his blood. *Why am I thinking about history when I'm about to* become *history?* The ridiculousness of the situation—the blatant unfairness—filled Corvus with a wild, uncontrollable energy.

He wrenched his arm free, not even feeling the *pop* of his shoulder dislocating. Blood splashed on his shoes as he dashed up the stairs and kicked Grigoth in the shins. It was a foolish move. Somewhere in the back of his mind, he knew that. But pure electricity arced through his veins, and without access to magic, he felt he would explode if he didn't get it out somehow.

The king looked more surprised than hurt, but Corvus savored his expression all the same. A fist collided with the back of his head, and the electricity vanished. Agony coursed through his body once more— doubling, tripling, quadrupling—until it was the only thing he knew. Somewhere far away, the guard's voice mumbled hasty apologies. The vice-like hand clamped onto his wrist and dragged him back to the stairs, making sure he felt every single bump on the way down.

To Corvus's disappointment, his act of rebellion didn't stop Grigoth for long. He heard the king chanting something, and his legs went numb as if they'd ceased to exist. When they got back to the dungeon, the guard threw him into his cell and slammed the door. The resulting metallic clang sounded like a death knell.

He was alone.

Somehow, the sense of isolation worsened the pain in Corvus's belly. He tried to roll into a more comfortable position, but his unresponsive legs made movement impossible. Taking a deep breath, he pried his shaking hands away from his belly. A thick layer of magenta blood squelched between his fingers.

Is it supposed to be that color? he wondered.

He couldn't bring himself to look at the wound itself. If he did, he might never stop screaming.

Chapter Forty-Two

BILLY AND HIS friends arrived on the outskirts of the castle around midday. He'd dozed most of the journey, partly due to exhaustion and partly to avoid the complaints of his empty stomach. Seisan shook him awake, his face haggard in the cold light.

"We have to go on foot from here," the older wraith said. "Walking through the front door is next to impossible, but I know a secret passage. It should be safe at this time of day."

He strode into the forest, and Rem jogged after him, pulling Billy along by the wrist. He still felt groggy from his sudden awakening, and the weirdness of being in a different dimension didn't help. Fortunately, it only took them a few minutes to reach Grigoth's castle.

"There's a drain in the outer wall," Seisan explained, scanning the area for guards. "There are steel bars blocking it, but I bent them out of the way during my last visit. Considering the damage is underwater, I doubt anyone's noticed, let alone attempted to fix it."

"And if they have, you can always break it again, right?" Rem asked.

"I can, but I'd rather not. If someone's in the area, they'll almost certainly notice the energy discharge."

The two wraiths scrambled down the banks and waded into the clear water. Billy paced back and forth a few times before following them. After his disastrous dive into Oilskin Lake, the idea of submerging himself again made him uneasy.

Come on, this is stupid, he berated himself. *They're both waiting for you. Get in the water!*

He trudged to the edge of the moat and eased himself in. Unlike Oilskin Lake, the liquid surrounding him felt and behaved like real water. It wasn't slimy, and it didn't try to drag him to the bottom. The knot in his gut loosened.

"It's a straight shot through," Seisan said when he joined them next to the drain hole. "You may not be able to see it from here, but there's an air pocket at the top of the tunnel. As soon as you clear the grate, go straight up and you'll reach it. Understand?"

Rem nodded.

"Good," Seisan said. "I'll kick the top of the grate three times when I'm safely on the other side. When you feel the bars vibrate, that will be your signal to follow. Hold on tight, won't you?"

"I will," Rem promised.

Seisan dove straight down, becoming a dark blur beneath the watery veil. After a few seconds, the blur morphed and disappeared.

"He made it," Rem reported, her fingers clutching the grate as instructed. "I'm going to go next. Did you hear what he said about the bars?"

"Yeah."

"Okay. Just checking."

Billy's stomach sank as he watched her go. The water didn't scare him anymore, but his vulnerability did. If a guard wandered past and saw him, how on earth would he explain himself? *Yes, officer, I'm a tourist from another dimension, and I thought this looked like a nice place for a swim.*

He grabbed the metal bars and waited for the signal, praying it wouldn't take too long. In fact, twenty seconds passed before the vibration jolted his arm. Billy took a deep breath and dived, groping the bars with both hands. When the gap widened, he propelled himself through. Strong hands grasped his shoulders and hauled his head above water.

"You okay, Billy?" Rem asked.

Billy blinked, taking in the low archway of the ceiling. If he treaded water too vigorously, he would be at serious risk of hitting his head.

"Yeah, I'm fine," he insisted. "Let's go."

They bobbed along the watery corridor with Seisan at the helm. Instead of paddling, Billy used the slippery walls to push himself forward. Water droplets plinked down around them, combining with their breaths and splashes to create an echoing soundscape. Soon, they reached a concrete embankment slathered in greenish-brown sludge. The drain continued for several hundred feet, but Seisan scrambled ashore instead of following it. Billy and Rem crawled out after him, grimacing at their filthy clothes.

"This isn't a sewer, is it?" Billy asked. The moat outside had been crystal clear, but here it bordered on the color of excrement.

Seisan cast a quick spell to dry them off and nullify their new, pungent odor. "Something like that. Don't worry. We can get out through the service entrance."

The service entrance turned out to be a rusting metal door at the far end of the embankment. Seisan pressed his ear against it, holding up a hand for silence. Apparently detecting no enemies on the other side, he stepped back and heaved the door open. The hinges squealed for all they were worth.

Billy winced. "Do you think someone heard that?"

"Maybe, maybe not," Seisan said. "Rem, can you use your sound-masking spell when I close the door?"

"I'll try."

Face lined with concentration, she cast the spell she'd invented. Once they'd all walked through, Seisan let the door go. It swung shut without the slightest squeak.

"Nice work," he whispered, leading them into the first corridor of the castle proper.

Billy gazed around in awe, wondering where the wraiths had found the materials to build a castle this big. *Maybe there's a quarry nearby. Or maybe they conjured the stone out of thin air. Is that even possible?* He resolved to ask Seisan about it later.

Torches lined the walls at infrequent intervals, each holding a ghostly ball of purple fire. Magic, Billy guessed, was a lot more reliable than real fire or electric light. He grabbed the closest torch and twisted it free from its socket, hoping to illuminate their path. The orb didn't move. *Well… never mind, then.*

"That's a werelight," Rem whispered as he replaced the torch. "They only respond to the wraith who made them."

"So even you couldn't…"

"No. But I can make a new one if you want me to."

Billy considered her offer. "Nah, it's fine. We don't have far to go anyway."

Seisan pushed open a door, filling the corridor with a faint silvery glow. Billy went through first, unsure of what to expect. When his eyes adjusted to the dim light, his heart quickened. Rows upon rows of shimmery, translucent fabric lined the room.

"You weren't kidding when you said they had a lot of glamours," Rem breathed.

Billy buried his fingers in the closest one, savoring the silky texture. Tingles raced up his arm when he lifted it from the hanger.

"We should use them to our advantage," Seisan said, draping a glamour over his arm and tossing another one to Rem. "We're too easily recognizable. Especially you, Billy. We need to look like ordinary servants or guards if we want to get close to the dungeon."

He pulled the shapeless garment over his head and let the edges fall to the floor. The fabric tightened around his body. Seconds later, a new wraith appeared to have taken his place. On the other side of the room, Rem's glamour turned her into an older version of Almwin.

"Are you ready?" Seisan asked, walking over to Billy. "Wrap the glamour around yourself, and I'll take care of the rest."

Billy obeyed, though his nerves were on tenterhooks. No matter what the wraiths said, he didn't want the fabric near his mouth. *Have they even tried these things on humans before?* Almost at once, the glamour molded to his shape, moving more like water than a solid object. It grew large enough to encompass his entire body, splitting apart to encase each limb and joining back together to form a seamless whole.

The ephemeral material settled on his face like a cool mist rather than a smothering blanket. He hated the way it wriggled up his nose and down his throat, but it didn't affect his breathing. The now-familiar thrum of electricity intensified for a split second, then relaxed to a gentle hum.

"There. How do you feel, Billy?" Seisan asked.

Billy opened his eyes. Tiny silver threads hovered around the edges of his vision, but other than that, he didn't feel any different.

"I'm fine," he answered, surprise coloring his voice. "Is there a mirror anywhere?"

Seisan jerked a thumb over his shoulder, and Billy hurried to check out his new appearance. His heart rate skyrocketed. *That can't be me.* The person in the mirror wore the same dusty, bloodstained outfit as him, but their skin was void-black and lined with pulsing violet runes. Prominent cheekbones replaced flat ones; inky hair replaced sandy brown. Indigo eyes with amorphous pupils peered back at him, devoid of the white sclera. Billy shivered and took a step back, disconcerted when his reflection copied the motion.

Rem gave him a thumbs-up. "Looking good, Billy."

He turned away from the mirror, unable to look at himself any longer. "Thanks. You too."

"Meh, I don't know. I could have done a better job with the hair."

"Enough idle chatter," Seisan said. "The official blood oath ceremony may not have started, but Grigoth usually holds a pre-ceremony for rebellious wraiths."

Rem's eyes widened. "You mean he could be torturing Corvus right now?"

"That's certainly a possibility."

"What are we wasting time for, then? Let's go!"

Seisan inclined his head and led them into the hallway. The door at the end took them into the heart of the kitchens, where a wraith hunched over the sink, scrubbing a soup ladle.

The famine must be pretty bad if Grigoth's own kitchen is this empty, Billy thought. *If someone stumbled in here by accident, they'd never guess there was a major ceremony coming up.*

The lone servant remained silent as they passed through, affording them no more than a cursory glance. A long corridor stretched out past the kitchen door, and Seisan followed it for a few paces before stopping. Two adjoining staircases, separated by a stone wall, descended into the bowels of the castle. He hesitated, considering them, then took the one on the right. Billy and Rem spiraled down after him.

The air grew thicker and mustier with every step, and the clank of metal boots met Billy's ears. *I hope Seisan knows what he's doing.* The guard at the bottom of the stairs stopped pacing when they came into view.

A deep but undeniably feminine voice boomed up at them. "Do you know how long I've been walking this post? Four days! That good-for-nothing Boren never showed up. If he hasn't starved to death by now, he has a lot to answer for."

Seisan held his hands up in a placating manner. "Boren was unavoidably detained. We're here to relieve you."

"All three of you?"

"Grigoth's orders."

"That's *King* Grigoth to you," the guard retorted. She blinked several times, as if waking from a dream, then shook her head. "You know what? I don't care. Just take your positions. I've earned my meal."

She stomped up the stairs and pushed past Billy, muttering something about the kitchens. *Boy, is she going to be disappointed.*

"This is the dungeon where Grigoth keeps his rebellious initiates," Seisan explained when the guard left earshot. "Corvus should be in one of these cells."

Billy and Rem dashed along the dungeon corridor on opposite sides, peering into each cell. Most were empty, but a few housed adult wraiths. They didn't speak when they saw Billy, but the despair in their eyes spoke volumes. A few had bones in their cells that looked suspiciously like a human's.

Or a wraith's, Billy supposed. *Our organs might be different, but our skeletons are the same. Did they starve to death or were they murdered?*

Either way, the idea of being stuck in a six-by-six foot room with a decomposing corpse churned his stomach. He glanced into another cell, making inadvertent eye contact with the wretches inside. He wanted to reassure them, but he couldn't think of anything comforting to say. Nothing that would put a dent in their suffering. *They would be better off dead.* Rather than dwelling on the morbid thought, Billy forced himself to move forward and check the remaining cells. He heard a low moan when he looked in the last one, but he couldn't see an occupant.

"Corvus?" he whispered.

The moaning stopped. "Is someone there?"

Billy's heart leapt. *It's him! He's alive!*

"Seisan! Over here!" he called in a stage whisper.

Seisan covered the ground faster than Billy thought possible and shattered the lock with magic. The door swung open, and Corvus's crumpled form fell out as though he'd been leaning against it. His eyes were glazed over, and his breath came in short, uneven pants. Seisan moved to grab him, but the boy yelped and folded in on himself.

"What's wrong?" Seisan demanded. "What have they done to you?"

"The oath," Corvus wheezed. "They made me. I didn't have a choice." Seisan reached for his son's hands, recoiling from the strangled cry his touch provoked. "Not there. My stomach."

"We can heal it," Rem said, rushing to his side. "Corvus, please. We can fix this. Let us help you."

"It's a blood oath scar. You might not be able to."

Agony ricocheted over his face as he attempted to roll onto his back, and he writhed into the fetal position instead.

Seisan cupped the boy's face with both hands. "We won't know unless we try. You've got to be brave, Son."

"So you are my father," Corvus said between gasps. "I thought so. You changed your face. Is that Rem with you?"

"Rem and Billy, yes," Seisan said. "They wanted to help you by any means necessary."

"And they did a great job of that, didn't they?" Corvus snapped, gesturing at his belly. A spasm racked his feeble frame, and the labored quality of his breathing intensified. "Sorry. I didn't mean to be rude. I'm a bad… a bad…"

"We know you're a bad patient," Rem said, placing a hand on his shoulder. "But that doesn't matter. We're still going to help you."

"It hurts," Corvus whimpered. "I can't stand it."

"The sooner we get to work, the better, then," Seisan said. His optimistic tone clashed with the concern on his face. "Billy, go and keep watch. Rem and I can handle this."

Billy nodded and obeyed; he'd seen enough. He made it to the foot of the stairs before the screams started.

Chapter Forty-Three

TEN MINUTES PASSED before Seisan called Billy back to him. Corvus sat slumped against the wall of his cell, his eyes half-closed. A violet scar glared out from the tattered remains of his shirt. Seisan and Rem had done an amazing job of staunching the wound, but he still looked ready to keel over.

"Hey," Billy said.

Corvus blinked and lifted his unfocused gaze. "Hey. You look different."

"Tell me about it." Billy glanced down at his glamour-clad arm, then back up at his friend. "How're you holding up?"

"Hard to say. The scar's throbbing a bit. It probably won't stop for the rest of my life."

Billy nodded, unsure of how to respond. If Corvus returned to Earth against Grigoth's will, the pain from the scar would increase with every passing moment. Unless Lothaire had another last-minute wonder spell up his sleeve—one that worked on the blood oath instead of the ceremony-based compulsions—Corvus would be reduced to a bedridden invalid.

"We need to get out of here," Seisan said, pacing back and forth beside the stairwell.

"I don't think I can walk," Corvus said. Grunting, he tried to push himself upright, but his trembling arms gave way and he collapsed. "Grigoth cast some kind of chaining spell on my legs."

Rem crouched next to him, her hands glowing. Corvus's left leg spasmed, but it remained limp and floppy like a dead fish. Frowning, she tried again. This time, both of Corvus's legs kicked out, flailing uselessly in the air.

"Can you stand?" Billy asked.

He pulled Corvus's arm around his shoulder and lifted him to his feet. The other boy lolled against him, his body a deadweight.

"It seems like it," Corvus said in a strained voice. "Don't ask me to walk, though."

"It might take a while for you to regain control of your legs," Rem said. "Remember when I took that botched potion and ended up switching between monster and wraith every day? I had balance problems too, but they always got better within a few hours. I'm sure it'll be the same for you."

"Okay, great, but what are we going to do *now*?" Corvus asked.

Billy looked at Seisan, taking in his hooded gaze and furrowed brow. The distant clanking of boots on stone echoed from the grand hallway above. The older wraith scratched his chin, his gaze shifting from the teenagers to the stairs.

"I fear we've stayed here too long already," he murmured. "I could carry Corvus out, but there are guards patrolling upstairs now. With the ceremony so close, they'll be keeping their eyes peeled for anything out of the ordinary."

"Can we outrun them?" Billy asked.

"Not in an open corridor."

"It's only a hundred feet from the stairs to the drain."

"Yes, but we'll be struck down in ten. We can't risk it."

"Would a spell of misdirection help?" Rem asked, tilting her head to one side. "I could trick their eyes into believing Corvus is an inanimate object."

"Like a potato sack or something?" Billy asked.

"In a famine?" Seisan asked.

Blood rushed to Billy's cheeks. "Okay, forget the potato sack. What about a plank of wood? Or a battle-axe?"

"A battle-axe could work," Rem agreed. "I saw an armory opposite the glamour room when we came in. If anyone stops us, we can tell them we found it in the dungeon and we're returning it to its rightful place."

"I can't say I like this plan," Seisan said, but he gestured for her to go ahead.

Rem released the spell from her cupped hands, transforming Corvus in front of their eyes. Billy *knew* it was him, but his vision played tricks on him. Two overlapping images competed for his attention, but in the end, the axe won out.

"Let's go," Seisan said, hefting the "axe" over one shoulder. "Quickly and quietly. If anyone *does* stop us, let me do the talking."

Billy nodded and followed him up the stairs. If someone questioned their actions, he'd be too busy evacuating his bladder to explain his presence.

True to Seisan's word, the corridor crawled with guards. Most of them wore ugly steel helmets jammed onto their heads like upside-down buckets. None of them wore body armor, but Billy suspected they had magical defenses instead.

The guards didn't give their arrival a second glance. Nevertheless, Billy felt an overwhelming desire to *run*. To throw caution to the wind and sprint the entire length of the corridor. To dash through the kitchens to the service hatch and the flooded drain that would carry him to safety. Seisan's sedate pace put a damper on his plan but not his frazzled nerves.

"Halt!"

Billy's blood ran cold, and his legs shuddered to a standstill. Invisible vipers coiled around his shins, doing their level best to squeeze the marrow out of his bones.

Move! he urged himself.

But it was no use. He could no more take a step forward than he could fly to the moon. He glanced at Rem and Seisan, who struggled against their own restraints. Was this the chaining spell Corvus told them about? And if so, why hadn't Rem done something about it?

"We're returning this axe to the armory—"

Seisan cut himself off with a strangled cry, clawing at his throat. His rune-like veins puffed out, his breath coming in tiny, choking hitches.

Footsteps approached from behind. "I know a falsehood when I smell one."

The silky voice made Billy's skin crawl. He wrenched around, trying to see its owner, but they might as well have been a ghost.

"Your name is Seisan Oathbreaker," the voice continued, purring with self-satisfaction. "Your fancy magic doesn't fool me. I see through your enchantments, and I shatter them."

All at once, the glamours were shucked from their bodies. Murmurs of surprise rippled through the guards, and Billy fought the urge to cover himself. Clothed or not, he felt naked without his disguise.

"Well, well, well," the voice simpered. "You brought me a little *human* to play with. How touching. A friend of the children, I presume?"

The mage stepped in front of Billy, his face perilously close. Black teeth zigzagged across his gums, their razor-sharp points angled toward his target. The smell of fried onions and rotten shrimp wafted past them.

"Please. I just want to go home," Billy whimpered.

"Then go," the mage said. "You're of no interest to me. Your companions on the other hand… well. It looks like young Corvus needs a reminder of where his loyalties lie."

Seisan jerked back, his eyes ablaze. Static electricity buzzed through the air like a nest of angry wasps. Snarls of pearl-gray smoke exploded into existence, filling the corridor with a bitter stench that burned Billy's throat. The smoke curled into clouds, darkening and lengthening into a full-blown thunderstorm. A bolt of lightning shot from Seisan's palm, striking their captor in the side. Billy's legs lurched forward. *I'm free!*

Seisan lowered Corvus to the ground, making eye contact with Billy.

The look said it all. *Take him home. Keep him safe.*

Tremors racked Corvus's frame when Billy hauled him to his feet. The wraith boy stumbled, his body sagging under its own weight. Seisan's sword whistled through the air, but the injured mage sidestepped the blow with ease.

"Come on, Billy," Rem urged. She pulled Corvus's other arm around her neck, and together, they dragged him toward the kitchens.

The servant was scrubbing the same soup ladle when they burst in. Upon seeing Corvus's battered state, the wraith yelped and flattened himself against the wall. Rem blasted open the door to the next corridor. This, apparently, was the final straw. The servant dropped the ladle and dashed into the corridor they'd entered from.

"Come on!" Rem repeated.

Billy obeyed, but he couldn't resist looking over his shoulder as they passed through the door. The other door hung open too, thanks to the dishwasher's departure, and the scene on the other side sent his mind into a tailspin.

Seisan moved in slow motion, as though the air around him had turned to honey. His blade stopped in midair. He swayed on his feet. A blast of golden light struck him square in the chest, and Seisan's body shrank in on itself, shriveling up like a plant deprived of water. He took a shuffling step forward and fell to his knees. Then his body exploded like a macabre firework, raining blood and viscera onto the floor below.

We've got to get out of here! Billy panicked, shoving Corvus and Rem aside in his desperation to reach the drain.

He couldn't process what he'd seen. Had the wraith mage just *killed* Seisan? In cold blood? It was the second murder he'd seen in as many days, but this one… He shuddered. There had been no hint of mercy in the mage's eyes. Not the slightest hint of compassion. If anything, Billy thought he'd been smirking.

The sound of Corvus's shoe scraping the concrete forced him back into the present. Even so, it took him a few seconds to realize his friend had fainted. *Why now of all times?* He lay Corvus flat next to the drain channel and splashed into the water, paying no mind to the filth surrounding him.

With Rem's help, he eased Corvus's legs into the discolored liquid, pulling him forward until his body could float unaided. Rem jumped in after him, holding the unconscious boy's head above the surface.

They swam through the drain as fast as they could, pushing and pulling Corvus along. The end of the tunnel came quickly, but not soon enough for Billy's nerves. *How are we going to get him through the underwater part?*

"Wait here," Rem said, as if reading his mind. "When I signal, dive down and pass him to me through the grate."

She disappeared under the water before Billy could argue. In her absence, he became acutely aware of the way his breathing echoed in the narrow passageway. For a terrifying moment, it sounded like it came from someone else. He imagined the mage creeping up behind him. Blowing him up like he had Seisan. No one in the Gloaming would care. He doubted they'd even notice.

His thoughts drifted to his parents. His brothers. His friends. The wraith kids. Shauna. All the petty drama seemed so meaningless now. Even Jeffrey Bancroft would be a welcome reprieve from the horror he'd witnessed here. More than anything, he wanted to go back to dealing with normal teenage problems. Things like acne and pop quizzes and awkward first dates. Not murderous sorcerers from other dimensions who liked to make people explode.

The steel bars vibrated, and Billy submerged. Corvus's limp body slowed him down, but he refused to let go. Rem's arms stretched through the deformed grate, waiting for him. Together, they maneuvered the unconscious boy to the other side. Billy's lungs burned for air as he squeezed through the gap himself.

Rem and Corvus rose high above him, making a break for the banks of the moat. Billy oriented himself toward them, kicking for all he was worth. When he reached the shore, Corvus lay flat on his back, half-in, half-out of the water. Death rattled in his chest.

"Hang in there, buddy. We've got you," Billy murmured.

He slung Corvus's arm across his shoulders, and Rem helped them up. Shouts of outrage followed them into the forest, no doubt from Grigoth's sentries.

Rem cursed. "Forget this. Let's go straight to the sleigh."

"What if there are archers?"

"There won't be. Ranged weapons aren't honorable."

"Yeah, well, freezing your opponent and blowing them up isn't very honorable either."

A spark of fear kindled in Rem's eyes. "You mean the mage…?"

Billy nodded.

Rem's mouth dropped open, closed, and then opened again. "I… I didn't know. Is there any chance Seisan…"

Billy shook his head.

"Oh… I see."

By unspoken agreement, they remained on their previous course. A couple of minutes later, they arrived at the sleigh. Rem and Billy shoved Corvus inside and jumped in after him. The sleigh hurtled forward, away from the castle and the horrors within. It didn't move as fast as it had with Seisan at the helm, but the mage would be hard-pressed to catch them without a sleigh of his own. Billy turned his attention back to Corvus. The boy's lips were fading in color, and a clammy sheen glazed his skin. No air passed through his nostrils.

"What's wrong with him? Is he drowning?" Billy asked. Panic rose in his chest. "Rem, we have to stop. You have to heal him!"

"I can't!" Rem responded, glancing over her shoulder for a split second. "If I stop, they could catch us."

"No one's coming! Rem, please. We can't let him die like this."

"He probably inhaled water from the moat. You'll have to help him expel it."

But how? Billy wanted to say. *I can't give him CPR. I don't even know where a wraith's heart is!*

Thinking fast, he turned Corvus onto his side and struck him on the back as hard as he could. A sharp *whoosh* of air escaped his friend's lungs. He thumped him again and again, unsure whether he was helping or doing more damage. On the sixth strike, water gushed out of Corvus's mouth. The boy gasped for breath, coughing and spluttering as the last drops dribbled down his chin. Overjoyed, Billy wrapped him in a hug.

"Never dunk me underwater again," Corvus groaned, leaning back against Billy's chest. "The least you could have done was give me some warning."

"Sorry," Billy said. "I would have warned you, but you were unconscious, and I was terrified that guy would catch us. Who was he anyway? He seemed to have us all figured out."

"I'm not sure, but he seemed too powerful to be a random foot soldier," Rem said. "He must have been one of the king's elite guard. Or…"

"Or what?" Billy asked.

"Or the king himself," Corvus finished. "I didn't get a good look at him, but the voice sounded about right. It had the same arrogance as Grigoth's did when he gutted me like a fish."

"But he was a soldier," Billy protested. "He was wearing a helmet like all the other guards."

"If there's one thing you need to know about Grigoth, it's that he loves to play little games with his subjects," Corvus said. "This kind of thing is funny to him. He was probably watching you guys from the start. Waiting for you to fall into his trap. Good thing we got away as fast as we did."

"Yeah, good thing," Billy echoed.

"There's only one thing I don't get," Corvus continued, squinting up at his friends. "I could have sworn my dad was in there with us. But that's crazy, right? I must have been hallucinating."

Rem and Billy exchanged a brief glance. *He doesn't remember?*

"It wasn't a hallucination," Billy told him. Stomach acid gurgled up his throat, and he swallowed a few times to force it back down.

Corvus's expression faltered. "Where is he, then? I can't wait to tell him everything I've been up to. Can you imagine his face when he finds out I've been rooming with you for three years?"

In the ensuing silence, all traces of positive emotion vanished.

"Why isn't he on the sleigh?" Corvus asked, his voice trembling on the last word.

"I'm so sorry, Corvus," Billy said. "I don't know how to tell you this, but your dad is dead."

Chapter Forty-Four

THE HOURS PASSED in uneasy silence. Billy expected Corvus to cry, scream, attack him, do *something*. But he didn't. He just sat there, staring at the skeletal branches overhead.

Seisan became dead to him the moment he left, Billy thought, swallowing hard. *Corvus has been grieving him for three years. He probably doesn't have any emotions left to give. And if that's true, then what I told him was the final, terrible confirmation of what he knew all along.*

"We're here," Rem announced, bringing the sleigh to a gradual halt.

Billy tore his gaze away from his injured friend. Oilskin Lake loomed in front of them, a dark blot on a dark landscape. *Home.*

He raked a hand through Corvus's slimy hair, feeling oddly protective. "Come on. I'll help you get out."

"I can do it myself," the other boy replied, his voice devoid of emotion.

He leaned over the edge of the sleigh, gripping the wood with what meager strength he had left. Rocking forward, he swung his legs over the side and lowered himself to the ground. His knees buckled, and he would have collapsed in a heap if Billy hadn't caught him in time.

"I can do it myself," Corvus repeated.

He freed himself from Billy's grasp and tottered toward the lake, tripping over every pebble he encountered along the way.

"I don't know how we're going to do this," Rem murmured.

"Do what?" Billy asked.

"Get him back to Earth without activating the blood oath spell. Bound wraiths aren't allowed to cross the portal without permission from Grigoth."

They rejoined Corvus, who walked in mindless circles through the shallows. The midnight-purple ooze didn't scare Billy anymore. Not as much as what lay behind him. He linked arms with Corvus, forcing the boy to stop moving. Rem looped her arms through Billy's and Corvus's, completing the chain. Although physical contact wasn't necessary to cross dimensions, something about it made Billy feel safer. Stronger. More in control.

"I'm ready when you are," Corvus said.

"I'm ready too," Rem said. "I'm just not sure it'll work."

"As long as you're the one doing it, it'll work."

Rem bit her lip and cast the spell that would transport them back to Earth. They arrived in a blinding flash, and Billy fell to his knees, trembling. He hadn't eaten in—what? Two days? Three? Adrenaline may have kept his body going, but now he was running on fumes. He crawled out of the lake on his hands and knees, his stomach clenched. Lothaire ran toward them, his eyes wide and his hair a mess.

"Where have you been?" the policeman exclaimed. Relief and fury fought for control of his voice, the former winning by a slim margin. "You've been gone for five days!"

Five days? Billy blanched. *My parents are going to kill me. I'll never...*

He didn't finish the thought. Mr. and Mrs. Porter stood at the edge of the park, their arms folded across their chests. *How did they know to come here?* He thought about waving to them, but their stony expressions convinced him to bide his time. He stood up, ducked his head, and scurried after his friends.

"A couple of Enforcers ambushed us," Rem explained. "They dragged Corvus back to Grigoth's castle and forced him to take the blood oath."

"They cut open my stomach," Corvus added. "I'm pretty sure my spleen fell out."

"You never had a spleen," Lothaire informed him, then turned to Rem. "What about you? Did you take the oath?"

"Billy and I didn't get captured. We went after Corvus to rescue him."

"What?" Lothaire's face purpled. "Do you have any idea how dangerous that was? You could have been killed! What on earth were you thinking?"

Rem glared daggers at her father. "Would you rather we left him to die?"

"I'm not saying that—"

"Lothaire, please," Corvus whimpered. All eyes turned to him. "The oath scar. It's burning me. Can't you do something?"

Concern extinguished the fire in Lothaire's eyes. He dropped to his knees next to Corvus and lifted the boy's tattered shirt. Billy gasped. The blood oath scar had grown. Tiny amber offshoots created a lattice across his skin, stretching toward his chest. An infection? Billy didn't know.

Lothaire placed a palm over the scar and hummed something under his breath. Corvus gasped and squirmed as a lavender glow enveloped his gut. A full minute passed before Lothaire removed his hand. The amber roots had receded, but faint, silvery lines streaked the area they used to be.

"How do you feel?" Lothaire asked.

"A little better," Corvus replied. The corner of his lip spasmed. "Actually, never mind. It's getting bad again."

"Hmmm, okay." Lothaire rocked back on his heels. "I've never dealt with anything like this before. I'll have to do some tests to refine the spell."

"That'll take months!"

"At the very least. I'm sorry, Corvus. I didn't expect you to end up in a situation like this."

"Isn't there something else you can do?" Corvus snapped. Tears filled his eyes, but he blinked them away.

"I can cast a spell to deaden and remove the nerve centers around the scar."

"Do it."

"It'll be permanent."

"I don't care, just do it. *Please*, Lothaire."

The desperation in his voice broke Billy's heart. The older wraith nodded and cast the spell. Something passed between the two of them, and Corvus's face slackened.

"Thank you," he whispered and passed out.

"Is he going to be okay?" Rem asked, worry saturating her voice.

"He'll be fine," Lothaire replied. "Corvus is a strong boy. He'll be back to his usual self in no time. He might be in some pain, but the deadening spell will place limits on how bad it can get. It'll be no worse than a mild toothache. Annoying, yes, but he won't feel like he's being stabbed with a thousand spears."

"That's better than nothing," Billy agreed. "There's one thing I don't get, though. How did *you* break your oath, Lothaire? Why can't you get Corvus to do the same thing you did?"

"I wish it were that easy. Back in my day, the ceremonial basin stayed in the banquet hall year-round. There were only two people to guard it, and it didn't take much to knock them out. Once they were out of the way, I simply reverse-engineered the oath spell and extracted my blood from the pool."

"And that released you?" Billy asked. Then he grimaced. "Wait, did you say there's a basin of *blood* sitting around in the *banquet* hall?"

"It's not like there's a lot of banquets going on these days," Lothaire said. "In any case, the basin is empty most of the time, except for the week of the blood oath ceremony. At that point, it fills up with the blood of every servant under Grigoth's command. It's a pretty clever spell. It took me a while to figure it out, but I freed myself in the end."

"So why can't we do the same thing with Corvus?" Billy asked.

"After our little stunt, Grigoth upped security on the basin. He moves it around the castle at random and keeps it under lock and key. Pigs will fly before we get a chance to reach it again."

"But if we did, we could free all of the wraiths, right?" Rem asked.

"I don't know about that," Lothaire said. "Separating out my own genetic material was easy. Blood calls out to blood. But separating the contents of the basin into its constituent parts? I fear that's beyond me."

"All the same," Billy pushed, "we *will* have to try it one day soon. Corvus shouldn't have to deal with this mess."

Lothaire regarded him with fondness. "I admire your courage and loyalty, but it's out of the question. We'll have to find a different way to help Corvus."

A flash of movement caught Billy's eye, and he looked up. His parents approached the scene, clutching each other's hands. Anxiety rose in his chest, and he studied the ground to avoid looking at them.

"You're alive," Mrs. Porter croaked. Tears streamed down her blotchy cheeks as she turned to Lothaire. "Sorry, Officer. I know you wanted to talk to them first, but Billy's our son. We couldn't wait any longer."

Lothaire inclined his head. "I understand."

"Are you okay, Billy?" Mrs. Porter asked. Her doleful eyes reminded him of the morning he'd returned from the Gloaming at age ten, bedraggled but otherwise unharmed. His father's tense expression mirrored Lothaire's.

"I'm fine, Mom," Billy said.

"I thought we'd lost you," she wailed. "Where's Corey? You both disappeared, and we didn't know what to do. Lothaire said you might have gone somewhere with a group of wraiths."

Billy's mouth clamped shut, and his mind raced to come up with an appropriate answer. *There's no point in lying. They already know what I've been doing.*

"Corey got hurt," he explained, trying to make the best of a bad situation. "If I hadn't helped him, he would be dead."

"Then where is he? Lothaire wouldn't explain."

Billy's gaze moved to Corvus's unconscious body before he could stop himself. Mr. Porter stepped forward, fists clenched.

"Did that freak kill my son?" he demanded. If he'd directed his fury anywhere else, Billy might have been comforted by the man's willingness to defend "Corey."

I don't have a choice, he thought. *I have to tell them the truth. I can't let them slander him like this.*

"No," Billy said, sucking in a deep breath. "That boy lying there. That's Corey."

Mr. Porter glared at him, his eyes burning like hot coals. "I've had enough of your disgusting jokes. Where's my boy?"

"Jerry, I think he's telling the truth," Mrs. Porter said, leaning over Corvus. "There's a definite resemblance there."

"Corey is *human*," Mr. Porter argued.

"Well, there I'm going to have to disagree with you," Lothaire cut in. "He's been disguising himself as a human for a few years now."

Mr. Porter stood perfectly still, his back rigid and his jaw clenched. He studied Corvus's prostrate form for a span of seconds, then jabbed an accusing finger into Billy's chest. "How long have you known about this?"

"Since the start," Billy admitted. "His dad left, and he needed a place to stay, so I thought—"

"You didn't think at all!" Mr. Porter raged. "I can't believe you would do something so irresponsible. What would Pastor Ryan say if he knew you were inviting demons into our house?"

"He's not a demon, he's a wraith," Billy retorted.

"Don't talk back to your father, dear," Mrs. Porter said.

"But he is," Billy insisted, no longer caring if he got in trouble. "Corey was a part of our family, and you loved him enough that you wanted to adopt him."

Mr. Porter spat at the ground. "That *thing* was never part of our family, and it never will be."

"But you loved him! Who cares if he looks different now? He's still the same person."

"He never was a person. He was a demon all along, and he can rot in hell for all I care. Get in the car, Billy. We're leaving."

"I'm not going anywhere."

"That's enough, Billy," Mrs. Porter said. "We'll talk about this at home."

She just wants to avoid making a scene, Billy fumed. *How can they do this after everything he's been through? At least he wasn't awake to hear his foster parents stabbing him in the back.*

"Don't worry, Billy. I'll take good care of him," Lothaire promised. "You go on home with your mom and dad."

Billy tried to argue, but Mr. Porter's fingers dug into his bicep and yanked him toward the waiting pickup truck. Tears pricked his eyes, turning the landscape blurry. *We're supposed to be safe here.* He crawled into the back seat, his wet clothes squelching against the leather. The stench of sewage and blood mixed with the musty car smell, growing stronger when the door slammed behind him.

He looked out the window, his stomach tight. Rem's hopeless eyes gazed back at him, and he realized with a pang of guilt what he'd sacrificed by telling the truth. *If Corvus moves in with her, their Promising spell will break. They'll never be able to get married or have children.* He buried his head in his hands as a second, more potent thought came to him. *What have I done?*

INTERLUDE

October 26, 2020

Three years and eight months later…

Chapter Forty-Five

Program: KSN National News Hour [Transcript]
Date: October 26, 2020
Time: 19:02:31—19:17:08

Pamela [interviewer]: The Wraithgate scandal is coming to a head in Paris this week. Half of the French cabinet were unmasked as wraiths this morning, fueling scenes of terror and rioting in the 8th arrondissement. All wraiths have been remanded in custody for questioning, but their origins and motives have not been shared with the general public until now. DS Tom Waters declined to comment on the unfolding investigation, but we've got three special guests on the show tonight to discuss all things Wraithgate. Dr. Aaron Crane, the esteemed biologist, is up first. Good evening, Dr. Crane.

Crane: Good evening, Pamela. It's a pleasure to be here.

Pamela: And it's a pleasure to have you with us. For those at home who don't know, tell us a little bit about what you do. What's your involvement in the Wraithgate scandal?

Crane: Right. Well, like you said, I'm a biologist. I've encountered wraiths many, many times before, back when most people still assumed they were a hoax. I've had more opportunity than most to study them. As soon as I heard about the situation in Paris, my team and I flew out to the detainment facility so we could interact with the wraiths and learn what we could.

Pamela: How did that go? Did you find out what they are and where they came from?

Crane: They refused to tell us where they came from or how they got here, but we believe they're an alien species of some kind. A few of my colleagues believe they have an affinity with water, but we've yet to get confirmation on that.

Pamela: So they're like fish people? Not the lizard people that so many conspiracy theorists have feared?

Crane: [laughing] No, no, no. They're definitely not lizard people *or* fish people. Having studied them in great detail, I can tell you that they're humanoid in shape and very much like us. For a while, I believed they were a subspecies of human—another stage of evolution, if you will—but MRI scans soon proved otherwise.

Pamela: Can you expand on that a little? What did the MRI scans show?

Crane: Internally, wraiths are very different from any creature I've ever studied. Their blood is bioluminescent, and they have a network of prominent veins that curve in unique ways. Some are interconnected, while others are dead ends with their own internal current system. We're unsure why this is, but we can assume it's for evolutionary reasons. The world they came from is probably very dark, much like the deep ocean, and we believe they use their blood to communicate and to attract prey. There's—

Pamela: Hold on a minute. Is it possible that they *are* from the deep ocean? You mentioned an affinity for water.

Crane: I find it extremely unlikely. The wraiths I studied were poor swimmers and had to be rescued before they drowned. An underwater city might be possible, but it raises the question of how they built it in the first place.

Pamela: Ah, I see. Sorry for interrupting. I was just curious. Tell us more about the wraiths' biology. What else makes them different from other creatures you've studied?

Crane: Well, their internal organs are different, for one thing. They have a heart and lungs and a skeleton, which are roughly the same as a human's, but the rest of their body deviates quite significantly. Their brains are slightly smaller than a human's but much more densely folded, which indicates they are highly intelligent. Possibly more intelligent than humans. We've only begun to guess at the function of their other organs, but we believe they fulfill a purpose specific to the biome they came from.

Pamela: That all sounds fascinating. Now, I know your role in the team is to study the biology of the wraiths and not their intentions, but I have to ask. What can you tell me about their purpose here on Earth? Why are they disguising themselves as public officials?

Crane: I'm afraid I'm going to have to disappoint you there, Pamela. I've been present for most of the interviews, and we've been unable to get a clear answer on that front. From what we *have* learned, though— from what they've told us, their general behavior, and so on—I believe they're refugees trying to assimilate into our culture. Almost all of the politicians these wraiths were impersonating have been lobbying for greater integration and acceptance of minorities. They were also vocal about updating the extraterrestrial incursion policy to allow exceptions for asylum seekers. Based on that, we believe they're trying to push law changes so that more of their kind can live here legally.

Pamela: You're saying there's *more* of them? How many are we talking about? Hundreds? Thousands?

Crane: By my estimates, around twenty thousand. Too many for any individual country to take on, especially after the Syrian crisis a few years back. We also have to consider how the public would react to something like this. Most people immediately turn to violence when they see a wraith on the street, as we saw in Japan back in 2017. In the face of that, we have to ask ourselves if integration is even a possibility.

Pamela: Yes, you're quite right. The incident in Japan was a tragic event, and I'm sure it didn't help the wraiths to form a favorable view of us.

Crane: No, it didn't. The wraiths I spoke to were, naturally, very angry about what happened.

Pamela: When you say "very angry," what do you mean? Did they ever try to hurt you?

Crane: No, never. They never gave me any reason to fear them. A few of them lashed out at the guards when they heard about the shooting, but they calmed down quickly. Given the severity of the situation, I'd hardly blame them for having an emotional outburst.

Pamela: With all the mass shootings in this country, I think we can all relate to their feelings on some level.

Crane: Right.

Pamela: So apart from that one occasion, they never showed violence toward you?

Crane: No, never.

Pamela: Okay. And based on your interactions with them, do you believe these creatures would be a threat to mankind if they lived among us?

Crane: I hesitate to say anything with absolute certainty, but I strongly believe they are not a threat. They've lived among us peacefully for years, and I see no reason why that would change. My colleagues have conducted intensive psychological testing on the wraiths in Paris, and there's no indication they would behave violently unless they were given a reason to do so.

Pamela: Like in self-defense?

Crane: Like in self-defense, exactly.

Pamela: I'm sure most people would find that reasonable. One of my other guests tonight, Reverend Pieter von Heidelberg, has been posting some controversial tweets about the wraiths, claiming they're demons sent by God to test us. What do you have to say about that?

Crane: [laughing] Well, I don't know much about the Bible, but I doubt they're demons. If they were, they'd be intangible, wouldn't they?

Pamela: Don't ask me; I'm not an expert [laughing]. But in all seriousness, do you think wraiths can safely integrate into our society when people believe these things about them? Because the Reverend isn't the only one who's been comparing them to demons. There are millions of people supporting his views, some of whom are calling for the death penalty.

Crane: Honestly, I don't know. People all over the world have had a big shock. They're scared, and they have every right to be. Over time, I do believe we have a chance at living together in harmony. But if people really are up in arms over this, perhaps we need to look at integration as more of a long-term goal, over several decades rather than months or years. But look, I'm just a biologist. I'm not the one making the decisions, and I'm very glad about that.

Pamela: You never know. We might not have any politicians left by the end of Wraithgate. Then we'll have to turn to your expert knowledge.

Crane: [laughing] Let's hope it doesn't come to that.

Pamela: All right, so I just have one more question, Dr. Crane. How did the wraiths manage to impersonate all those people? Were they wearing costume makeup, skin suits, what?

Crane: I'm afraid I can't comment on the specifics of the situation, but I can tell you it involves very advanced technology.

Pamela: More advanced than our technology?

Crane: I wouldn't say that. It's like a magic trick, really. A good trick, but at the end of the day, that's all it is: a trick. And despite having this technology, they still haven't mastered ours in all their years on Earth, so I think it's safe to say we're more advanced than they are in that regard.

Pamela: So if Grandma doesn't know how to use the TV remote, do we need to panic?

Crane: [smiling] No, no, no. I'm not saying that. But do keep an eye out for anything suspicious. I believe the police are still looking for suspects, and personally, I would love to speak to any other wraiths out there.

Pamela: You heard it, folks. If there are any wraiths watching, please get in contact with us. We'd love to hear from you. Thanks for agreeing to speak with me, Dr. Crane. It was a pleasure having you on the show.

Crane: Thanks, Pamela.

Pamela: All right. That was Dr. Aaron Crane, lead biologist in the Wraithgate saga. Next up, we'll be talking to Reverend Pieter von Heidelberg, who leads the Hudson Valley Megachurch. Good evening, Reverend.

Pieter: Good evening, Pamela.

Pamela: I understand you've been posting pretty extensively on Twitter about what you call the "demon invasion." Can you tell us more about that?

Pieter: Sure. So, as you know, there's been a recent influx of those demonic entities you call wraiths. They've been hiding among us, disguising themselves as humans—as people we should be able to trust. They have been undermining our society from within and sowing seeds of doubt wherever they go. They've been manipulating important decisions about the well-being of our country to let all kinds of degenerates in.

Pamela: And by degenerates, I take it you mean more of their kind.

Pieter: Exactly. As it says in Peter 5:8, we need to be alert and of sober mind, because the devil prowls around like a roaring lion looking for someone to devour. These so-called wraiths are exactly what God was warning us about. We should be fighting against them to keep our families and children safe, not discussing how to integrate them into society. We need to take a stand against evil and let these demons know they're not welcome here.

Pamela: Just to be clear, you believe these wraiths are genuine demonic entities? Not a subspecies of humans or some kind of alien race?

Pieter: That's correct. People these days seem to think demons are just make-believe creatures, but I can assure you they're not. They are powerful, malevolent beings who destroy people's lives. These wraiths have done that and more in the time they've been among us. They're not just impersonating people, they're tearing communities apart. We don't know what they've done to the real John Smith. The real Barbara Stone. They could be dead for all we know, and their families have to live with that.

Pamela: There have been a lot of unsolved missing persons cases in the past month, so I suppose we have to consider that as a possibility. You've made your position pretty clear on the matter of integration, but how do you feel about the scientists who are currently studying the wraiths? Should they be doing that? Or do you think they should be staying as far away as possible?

Pieter: They should leave, one hundred percent. I have nothing against science, but willingly spending time around these demons is lunacy. The servants of Satan mislead people all the time, and this is no different. They'll brainwash the scientists into believing all kinds of lies about them—about how they're refugees, how they're just misunderstood—and then they'll strike.

Pamela: So you're saying we shouldn't help them?

Pieter: That's right. They're not humans. They're not creatures of Light. They're abominations bent on destroying us all.

Pamela: I understand you haven't spoken to any of these wraiths yet. Is that correct?

Pieter: It is.

Pamela: Some of our viewers—well, a lot of them actually—have written in on Twitter and Facebook about this interview. Thousands of them are saying you wouldn't be saying these things if you talked to a wraith in person. What do you have to say about that?

Pieter: No. I... Well, first of all, I'm going to emphatically disagree with that. The Bible specifically warns against communicating with spirits and evil entities. Talking to a wraith would be like poking an alligator with a stick just to see what happens. You already *know* what will happen, and that it's going to be bad. I don't see any reason to put myself through that. I don't see why *anyone* would want to go down such a dark, miserable path.

Pamela: All right. Thank you for sharing your perspective with us, Reverend.

Pieter: You're welcome, Pamela. Take care and God bless.

Pamela: Next up this evening, we've got Senator Antony Bell—one of the few politicians unaffected by the current scandal. Good evening, Antony.

Antony: Good evening, Pamela. Lovely to see you again.

Pamela: It's great to see you too. I understand you've had a very difficult month with the ongoing Wraithgate scandal, so thank you for agreeing to come and talk to us.

Antony: You're very welcome. It has indeed been a difficult month—

a difficult year, really. Dealing with the fallout from Wraithgate has been a nightmare, but we're doing our best to contain the damage.

Pamela: Now, Antony. You've always been open about issues in the House.

Antony: [smiling] Are you calling me a brash loudmouth?

Pamela: [blushing] No, no! Of course not. But because you're so open and honest, I was wondering if you could tell the viewers at home a little more about why this scandal is so serious.

Antony: Of course [pause]. I'm sure you can imagine how harrowing the whole experience has been for all of us in Congress. It's not every day your friends dissolve into shadow creatures. But on a wider scale, it's even more terrifying. We don't know who these wraiths are. We don't know what they want. But we do know they were making decisions on our behalf for months—possibly years—and those decisions may not have been in our best interests. These wraiths were in positions of trust. They had access to top-secret information. We have no way of knowing if that information was leaked to our enemies, or if it was used in a scheme of their own, or if… [shaking head] I mean, we just don't know.

Pamela: When you put it that way, it's even more terrifying than I imagined.

Antony: Yes. My colleagues won't thank me for telling you, but everyone deserves to know the truth.

Pamela: Well, we don't want you to get in trouble, but we appreciate your honesty. What do *you* think should be done about the wraiths in custody? Do we move them to a more secure facility? Sentence them to the death penalty? Deport them? What?

Antony: [laughing] Where are we going to deport them to? The bottom of the ocean? No, for now, I think we should just hold them where they are, and… uh, hope that no other wraiths show up.

Pamela: Okay. Now, I know you were listening to the previous interviews from the wings. What did you make of Reverend von Heidelberg's comments? Do you believe the wraiths are demons or are they some kind of alien like Dr. Crane says?

Antony: I really don't know, Pamela. I'm going to leave that one for the experts to decide.

Pamela: All right. That's fair enough [turns to camera]. We're going to a commercial break, but when we come back, we'll be continuing our discussion with Senator Antony Bell. What do *you* think about the unfolding wraith controversy? Share your thoughts on Facebook and Twitter, or email us at the link on our website. Don't go anywhere. We'll be back very soon.

PART THREE

October 29, 2020

Three days later…

Chapter Forty-Six

CHEFS BUSTLED AROUND the humid kitchen, their bloodstained knives glinting through the steam. Billy stood hunched over the sink, his forearms bathed in soapy water. His coworkers elbowed him every time they walked past, but he did his best to ignore them. He'd take a stray elbow over a knife to the gut any day, and everyone seemed stressed enough that a rebuke might trigger a violent reaction.

Lifting a plate from the lukewarm water, Billy scrubbed away the crusted remains of beef stroganoff. Being a dishwasher at the local mom-and-pop restaurant wasn't a glamorous job, but it earned him a few bucks after school. Better yet, it took his mind off the tensions at home. Tensions that were somehow more palpable than those in the restaurant's cramped kitchen during the dinner rush.

Something pale green flew past Billy and splattered against the plate. He glanced at his neighbor, eyebrow raised.

"Sorry," Elmer muttered, tightening his grip on the celery he'd been dicing.

A high school dropout, Elmer had been working at the restaurant for three years—two years longer than Billy. Now eighteen, he was working his way up to a chef position.

"Don't worry about it," Billy replied. He wiped the plate clean again and stacked it on top of the others. "Do you need a hand with anything? I wouldn't mind doing something else for a while."

"Nah, I'm fine," Elmer said. His knife flashed under the fluorescent lights, creating a pile of tiny celery rings.

Billy watched in awe. "You're getting pretty fast."

"Thanks. I've had a lot of time to practice. Maybe I can teach you one day."

"Maybe."

He snuck a glance at the clock. *Seven fifty-five. Orders will close soon.* The thought came with no small measure of relief. His legs ached from standing on the hard floor for hours on end, and he longed to stretch them out.

Elmer handed his prepped vegetables to a passing chef and wiped his hands on a rag. "That's me done. Want some help with the dishes, Billy?"

"Nah, I'm fine."

"You sure? They're starting to stack up a little."

"Yeah, don't worry. I've got it under control."

"I like your confidence. See you tomorrow, eh?"

He walked away with a spring in his step, and Billy swallowed the lump in his throat. *Bye, Elmer.*

Another ten minutes dragged by. One by one, the chefs traded their white jackets for wool overcoats and slipped out into the night. Five minutes after the last departure, his boss strode into the kitchen with a stack of empty plates balanced on his arm.

"Good shift, Bill?" Mr. Thurston asked.

Billy took the plates and dunked them in the sink. "Of course."

Mr. Thurston grabbed a clean dish towel and started drying the dishes on the counter. "Are you sure I can't do anything to change your mind?"

"I'm sure. I've really enjoyed working here, but I have other things I need to focus on."

"I understand. Exams and everything. It's such a pity. You're one of the most hard-working members of the team. Unlike all the other dishwashers I've hired, you actually get things *clean*. I was thinking about giving you a raise…"

Sure you were, Billy thought, suppressing the urge to roll his eyes. *It doesn't matter anyway. Corvus and Rem need me, and I wouldn't abandon them for all the money in the world.*

He worked in silence, scrubbing every dish until it sparkled with his reflection. When he finished, he drained the sink and washed away the lingering soap suds.

Mr. Thurston placed the stack of clean plates in the cupboard. "I'd better go and get your final paycheck. Are you sure you won't reconsider?"

Billy nodded, eliciting another sigh from his boss. Mr. Thurston retreated to his office, his steps heavy with defeat. Billy dried his arms with the dish towel and pulled down his sleeves. Prune-like ridges protruded from the pads of his fingers, a side effect of keeping them submerged for so long. Experience told him they'd disappear by the time he got home.

Mr. Thurston re-emerged from his office, waving an envelope. "Here's your money."

Billy took it. "Thank you, sir. It's been a pleasure to work for you."

It hadn't been, but he didn't want to be rude. Besides, washing dishes was a much safer job than Murdock's gig at the local mechanic shop. On his first day, his friend had been hit by a car and spent the next six weeks on crutches.

Nervous excitement welled up inside Billy as he stepped into the cool evening air. As bad as he felt about resigning, dishwashers were a dime a dozen. His old boss would be inundated with résumés the moment he advertised an open vacancy. Billy's spot would be filled by the end of the week, and Mr. Thurston's life would go on as normal.

Which is more than can be said for my life, Billy thought, turning his collar up against the wind.

Yellow light pooled on the sidewalk, cast by fluttering street lamps and the steady glow of shop windows. Despite the popularity of late-night shopping elsewhere, Morton had only adopted the trend a few weeks ago. The lack of people on Main Street suggested the residents either didn't know or didn't care about the new hours.

Billy strolled into Euler's Sporting Goods, flinching when a bell tinkled to announce his arrival. The clerk, who had been slumped over his desk, jolted upright and mumbled an unintelligible greeting. Billy nodded in his direction before proceeding to the camping section. His mind drifted back to the previous afternoon and the two-word message he'd received from Corvus.

Tomorrow night.

He'd clapped the magic notebook shut after reading it, filled with a sense of finality. Those two tiny words terrified him as much as they invigorated him. With Wraithgate dominating the media, hundreds of new conspiracy theories were popping up every day. Someone in Portugal—a Morton-born expat—had even leaked information about wraithkind's culpability in the 2001 Halloween Massacre.

One eagle-eyed commenter noted that the murders took place during a full moon—a blue moon, no less—and that Halloween coincided with these events once every nineteen years. The wraiths' appearance now, so close to the nineteenth anniversary of the massacre, must be an omen of further bloodshed.

Billy asked Lothaire about it during one of their joint planning sessions, and the older wraith responded with a sad smile. "*The full moon strengthens the portal between our worlds and allows us to cross without expending as much energy. Halloween has a similar effect, and when the two are combined, even the weakest wraith can pass through with ease. Grigoth took advantage of it last time, and I have no doubts he's planning to do it again on a wider scale.*"

Billy considered Lothaire's words as he scanned a row of hiking backpacks. He had to admit, they made a certain sense. After all, the moon controlled the tides of the ocean. Why not the rift between dimensions as well?

The one thing Billy didn't understand was Lothaire's insistence on crossing the portal themselves. Four years ago, the older wraith had warned them to stay away from the Gloaming. Now, he not only expected them to go back there but to dive into the heart of danger— Grigoth's castle itself. *Madness.*

Billy chose a backpack with a built-in hydration system and carried it to the counter.

The bleary-eyed clerk rang him up. "That'll be seventy-nine ninety-nine."

Billy opened the envelope containing his final paycheck and handed over the entire wad of banknotes. The clerk's eyes widened into something resembling alertness for the first time that evening.

"Keep the change," Billy told him, shouldering his new backpack.

He walked home with a spring in his step. Hamish and James were in bed by the time he arrived, but his parents were watching TV in the lounge. Mrs. Porter called out a sleepy greeting, which Billy returned stiffly before retiring to his room. He threw open his dresser, shrugged off his backpack, and shoved some T-shirts and jeans into the main pocket. Midway through zipping it up, Mrs. Porter burst through the door.

"Are you hungry, Billy? I put some leftovers in the fridge for you."

"No thanks, Mom. I ate at the restaurant."

She watched him fill the backpack's hydration bladder. "What are you doing?"

He met her gaze, studying her pale face and the spark of fear behind her eyes. He didn't blame her for being scared. The last time she found him packing a bag like this, he'd punched a wall and screamed about running away.

"We have a field trip tomorrow," Billy lied. "We'll be walking around in the woods for a few hours, so I thought I should be prepared."

"I don't remember signing a permission slip for that."

"You did it last week."

"Did I?"

"Yup."

She tilted her head to the side, studying him. "Is that a new bag?"

"Yeah. My old one had a hole in the bottom."

"Oh. Okay." She paused, her lips pressed into a thin line. "Are you sure you don't want some spaghetti? I know you ate at work, but maybe you could manage a few bites. It's still your favorite, isn't it?"

"Yeah. It is."

They stood in silence, staring each other down. Mrs. Porter stepped forward and cupped his cheek, her voice gentle. "Please come and eat, Billy. You've been so busy with school and work. It's like we never see you anymore."

He hesitated. "I guess I could have a little bit."

His mother's face lit up, the same way it used to when he did well at school or when he complimented her cooking. He hadn't seen that expression in years. Not since Corvus left. He dropped the backpack on his bed and followed her to the kitchen. Complying with her requests wasn't part of the plan, but if this was his last chance to spend time with her, he wanted to make the most of it.

The glowing hands of Billy's watch pointed to ten fifty-five when he shuffled back to his room. Mrs. Porter's reheated spaghetti could have warmed him from head to toe, but her questions froze him to the core. Why hadn't he told her about the field trip? How long would he be away? Why was he bringing extra clothes with him? Why, why, why?

Mr. Porter's questions were no less difficult. What would he be doing on the field trip? Would there be any wraiths? Had he seen any suspicious characters hanging around that might be wraiths in disguise? Did his boss know he wouldn't be there for his shift tomorrow?

A frustrated scream built up in Billy's chest, but he refused to let it out. Instead, he answered their questions in the most nonchalant voice he could muster, lying through his teeth with every word. Eventually, they'd given up and let him go to bed.

Unable to sleep, he sat with his ear pressed against his bedroom door and waited until their anxious whispers turned into snores. He glanced at his watch. *Twelve fifty-nine. Time to move.* Shivers of dread and excitement coursed through him as he grabbed his backpack and tiptoed to the window. With one hand, he swished open the curtain. The metal gliders scraped across the curtain rod like nails on a chalkboard. As he reached for the sash, something creaked outside his bedroom door.

Billy held his breath, ears straining. His parents' snores clashed together, one rough and rattling, and the other a high-pitched whistle. Billy returned his attention to the window, satisfied they were out for the count. Before he could lift the sash, the door squeaked open, and a small blond-haired boy entered.

"Hamish?" Billy murmured, his heart rate creeping up.

The boy closed the door with a soft click and turned to face him. Fear shone in his eyes, and his breath came in short hitches.

"There are wraiths outside," Hamish whispered. "Big ones."

Billy pressed his nose against the window, squinting into the darkness. He caught a glimpse of three familiar figures before his breath fogged up the glass. "Don't worry. They're friends of mine."

"All of them?"

"All of them."

The fear faded from Hamish's demeanor, but it didn't disappear. He appraised Billy doubtfully, his lower lip quivering. "I thought they might be like the wraiths on the news."

"Nope. It's just Corvus, Rem, and Lothaire. They're good people."

"Corey's out there?"

Hamish hadn't been there when Mr. Porter disowned Corvus, but he'd heard about it as soon as he got home. Instead of shunning the wraith like he'd been told to, Hamish relayed messages to him through Billy. On rare occasions, he joined them on their outings too. The simple display of loyalty strengthened their bond more than video games ever could.

"Yeah, he's out there," Billy said. "And no, before you ask, you can't see him tonight."

"Why not?"

"Do you remember what I told you about Grigoth?"

Hamish pouted. "You're going away, aren't you? You're going to try to defeat him."

"That's right."

Billy tried to ruffle his brother's hair, but the small boy crushed him in a hug.

"I don't want you to go," Hamish mumbled.

"I don't have a choice," Billy said, patting his shoulder. "If I don't go, Grigoth is going to come here, and then where will we be? People will get hurt and killed. I can't let that happen."

Hamish pulled away, his gaze fixed on his slippers. When he met Billy's eye, he looked much older than his twelve years. "Let me come with you."

Billy studied his brother's expression. *Is he serious? He's way too young!* Sure, he'd been younger than Hamish when he first traveled through the portal. But a brief trip to the edge of the Gloaming was different from sneaking deep into enemy territory.

"No," Billy said. "You need to stay here and look after Mom and Dad. Stall for me. Say you heard me leave early in the morning for my trip. It's not technically a lie."

"I'm not a baby anymore," Hamish retorted. "I want to help now. Jarsha does too, and he should be allowed to. The Gloaming is his world."

"Trust me, Hamish, you're both better off here. Besides, someone has to look after Mom and Dad and James."

Hamish's brow furrowed as he considered the matter. "Fine. I'll take care of them. But only if you leave a note. I don't want to explain everything."

"Okay."

"And look after Corey. I don't want anything bad to happen to him."

"It's a deal," Billy said, glancing out the window. "Look, I've got to get going, so I'll see you in a few days, okay?"

"Okay. Don't forget the note."

With a final hug, Hamish crept out of the room. Billy watched him go, his heart contracting in his chest. *I would never forgive myself if something happened to him. I was right to put my foot down.* Grabbing a pen and paper from his school satchel, Billy penned a quick message. He'd hoped to avoid leaving one; after all, explaining his intentions gave the game away. However, a promise was a promise, and Billy didn't want to throw his brothers under a bus.

Mom and Dad—

If you're reading this, I've left for my trip and won't be back until the 31st. There's nothing to worry about. I'm with my friends, and we have adult supervision. I know you want me to focus on my exams, but this is more important. I can't explain more, but you'll understand everything by the time I get back. Keep yourselves safe. Keep James and Hamish safe. Don't go outside on Halloween. I love you.

—Billy

He folded the note in half and placed it on the dresser. Having fulfilled his duty to Hamish, Billy returned to the window. Corvus's shadowy form raised an arm in the air. At first, it looked like a wave. Then the boy pointed at his wrist in an exaggerated fashion, making Billy's cheeks grow warm. *He's telling me to hurry up.*

Billy slid open the window sash and threw his bag onto the grass, where it landed with a soft thump. Squeezing himself through the tiny gap proved harder, but he did it without crushing his mother's flowers this time. He wasted a few seconds shutting the window, then jumped the fence to meet his friends.

"Took you long enough," Corvus groused. "We've been waiting for hours!"

"I had to have dinner and pack my stuff," Billy explained.

"Yeah, and then what? Take a nap?"

"I had to make sure my parents were asleep first."

"Why?" Lothaire asked, confusion knitting his brow. "You're old enough to make your own decisions, you know."

"Trust me, it's easier this way," Billy said. "Are we leaving or what? It's too cold to be standing around."

Lothaire inclined his head and marched toward Oilskin Lake, his flashlight waving from side to side. Corvus stalked after him, a gentle breeze tousling the hair. Even in the dark, Billy could make out the tense outline of his jaw and the permanent wince gracing his features.

Billy fell in step with Rem, who dawdled a few paces behind the others. "How is he?"

The ghost of a smile touched Rem's lips. "Coping. Some days are better than others."

After their ordeal in the Gloaming, Corvus and Rem had dropped out of school to focus on their magical education. For the first year, Billy stopped by their house every afternoon. As his workload increased, though, his visits became fewer and farther between. Tonight was the first time he'd seen them in two weeks.

"No progress on the scar, then?" he asked.

"Nope. Dad's tried everything he knows. The only sure way to free Corvus from the pain is to kill Grigoth, and that's not exactly a piece of cake."

"We'll find a way," Billy promised. *I don't know how, but we'll do it.*

"Of course we will."

They walked in silence for the rest of the journey, unwilling to draw attention to themselves. The streets were unnaturally still, as though all ambient sounds had been sucked out. Oilskin Lake lay dormant under the starless skies, absorbing the beam from Lothaire's flashlight. The older wraith stopped by the water's edge and shrugged off his backpack. Crouching, he unzipped it and pulled out a length of shimmering fabric, which he thrust into Corvus's arms.

"I made glamours for all of us," he explained.

"Are you sure this is a good idea?" Billy asked. "Grigoth saw through our glamours last time."

"Grigoth isn't the only danger in the Gloaming," Lothaire replied, handing the next glamour to Rem. "I'd like to keep our identities hidden from the other wraiths as much as possible. Especially yours, Billy."

Something cold spilled over Billy's head and wrapped around his body. He glanced at his newly void-black arm, disconcerted. Lothaire must have applied the glamour for him.

"Why me?" Billy asked. "I know I'm human, but I've walked around the Gloaming without a glamour before."

"And you were lucky no one saw you. The bound wraiths have all had bad experiences with humans, and your presence might provoke them. It's best to be discreet."

"I understand," Billy said, but his stomach sank. *This must be what Corvus felt like when he was still living with me.*

Lothaire gestured toward the lake. "Come on. Time to go."

The wraiths waded in first, the stagnant water girding their knees. Billy stood frozen on the bank, willing himself to follow their lead. *This is it. This is really happening.*

They'd been planning it for years, but now that the time was upon them, everything felt too real. War meant death—potentially his own—and he was all too aware this might be the last time he laid eyes on his hometown. Billy stepped into the water, his gaze fixed on the silhouettes of distant houses. A lump formed in his throat.

"Goodbye, Morton."

A flash of light illuminated the clearing, and his vision went black.

Chapter Forty-Seven

"—AIRE, IS THAT you?"

The crackle of an unfamiliar voice assaulted Billy's ears when he arrived in the Gloaming. Portal water dripped from his eyelashes, slid down his nose, and landed between his lips. Grimacing, he wiped it away with his sleeve and clambered up the muddy banks.

"Yes, it's me," Lothaire said, extending his hand toward a stocky wraith. "Good to see you again, Darthan. It's been a few years."

"Aye, it has," the wraith—Darthan—responded. "I've been keeping an ear to the ground like you asked, but I haven't been able to keep track of the human calendar. Time seems to be in flux these days— even more than it usually is. Just last week, our timestream was ahead of Earth's. Yesterday, it was behind again. Now, it seems to be in synch. Something weird is going on."

"That *does* sound weird," Lothaire agreed. "Grigoth must be behind it. But no matter. The only important thing is that we both arrived here at the same time on the same day."

"I'll toast to that." Darthan lifted a small silver flask from his waist and took a swig. He offered it to Lothaire, who held up a restraining hand. The stocky wraith shrugged and returned it to his belt. "Who are the kids?"

A flash of annoyance raced through Billy. *He thinks we're going to get in the way.* He trudged over to his friends, reining in his emotions before the newcomer could see them.

Lothaire pointed to each of them in turn. "This is my daughter, Rem, and her friends, Corvus and William."

Billy fought back a wince. He'd always hated his full name, but the wraiths had insisted on using it during their mission. "Billy" was an unusual name in the Gloaming and sure to arouse suspicion, but no one would bat an eye at "William."

"Nice to meet you," Darthan said, bowing. "My name is Darthan, but I'm sure you've guessed that already." He turned to Lothaire. "I didn't know your friends would be so young. Are you sure they can handle a blade?"

"Rem and Corvus have been trained by the best," Lothaire answered, ignoring his friend's incredulous tone. He clapped a hand to Billy's shoulder and gave it a gentle squeeze. "William grew up in the homestead, but he's keen to learn. Aren't you, my boy?"

Billy nodded, excitement bubbling up inside him. *I get to wield a sword? That's awesome!*

"I suppose his inexperience can't be helped," Darthan said. His piercing eyes zeroed in on Corvus. "Is this Seisan's boy?"

"I am," Corvus said before Lothaire could answer. His eyes burned somewhere between determination and quiet fury. "Are you the rat who dragged my dad back to the Gloaming?"

Darthan's jaw dropped. "I… I didn't force him to. He volunteered."

"And now he's dead."

"Yes. He is." Darthan's lips set in a grim line. "I'm… s-s-s-s—" He paused. "It should never have happened. Seisan was a great m-m-m—" Another pause. "Sorry. This is difficult to talk about."

"Why weren't you there to help us at the castle?" Corvus persisted. "You were meant to be working together. If you'd bothered to show up, he might have made it out of there alive."

"Corvus—" Lothaire began, but Darthan held up a hand.

"It's all right, Lothaire," he said, his voice pained. "The boy's right. I *should* have been there. If I hadn't broken my ankle, believe me, I would have been."

Corvus narrowed his eyes. "You broke your ankle?"

"That's right," Darthan said. "We had a run-in with a couple of soldiers. One put an arrow clean through the bone. We fled and cleaned it up as best we could, but without potions, there was only so much we could do. Casting a healing spell on an injury that severe would have attracted every Enforcer in a fifty-mile radius. Seisan had no choice but to continue alone."

Corvus stared at him, unflinching. "You should have done something."

Darthan lowered his gaze. When he looked up again, steely determination imbued his features. "I can't change what happened, Corvus. All I can do is help you to smite the person who killed him. I hope that's good enough for you, because I'm here at Lothaire's invitation. I'm staying whether you like it or not."

"Fine. Let's hope you don't get hit by any more arrows."

"I'm going to pretend that wasn't sarcasm," Darthan said, turning back to Lothaire. "Now that we've cleared the air, I need to go and dig up the weapons and armor I promised you. Do you mind waiting here for a few minutes?"

"Not at all," Lothaire replied, gesturing for him to go ahead.

Darthan all but sprinted into the woods, and Billy felt an unexpected pang of sympathy for him. While the wraith's demeanor rubbed him the wrong way, his remorse seemed genuine.

"Are you sure he's trustworthy, Dad?" Rem asked.

"As sure as anyone can be these days," Lothaire said. "I've known Darthan since we were children. He may be bound by the blood oath, but he's no fan of the king."

"Really?" Corvus scoffed. "He seems a bit nervous to me. Maybe he's working for Grigoth after all, and he's scared we're going to find out. Why else would he stutter so much?"

"You know why," Lothaire said. "The oath prevents him from speaking out against the king, the same way it stops you. Stuttering is a natural side effect of trying to do it anyway."

"He wasn't trying to speak out against the king," Corvus retorted.

"No, but he *was* trying to show vocal support for Seisan. Standing up for Grigoth's worst enemies counts as a betrayal in his book, and the oath wouldn't allow it."

They waited in tense silence as five minutes turned into ten. Billy shifted his weight from foot to foot, his gaze fixed on the dark tree line. Another five minutes passed before Darthan returned. A tartan golf bag trundled along in front of him, sustained by magic rather than physical contact.

"This is it," Darthan said, wheeling it over to them. "Weapons and armor for everyone."

Lothaire reached into the bag and pulled out a gleaming sword. "You've outdone yourself, Darthan."

"Thank you. I tried my best." The wraith tilted his head to one side. "I don't suppose you've got any food on you?"

"We brought some with us, but it turned to dust the same way it always does when we cross the portal," Lothaire said. "I invented a spell to make it look and taste like food again, but I don't recommend eating it unless you're desperate. At the end of the day, you'd still be eating ashes, and they're not very nutritious."

Darthan grimaced. "In that case, I'll wait for something better. We're going to visit the labor camps tomorrow, aren't we? They usually have food depots nearby."

"Yes. We'll take the food once the guards are neutralized."

Shivers raced down Billy's spine. He'd heard Corvus talk about the labor camps a few times, and they sounded like one of the worst places a person could live. Lothaire's plan involved bribing the laborers to stage an uprising against their guards, and then convincing them to continue their campaign to Grigoth's castle. There, they would help to overthrow the tyrant king and, in time, restore their beloved homeland to its former glory.

That's the idea, anyway, Billy thought, biting his lip. *The oath only allows them to fight in self-defense, so we're on the back foot from the get-go. Plus, there's no guarantee Grigoth won't use magic or mind control to stop us.*

Pushing the thought away, Billy approached the golf bag. Darthan handed him a long, slim blade, and he staggered forward under its weight.

"Take a belt and sheath too, William," Lothaire prompted.

Billy buried the tip of his sword in the dirt and donned the belt Darthan offered him. Sheathing his sword without stabbing himself proved difficult, but in the end, he managed it. *How on earth did squires do this back in the day? They were fourteen! I'm seventeen and I'm having trouble.*

"These are charmed swords from the Forge," Darthan explained when they'd chosen their weapons. "All of them were created before Grigoth's reign and never fell into his hands. I checked each one personally to make sure the spells were pure."

"Good," Lothaire said, stepping back. "The last thing we need is for our swords to betray us in the heat of battle. It's risky enough relying on wraiths who've been bound by the blood oath."

No one opted to wear the hardened leather armor Darthan procured. Rather, they shrank it down to the size of a peanut and shoved it in their pockets for safekeeping. Rem helped Billy with his. Having done his job, Darthan wheeled the cart back into the forest.

"Hey, Lothaire?" Billy asked. "Are you sure it's safe for us to fight alongside oath-bound wraiths? I mean, what if Grigoth makes them turn on us?"

Lothaire's eyebrow quirked upward. "Have I not explained this before?"

Billy shook his head.

"The oath *suppresses* certain actions. It can't force a wraith to do something. It's even possible to get around the oath with a bit of creativity. Grigoth's telepathic abilities are another story. If he's close by, he can use them to force someone to behave in a certain way, regardless of whether the oath binds them. I think our best chance is to overwhelm him with numbers. With a bit of luck, Grigoth will be dead before he knows what hit him."

"He'll know," Corvus snapped. "He always knows."

His hands drifted to his abdomen, brushing the part of his shirt that hid the blood oath scar. Billy's stomach twinged in sympathy. Of their group, Corvus was the most recent victim of Grigoth's brutality. Nearly four years on, his suffering had yet to end.

"We can't give up," Rem said. "Everyone's depending on us."

"That they are," Darthan agreed, strolling over to join them. "Most of my friends will be slaughtered if ol' Griggles goes ahead with his plan. I'm not going to let that happen while I've got air in my lungs."

"Me neither," Billy echoed. Seisan's violent death flashed through his mind, and he squeezed the hilt of his new sword. He didn't want to think of the horrors his family would face if Grigoth's minions crossed the barrier en masse.

"I never said anything about giving up," Corvus bristled. "I'm just pointing out how dangerous this is going to be."

Rem patted him on the shoulder. "I know. We'll get through this together."

The group set off at a brisk pace, with the adults at the front and the teenagers bringing up the rear. The last time Billy traversed this dusty path, he'd been fleeing Grigoth's castle on a magic-powered sleigh. He scanned his surroundings, hoping to find the sleigh where they'd abandoned it. No such luck. *Too bad. We'd save a lot of time by driving.*

"Tell me, Lothaire," Darthan said as they walked. "How have wraithkind been treated on Earth in recent years? Are humans starting to accept them?"

"Quite the opposite," Lothaire replied. "Grigoth ordered some of his subjects to disguise themselves as humans and work their way into positions of power. It only took one unmasking for the witch hunt to begin, and there have been hundreds of unmaskings since then. The president of America. The former president. The British prime minister. A couple of sheiks in the United Arab Emirates. Half the French parliament. People are scared and angry. They don't want anything to do with us."

"That shouldn't have happened. Grigoth would have wanted them to stay hidden," Darthan said. "How did the humans respond? Are they attacking wraiths in the streets?"

"No more than usual. The internet storm was worse than the physical one."

Darthan gave him a puzzled glance. "Internet?"

"The internet is… uh… never mind."

"It's a place people can talk to each other, like with magic notebooks," Billy said, sticking with the simplest explanation.

"Oh, I see," Darthan said. "People talked about it a lot on this… internet?"

"That's right," Lothaire said, shooting Billy a thankful look. "Millions of them talked about it, but very few of them tried to contact the impostors."

"Interesting. I take it the impostor wraiths are imprisoned now?"

"Not in jail, but yes. They're in a secure research facility."

"Grigoth won't be happy about that. If he wasn't going to attack Earth before, he will now. He doesn't have another choice, short of dying to the Oncoming Abyss."

"Were you able to confirm that the invasion is set for Halloween?"

"I haven't dared to get close enough to find out, but I have no doubts your theory is correct. The full moon, the blue moon, and the Samhain moon will create the perfect storm to open the portal completely. The last time that happened was nineteen years ago, and we all know what happened then."

A wave of nausea rolled through Billy's stomach. *That was the day Heather died. The sister I never knew.*

"Of course, things were different back then," Darthan continued. "Grigoth wanted to test the waters, but he wasn't desperate enough to risk a full invasion. The darkness is rolling in faster than ever now, and his castle is within weeks of being consumed. Once that's gone, the rate of destruction will speed up. The Gloaming will be gone before this opportunity opens to him again. He has no choice but to act now unless he wants to lose everything."

A somber silence met the wraith's bombshell. The forest obscured the promised wall of shadows, but Billy's heart rate crept up anyway. He felt the truth in Darthan's words, and they clouded his mind until he could think of little else. What would it be like to fall victim to the ravenous Abyss? Would it be violent like a tsunami? Or would he pop out of existence in the blink of an eye? Regardless of the method, Billy didn't want to find out, and he was pretty sure Grigoth didn't either.

He's been backed into a corner. He'll be more dangerous than ever. My family… Images of blood and violence tore through his mind and he shuddered, blinking away a film of tears. Despite their differences over the years, he loved his parents. His brothers. The idea of losing them to a madman's plot sent his heart into an anxious frenzy. *I won't let that happen. I'll stop Grigoth no matter what.*

A few minutes before nightfall, the party veered off the path and into the forest. Lothaire conjured a werelight to illuminate their path, but its faint glow didn't reach Billy. If it weren't for the wraiths' panting breaths, he would have assumed they left him behind. After a short trek, the outline of a wooden shack came into view. Judging by its compact frame, the five of them would struggle to fit inside.

Darthan cleared his throat. "This is it. Home, sweet home."

"It's a bit small," Corvus muttered.

"Small, but safe," Darthan said. "There's a swamp out the back, and it's enchanted to take down intruders. If anyone wants to attack us, they'll be funneled to the front of the house."

"But that means we won't be able to get out," Billy protested.

"There's always a way out," Darthan said, tapping the side of his nose. "Anyway, I wouldn't worry about it. If we're lucky, ol' Griggles and his associates will be too busy with war preparations to bother us."

Billy took a deep breath and followed his friends into the shack. *We need all the luck we can get.*

Chapter Forty-Eight

HAMISH LEANED OVER James's bed, jabbing the cotton duvet. He blew out a frustrated breath when his brother failed to stir.

"James," he hissed.

The boy in the blanket cocoon inhaled deeply, his right eye fluttering open. "Mmph. What do you want?" He made a half-hearted attempt to sit up, then subsided back onto the pillow. "It's creepy to watch someone sleep, you know."

Hamish plopped down next to him. "I know. But I need to talk to you."

"*Now?*" James asked. Exhaustion rumbled in his throat. "We can talk in the morning, Hamish. I'm trying to sleep."

Undaunted, Hamish threw himself on top of his brother's sprawling form and bounced up and down. The bedsprings squealed a warning. "*Ja-ames.*"

James rolled out from under him and tumbled to the floor, clutching his side. "What did you do that for?"

"It's not my fault you fell."

"No, but why did you have to hit me in the ribs?"

"I'm sorry. I didn't mean to."

James got to his feet, avoiding the Lego bricks they'd left strewn across the floor. "Go to bed, Hamish. We have school in the morning."

"There are more important things than school," Hamish said, grabbing his brother's arm. "Billy's gone."

"So what? He's seventeen. He can do what he wants."

"He snuck out the window to meet a group of wraiths."

James's spine jerked ramrod straight as though he'd been electrocuted. "*What?*"

Hamish allowed himself a small smile at his brother's reaction. He hadn't seen James so panicked since the first time he met Jarsha.

"Corey's with him," Hamish said. "They're going to Wraithland to fight the bad wraiths who want to take over the planet."

"What do we do? Do we tell Mom and Dad?"

"No. I promised him I wouldn't. I think we should follow him and do whatever we can to help."

"You're crazy. We can't go wandering around the neighborhood at two in the morning."

"Why not? Come on, James. He's going to need us."

"For what? We don't know anything about wraiths and how to stop them."

"You don't, but I do. Do you remember my friend Jarsha?"

"The wraith?"

"Yeah. He thinks there might be some magical songs we can use to stop the bad wraiths. I asked Corey about it a couple of years ago, but he'd never heard of music magic. If the bad wraiths don't know about it either, then they might not know they have to defend against it. Jarsha thinks we could find some scores for music magic in Wraithland, and this is the perfect time to help him look. We can all go together."

"I don't think so," James said. "I have training in the afternoon. I'm not going to Wraithland in the middle of the night to find some 'magical songs,' whatever that means. You're talking nonsense, Hamish. Just go to bed."

"I'll leave without you."

"You can't do that."

"I will."

"You wouldn't dare."

"Try me."

James stared at him without blinking. "You're serious about this, aren't you?"

Hamish nodded, eliciting a strangled groan from his brother.

"*Fine.* I'll come. Are you sure we won't meet any of the bad wraiths?"

"Pretty sure."

James sighed and threw his hands in the air. "Good enough, I guess."

The boys shuffled across the Lego minefield and opened their shared closet. The musty odor of mothballs permeated the air, encouraging the haste with which they picked their outfits. Hamish pulled on a pair of jeans, hopping from foot to foot as the cold denim settled against his skin. A turtleneck and a puffer jacket came next, followed by a pair of ratty sneakers his mother hated.

The window sash grated against the frame when James lifted it. At fifteen, he was as tall as Billy and twice as muscular, and he climbed outside with ease. Hamish swung his legs over the sill, pointing his toes in an attempt to find solid ground. Nothing but air met his sneakers. James wrapped his arms around his brother's waist and helped him down.

"Thanks," Hamish mouthed.

He closed the window, shivering as a wave of cold air washed over him. He'd never been outside at night before. Not at the hour when stars ruled the inky blackness. The Monster of Morton had been defeated seven years ago, but the memory of its nightly reign terrified him enough to stay indoors.

Until tonight, he thought, stifling another shiver.

"How do we even get to Wraithland?" James asked.

"I'm not sure," Hamish admitted. "We have to pick up Jarsha first, anyway. He'll know what to do."

"So… what? You're going to go there and knock on the front door? At this hour?"

"I don't have to. I know where his bedroom window is."

Shoving his hands in his pockets, Hamish set off for Mrs. Price's house with James trudging alongside him. Streetlamps flickered overhead, sometimes blinding him, sometimes plunging their path into darkness. In the absence of light, the bushes looked like crouching monsters ready to pounce. He drew closer to James, clenching and unclenching the handkerchief in his pocket. Parked cars lined the sidewalk, their wheels half on the curb. Old petrol fumes lingered in the air, the scent a mere echo of the day's hustle and bustle.

In the dim light, Hamish almost walked past Mrs. Price's house. Tall hedges loomed over him, their shadows gathering an army at his feet. Heart racing, he opened the gate he'd passed through a hundred times before. The house's security lights flared to life, chasing the shadows back to their dens. Hamish left his brother by the road and beelined for Jarsha's window. He would have felt more confident with James by his side, but the older boy seemed content to stay put.

He rapped his knuckles against the cold glass. After a minute, the curtains slid open and Jarsha's sleepy face peered out at him. The wraith's eyes widened, and he opened the window.

"What's wrong?" Jarsha asked, concern lining his face. "Is it time to put our plan into action?"

"Yeah, it's time," Hamish said. "Billy and Corey left an hour ago. We should hurry."

"Okay. I'll be right out."

He climbed through the window with surprising agility, his feet hitting the grass with a soft thump. James looked up when they retreated to the sidewalk, something akin to fear in his eyes.

"Which way, Jarsha?" Hamish asked.

The wraith looked both ways, then pointed left. "This way."

"How far?"

"Not far. Just to Oilskin Lake."

Hamish's stomach squirmed at the name; he couldn't help it. *That's where the monster lived.*

"Is that safe?"

"Of course it is. My friends hang out there all the time."

Jarsha's reassurances didn't loosen the knot in Hamish's gut. On a surface level, he knew the Monster of Morton was gone, but the thought of visiting its former lair freaked him out. When they arrived, Jarsha leapt the barrier. Hamish followed suit, albeit reluctantly. The water looked like blackcurrant juice, but it smelled corrosive, like the bleach his mother used to clean the bathroom. He toed the fetid liquid and jumped back, half-expecting to find a hole in his sneaker.

"So, how do we get to Wraithland?" Hamish asked.

"I'm not a hundred percent sure," Jarsha said. He edged his way to the water, eyes wide as though he expected something to jump out and drag him to the bottom. "I know there's a portal here because I've seen those two older kids go through it. There's a spell to make it work, but I don't remember what it is."

James rolled his eyes. "Oh, come on. It can't be that hard. Abracadabra! Alakazam!"

Nothing happened.

"I don't think you're supposed to say the spell out loud," Jarsha said. "The others never did."

The smug grin on James's face dissolved. "You're serious about the magic, aren't you? I thought you were playing around, but you actually mean it."

"Of course we mean it," Hamish retorted.

"And there's a portal to this… Wraithland?"

"Yeah, but I don't know if I'll be able to activate it," Jarsha said. "I haven't spent much time around other wraiths since Mrs. Price adopted me. There hasn't been anyone I could ask, and I didn't really want to go back anyway. The only thing I know for sure is that we all have to be touching the water. I'll have to experiment to figure out the rest."

Grimacing, Hamish waded ankle-deep into the lake. Mud sucked at his feet, drenching his socks and filling his shoes with silt. James and Jarsha splashed in behind him, disgust marring their features. Jarsha crouched on his heels, water lapping at the seat of his pants. At any other time, Hamish would have teased him for "wetting" himself, but jokes were the furthest thing from his mind. His limbs tingled when Jarsha stood up.

"I think I've got it," the wraith announced. "Are you ready to go?"

"Ready," the Porter brothers answered in unison.

A high-pitched hum pierced Hamish's ears, dragging him back to the land of the living. The pressure in his head built to unbearable levels. Then, as if a switch had been flipped, it dissipated into nothingness. Blessed relief flooded the space it left, and he would have sighed, had his mouth not filled with brackish water. He reeled back, coughing and spluttering. His arms flailed against the stagnant lake.

Finding his feet at last, he staggered out of the water. *Did it work? Are we in Wraithland?* One look at his surroundings answered the question for him. Long-dead trees speared the sky, a stark contrast to the lush foliage around Oilskin Lake. The skies themselves were bruised purple, as if they'd been pummeled by a giant's fists. Hamish's gaze drifted to a human-sized lump lying half-in, half-out of the water. His heart skipped a beat.

"James!"

He sprinted over and fell to his knees, pushing damp hair out of his brother's eyes.

"It's okay, Hamish. He's fine," Jarsha reassured him. "The first trip is rough for most people. I should have warned you."

As if to illustrate his point, James sat up and groaned. "Why did I agree to this stupid plan?"

Hamish tackled him in a hug. "You're alive!"

"Whoa, easy," James panted. He rubbed his sternum and pushed Hamish away. "I won't be alive much longer if you keep slamming into me like that."

"I didn't mean to. I was just worried."

"Yeah, well, don't be." James scrambled to his feet and gazed around the clearing. "Did we make it to Wraithland?"

"Looks like it," Jarsha said. "I don't remember a whole lot, but this definitely looks familiar."

"It's not Earth, that's for sure," James agreed. "Why are the trees all dead? Was there a forest fire?"

"I don't know," Jarsha said, running a hand through his hair. "Come on. We need to stay focused. I think we should go to the Hatchery first. That's where I first heard the song, so we're most likely to find something there. We need to get back before morning, right?"

"Preferably."

"Then we'd better run."

Jarsha took off down the path with James hot on his heels.

"Hey! Wait up!" Hamish shouted, running after them.

He was pretty fit despite not playing any sports, but his two companions had the endurance to run rings around him. Plus, their longer legs meant they could cover more ground, faster.

It's not fair. Why did James have to steal all the tall genes?

The Hatchery came into sight after nearly an hour of running. They'd stopped a handful of times—once so James could remove a stone from his shoe and four times so Hamish could catch his breath. Jarsha never berated them for it, but an agitated aura emanated from him nonetheless. His gaze darted around, and he startled at the slightest noise, as though he knew something they didn't. *Are we in danger? Should I have stayed home like Billy wanted me to?* A pang of guilt shot through Hamish.

He'd promised to take care of their family. While he hadn't broken that promise, he was flirting with the edge of disaster by leaving Earth with James.

"This is it," Jarsha said, pointing at a yawning cave at the base of the hill.

Multi-colored lights floated inside the mouth of the cave, flitting back and forth like fireflies. Jarsha skidded down the scree slope, a cloud of dust accompanying his descent. Hamish and James scrambled after him, kicking up stones as they went. Hamish lost his balance a couple of times but managed to remain upright.

"Follow me," Jarsha said when they reached the bottom.

Hamish's heart beat faster and faster as they approached the cave entrance. He suspected there were wraiths inside, both infant and adult. The former didn't scare him, but the latter…

They're just nurses, he tried to reassure himself. *They won't hurt kids like us. Especially not when Jarsha's with us. Right?*

Although the cave's craggy exterior looked natural, its heart was anything but. The sandstone foyer gave way to a winding marble corridor, where their echoing footsteps mingled with soft strains of music.

Jarsha's song, Hamish thought with a flicker of recognition.

The corridor led to a round, sparsely decorated atrium. Fogged-up crystal jars bathed every surface in purple light, adding to the otherworldly feel. Doors lined the walls, and beyond them, Hamish heard babies crying.

He moved toward the closest door, intending to go through it, but the music swelled to a crescendo, filling him with a profound sense of peace. In that instant, he knew he had nothing to fear. No one who spent their days listening to this song could be capable of anything but love. He didn't know *how* he knew that, only that he believed it with all his soul.

"This is the song you were playing on the keyboard," James whispered.

Hamish nodded, mesmerized.

"It is the Song of Life," a musical voice greeted them. "Welcome, children. You've come from far away."

All three boys spun around. A wraith nurse curtseyed in their direction, her apron splitting at the hem. Hamish wondered if it was meant to be like that or if it had been damaged in the line of duty.

"We're from Morton on Earth," Jarsha said on their behalf. "We've come to learn everything we can about music magic. We know how to play the Song of Life, but we don't know what it's for. What can it do? And are there any other songs we can learn?"

The nurse's eyebrows quirked upward. "You ask a lot. I can tell you a little about the Song of Life, certainly. It was gifted to us hundreds of years ago by one of the Great Virtuosos. His name was Elin, and he was the best composer wraithkind have ever known. Since then, none have been able to replicate his music perfectly. You must excuse me if I'm a little skeptical when you say you can play it."

"Do you have a piano?" Jarsha asked. "My friend and I can prove it."

"A piano?" Confusion laced the nurse's voice. "As I understand it, the piece must be played on the versailliad to produce its full effect."

"What's a versailliad?" Hamish asked.

"It's an instrument unique to the Gloaming," the nurse explained. "Or at least it used to be. They were destroyed when Grigoth came to power. All of our great compositions were burned with them and lost to time. The only way to discover them now is to hear the ones that play eternal, as the Song of Life does, or to learn from a musician."

"So the Song of Life is the only one you can play for us?" James asked.

"Of course," the nurse said. "Is that not enough? The Hatchery aims to raise its young into strong children. Ones who are capable of crossing the portal to a better life. It's a shame they have to return later on. I think we would all be better off living a life of peace and plenty on Earth."

"Have you heard about the upcoming war?" Hamish asked. "Apparently, Grigoth is going to force the portal open and unleash his entire army on the humans. You'll probably get to live on Earth if he wins."

"Is that so?" The nurse's gaze dropped. "I do not care for war, but I want the best for the children here. Just as I want the best for you three.

You are young. This is not your battle. You should go back to Morton. Find a safe place to hide."

"We can't go back yet," Hamish protested. "We need the music to protect ourselves. Grigoth will kill us if we don't have it."

"He's right," Jarsha said. "Please help us. We need the songs to keep ourselves safe."

The nurse swept a wrinkled hand through her hair. She looked exhausted. "Apart from the Song of Life, no eternal songs exist to my knowledge. The only way to find out for sure is to ask a composer."

"Okay, great," James said. "Where do we find one of those?"

"You cannot. They were executed decades ago."

Hamish took a step back. *Executed? For writing songs?*

"All of them?" Jarsha asked. His voice wavered. "There must be archives or something, though, right?"

"The archives were destroyed, along with much of our art and literature. As for the composers, well… no… I don't think… that is, I mean to say, there isn't anything you can do."

"There *is* something we can do," James persisted. "I saw it in your eyes. What is it?"

"You saw nothing."

"Please tell us," Hamish begged. He didn't know what his brother was talking about, but he trusted his judgment.

"It's not safe for children. My duty is to protect, never to endanger."

"We'll be in more danger if you don't tell us," Jarsha argued. "We're not the only ones who need this, either. There are hundreds of kids in Morton, and we could save them if we knew more songs. Please help us. We'll be careful, we promise."

The nurse lowered her head, and for a moment, Hamish feared she would yell at them. But when she looked up, defeat filled her eyes.

"My loyalty is blood-bound to King Grigoth, and I cannot betray him. However, if I were looking for music-based magic, I would head a few miles west to Blackbriar Cemetery. There might be something of interest there."

Jarsha dipped his head in a bow. "Thank you."

The nurse curtseyed and glided into one of the side rooms. "Goodbye, children."

She closed the door with a resounding click. The Song of Life faded out, bringing a heart-rending stillness to the air. Hamish froze to the spot, his stomach squirming into unpleasant shapes. After a few beats, the song restarted, filling the room with joy once more. By unspoken agreement, the boys dashed out of the cave and didn't stop running until they reached a rock ledge several hundred feet above it.

"The Hatchery feels empty without the song," Jarsha reflected, gazing down at the entrance. "I remember that from when I was little. Every time the song stopped, we all started crying. It felt like the air was being sucked out of the place."

"Sounds like a drug," James said. "Maybe you were all addicted to this music magic, and when it stopped, it was like going through withdrawal."

"I don't know," Jarsha said. "If that was really the reason, I think more wraiths would remember the music."

"What's your theory, then?"

"The nurse said it was the Song of Life, right? I think it helps us to grow. Maybe if we don't have it when we're young, our bodies die. Maybe it's an important part of the hatching process."

"Wait, you guys *hatch?*" James's mouth dropped open. "Like, out of giant eggs? How could the mother even lay an egg that big? Are wraith babies tiny or something?"

Jarsha blushed. "Not exactly."

"Then how?"

"I don't want to talk about it."

"Oh, come on. It's only us. We won't make fun of you."

Jarsha studied the dust between his boots as though it were the most interesting thing in the world. A lilac blush tinted his cheeks.

"The blood donations of two bonded wraiths are added to a special potion," he said. "After a while, a baby forms and the potion turns into a clear jelly. The nurses pour it into a bath, and the surface hardens like an eggshell. The baby grows until they're ready to hatch and then they, uh… hatch."

"Whoa." Hamish's eyes widened. "That's actually pretty cool. I was expecting something way grosser."

"Same," James agreed.

"If you say so," Jarsha said, scrubbing the dirt with his shoe. In the faint light, Hamish noticed his cheeks had purpled further. "We never get to meet our parents after we hatch, so that part's not cool. I think that's another reason why they play the Song of Life. Because it's a song of love as well."

"Love?" James wrinkled his nose.

"Yeah. Pure love. Parental love. Maybe they play the song to make up for our parents not being there."

The thought sobered Hamish, distracting him from the oddness of wraith biology. "Maybe."

"This is all very interesting, but we don't have time to stand around chatting," James said, bouncing on his toes. "Are we going to Blackbriar Cemetery or what?"

"Yup." Jarsha bent down and tightened his shoelaces. "The nurse said it's a few miles west of here. It shouldn't be too hard to find. Ready for another run?"

Hamish groaned. No matter how much he hated running, he'd do it if it meant helping his friends and family.

"I'm ready," he said.

And so they ran.

Chapter Forty-Nine

HAMISH FELL TO his knees outside Blackbriar Cemetery, cold air piercing his strained lungs. A further fifty minutes of running had left him with muscle spasms in both legs and a stabbing pain in his side. Sharp and persistent, it felt like someone was attempting to sew his stomach to his liver. *I guess that's why they call it "the stitch."* Jarsha leaned against a tree, hunched over and panting, while James lay flat on the ground. It seemed not even athletes were immune from the effects of vigorous exercise.

As his breathing slowed, Hamish turned his focus to the spikes atop the cemetery fence and the slew of tombstones beyond. Bruised sunlight bathed them in an eerie glow, and he couldn't hold back a shiver of unease. He hated cemeteries. Even at the best of times, they reminded him of the sister he'd never met. The Porter family visited her grave once a year to pay their respects, and he knew the engraving on it by heart. *Here lies Heather Porter, daughter of Jeremy and Margaret Porter. Born October 26, 2001. Died October 31, 2001.*

"What do you think we'll find in there?" James asked, breaking through Hamish's thoughts.

"Other than graves?" Jarsha tilted his head to one side. "I dunno. I think a song of death would be fitting."

Hamish paled. "A song of death? You mean, like… killing?"

His chest constricted at the idea. *We should have gone straight home after visiting the Hatchery. No, scratch that—we shouldn't have come here at all. Then we could have had a good night's sleep, and Mom and Dad wouldn't be having heart attacks right now.*

"No, not killing," Jarsha said. "Think about it. The Song of Life played in the Hatchery, right? It didn't give us life, but it helped us grow. Maybe the Song of Death helps people find peace when they die."

"Still sounds creepy to me," James said. "And anyway, wouldn't a spell to kill people be more useful against the bad guys? Who cares if their death is peaceful or not? You just want to get rid of them, don't you?"

"Well, yeah, obviously," Jarsha said. "But I think there's more than one song hidden here. The nurse hinted that there's a musician living inside Blackbriar Cemetery—or close to it."

Hamish wrinkled his nose. "Who would want to live in a cemetery?"

"I guess we're about to find out," Jarsha said, tramping toward the gates.

Rather than opening them, the wraith boy clambered to the top and dropped to the dust on the other side. Willing himself to ignore the pain in his gut, Hamish followed suit. His palms snagged on the rough-hewn metal, stippling the bars with tiny pearls of blood.

His shoulders ached with effort as he pulled himself up, hand over hand, to the spot where Jarsha had crossed. The gate swayed under his weight. Careful not to impale himself, he climbed over the spikes and jumped to the ground on the other side. Mild pain shot through his ankles.

"Good job, Hamish," Jarsha cheered. "Come on, James. You're next."

James joined them in seconds, his height negating the need to copy the other boys' acrobatics. The sight sent prickles of envy down Hamish's spine. *I wish I could be as fit as him.*

They strolled across the cemetery, eyeing the patches of raised dirt and the stone markers that jutted from them like broken teeth. No names were etched into the markers, although some bore splatters of mud that resembled letters. A coven of dead trees surrounded a small cottage in the distance, their lower limbs grasping the thatched roof.

Tremors of anticipation racked Hamish's frame as he beheld the structure. *Someone really does live here.* A wooden arch marked the entryway, the topmost board proclaiming it to be the caretaker's house. A weathered door hung in the frame, half open, as though the occupant had dashed out to grab the mail. The cloying odor of compost emanated from inside.

"Hello?" Jarsha shouted.

The rasping reply was immediate. "Who's there? What do you want?"

A wraith hobbled over the threshold, his posture hunched. White hair clung to his cheeks like broken cobwebs, and he wrung his hands as though they pained him.

"I wanted to talk to you," Jarsha said. His voice didn't waver, but he flinched when the man approached him. "One of the nurses at the Hatchery said you could teach me something."

A wheezy laugh blew past the old wraith's lips. "Been misbehaving, eh?"

"No, sir. I want to learn more about music magic, and I was told I'd find something here."

"Hmmm." The old man stroked his chin. "You must be talking about the catacombs."

"There are catacombs?" James asked.

The man took another shambling step forward. "Who's that with you? A friend?"

Pale light bathed his face, revealing a milky film over his left eye.

He's going blind, Hamish thought, transfixed. *But it's not just that. He looks old—like, really old. Older than Mrs. Price, and she's the oldest person I know.*

"Yes, these are my friends," Jarsha explained. "My name is Jarsha, and this is James and Hamish."

"Humans!"

Hamish stepped back, ready to sprint headlong through the cemetery, but the stranger looked too relaxed to attack them.

"You three are the first company I've had in months," the old wraith said, beaming through a mouthful of rotten teeth. "My name is Wolpeth, and it's a great pleasure to meet you. You must forgive me. I'm not prepared for visitors. I haven't got any rations to offer you. Not even a drop of water, unless you want to try digging in the old well."

"It's all right. We don't need refreshments," Jarsha reassured him.

Hamish begged to differ. His throat was parched from running, and his stomach growled for sustenance. *We should have brought some food and water with us.*

"I haven't seen youngsters like you in two decades," Wolpeth said. "In some ways, that's a good thing because it means none of you have died. I spend most of my time as a groundskeeper, you see, but I also dabble in the undertaking business. It's a hard job. The dead aren't a talkative bunch."

"Do you bury many people?" Hamish asked.

"*Bury* them? Goodness, no. Most ask for their bodies to be vaporized. There are a few oddballs who prefer human customs, and I honor their wishes the same as everyone else's, but I only get one or two burials a year."

Jarsha cleared his throat. "I don't mean to be rude, but we don't have a lot of time for chit-chat. Do you know anything about music, Wolpeth?"

The light behind Wolpeth's good eye faded. "Again with the music." He shook his head. "Your nurse was mistaken. I don't play any instruments. Not properly, anyway. And I don't know any songs either."

"You must know something," Jarsha persisted. "You have an instrument hidden somewhere, don't you? One that survived Grigoth's destruction."

The veins in Wolpeth's neck bulged. "Why would that matter to you?"

"Because Grigoth is going to attack Earth," Hamish said. "We want to use music magic to stop him."

"Stop him?" Wolpeth repeated. "If Grigoth wants to invade, he will. No force, magical or otherwise, can stop him. Music-based magic needs to be performed perfectly to reach its full potential, and even if you do that, it won't make a dent in his efforts."

"You don't sound very surprised about what we're doing," Hamish said.

"You're humans. Why would you be supporting a wraith who hates you?"

"You're not bothered by it?"

"Why should I be? I've never met Grigoth. I was already a hundred and twenty-four years old when he took over, and my blood oath ceremony had been and gone. I've been keeping my head down ever since."

"Aren't you afraid he'll catch you?"

"Why? Are you planning to report me?" Wolpeth's mouth twisted into a smile as Hamish's eyes widened. "I'm just kidding. I trust you boys. Do you know the one thing he fears more than anything else?"

They shook their heads.

"Losing his reign. Death is a reminder of what's waiting for him. The cemetery is an extension of that. I doubt he would ever come here, but if he did, I could easily hide in the catacombs. The Song of Death rings down every corridor, and that would be enough to keep him out."

Jarsha's eyes lit up. "So there *is* a Song of Death in the catacombs, and it *does* have an effect on Grigoth."

Wolpeth deflated, his head drooping. "Yes, but it isn't safe for children to hear. The effect it would have on you… You'd lose your minds."

"We have to hear it!" Hamish insisted. "If my brother can't stop Grigoth in time, we can play the song to slow him down. How are we supposed to do that if you won't let us learn it?"

The wrinkles on Wolpeth's forehead multiplied. "Your brother is trying to stop Grigoth?"

"That's right. He came here with a bunch of his friends."

"Then I'm sorry to tell you this, but your brother will be dead soon," Wolpeth said. "No one can stop Grigoth, especially not a human. You should go home before you meet the same fate."

"No," Jarsha said, crossing his arms. "We're not leaving until we've heard the song. A lot of lives are going to depend on it, especially if something happens to Billy."

Something deep and unfathomable passed through Wolpeth's good eye, and he sighed. "All right. I'll take you into the catacombs. But don't blame me if you suffer for it."

Struggling to get his legs under him, he hobbled around the corner of his house. Excitement bubbled through Hamish. *We're actually going to do it!*

A black granite igloo sat behind Wolpeth's cottage, nestled between a handful of rotting tree stumps. Inside, Hamish spotted a set of skinny stairs that descended into the bowels of the earth. Their guide went in first, disappearing into the darkness below. Gritting his teeth, Hamish padded after him.

The sandstone felt brittle under his heels, and his toes hung over the edge of each step. It wouldn't take much to plummet to his death. Ragged breaths echoed down the stairs, some his own and some belonging to James and Jarsha. Five steps from the bottom, a purple light winked into existence, revealing the path ahead. Strings of dead ivy strangled the walls, burrowing through the cracks and imperfections. The blighted leaves crumbled to ash at the slightest touch.

"Keep up, children," Wolpeth's voice echoed back to them. "We mustn't tarry here."

The boys jogged down the narrow passage, their features cast in sharp relief as more and more werelights woke from their slumber. A shuddering, droning noise filtered down the corridor, growing stronger with every step.

"What *is* that?" James asked, unable to keep the fear out of his voice.

Wolpeth's face loomed in front of them, his cataract-blinded eye glowing yellow in the dim light. "It's the Song of Death. I told you it was a bad idea to come here."

Hamish inched back a few steps, his heart thumping against his rib cage. The other boys stood their ground.

"Where is it coming from?" Jarsha asked.

"The walls have been enchanted to play the song until the end of time," Wolpeth explained. "My great-great-great-grandfather placed the spell himself to ease the burdens of the dying and to guide the dead into the afterlife."

"So you're related to a musician," Jarsha said. "Did your grandfather pass any of his songs on to you?"

"Great-great-great-grandfather," Wolpeth corrected. "And yes, he did. Elin the Virtuoso, they called him. I don't suppose that rings any bells?"

"The nurse told us about him," Hamish piped up.

"Yeah, that's right," Jarsha said. "I don't know much about his songs except that they were powerful. Which ones do you have? And what do they do?"

Wolpeth gestured to the passage ahead. "Why don't you come and see for yourself?"

He staggered forward, prompting the others to follow. Deeper and deeper, they wove their way into the heart of the catacombs.

How big is *this place?* Hamish wondered.

Another five minutes passed before they arrived in a cavernous chamber. A lumpy mattress had been pushed into one corner, its surface littered with miscellaneous clutter. Sandstone pillars made a show of holding up the ceiling, but the thick dust at his feet spoke of previous cave-ins. *If the whole thing collapses while we're down here, we'll be buried alive.* Hamish sucked in a deep breath, marinating his lungs in the musty air. *No. Don't think about that. We're going to be fine. Focus on the present.*

"Do you sleep here?" James asked, gesturing at the mattress.

"Sometimes," Wolpeth said. "To be honest, it's more of a storage room these days. The location makes it useful for keeping certain items away from prying eyes."

He dug through his meager possessions and pulled out a small book, which he handed to Jarsha. The wraith boy eased it open, the aged paper crackling at his touch. Hamish peeked over his shoulder. Staves, clefs, and notes covered the pages, no different from the ones he'd seen in his music lessons.

"That's Elin's composition notebook," Wolpeth explained. "I can't make heads or tails out of it, but if you think it's important, then you need it more than I do."

"You're giving it to us?" Hamish asked, his jaw dropping.

"Consider it a loan," Wolpeth said. He pressed a conch-shaped object into Jarsha's free hand. "You'd better take this too."

"What is it?" James asked. "Is that one of those versilly things the nurse was talking about?"

"A versailliad," Jarsha corrected, brushing his fingers over the metal curves. "How do you play it?"

"I don't have the faintest idea," Wolpeth said. "I've tried to make music with it, but it comes out as noise. You're bright children. I'm sure you'll work it out."

Something in the caretaker's speech stirred Hamish's heart, and he forgot his fear. He wrapped his arms around the older wraith's waist, hugging him tightly. "Thanks, Wolpeth."

Wolpeth patted his head. "You're very welcome. Now, you three should head off home. The Song of Death is recorded in the book, but you'll need to work hard if you want to learn it before Grigoth makes his move."

"All right," Jarsha agreed, bouncing on the balls of his feet. "How do we get out of here?"

Wolpeth led them through the twisting sandstone corridors, his footsteps frail but certain. Cold air swirled around them as they got closer to the surface. When they breached, Hamish's breath came out in small, frosted puffs. Rather than retiring to his cottage, Wolpeth heaved the cemetery gates open for them with a strength that belied his age. They tried to thank him, but he waved it off and encouraged them again to hurry home.

"Work hard, boys!" Wolpeth shouted after them. "Remember what I told you!"

The return run took longer than their initial foray into the Gloaming. Hamish's muscles ached and, having reached the limit of their endurance, let the pain spread to his bones and joints. His lungs cramped in the frigid air, constricting his chest. This time, he wasn't alone in his suffering. James and Jarsha, fit though they were, requested more and more frequent breaks. The novelty of being in a brand-new world was well and truly over.

The moment they reached the portal, Jarsha unleashed the sizzling magical currents that would suck them back to Earth. Hamish clung to consciousness as Oilskin Lake spat him out on its muddy banks. The violet sky deepened to sapphire blue, the color preceding dawn, and the dead forest vanished in favor of lush vegetation. Only the lake remained the same—tepid, stagnant, and eerily dark.

"We'd better get home," Jarsha said, heading for the exit. "See ya tomorrow, Hamish."

"Yeah. See ya," Hamish said. He turned to James. "Ready?"

"Yeah, I'm ready. Let's take it easy the rest of the way. I have basketball training after school, and I'm not sure I'm going to survive it."

Silence surrounded them as they trudged along the empty streets. When they reached their house, they jumped the fence, crawled through their bedroom window, and collapsed on the floor, spent. Lego bricks dug into Hamish's back, but he couldn't bring himself to move. Soft snores echoed from down the hallway. *Mom and Dad didn't wake up. We actually got away with it.* Elated though he was, a sleepy darkness rose within him and his eyelids drifted shut.

"G'night, James."

He was asleep before his brother responded.

Chapter Fifty

BILLY WOKE AT dawn to the clanging of pots and pans. He rubbed his eyes, inhaling the rich scent of tomato broth, and the fuzz of sleep receded from his brain. Abandoned bedrolls blanketed the floor around him. *Where is everyone?*

Yawning, he rolled to his feet and shuffled outside. The dead branches formed an imperfect ceiling, shrouding him in partial darkness. Muffled voices hummed from the side of the shack, accompanied by a hearty laugh—*Darthan's.* Billy jogged toward the sound, blinking when he spied the orange glow of a campfire. His companions lounged around it, light and shadow dancing across their haggard faces. Lothaire held a cast-iron skillet over the fire, tossing and catching the contents with an expert hand.

Rem glanced up when he approached. "Hey, B—William. How'd you sleep?"

"Like a rock," he admitted, taking a seat between her and Corvus. "What's for breakfast?"

"Beans and minced beef," Darthan answered, rubbing his hands together. "It doesn't get much better than this."

"I hate beans," Corvus muttered.

"Yeah, I'm not a big fan of them either," Billy said. He eyed the brown sludge lining the skillet. "Can I have an energy bar instead?"

Lothaire tossed him two rectangles wrapped in bright green foil. "I don't see why not. It's all the same thing anyway."

Billy grimaced at the reminder. Eating the ashes of disintegrated food wasn't high on his wishlist, but it would be rude not to sample the fruits of Lothaire's labor.

He peeled back the wrapper of the first bar and stared at the cobblestone pattern of exposed grains. "This looks identical to the energy bar I ate yesterday. Are you sure it's made from ashes?"

"Positive," Lothaire said, his face glowing at the indirect praise. "I performed the spell an hour ago."

Billy took a deep breath and sank his teeth into the energy bar. The crunch of mixed nuts combined with the chewy sweetness of a fruit he couldn't identify. It tasted like an energy bar should, and after the second bite, the true content of the food no longer mattered to him. Ash or not, it eased the ache in his belly. He pocketed the second bar for later rather than indulging himself.

"All right," Lothaire said once they were done eating. "Darthan and I need to discuss a few things. The rest of you should grab your swords and get some practice in."

Corvus wrinkled his nose. "Do we have to?"

"For William's sake, yes. He hasn't used a sword before, and I don't want his first time to be on the battlefield."

"In that case, I'll do my best to teach him."

"I'm glad to hear it."

They all retreated to the shack, but the teenagers only stayed long enough to pack up their belongings. Leaving Lothaire and Darthan to talk, they headed back to their breakfast spot, dropped their bags next to the dying campfire, and converged on the widest part of the clearing. Rem lowered herself to the dead grass, content to watch instead of participating. Corvus drew his sword and slid a glowing hand over the flat of the blade. Satisfied, he grabbed Billy's sword and repeated the motion.

"What are you doing?" Billy asked.

"Dulling the blades so we don't slice each other to ribbons."

"Oh." Billy thought about it, then nodded toward the shack. "What do you think they're talking about?"

"Does it matter?"

"You're not the least bit curious?"

"Not really, no."

"But if it's something to do with the mission, they should tell us, right? Why are they being all secretive?"

"They'll tell us when they're ready," Corvus said, returning Billy's sword. "Unless you want to listen to them bickering for an hour straight, you should stop worrying about them and focus on what we're doing here."

He's trying to help me. The least I can do is let him. "Okay. Teach me what I need to know."

"Sword fighting is very simple," Corvus explained. "Keep the sharp end pointed toward your enemies, and wave it around. Lesson over."

"Oh, come *on*, Corvus," Rem interrupted from the sidelines. "There's more to sword fighting than 'waving it around.' If you aren't going to teach him properly, then maybe I should take over."

"We don't have time to teach him properly," Corvus retorted. "Wildly waving your sword is a legitimate tactic. If someone came running at me like that, I'd probably wet myself and do everything in my power to get away from them."

Rem leaned back on her elbows. "Fine. Do it your way, then."

"All right, let's try a few rounds of sparring," Corvus said. "The swords may be dull, but they can still cause nasty injuries if you bash your opponent too hard. So try not to bash me, okay?"

"Okay."

Billy settled into a comfortable fighting stance. *He's in chronic pain from the blood oath scar, so his reflexes are slower than they used to be. If I strike fast, I should—*

A flash of silver whistled through the air, and something hard punched him in the side. He staggered away from it, arms rigid with shock.

Corvus retracted his own sword arm, scrutinizing Billy's expression. "Are you okay?"

"Fine," Billy said, but his mind raced a mile a minute. *How did he move that fast?* "I wasn't ready. Could you go a bit slower?"

"I could, but I wouldn't be doing you any favors," Corvus said. "Grigoth's soldiers aren't going to go easy on you because you're new."

"But you haven't even taught me the basics."

"You already know them. Remember all those times we went on camping trips and you wanted to play-fight with sticks?"

"Yeah. You always refused."

"That's not the point. I watched you spar with James and Hamish. You know the basics of how to strike and block with a stick. You just need to put it into practice with a sword."

Easier said than done, Billy thought, settling back into his fighting stance.

Lifting the sword over his head, he lunged forward. The blade's weight propelled it in a downward arc toward Corvus. The wraith deflected the blow with a lazy flick of his wrist, countering with a strike to the shoulder. Billy's teetering weapon clashed with Corvus's, jarring his bones until they hummed and vibrated with songs of war.

A second, more powerful attack cut through Billy's guard and clobbered him in the stomach. He stumbled, gasping as the sword slipped through his fingers. Metal hit dust with a muffled thump, and seconds later, he lost his balance and followed suit.

Corvus stepped back, pinwheeling his sword and sheathing it in one smooth motion. "Lesson two: don't drop your sword."

"I know that! It's not like I did it on purpose," Billy said, glaring at him. He rose to his feet and retrieved his fallen blade. "This thing's heavy, you know."

"Is it? Let me try."

Billy handed the sword to Corvus, who lifted it into an upright position. The wraith scrutinized the steel with wolfish intensity, twisting it in his hands. Satisfied, he bounced the hilt against his palm and took a few experimental swings.

"Now you're just showing off," Billy grumbled.

Corvus ignored him. "It's slightly tip-heavy, but otherwise it seems fine to me."

In other words, I'm a weakling. "How am I supposed to get used to it in two days? That's not going to be enough time, is it?"

"Not even close. But two days of training is a lot better than no training, and you'll have us backing you up. You'll be fine."

Corvus returned the sword to him, and Billy grimaced at the unfamiliar weight. He heaved it into the air, ready for another clash, but the wraith boy retreated to Rem's side.

"My scar hurts," he told her in a low voice. "Do you mind taking over?"

Rem patted his shoulder and whispered something Billy couldn't make out. Then she straightened and whipped out her sword. "Ready, Billy?"

He nodded, widening his stance and bending his knees for extra stability. The adjustments would slow his reactions, but they'd also make it easier to control the capricious sword. In turn, the risk of hurting Rem would decrease, and that was always a good thing as far as Billy was concerned. Rem dulled her sword and lifted it over her head, turning sideways to make herself a smaller target.

I don't want to hurt a girl, Billy thought. *Maybe I should take it easy on her.*

His concerns were groundless. From the moment Rem sprang toward him, he knew he'd underestimated her. She spun around him like a whirlwind, landing blows left and right, her every movement a picture of elegance and deadly precision. Fireworks of pain exploded across his nerve centers, each burst stronger than the last.

She couldn't match Corvus's raw physical power, but her speed and agility made up for it. Billy backpedaled, the tip of his blade plunging into the dirt. *How can she do that? I can barely* lift *a sword, and she's cutting me down to size like it's nothing.*

He threw a half-hearted parry, wincing as the flat of her blade left a welt on his shoulder. Another flurry of blows rained down on him, and he tumbled to the ground, swordless, for the second time in as many minutes.

"Ow! I give up! I give up!"

Rem paused, the tip of her sword quivering in front of his chest. Then she withdrew with a bright smile. *How can she go from ruthless killer one minute to a ball of sunshine the next?*

"Do you need a break?" she asked.

He rose to his feet with a wince. "A *long* break. A very, *very* long break. Like, maybe forever."

"We don't have that long," Rem teased. A moment later, her expression sobered. "I didn't hurt you, did I?"

"You hit me with a sword. Repeatedly. Of course it hurt."

"I'm sorry."

"It's okay. I'll live."

Billy left the sword where it lay and hobbled over to Corvus. The ground rushed up to meet him again, and he groaned when the impact jarred his injuries. None of Rem's blows had drawn blood, but he'd have some wicked-looking bruises tomorrow. He rolled onto his back and gazed at the deadwood canopy.

"How strong do you think Grigoth's soldiers are?" he asked. "I know I'm pretty useless at the moment, but you guys have been training for years. Do you think you can beat them?"

Out of the corner of his eye, he saw Corvus tense up. "One on one? Probably. But anything can happen in the heat of battle. It doesn't matter how good you are or how well you've trained. If luck's not on your side, you're a goner."

"Maybe, but that goes for Grigoth and his soldiers too. They're not infallible."

"I admire your optimism, but we need to be realistic. Most of the people we're recruiting to fight alongside us aren't trained. It's going to be a hard-fought battle."

"What do you think, Rem?" Billy asked, undaunted. "Do we have any chance of winning?"

"We've definitely got a chance," she said, tucking a strand of hair behind her ear. "An army marches on its stomach, and we'll be feeding our army better than Grigoth feeds his. I doubt his soldiers have done much real training since they left the Academy, so we might end up evenly matched."

Billy cocked his eyebrows. "You really think so?"

"I don't see why not. The people on our side have a lot more to fight for than Grigoth's soldiers. Sometimes that's enough to turn the tide of a battle."

"I guess that's true. They're still going to be a lot better at fighting than I am, aren't they?"

"No offense, but that wouldn't be hard," Corvus said, jerking a thumb over his shoulder. "That *tree* could handle a sword better than you."

Billy gave him a playful shove. "Why don't you recruit that tree, then, if it's so talented?"

"Maybe I will."

"Oh, leave it alone you two," Rem interrupted. "Can't we enjoy each other's company for a few hours without bickering?"

Corvus and Billy looked at each other, impish grins plastered across their faces. They replied in unison. "Nope."

Rem shook her head and went to retrieve the swords. Her hands glowed as she reversed the dulling spells.

"How come you can you lift them so easily?" Billy complained.

"They're not heavy."

"Yes, they are!"

Rem placed her sword back in its sheath and focused her attention on Billy's. Purple light spilled between her fingers, and she handed the sword back to him. A pensive expression fell across her features.

"What?" Billy asked.

"Your sword has been charmed to weigh more in human hands," she said. "That must be why you're having trouble. I never even considered…"

"Why would the Master Forger put a spell like that on a sword?" Corvus asked. "That doesn't make any sense."

"Actually, it makes plenty of sense," Rem said. "Your dad told us about this years ago. If an enemy gets hold of your sword, you don't want them using it against you. Making it heavier is one way to stop that."

"Why is the charm specific to humans, though?" Corvus asked. "We've never fought against them before, have we?"

"Not since the middle ages," Rem replied. "This sword is old. I'd get rid of the enchantments if I could, but I'm not sure it would be safe. They're built into the steel."

"If it's not safe, then don't do it," Billy said, examining the blade. "I can put up with the extra weight. Hey, who knows? Maybe I'll get some muscles along the way."

"Maybe," Rem agreed. The hint of a frown tugged her lips. "I should check if all of the swords are like that or just yours."

Billy watched with bated breath as she tested Corvus's sword and then her own.

"I was right. They're all the same," she said at last. "I'd hoped we could swap them around so you could have one that's easier to manage, but it looks like we're out of luck."

"Do you think Excalibur had that spell placed on it too?" Billy asked. Confusion flitted across his friends' faces, compelling him to explain. "You've heard of Excalibur, right? It's the sword from the legend of King Arthur. It was stuck in the rock until the right person came along to pull it out. Arthur wasn't particularly strong, but he *was* the right person, so he managed to do it. You said the spell on my sword could distinguish between people, so I thought it might be the same thing."

Corvus and Rem exchanged a pained look, and his curiosity evaporated. *Now is not the right time to compare our situation to a movie.*

"Billy?" Corvus placed a hand on his shoulder. "Shut up."

Billy was only too happy to obey.

Chapter Fifty-One

BILLY REFUSED TO get up until the adult wraiths emerged from the shack. Dark gray worry lines criss-crossed their foreheads, contrasting with the purple veins there. As they got closer, their frowns morphed into smiles, but their fists remained clenched.

"You kids didn't burn yourselves out, did you?" Darthan asked.

Rem rose to her feet. "We're a little tired, but we're ready to go."

"I'm glad to hear it."

Lothaire crouched and planted a hand on Billy's shoulder. "How did the lesson go, William?"

Billy fought the urge to grimace. "It was terrible. Corvus and Rem are good teachers, but I'm no good at learning. I'm too weak and clumsy to handle a sword properly."

"I'll say," Corvus muttered under his breath.

"Ah well, that can't be helped," Lothaire said. "If you're lucky, it might even work in your favor. I believe there's a human saying along the lines of, 'I do not fear the master swordsman but the beginner, because there's no telling what the idiot will do next.'"

Billy's cheeks burned. "Oh, so now I'm an idiot. Thanks."

"I wasn't calling you an idiot. I was saying you're fearsome," Lothaire said, saving the comparison. "You'll be just like those action heroes on TV."

"I wish," Billy said, forcing himself to stand. He buckled on his sword belt, unsettled by the lopsided weight. "I don't think I'm cut out for all this athletic stuff."

"Well, you'd better get used to it," Darthan said. "We've got a long walk ahead of us and a tough fight to boot."

He marched off down the trail, kicking up clouds of dust as he went.

Lothaire scooped Billy's backpack off the ground and guided it onto his shoulders. "Come on. We'd better go."

The three wraiths hurried after Darthan, but Billy trailed behind. In a few hours, he'd have to fight someone for real. Not just one someone either, but several someones, all of whom would be bent on killing him. *I'll have to kill them before they kill me.*

Bile rose in his throat. He'd killed a lot of deer on hunting trips with his father. It was all so easy—a held breath, the squeeze of a trigger, and the rifle kicking back into his shoulder. Everyone went home happy, save for the hapless animals and their young. But firing a bullet from half a mile away didn't compare to the desperate struggle of hand-to-hand combat. Without a long-distance weapon and a bush to hide in, he was next to useless.

Pinpricks of black static framed his vision when he snapped back to reality. His friends' silhouettes were so far ahead they blended into the surrounding trees. Sensing his own vulnerability, Billy loped down the path after them. Rem regarded him with concern when he caught up, but he refused to meet her gaze. If she could handle this, then so could he.

The labor camp came into view a couple of hours before sunset. Wraiths in sackcloth tunics shambled across dusty fields, while others sat in small groups, hunched over their work. Guards in navy blue robes stood over them, barking instructions. A contingent of leather-armored soldiers congregated outside a large concrete building, their eyes dulled with boredom. Only two of them actively patrolled in front of the door. The others clustered around a fire pit, brooding over the flames and picking their teeth with dead twigs.

The military presence didn't surprise Billy, but the lack of physical barriers did. He'd envisioned a prison with tall stone walls topped with barbed wire. The camp in front of them didn't have so much as a picket fence surrounding it.

"They could run away if they wanted to," he commented.

"Yeah, and then what?" Rem said. "Starve to death? Working in a labor camp is the only way they can get food. Grigoth knows that. The guards know that. The soldiers know that. All the physical barriers in the world are nothing compared to the desperation that comes with hunger."

"So the guards and soldiers aren't here to stop the laborers from leaving."

"Nope. They're here to stop them from breaking into the depot. Can't have laborers stealing rations."

"Enough chatter," Lothaire interrupted. "We need to disguise ourselves before we get any closer."

He loosed a stream of magic, turning their clothes into perfect copies of the laborers'. Billy looked down at his new tunic, unnerved. The sackcloth stopped at his knees, revealing spindly void-black legs. Even so, he could feel the cotton lining of his sweatpants clinging to his calves. The spell must have been an illusion rather than a physical transformation.

"We should hide our swords too," Lothaire continued when their disguises were in place. "Laborers wouldn't carry them."

This time, the wraiths cast the necessary spell themselves, moving so fast that Billy missed it by blinking. Rem sidled up to him, hand extended, and he heaved his blade free of the sheath. A purple glow enveloped the weapon, and it shrank to the size of a dagger, a letter opener, and then a Playmobil sword. Pinching it between her thumb and forefinger, Rem deposited the tiny weapon in his palm. Despite its diminutive size, its weight did not decrease.

"I added a trigger spell to it," Rem explained as he fumbled the shrunken sword into his pocket. "It's the same spell I added to your armor. If you tap it three times, it'll grow back to its original size. You'd better keep your hands out of your pockets until you're ready to use it. And take it out before you activate it. I don't want you to stab yourself by accident."

"Thanks, Rem."

The sword's unnatural weight disappeared as soon as it left his hand, but the weight of impending bloodshed couldn't be cast off so easily.

"Right," Lothaire said. "You know why we're here. We need the laborers to fight alongside us if we're to have any hope of defeating Grigoth. The plan is simple. We're going to split up and act like we're laborers too. You need to talk to everyone you can and try to convince them to join us. Promise them food if you have to. When I give the signal, we'll take out the soldiers and guards, raid the depot, and find a safe place to hide before reinforcements arrive. Everyone understand?"

Billy nodded, his gaze fixed on the laborers. Until this moment, he'd never imagined what it would be like to live in a situation like theirs. What it would be like to work himself to the bone for no reward beyond a few dry scraps. His family wasn't rich by any means, but his needs had been provided for. If he was hungry, he could grab something from the pantry or the fridge. If they were out of snacks, he could stroll down to the shops and pick up a candy bar or a bag of chips. The laborers had never known such luxuries.

I've been lucky, he thought, studying the way their skin pulled taut against their bones. *No one should have to live like this.*

Lothaire led them to the camp at a cautious pace, trying to avoid notice. He needn't have bothered. None of the laborers seemed interested in them. Some milled around the compound with blank expressions. Others worked in the field, half-heartedly slamming their rakes into the soil. In preparation for future planting? Billy doubted it.

The others split away from Billy as soon as they arrived—Rem to the blacksmiths, Corvus to the builders, Darthan to the miners, and Lothaire to the potion brewers—and he found himself alone in the middle of the field. Determined not to be the weak link, he hurried forward to join a group of woodcarvers. The pungent stench of sweat washed over him, and he fought to keep from gagging. He was so distracted by the smell that he crashed into the broad chest of an otherwise emaciated laborer.

"Sorry," Billy mumbled. He tried to sidestep, but the man copied his movement, blocking his path.

"I haven't seen you around here before," the wraith rasped. "Are you new?"

"Uh… yeah. My name's William."

"Like William Wallace, eh?" The wraith grunted. "That's my name too. Your nurse was obsessed with Scotland like mine was, I suppose."

Billy didn't know what that meant, but he went along with it anyway. "Scotland has a fascinating history."

"That it does," William said. "I remember going to school in Morton… ooh, twenty years ago now. I did a summer project on my namesake."

"Me too," Billy lied. "So anyway, what are we supposed to be carving?"

William eyed him suspiciously. "You really are new. Fail out of the Academy?"

"Yeah. My aptitude for magic wasn't as strong as they thought it was."

"Well, it's pretty simple here," William said, handing him a small carving knife and a slab of wood. "We're making little round projectiles for Grigoth's mages to enchant. If we meet our daily quota, we get fed. So make sure you don't slack off, eh?"

"I won't," Billy promised.

His father had taught him to whittle during their first camping trip together, but he'd never taken it up as a hobby. Even so, he remembered how it felt. The blade gliding along the grain of the wood. The long, corkscrew shavings dropping to the ground between his boots. Making a sphere was no easy feat, but muscle memory helped him to control the knife. William glanced over, his projectile more of an indistinct blob than a sphere.

"Hey, that's real nice," the wraith said, giving him a gentle nudge. "You're a natural."

"What are they using these for anyway?" Billy asked. He tossed his ball into the basket and started on the next one. "You said something about projectiles."

"Yeah. Projectiles. The mages are going to enchant them to explode on our enemies."

"You mean humans?"

"That's right. There aren't any foreign wraiths left to fight now that the Abyss is rolling in."

"And you're okay with that?" Billy asked. "I mean, humans are pretty decent most of the time."

"I know, I know. I wouldn't attack them if I had a choice, but we're starving to death out here. People are *dying*. It's either us or them. If the humans won't help us, then we'll take what we need by force."

Defensive remarks swarmed to the front of Billy's mind, but pity gave him the strength to hold his tongue. *I'd do the same thing if I was in his position.*

"You're right," Billy said. His second ball looked more like an egg than a sphere, but he tossed it into the basket anyway. "William, what would you say if I could guarantee an endless supply of food for you and everyone else here?"

The wraith laughed. "I'd say you're a better mage than anyone in the Gloaming. I'd also say that the guy who expelled you from the Academy has a lot of explaining to do."

"There's no magic involved," Billy said. His heart thundered in anticipation of his next words. "I'm not actually interned here. My friends and I snuck in because we want to help you. We've got food, and we'll give you as much as you want if you help us."

William's eyes narrowed, studying him with a mixture of hope and distrust. "I'm listening."

A guard walked past, and they both fell silent until the blue robes vanished around a corner.

"The first thing we need to do is take over this camp," Billy said, keeping his voice low. "If we all rise up, the guards won't be able to stop us. After we take them down, we'll break into the supply depot, and you can take as much food as you want. But we can't stop there. All the food in the world won't matter if the Gloaming is wiped out by the Oncoming Abyss. Grigoth caused the Abyss the same way he caused the famine, and the only way to stop its path of destruction is to kill him."

A gasp split William's lips. "How can you say that? The oath—"

"Doesn't affect me," Billy finished for him. He lifted his hands, showing off his unblemished palms. "I'm a free wraith. I never took the oath, and that means I can say whatever I want. I can help you break free of your oath too, if that's what you want."

The lie stung his conscience, but William didn't seem to notice. The wraith stared at Billy's unsullied skin, his fingers tracing the scar emblazoned on his own palm. "Why would you offer me this?"

"Because it's honorable," Billy said, opting for the most culturally appropriate answer. After a moment, he added: "And because I care."

William stared at him, sizing him up. "How do I know I can trust you?"

Billy reached inside his tunic, relieved he could still access the pockets of his invisible coat. Careful to avoid touching the miniaturized sword, he pulled out the energy bar he'd been saving.

"It's not much, but you can have it."

William looked at the bar as though he'd been given a slab of pure gold. His eyes lit up, and he ripped open the foil, tearing into the contents with his teeth. Billy wondered if he should warn him to slow down, but he doubted the wraith would listen. William wolfed down the rest of the bar and stared longingly at the empty wrapper.

"There's more where that came from," Billy said. "I hate to ask a favor in exchange for food. If it were up to me, I'd just give it to you. But we need help to stop Grigoth and the endless cycle of misery he's created."

William held up a hand. "No need to explain. Just tell me what you need me to do."

Billy smiled. "The first thing we need to do is…"

Chapter Fifty-Two

Convincing the laborers to join their cause was easier than Corvus expected. The promise of a full belly was a powerful motivator, yes. But after failing to lure his peers away from the blood oath ceremony four years prior, nothing seemed certain anymore.

He watched the builders splinter off from their impromptu meeting, stone hammers clenched in their fists. A guard in blue robes marched toward them, and Corvus dashed into the crowd. Wearing a glamour might hide his identity, but it wouldn't stop Grigoth's officials from trying to subdue him.

Come on, Lothaire, Corvus pleaded. *Give us the signal.*

No such luck. He gritted his teeth and pushed a path through the multitude of wraiths. Hammers thudded in his ears. A flash of bright purple caught his eye, and he glanced up. Amidst the sea of void-black faces, a wraith with blood-matted hair stood in a daze. Something about the wraith looked familiar.

"Volner?"

Their eyes met for a fraction of a second. Then Volner's widened, and he scurried away, disappearing into the crowd. Corvus surged after him, murmuring an apology when his shoulder collided with someone else's. *What's he doing here? He should be at the Academy.*

"Hey! Volner! Wait!"

The din and clamor of the building site swallowed his words. He forced himself to push forward, squeezing his way through the dispersing workers. Despite losing sight of Volner for a few seconds, the boy's bloodied state made him stand out like a sore thumb, and Corvus soon picked up the trail again.

"Volner!"

The boy stopped. Swayed. His chin tilted to his chest, his shoulders heaving. Then he plunked himself down next to a stack of wood. The hammer slipped out of his hand, but he didn't seem to notice. Corvus jogged up to him, questions racing through his mind and evaporating before they reached his tongue. He wanted to demand answers. To find out why his former classmate had ended up in a labor camp and why he was ignoring him. Instead, he crouched in the dust in front of Volner, picked up the fallen hammer, and offered it to him.

Volner took the hammer without looking up. "Th-thanks."

Corvus blinked. The other boy had never been much of a revolutionary, but he'd stood up for what he believed in. Now it was like all the fight had been beaten out of him.

"Volner, it's me, Corvus. What happened to you?"

Volner bit his lip, worrying the dark flesh between his teeth. "It's a long story."

"I can tell," Corvus said. When no response seemed forthcoming, he added: "I can heal you if you want."

Volner stayed silent, picking at the chips and imperfections of the hammer. Corvus blew out a frustrated breath. Under ordinary circumstances, he would have stormed off and left Rem to deal with the situation. She was much better at this sort of thing. But on the eve of battle, he didn't have the luxury of waiting for Volner's permission. Nor could he afford to wait for a more skilled healer.

With a wave of his hand, he staunched the blood flow and summoned a rag from the shrunken backpack in his pocket. He threw the rag into Volner's lap, startling the boy out of his torpor.

"I didn't think I'd see you here," Corvus said, trying a different tack. "You were so bent on going to the Academy. I thought nothing would stop you."

"Yeah, well, it did," Volner replied, picking up the rag. He stared at it for a moment, then pressed it to his forehead, soaking the fabric purple. "I… I failed out in my second year."

"And they sent you here? I thought they had to wait until the end of your tenth year to pass judgment."

Volner shook his head, a bitter smile edging onto his lips. "Not if you have no magical aptitude whatsoever. I can barely lift a pebble. A *pebble!*" He dropped the bloodied rag into his lap, hands shaking. "I should have listened to you back in Morton. Everything you said was true. All of it."

Four years ago, Corvus would have given anything to hear those words. Now, faced with the miserable reality, he derived no pleasure from them.

"I'm sorry," he said. The words sounded hollow to his ears, but he meant them with all his heart. No one deserved to suffer as much as Volner had. "At least things are going to change, though, right?"

A shiver racked Volner's slight frame. "Yeah. I suppose you're right. I'm not sure what we're supposed to do without weapons or magic, though."

"The soldiers can be overwhelmed through sheer numbers," Corvus said. "There's at least a hundred of us in this camp and only thirty of them. They won't be expecting an attack. Besides, you're not entirely defenseless." He pointed at the hammer trailing from Volner's hand. "Being hit with one of those things is bound to do some serious damage."

"If you say s—"

Volner didn't get a chance to finish his sentence. A magically enhanced bugle blasted their ears, blocking out every other sound. Before it faded, Corvus pulled out his armor and enlarged it to its original size. Laborers stampeded past him, sweeping Volner along on their crusade. Battle cries tore from their throats. Corvus jumped out of their way and yanked the reinforced leather cuirass over his head. He reached for the accompanying trousers, flinching when a high-pitched scream filled the air. *Rem!*

He sprinted toward the center of the camp, letting go of the extra armor and whipping out his sword. In a flash, it returned to its usual size, and he put it to good use, decapitating the guard in front of him.

A plume of smoke rose from the fire pit area, and Corvus oriented himself toward it. The soldiers had scattered. Three of them had been knocked down by Rem and Darthan's sneak attack on the flanks. A fourth fought for his life against a mob of laborers.

As he watched, though, the soldiers recovered from their shock and regrouped with their backs to the supply depot. One of them shot a bolt of purple light into the crowd, ripping laborers off their feet like ragdolls and flinging them at their comrades. Like macabre bowling balls, they knocked down everyone they touched.

Rage and desperation filled Corvus, and a burst of energy exploded from his palm. The soldiers dropped to their knees, but their weakness dissipated after a few seconds. They leapt up again, scanning the chaotic masses for the person who attacked them. Corvus slipped away, cursing to himself. *I should have killed them.*

Stunning the soldiers might have given the laborers a respite, but it hadn't helped them to gain any ground. He hurried forward, cutting down the dazed guard who got in his way. The dry dust became slick under his boots, and he felt the squelch of blood before he heard it. Despite this—or perhaps because of it—he refused to look down. He could deal with the morality of his actions later.

Where *was* Rem? He tried to convince himself the scream belonged to someone else, but his gut didn't believe it.

A lone soldier stepped in front of him, sword raised. Corvus swung at him, cutting through the air with ease. He'd trained for this his whole life. One-on-one fighting, blocking out distractions, total victory. A jolt of pain shuddered up his arm as his blade collided with the soldier's. *He blocked me.* It shouldn't have come as a surprise. Rem blocked him all the time in practice. But Rem never snarled at him the way the wraith in front of him did.

Corvus stumbled, then struck again, aiming for the ribs. Another block. They sparred back and forth, neither gaining the upper hand for more than a split second, until someone bumped into the soldier. Corvus's blade buried itself in his opponent's throat, spraying both of them with blood. Another soldier popped up and punched Corvus in the hip before he could react. He dispatched them too, watching them fall with a savage sense of satisfaction.

And that's when he saw it.

The tip of a foreign dagger jutted from his hip, turning his tunic purple. Cold panic set in. Without thinking, he gripped the obsidian hilt and yanked the blade free. Blood cascaded down his leg.

You're not supposed to pull a knife out of a wound, he remembered with a flash of regret. *It makes you bleed out faster.*

He didn't have time to rue his decision, because a second later, two more wraiths launched themselves at him. Corvus limped backward and tripped over the body of a fallen laborer. The impact jarred his spine, sending waves of pain through his stomach and injured hip. The soldiers loomed closer, their faces twisted in ugly scowls.

Corvus leapt up, his sword lifted in preparation. Smiling was the last thing he felt like doing, but he forced his lips into a deranged grin anyway. Fewer things were more unnerving than a smiling enemy, especially if said enemy was covered in blood and apparently hungry for more.

The soldiers hesitated, and Corvus sprang forward, severing the first one's neck. The second soldier flinched as his companion's head bounced off his shoulder. He paid for his mistake with a sword through the chest. Shaking, Corvus pulled his weapon free. *I didn't think that would actually work. Thanks, Billy.*

He'd learned a lot of unconventional techniques from the movies Billy made him watch when they lived together. While he would never admit to liking them, he appreciated what they added to his repertoire. Unease coursed through him at the memory of his friend. *Where is Billy? I was supposed to be keeping an eye on him.*

Rem's lithe form danced into view, and he shunted the thought from his mind. She was fighting three wraiths at once, ducking and weaving to escape the reach of their blades. Despite her acrobatics, Corvus knew from her harried posture that she was sorely pressed. The tension in her shoulders was all too familiar from their training sessions.

He dashed through the chaos, his approach masked by the clamor of the battlefield. With a mighty horizontal swing, he cleaved one of the soldiers clean in half. Caught off-guard, the other two soldiers tried to scramble away. A crouching whirlwind slice from Rem sent them tumbling to the ground, their legs no longer attached to their bodies.

"Where's Billy?" Rem asked over the din.

"No idea!" Corvus shouted back. "I thought he might be with you."

A wave of pain shot through his injured hip, and he doubled over, static clouding the corners of his vision. When he straightened, the world seemed brighter, more saturated. Every tiny detail, from the individual dust motes to the glossy cut on Rem's cheek, took on a new importance. He gazed down at his hip. Glowing purple blood spurted out of him, pulsating like a strobe light. A strange feeling wriggled through his gut. *I'm watching myself die in Ultra HD. Mr. Porter would be dancing in the streets if he could see me now.*

"You're hurt!"

Rem's voice broke through his morbid thoughts. She reached out to touch the bloodied mess, but he batted her hand away.

"Not now. I'll be fine. I need to go find Billy."

"You're not fine," Rem retorted. She summoned a healing potion from her hidden pockets, unstoppered it, and pressed the glass rim to his lips. "Drink it, Corvus, and don't argue."

The briny liquid soaked into his taste buds, making him gag. Warmth bloomed in his injured hip as the potion stitched the muscle and sinew back together. He resisted the urge to scratch it.

"Thanks."

Rem vanished the potion flask and resumed scanning the horizon. Corvus followed her gaze, flinching when a wave of magic knocked the laborers off their feet.

"I'll help them," Rem said, adjusting her grip on her sword. "You can go and look for Billy."

"All right." He nearly leaned over to kiss her cheek, but the determined glint in her eye held him back. *Plenty of time for that later.*

Chapter Fifty-Three

BILLY COWERED UNDER an upturned basket with a pile of wooden balls at his feet. It was, quite possibly, the worst disguise in existence, but the thick barrier made him feel better about his odds of survival. Through a gap in the thatching, he saw a guard fall to his knees, magenta blood spurting from his neck. Billy's eyes snapped shut again, his breath coming in labored pants.

Get it together, he admonished himself.

But getting it together was easier said than done. William had gone to spread the attack plan amongst the other laborers, leaving Billy by himself. Minutes later, Lothaire's signal blasted through the camp. In the resulting tumult, Billy dropped his shrunken armor, and it skittered out of sight, trampled by the mob of wraiths. The sword had nearly gone the way of his armor, but not before he returned it to its original size. It lay in front of him now, a mere two feet away, but too far to reach without stepping outside the safety of the basket. Hence his dilemma.

He inched his fingers onto the hilt and tried to pull the sword toward him, but to no avail. *Of course it's not going to work. I can barely lift it when I'm using all of my muscles. Why would I be able to move it with my fingers?*

The pitter-patter of footsteps on dry earth filled his ears, growing louder by the second. He yanked his hand back, heart racing. William emerged from the jumble of baskets and wood, his eyes wide and fearful.

"William? Where are you?"

For a moment, Billy wondered why he was calling his own name. Then he remembered it was supposed to be *his* name as well. He moved to lift the basket, but a streak of navy caught his eye. The next thing he knew, William was falling, crying out, clutching his head in agony. A guard stood over him, fist raised. Then the hand descended, snatching William by the scruff of his tunic and dragging him through the dust. Every muscle in Billy's body tensed, locking him in place as his new friend disappeared into the forest.

Move!

The potency of the thought broke through his paralysis, and he threw off the basket. Seeing no enemies nearby, he hauled his sword back into its sheath. He would have felt safer holding it in front of him, but his puny arms would never survive the journey. Ignoring the battle behind him, Billy sprinted for the place where William entered the forest.

Part of him knew he should be going back to help his friends. They'd trusted him to join their crusade against the king, and running away abused that trust. On the other hand, they didn't need him. Not really. Hadn't Lothaire said as much after his failed training session? *I can't compete with them. But if I save William, maybe they won't look at me like I'm useless anymore.*

Long-dead twigs stretched toward him, whipping his torso as he dashed past. Warm blood trickled down his belly and stuck to his shirt. He didn't look down to see if the glamour would render it purple like a wraith's. There were more important things at stake. Something blue flashed through the trees ahead, and he redoubled his speed.

The guard stood two hundred feet away, pinching William's throat with the crook of his elbow. His eyes met Billy's as though he'd been expecting him, and a smirk tugged the corner of his lips. He waited until the distance between them halved, then resumed running, lugging William behind him like an oversized ragdoll.

What's going on? Was he waiting for me? Slowing his pace, Billy pulled the cumbersome sword out of its scabbard. *Better to be exhausted than dead.*

The retreating guard disappeared when Billy stopped to rebalance his sword, and it cost him a few precious minutes to pick up their trail again. When he did, his quarry leaned against the mouth of a cave, the roof of which hovered a few inches above his head. William was nowhere to be seen. The guard's rotting teeth formed a crude approximation of a smile, daring Billy to come closer. The soulless orbs staring out of his gaunt face warned him not to. When Billy came within fifty feet of him, the guard receded into the shadows of the cave.

Billy hesitated. Everything about the situation screamed "trap," and he'd seen enough horror movies to know how things could end. But why would a guard do this? Why leave the camp in the middle of a battle? And why drag someone along for the ride? William was a laborer who owned nothing but the sackcloth on his back—hardly a valuable hostage. Besides, no one had been there to witness the kidnapping except for Billy himself, and he'd been hidden. It couldn't be a deliberate attempt to lure him away.

Hefting his sword into a more defensive position, Billy let the cave swallow him whole. Darkness pressed in on him, squeezing the air from his lungs. He paused, trying to sense the guard's proximity. The narrow passage guaranteed the wraith was somewhere in front of him, but where? Billy stepped forward and his shoulder collided with something solid. Without thinking, he swung his sword at it.

Metal reverberated off rock, and he realized with a flush of embarrassment that he'd walked into a wall. Running his fingers along the rough surface, he rounded a hairpin corner. The ceiling sloped downward, forcing him to crouch as he walked. Pinpricks of light dotted the ceiling, hundreds of them banding together to illuminate the sandstone below. Werelights or windows to the outside world? Billy couldn't tell.

A muffled scream tore through the air for half a second. After it cut off, it continued to bounce around the rocky walls, echoing back and forth like a chant. Egging him on. Warning him off. Billy froze in place, listening for more disturbances. Had the guard killed William? The stillness of the cave suggested yes, but he refused to believe it. Not until he saw it with his own eyes.

Half a minute later, he reached the threshold of a wide-open chamber. The tattered remains of a blue robe lay next to a pool of water. Blood stained the surrounding rock purple. A wild hope took hold of Billy's heart. *Did William kill the guard and get away?*

He scanned the room again, taking note of every crack and crevice. William and the guard were gone. *There aren't any other exits! They would've had to double back past me, and I would've seen them. Where are they?* He leaned the tip of his sword against the wall and dried his sweaty palms one by one.

Still sweating, he reaffirmed his grip on the hilt. *I'm not crazy. They didn't go past me. Unless they magicked themselves through a wall of solid rock, they must be here somewhere. Maybe in the water?* The explanation made sense. Plenty of caves on Earth had underwater tunnel systems. Why should the Gloaming be any different? A quick look at the pool would satisfy his curiosity, and then he'd go back to help Corvus and Rem. He'd done all he could for William.

The blood spatter and damaged robes weighed on Billy's mind as he edged closer to the pool. He forced himself to look past them and into the water. To his surprise, it was shallow, no more than knee-deep. Traces of color gamboled across the sandy bottom, joining together to form slow-spinning galaxies in every hue of the rainbow. He'd never seen so many colors in the Gloaming before. Two gray specks festered above them, darkening with each passing second.

The swirling pigments radiated outward, shifting between crimson and yellow and azure blue. After a while, purple reclaimed its rightful place at the helm, the water coruscating like a giant amethyst. A droplet plinked into the pool from above, fragmenting it into thousands of tiny gems. Something moved in the corner of Billy's eye, and he whirled around. The colors were no trick of the light; they were a reflection.

Standing behind him, larger than life, was a dragon.

A kaleidoscope of colors shivered through its scales, reminiscent of the ones he'd seen in the pool. Each tinted thread slithered toward the tail, leaving streaks of purple in its wake. The threads winked out of existence upon reaching their destination. Stormy black eyes, each as large as a dinner plate, studied him from head to toe.

What do I do? Billy despaired. *I didn't know they had dragons in the Gloaming! Why didn't Corvus tell me? And how are you supposed to stop one anyway? Oh, forget it. I can't even hold a sword properly. I'm doomed.*

"Nice dragon," he said tentatively. He didn't know how sentient these things were, but he figured he should err on the side of caution.

"I am not a dragon," the beast intoned, blinking one glittering eye. "My name is Thoggri."

Billy jumped back. *It can talk?* "I'm very sorry for the misunderstanding, Thoggri, sir."

A deep rumbling filled the cave, and the stone beneath his feet vibrated. It almost sounded like a laugh. "Of course. And you are young Billy Porter. Species: human."

Billy's mouth went dry. "I don't know what you're talking about. I'm a wraith."

"A wraith, you say? It is a clever glamour, but a glamour nonetheless. I know what you are, Billy Porter."

"May I ask what you are?"

"I'm a wraith, of course," Thoggri replied. His lips peeled back to reveal a mountain range of jagged teeth. "Some would call me a trickster. Others, like you, erroneously call me a dragon. Do you know why some believe I am a dragon?"

Given the wraith's appearance, the answer seemed obvious, but Billy shook his head. He didn't want to risk provoking Thoggri's ire.

"It's because I like to hoard things." Thoggri leaned close, his sour breath overwhelming Billy's senses. Magenta blood stained his teeth, too fresh for comfort. "Unlike dragons, who hoard gold, I choose to hoard memories. Do you know what that means?" Billy shook his head again, and Thoggri withdrew, eyes narrowed. "Interesting."

Asking exactly *what* the trickster found interesting was a step too far, so Billy changed the subject. "What happened to the guard I followed in here? And William?"

The dragon-wraith shrugged its massive shoulders. "I was hungry. They made for a light snack."

The gleam in his eye unnerved Billy. *Did he really eat William?* Nausea churned in his belly, and he swallowed several times to avoid throwing up. He might not have known the man for long, but no one deserved to die like that.

"Right," he squeaked. "Um… okay. If you don't mind, I'll just be going."

"I think not, Billy Porter. We have so much to discuss."

They stood, unmoving, for the better part of a minute. Billy dared not break the silence for fear he'd become Thoggri's next victim. *Why didn't Corvus tell me about these things?*

"You're here with your friends," Thoggri said at last. "Rem and Corvus. Lothaire and Darthan. An oathbreaker and three would-be rebels."

Billy's jaw would have dropped if his muscles weren't so tense. "How did you know?"

"The same reason I knew you were wearing a glamour. I'm omniscient."

Is he serious? No, he can't be. He probably cast a spell to learn our names. It isn't impossible to pick out a glamour either. I bet plenty of wraiths can do that with the proper training. Who knows how good this dragon's eyesight is?

"Speaking of glamours," Thoggri continued, "I'm most interested to see what you look like as a human. Would you remove it for me?"

"I can't." Billy's knees quaked when Thoggri moved closer. "I mean, I would if I knew how. I didn't cast the magic."

"I see," Thoggri said, his tone a sliver above condescending. "Let me help you."

Billy stumbled back, his heels splashing the pool. "I'd rather you didn't."

"Let me put it this way," Thoggri growled, his eyes ablaze. "If you don't remove it, I will rip out your guts and hang them as decorations. Are we clear?"

"Yes, sir."

Billy squeezed his eyes shut as the beast moved in. With a single, foul-smelling breath, the glamour loosened enough for him to climb out of it. Despite keeping his outer clothing on, he felt naked under Thoggri's gaze.

"Most interesting," the dragon-wraith purred. He stepped back, tapping a giant claw against the blood-spattered stone. "So tell me, Billy Porter: why are you here?"

"To free the laborers."

"Come now. You don't expect a half-truth to satisfy me, do you? Why free the laborers?"

"It's the right thing to do."

"A blatant lie based on sentiment."

"What do you want me to say?" Billy asked. He'd intended it to come out as a demand, but fear made a mockery of him. The pitch of his voice rose, sending each word out as timid as a church mouse.

"The truth, nothing less. I'm omniscient, remember? I know when you're lying."

"Then why ask me at all?"

"Because it's fun to watch you squirm. Now answer the question. I answered yours. It's only fair."

The back of Billy's head prickled. "We need their help to fight the king."

"Indeed," Thoggri said. "That one tastes like truth. Do you believe you can succeed in this mission?"

"I don't know, but I hope so. A lot of people, both humans and wraiths, will die unnecessarily in the upcoming war. There's a better way to fix things. One that saves the Gloaming. We want to make that happen."

"Very interesting. I must commend you on your lofty venture. How do you plan to carry out this little escapade? The laborers won't get very far without magic and neither will you."

"I don't know what the plan is. Lothaire's in charge of that stuff, not me. And I already know I'm terrible with a sword. You don't have to rub it in."

Thoggri thought for a while. "What would you say if I granted you the ability to use magic?"

Billy's eyes bugged out of his head. "You can do that?"

He sobered an instant later. As much as he wanted to use magic, he didn't want to accept anything from a creature who called himself a trickster.

"Of course I can do it," Thoggri replied breezily. "Granting magic to another being is an ability all tricksters have."

"There are more of you?"

"Hundreds."

"Aren't you on Grigoth's side, though? What's the catch?"

The trickster stepped back as if the questions offended him. "I am, and have always been, a loyal wraith. I live to serve the king. However, the idea of a human using magic is amusing to me. It might make the battle interesting."

"Would your king find that interesting too?"

"He would see the humor in it. After all, he loves games as much as I do."

"You haven't answered my other question."

"Which is?"

"What's the catch? What do you want in return? You say it's amusing to you, but that's not good enough. If you're not going to be there for the battle, then you won't get to watch your 'game' unfold. You must want something else from me as well."

"I don't need to be there," Thoggri said. "I'm omniscient, remember? I will know exactly how things turn out even if I'm not physically present. But you're right. There is something I want."

Attack butterflies took up residence in Billy's stomach. "What?"

"As I mentioned earlier, I hoard memories. Visitors to my cave have been few and far between lately, and I was so hungry that I feasted on the last two before I could take theirs. It was a great shame. I need new memories for my collection. Powerful memories. If you share some of yours with me, I will grant you power beyond your wildest dreams."

"What kind of memories?"

"Ones of great value to you. Ones with sentimental meaning. They don't have to be of an event. They could be of a person. Or several persons."

Billy's stomach sank at the implication. *I can't share any of my memories involving Corvus or Rem. Or Lothaire. Or any of my wraith friends. It'd be too easy for him to use it against me. He could find out what we're planning and tell Grigoth about it. That just leaves…*

"My family?"

The words hung in the air between them, heavy with the sense of betrayal. He wished he could swallow them again.

Thoggri's eyes glittered. "Ah, yes. I had forgotten that humans value family relationships. That would do nicely. Are you prepared to relinquish all memory of them?"

Uncertainty sealed Billy's lips. *I can't do this. If it was a copy of my memories, maybe. But giving them up altogether?* He cleared his throat. "I'm sorry, but no. I could never do that. If I did, I'd lose my sense of purpose. I might forget why I'm here."

The dragon-wraith fixed an eye on him. "So you're only here because you want to save your family. You don't care what happens to everyone else."

"Of course I care! I'm not just here to protect my family. I want to help my friends as well. I want to save everyone if I can."

"The decision should be easy, then." Thoggri's gaze penetrated deeper. "If you love your family, you'll do anything to save them. If you want to save them, or anyone at all, you need magic. There is no other way."

"I'll take my chances."

Billy spun on his heel and marched away, his neck pulsing in anticipation of an attack. Thoggri claimed not to be a dragon, but he looked capable of breathing fire (or at least producing it with magic). Turning his back had been a stupid idea.

"They'll die, Billy. All of them. And it will be your fault."

He froze on the spot, skin prickling. *No, that's not true. Corvus and Rem can win without me. I'm here as moral support. I don't need magic. I don't!* But deep down inside him, desperation welled up like a dam about to burst.

This was something he'd wanted his whole life. How many times had he wished he was Harry Potter? Pestered his friends into showing him some basic spells? Tried to feel the flow of energy Rem talked about? He'd be mad to turn down Thoggri's offer. Besides, they were in the middle of a war. Evenly matched. Having an extra mage on their side could be the domino to tip the final battle in their favor.

"How powerful will my magic be?" Billy asked.

"As powerful as the love you have for your brothers. If I'm reading your heart correctly, that means you will be very powerful indeed. Strong enough, perhaps, to take down the king single-handedly. Now *that* would be interesting. I might even leave my cave to see it firsthand."

Billy thought it over, his shoe scuffing the rock in front of him. *I hate this.*

Unbidden, a series of images flashed through his mind. Hamish in a tuxedo, his hands dancing across the piano. James sinking a three-point shot against Platte County Middle School. Sleeping under the stars with his father. Walking to the swimming pool with his mother. Attending church as a family, the collar of his shirt so starchy it made his neck itch. Pastor Ryan had waxed lyrical about the evils of witchcraft and the importance of following in Jesus' footsteps. Billy's heart ached.

Do I sacrifice my soul to Thoggri and save thousands—millions—of lives in the process? Or do I walk out of here and risk letting them die? He scowled in frustration. *I wish Corvus were here. He always tells me if I'm doing something stupid.*

Thoggri growled, interrupting his thoughts. "What is your decision, Billy Porter?"

A sense of finality entered the trickster's tone, as if his patience were hanging by a thread. The next time he opened his mouth, it would be to incinerate the boy in front of him. Nausea rocketed up Billy's throat as he turned around.

"All right. Let's do it."

Chapter Fifty-Four

BILLY AMBLED OUT of the cave half an hour later, nausea tugging his stomach in four different directions. The pale sun stared down at him, bathing his glamour-clad skin in glacial light. The runes on his arms glowed brighter than before, like someone had underlaid them with conductive mesh. A strange energy thrummed through his body.

He supposed it could have been nerves, but it felt more powerful than that. More *alive*. Like he shared his body with a creature made of pure electricity. A creature that writhed through his veins and injected his worn-out muscle fibers with new life.

A cloudy thought drifted across his mind, bringing a smile to his lips. *I can use magic.*

In their final moments together, Thoggri had given him a crash course in the basics. How to delve into the flow of energy. How to channel it through a focal point. How to bind it to his will. Mauve light had spilled from his palm like water, tickling his skin, and he'd been unable to bite back a delighted chuckle. It was his turn to pull the strings. For the first time since he entered the Gloaming, he could take care of himself.

Billy trudged through the dead forest, exhausted but for the elation bubbling through his veins. Something niggled him in the back of his mind, a persistent ache he couldn't quite put his finger on, but he pushed it away. *Nothing a good night's sleep won't fix.*

He marched halfway across the camp before Corvus came into view.

The wraith was deep in conversation with one of the laborers, but he looked up when Billy approached.

"There you are!" Corvus exclaimed, limping over to greet him. "I've been looking everywhere for you."

"A guard kidnapped one of the laborers and dragged him into the forest," Billy explained. "I tried to help him, but they're both dead now. There was this—whoa, are you okay?"

Magenta blotches stained the front of Corvus's tunic, providing a sickening contrast to the beige fabric.

"It looks worse than it is," Corvus said. "Come on, let's go and meet up with the others. They've been worried about you too."

"But not worried enough to look for me?" Billy teased.

He expected Corvus to roll his eyes, but the boy just smiled. "They knew I'd be able to find you by myself. Besides, they're busy handing out ration cubes to the laborers. We did promise to feed them. Oh! And you'll never guess who I was just talking to."

"Who?"

"Volner! Remember him? I never expected to see one of our old classmates here. The old geezers who run the Academy kicked him out because he wasn't learning as fast as they wanted him to. Ridiculous, really. Anyway, we were talking about the fight with ol' Griggles and how dangerous it's going to be for our new recruits. You know, since they don't have armor or anything.

"I was worried because we already lost half of them today, but then Volner told me about this room at the Academy that's completely packed with armor and weapons. Like, top-of-the-line stuff. Long story short, we're going to break into it before we storm the castle. How awesome is that?"

"Um..." Billy paused, disconcerted. In all their years together, Corvus had never shown this level of enthusiasm about anything. Not magic, not entertainment, not even friendship.

He must be in shock or something, Billy thought. He opened his mouth to respond, but Corvus kept nattering away.

"I'd love to talk to some of our old classmates while we're there, if I can. I know I didn't do a very good job of convincing them last time, but I really think they might join us now. There's a huge difference between talking about starvation and actually experiencing it. Volner said there was a lot of dissent in the dorms, even from the stronger students. Winning them over would be a huge bonus for our side, especially since the laborers don't have much magic of their own. We could get them to set up energy shields for us and everything."

Billy nodded, unable to get a word in edgewise. They muscled their way to the front of the crowd, where they found Lothaire and Rem tossing two-inch ration cubes to any wraith who asked for one. The masses quivered and salivated, tearing into the blocks with their teeth and crying out for more.

Billy's stomach rumbled, but he refused to entertain the possibility of eating. He'd had three full meals the day before and a filling, if not nutritious, breakfast that morning. The laborers had spent their whole lives starving. The thought of further delaying their access to food made him sick.

He grabbed a ration cube from the pile and threw it into the sea of bloodstained hands. A second followed, then a third and a fourth. Soon, he lobbed them at the same rate as Lothaire and Rem.

"Glad to see you're all right, William," Lothaire commented.

Billy flinched at the name, unable to stop the torrent of recent memories. William being dragged through the forest. The guard's smirk. The blood on the cave floor. *I couldn't save him. I made a pact with his murderer. What was I thinking? And what kind of idiot makes a deal with a trickster?*

A hand touched his shoulder, startling him out of his melancholic spiral. Rem stood in front of him, her head tilted as if she expected a response.

Billy blinked. "Sorry, what?"

"I was wondering if Corvus told you the plan."

"About the Academy? Yeah, he did."

"Okay, good." She paused, her lilac eyes searching his brown ones. "Are you all right, Billy? We tried to find you, but it was so chaotic out there. Did you get hurt?"

He looked away from her intense stare. "No. I'm fine."

"Are you sure? I can heal you if you need me to."

"I'm sure."

Rem folded her arms, unconvinced. "You and Corvus are as bad as each other. Stubborn as a pair of mules."

The comment, misplaced though it was, brought a smile to Billy's lips. He turned to look at Corvus, but the other boy had disappeared.

"Where did he go?" Billy asked.

"Corvus? He went to join Darthan," Lothaire said. He tossed another ration cube into the crowd. "You two should head over there too. We need to move on as soon as possible in case Grigoth sends reinforcements."

"But we killed all the soldiers," Billy said. "How would he know we attacked the camp? It's not like they have surveillance cameras."

"No, but he'll sense it through the blood bond," Lothaire said, dusting off his hands. "Right. I've got to shrink all the remaining food down and add it to my pack. Shouldn't take longer than five minutes. Do you think you can keep Corvus and Darthan from killing each other for that long?"

"We'll try our best," Rem promised. She grabbed Billy by the shoulder and guided him away from the hustle and bustle. When they were a respectable distance from the depot, Rem cleared her throat. "It's just you and me now. You don't have to put up a front. How are you really?"

"I told you, I'm fine. I didn't get a scratch on me the whole battle."

"That's not what I was asking." Rem bit her lip, gathering her thoughts. "Billy… sometimes people see things on the battlefield that upset them. That's completely normal, but I've read that some humans go on to develop post-traumatic stress disorder and, well… it sounds terrifying. So if you *are* feeling sad or scared, I want you to know that

I'm here for you, and Corvus is too."

Billy's cheeks heated up, tears stinging his eyes. *I don't deserve a friend like her.*

"Well… I was pretty scared," he confessed.

"Same here. Is that why you're acting different?"

"Kind of. I don't want to talk about it right now."

"Okay. Just let me know when you're ready. We're in this together."

The idea of admitting his stupid decision to Rem made his stomach churn, but he nodded anyway. They walked in companionable silence to the copse of trees where Corvus and Darthan stood. The latter held a fist-sized rock in each hand.

"Are you sure these things will work?" Darthan was asking when they came within earshot.

"Obviously," Corvus replied. He held out his hand, and Darthan deposited one of the rocks into it.

"Incredible. What did you say it was modeled after? A portable telephone?"

"A cell phone. Yes."

"Incredible," Darthan repeated. He turned to Rem and Billy. "Can you believe the things humans come up with? They carry little boxes that let them talk to people on the other side of the world. Earth technology is amazing."

"It is pretty great," Billy agreed, perturbed by the civility of their conversation. "What are you guys talking about?"

Corvus held up his rock. "I charmed these to act as two-way radios. I thought it might be helpful for coordinating our attack on the castle."

Billy's eyebrows shot up. "You can do that? Magic is amazing."

"Amazing, yes, but I think human technology is better," Darthan said. "It's more stable. If a robot goes rogue, it's still bound by the laws of physics. You can still destroy it. If ol' Griggles changes the laws of magic, we risk being wiped out of existence. That's an awful lot of power for one person to have, don't you think?"

"Yeah, but that's why we're here," Billy said. A dull throb formed at the base of his skull. "To fix things. To make sure this never happens again."

"Yes. Well. Let's hope we're successful."

"You don't think we can do it?"

"I'm a realist, William. It's possible, sure, but it's not probable. How do you beat someone who can change magic at will? How do you win a game when someone keeps changing the rules?"

"Things are fragile at the moment, though," Corvus said. "Ol' Griggles isn't stupid enough to risk damaging magic even further. If he does, he won't have enough residual energy to travel through the portal."

"How do *you* know?" Darthan asked.

Corvus rolled his eyes. "It's magic one-oh-one. A better question is, how don't *you* know?"

The two stared each other down, glowering. Lothaire showed up and stepped between them, interrupting their contest of wills.

"We need to press on," he announced. "There's an abandoned outpost five miles from here. Volner tells me it's completely fenced in, so we're going to make camp there tonight." He paused, looking between Corvus and Darthan. "Is there a problem here?"

"No problem," Corvus said, turning his back on the antagonistic wraith. "Say, Lothaire, have you decided who's going on the mission to the Academy?"

"No. I'm going to let you decide that amongst yourselves. Seeing as it's a stealth mission, I don't want more than three of you going in, so choose wisely."

"You're not going, Dad?" Rem asked.

"I don't have a fresh glamour, nor the materials to make one," he replied. "Even if I did, there are probably wards in place to detect the presence of oathbreakers. It'll be safer for everyone if I keep my distance. Besides, you're much younger than I am. You're much more likely to fit in without getting caught."

"Looks like it's up to us," Billy said, throwing his arms around his friends' shoulders.

The smile faded from Corvus's face. "Actually, I was thinking Volner should be our third person. He can't use magic, but he knows the Academy like the back of his hand. Sorry, Billy."

"But Volner's in bad shape," Billy protested. "I'm stronger than he is. How are you going to carry all that armor out between the two of you?" Corvus shot him a look, and a light bulb went off in Billy's head. "Oh. Right. You're going to shrink it down. Got it."

Another wave of nausea crashed into him, and he pulled back, hugging his stomach. Uncontrolled energy seeped through his forearms, soothing him. Telling him everything would be fine. He didn't quite believe it, but he clung to the thought like a drowning man to a life raft. *What did Thoggri do to me?* Shaking, Billy turned to Rem, a confession already on his lips, but the approaching laborers drowned him out. He bit the insides of his cheeks. *I'm fine. My body's getting used to the flow of magic, that's all. I don't need Rem's help. I can handle this.*

With every repetition, the lie became a little bit easier to believe.

Chapter Fifty-Five

A COOL BREEZE filtered through Mrs. Price's yard, catching strands of Hamish's hair and splaying them across his forehead. The trees overhead were resplendent with reds and oranges, their leaves fluttering like a living mosaic. Rust-brown leaves crunched under his feet as he skipped up the stairs and pressed the silent doorbell. Mrs. Price's silhouette bloomed behind the mullioned windows, and the door creaked open.

"Hamish? What are you doing here today?" Mrs. Price squinted at him over the rim of her glasses. "I thought we didn't have another piano lesson until tomorrow."

"We don't, Mrs. Price. I'm here to see Jarsha, if that's okay."

"Of course you can see him, sweetheart. You must have missed him at school today. The poor little possum caught a cold, and he looked simply dreadful this morning. I thought it was best to keep him home."

"I hope he's feeling a bit better now," Hamish said, kicking off his shoes and following her into the kitchen.

The tiles were cool under his sock-clad feet, but the air around him was toasty warm. Two mugs and a batter-striped mixing bowl sat next to the sink, emitting the sweet aroma of freshly baked cookies and the salty tang of chicken noodle soup.

"He brightened up a little this afternoon, but I think I'll keep him home tomorrow too. Better safe than sorry," Mrs. Price said. She scooped her keys off the granite countertop. "I need to pop out to get some more soup. You'll be okay here, won't you?"

"Yeah, I'll be fine."

"Good boy. Feel free to make yourself a cup of tea if you want one. There are cookies in the pantry if you get hungry."

"Thanks, Mrs. Price!"

"You're welcome, dear. Make sure Jarsha stays in bed for me."

"I will."

Favoring him with a pat on the shoulder, Mrs. Price walked out the front door and closed it behind her with a decided click. She rattled the handle a few times, as if to double-check it was locked, and then her footsteps receded down the garden path. The promise of cookies tempted Hamish to scope out the pantry, but he resisted the urge. *I'll talk to Jarsha first.*

He padded into the lounge, his gaze drawn to the dying embers in the fireplace. Warmth radiated from the alcove, spreading through the room despite the lack of flames. Fluffy the ragdoll cat snoozed on the arm of the sofa, his paws wrapped around Mrs. Price's latest knitting project. Hamish tiptoed past him and scurried down the hallway to Jarsha's room. The door was open, so he went in without knocking.

Jarsha sat up in bed, his eyes bright and alert. "Hey."

"Hey," Hamish replied. He plopped down on the bed next to his friend. "How are you feeling?"

"Fantastic," Jarsha said. "I've been reading Elin's composition notebook all day, and I've got a pretty good idea of what the songs are supposed to sound like."

"That's great! Any luck with the versailliad?"

"Not yet. Gran's been hanging around my room all day, so I haven't had a chance to play it."

"That's too bad."

"Do you want to see what I learned?" Without waiting for an answer, Jarsha pulled Elin's notebook out from under the covers and flipped to the center page. "There's sheet music for the Song of Life, the Song of Death, and a bunch of other ones. Misdirection, confusion, fear… I think fear would be a good one to use."

"We could scare the bad wraiths all the way back to Wraithland," Hamish said.

"Yeah, and hopefully scare the humans away from the battle at the same time. That way, Grigoth won't be able to kill them." Jarsha opened the bottom drawer of his nightstand and pulled out the instrument they'd been given the previous night. "Wolpeth said Grigoth is scared of dying, so the Song of Death would be a good choice too. Maybe we can play a mashup of both of them."

"Are you sure that would work?" Hamish asked. "Wolpeth said the songs had to be played *perfectly* for it to have an effect."

Jarsha's shoulders deflated. "I guess you're right. Still, we won't know 'til we try."

He lifted the versailliad to eye level, the bronzed metal glinting in the soft afternoon sunlight. In the Gloaming, Hamish hadn't had a chance to study the mysterious instrument. Here, in the safety of Jarsha's room, it entranced him. Winged engravings hugged the outer curves of the conch, the designs growing more intricate as they neared the center. A band of seven gem-like protuberances wrapped around the midline, each containing a tiny purple dot.

Tilting the versailliad forward, Jarsha puckered his lips around one end and blew. The purple dots tripled in size, swirling like mini tornados within the confines of their transparent cabochons. A reedy, mournful tone wobbled through the air, then diminished into silence. Jarsha blew again, his slender fingers grazing the gems. This time, a lilting tune filled the room. Hamish's legs gave an involuntary twitch, as though they wanted to dance a jig all on their own. The music could be none other than the Song of Life.

"You did it!" Hamish exclaimed when the final note faded.

"I know! I can hardly believe it." Jarsha lowered the versailliad and held it out to his friend. "Do you want to have a go?"

"Sure!"

Hamish brought the versailliad to his lips the way Jarsha had. The metal tasted warm and coppery, like the old saxophone in his grandparents' attic. He blew a steady stream of air through the mouthpiece. No sound came out. He pulled back and looked at the gemstones. The purple dots had vanished.

"I can't do it," Hamish said, handing the versailliad back to Jarsha. When the metal touched his friend's hand, the gems flared back to life. "Maybe only wraiths can play it."

"Maybe," Jarsha said. "I can feel it inside my head when I touch it. Like, it reads my mind and plays whatever I want it to. There's some kind of magical energy too. I can't explain it."

"A psychic instrument with magical powers. I bet you ten bucks Grigoth doesn't have anything like this."

Jarsha grinned and turned to another page in Elin's notebook. "I think the Song of Death will be the most effective against Grigoth, so I'll play that one. The versailliad will give it the power it needs to knock him flat. Are you okay with playing the Song of Fear?"

Hamish eyed the chaotic arrangement of notes. "It looks hard, but I'll do my best."

"That's all I can ask for," Jarsha said, bringing the versailliad back to his lips.

A sonorous note rang out, underscored by a fainter droning sound that made Hamish's stomach drop. Six seconds passed before a second note followed the first—deep and heavy with the weight of a thousand lifetimes. Like a single footstep in a never-ending funeral march. Hamish's eyelids drifted closed. Everything in him wanted to lie down and surrender to the music. A moment before he tipped over, the song ended, and he snapped back to reality.

"That..." Hamish's voice cracked, and he cleared his throat. "That was powerful. I recognized it from the catacombs, but this... the way you played it..."

He shook his head, unable to continue. His lips went rubbery and numb, like they'd been pumped full of novocaine.

"It was more powerful," Jarsha said quietly. "Yeah. We didn't hear the Song of Death at its full volume in the catacombs. The walls down there dampened the sound, so we only heard the echoes. Playing it here… it was the real thing." He fell silent and pulled back the covers, revealing his plaid pajamas. "I have an idea."

"What?"

Jarsha leapt out of bed and jogged down the hallway, leaving Hamish alone in the room. He returned half a minute later, clutching something in his fist.

"Mrs. Price said you were sick," Hamish admonished him. "She said to make sure you stayed in bed."

"I'm not really sick," Jarsha protested, reclining against his pillow. "I didn't get enough sleep, that's all. Gran just worries a lot. You know how she is."

Hamish did. Over the years, she'd kept Jarsha home at the slightest hint of illness. As a result, he'd missed more days of school than he'd attended. Jarsha didn't mind staying home, but he missed his friends during those lonely "sick" days.

"Missing a day or two won't matter," Hamish said. "Not if you're doing it to save the world."

"Yeah, you're right," Jarsha said. He dropped four foam capsules onto the duvet in front of him. "These are Gran's special musician earplugs. They should make the music more bearable for us."

Hamish grabbed a pair, pinched the foam tips, and inserted them in his ears. The sounds around him became quieter, but they didn't lose any of their clarity. *Let's hope these things work on magical instruments as well as they work on regular sounds.* Jarsha blew into the versailliad, releasing a muted yet distinct melody. Suppressed, the instrument failed to stir Hamish's soul the same way it did with its full-bodied tone. When the final note quavered into oblivion, he pulled out the earplugs.

"That solves that problem," Jarsha said, putting the versailliad back in the drawer. "Now we just have to hope Grigoth doesn't have earplugs as well."

"Do you think he does?"

"I don't know. He could probably magic some up if he wanted them."

"Then we'll have to strike first. Before he catches on to what we're doing."

Jarsha nodded and thrust the composition notebook into Hamish's arms. "You should take this. You've got a photocopier at home, right?"

"I think so."

"Okay, that's good. You should make a copy of the Song of Fear and get the book back to me as soon as you can."

"But you need it more than me," Hamish said. "Are you sure it's okay for me to take it? I mean… it's super important to your culture, isn't it?"

"I'm sure," Jarsha replied. "I trust you to take good care of it. Besides, I'm going to need your help to pull this off. The Song of Death won't be strong enough by itself. You heard what the nurse said. And Wolpeth."

"You're right," Hamish said. He forced his aching body to stand. "I'll stop by your window tomorrow morning. That way, you can keep memorizing the Song of Death while I'm at school."

"And you can memorize the Song of Fear whenever you have time. We can try a duet after your piano lesson tomorrow."

The front door screeched open, and Hamish backed up to the threshold of Jarsha's room.

"What if Mrs. Price hears our duet?" he asked in a quieter voice.

"She won't. She's got a garden club meeting straight after your lesson. We'll have at least an hour to practice."

"Okay. That's good." Hamish glanced over his shoulder, half-expecting Mrs. Price to pop up behind him. "I'd better go. See you tomorrow."

"See ya."

Hamish ambled down the hallway, dragging his feet on the carpet. Mrs. Price sat on one of the brown suede sofas when he entered the lounge. Grainy images flickered across the TV—the same TV she usually refused to watch for fear of it rotting her brain. A single plastic bag sat by the front door.

"I'm leaving now, Mrs. Price," Hamish said. "Would you like me to put the groceries on the counter for you?"

"Thank you, dear. That would be a great help."

Hamish picked up the plastic bag and placed it next to the sink. A folded newspaper stood between the boxes of instant soup, its headline bold and imposing. *Wraithgate Heats Up: Senator Antony Bell Arrested.* Hamish's heart leapt into his throat. The name meant nothing to him, but he recognized the balding man in the photo. He'd seen him on TV not four days ago, speaking out against the wraiths' invasion. *What's going on?*

Shivering, Hamish returned to the lounge. Mrs. Price perched on the edge of her seat, stroking Fluffy's head. The cat tolerated the attention with nary a flick of his tail. Hamish snuck a glance at the screen. Although the TV was muted, the news ticker told him everything he needed to know.

Arrested senator Antony Bell unmasked as wraith, beaten to death by inmates.

"They're spreading horrible lies," Mrs. Price said. "How can they be so heartless, killing an innocent man like that? It's not his fault he caught the wraith disease. Oh, Hamish, do you think they'd do the same to Jarsha? Maybe… maybe I ought to take him out of school. What if they hurt him too?"

"No! They wouldn't," Hamish said. "Everyone loves him at school. They wouldn't even be mean to him, let alone beat him up."

"It's only a matter of time before it happens again," Mrs. Price continued as if she hadn't heard him. A solitary tear trailed down her cheek as she lifted her gaze to the photos on the mantelpiece. "Are the schools safe, Hamish?"

"Yeah, they're safe," he said. But as soon as the words left his mouth, he wasn't so sure.

"I hope so." Mrs. Price sniffled, dabbing at her eyes with an embroidered handkerchief. "Forgive me. I lost my head for a moment there. Would you like to stay for supper? I can set up a little table in Jarsha's room for you."

"Thanks for the offer, but I should really get going. Mom will be wondering where I am."

"Ah, yes. Quite right. Silly of me. Of course, you could always phone her?"

Hamish hesitated. The latest Wraithgate news had unsettled him. What if Mrs. Price was a wraith too—one of the bad ones? There was no way of telling. Antony Bell had denounced them less than a week ago, and he turned out to be the very thing he preached against. Anyone could be a wraith in disguise. Anyone at all. He studied the veins webbing through Mrs. Price's hands. Imagined they were secretly purple.

Guilt washed over him. Aside from being an elderly lady, Mrs. Price had given him free piano lessons for years. Baked him cookies. Adopted a child in need. How could he be suspicious of her? A small voice in the back of his head reminded him that the real Mrs. Price could have been replaced with a doppelgänger. The breath caught in his throat.

"I think I'll head home," Hamish repeated. "Mom's already on edge because Billy's gone, and I don't want to worry her. Thanks for having me over, Mrs. Price. I'll see you tomorrow."

He skidded out of the house and didn't slow down until he reached the sidewalk. There was a good chance he'd run out on an elderly lady in need of comfort, but he couldn't bring himself to regret his decision. Muscles aching, Hamish settled into an even jog, clutching Elin's notebook under his jacket. His anxious feet pounded the pavement toward home.

Chapter Fifty-Six

BILLY ROLLED OVER in his sleep, bumping into the hard bone of someone's shoulder. His eyes fluttered open. Corvus sprawled next to him, his breathing deep and even. All around him, the laborers lay prone, packed together like sardines. A ragged cacophony of snores filled the air.

Despite Lothaire's best efforts, they'd been unable to find the abandoned outpost. Too tired to go on, they'd spent the night on the forest floor. The first strains of sunlight filtered through the barren trees, caressing Billy's skin with cold fingers. He pushed himself into a sitting position, eliciting a grunt from Corvus.

"Morning," Billy mumbled.

Corvus squinted at him, rubbing his eyes. "You're covered in dirt."

"So are you."

"Touché."

"You know, I think I saw a river on the way here."

"How far?"

"Less than a quarter of a mile back."

"Not bad."

"Are you thinking what I'm thinking?"

"I hope so."

Corvus got to his feet, extending a hand to help Billy up. The latter shouldered his backpack, and the two boys picked their way through the sleeping wraiths. Dead branches leered at Billy in the lambent darkness, but he pushed them away without fear. The magic boiling through his veins would leap free at the slightest hint of danger. No denizen of the Gloaming could overpower him. He knew it in his bones. If Grigoth's minions dared to show up, he'd teach them a lesson they'd never forget.

Billy and Corvus didn't speak again until the river came into sight. Unlike the murky depths of Oilskin Lake, its water ran clear and flowed freely.

"You go first. I'll keep watch," Corvus said, drawing his sword.

Billy scrambled down the banks, reaching into the wellspring of energy nestled deep inside him. The glamour prickled against his skin as it loosened. He pulled it over his head and hung it on the smoothest tree branch he could find.

That was probably a dumb idea, Billy thought. *The laborers aren't likely to come looking for us, but if they do, they're going to know I'm human. Things could get dicey.*

He caught a whiff of his own body odor and dismissed the thought. Two days had passed since his last shower. He was going to get clean if it was the last thing he ever did. Billy grabbed an old T-shirt from his backpack, stripped off, and waded waist-deep into the water. Smooth, palm-sized rocks rolled under the soles of his feet.

Water surged past him, not strong enough to sweep him away, but strong enough to give him second thoughts. He balled up the T-shirt, dunked it underwater, and used it to scrub the grime from his skin. Aided by the current, the worst of the dust came off easily, and he soon felt more like himself. *I should have brought soap, though. Not to mention shampoo.*

He tipped his head forward, intending to splash some water on his hair, when something dark flashed past his ankles. Yelping, he stumbled sideways. His ankle rolled on a loose rock, sending him face-first into the water. The cool liquid shot up his nose. He inhaled without meaning to, flailing as he choked and spluttered his way back to the surface.

"Billy!" Corvus's panicked voice charged toward him. "Are you okay?"

Wiping away the droplets that glued his eyelashes together, Billy squinted up the bank.

"I'm okay." He coughed up a thimbleful of water, relieving the pressure in his chest. "I slipped, that's all."

"You need to get out of there."

"In a minute. I'm nearly done."

"I said, get out."

The hard edge in Corvus's second demand spurred Billy into action. He wrapped the old T-shirt around his waist and paddled back to shore. As soon as he was out of the water, Corvus spun him around and kneaded the skin of his right shoulder. Pain lanced down Billy's arm.

"Why aren't you wearing your glamour?" Corvus demanded. "And how did you take it off?"

"I just did," Billy said, pulling away. "Does it matter?"

"Of course it matters! Billy, you've got a scar on your shoulder."

"So? I probably got it when I slipped. The current's strong. There are a lot of rocks floating around."

"No, you're not listening. A scar. Not an open wound. It's identical to the one on my stomach."

Corvus lifted the hem of his shirt, exposing the puckered silver tissue.

The world tilted around Billy. "What does that mean?"

"Well, it could be a coincidence."

"But you don't think it is?"

"No. I've been around you the whole time we've been in the Gloaming, except for during the battle. Did it happen then?"

"I don't know," Billy croaked. His mind swam with confusion. "It's like I told you. I went to help William. I didn't do any actual fighting, but there's... there's a lot I can't remember about yesterday. Maybe that *is* what happened."

Corvus's hands found his shoulders again, gentle this time. "Tell me everything you *do* remember."

Billy hesitated, trying to make sense of his thoughts. "A guard grabbed William and took him to this cave thing. He was acting weird. He definitely knew I was following him. It was like he *wanted* me to. But after I got there, both the guard and William were gone. This dragon snuck up on me—well, he called himself a trickster, but he looked an awful lot like a dragon—and he said he'd eaten both of them. He wouldn't let me leave until I talked to him."

"Hold on a minute. You met a *trickster*? And you didn't tell me?"

"I didn't get a chance to."

"Billy, this is serious." Corvus raked a hand through his hair, a pained expression on his face. "What did you talk about?"

"He wanted to know what we were doing," Billy said. "I wasn't going to tell him anything, but he already knew somehow. He said he wanted to hear me say it. Then he asked me if I wanted to make a deal with him."

"What kind of deal?"

"I had to give up some of my memories in exchange for the ability to use magic."

"You took it, didn't you?"

"How did you know?"

"You managed to remove the glamour by yourself."

"Good point."

"So, what memories did you give up?"

"I can't remember."

"Oh. Of course you wouldn't. That was a stupid question. Sorry."

"That makes a change."

"Yeah. I'm picking up your bad habits, and you're picking up my good ones."

Silence, deep and uneasy, stretched between them, making Billy wring his hands.

"Do you think I made the wrong decision?"

"I really don't know," Corvus said. He stood up and rummaged through Billy's backpack. "Everything about this rubs me the wrong way. Tricksters usually take advantage of wraiths for their own gain. I can't imagine what they'd do with a human, but the scar thing is really worrying me. Do you feel any different? Any compulsions?"

"I can feel the flow of magic now, but there haven't been any compulsions."

"That's good, but I still don't like anything about this. We should get Lothaire to take a look at it." Corvus pulled some clothes out of the backpack and tossed them at Billy. "You'd better get dressed first, though. You look completely ridiculous."

The wraith boy shuffled past him to bathe, giving him a modicum of privacy. Billy donned a pair of sweatpants and a hooded pullover, topping off the outfit with his glamour. Once dressed, he surveyed the tree line for intruders. *Looks like we're in the clear.* Corvus rejoined him two minutes later, and together, they made the silent return trip to camp.

The festering sun illuminated the bustle of activity in the clearing. A large group of laborers clustered around Darthan, Lothaire, and Rem. Others sat cross-legged in the leaf litter, stuffing their cheeks like chipmunks. Billy's heart warmed at the sight; the spoils of war were being put to good use. He'd eaten a couple of ration cubes the night before, but the dry texture made them stick in his throat. He wasn't desperate enough to suffer a repeat experience. Not yet, anyway.

"Good morning, boys," Lothaire greeted them. "Ready for another day of walking?"

"Actually, we need to talk to you first," Corvus said, drawing himself up to his full height. When he spoke again, his voice deepened into a fair imitation of his late father's—a voice that left no room for negotiation. "Rem, you need to be there too. It's a delicate matter, so we'd prefer to meet in private."

"Very well. Darthan, you'll be in charge until I get back."

Darthan regarded them with mild curiosity but inclined his head in a curt nod. With that taken care of, Rem and Lothaire accompanied them into the trees.

"What can I help you with?" Lothaire asked when they were a reasonable distance away.

"Billy met a trickster yesterday," Corvus explained. "He's got a scar on his right shoulder, and it looks identical to my blood oath scar."

"Let me see," Lothaire ordered. He placed a hand on the offending shoulder and loosened the glamour with a stream of magic. The opalescent fabric split apart, followed by the cotton of Billy's hoodie, exposing the scar. Lothaire traced the gnarled flesh with his finger, hissing in sympathy. Once he'd seen enough, he used magic to repair Billy's clothing and glamour.

"What do you think?" Billy asked.

"This trickster… did he ask you to make a deal for something?"

In halting words, Billy recounted Thoggri's demands. "I'm pretty sure I didn't give him any memories involving you guys," he finished, heaving a helpless sigh. "Not that it'll do much good since he's omniscient."

"Tricksters are powerful telepaths, but they're not truly omniscient," Lothaire said. "Asking you questions was a means to an end. It forced you to think of the answers, which allowed him to read the truth in your mind. You didn't stand a chance against him, and neither would any of us. As for your memories… I'm sure we can find a way to restore them."

"I don't think now is the right time for optimism," Corvus cut in. "He has a blood oath scar on his shoulder. The trickster might have taken a lot more than memories."

"If that's the case, we'll deal with it when the time comes," Lothaire said. "For now, we should just be thankful he made it out alive."

"William didn't," Billy mumbled.

Lothaire gave him a sympathetic look. "No, he didn't. But the sooner we put an end to this war, the sooner we can stop this sort of thing from happening again."

"Hey, Dad," Rem said, curiosity coloring her voice. "How is it possible for a trickster to give Billy magic? I thought only the king held that power."

"Ordinarily, yes, but tricksters are more than capable of it if the urge arises," Lothaire explained. "They're masters of three things: disguise, telepathy, and energy manipulation. What is magic but a manifestation of energy?"

"True," Rem said, her tone hesitant. "But do you think it's safe? What he did to Billy?"

"We'll have to test his newfound powers to find out."

"How are you going to do that?"

Lothaire grabbed a low-hanging branch and snapped it free. He balanced it across his open palms and presented it to Billy. "Try breaking this in half."

Billy stared at the branch. It was thick, almost the width of his wrist, and it looked like obsidian rather than wood. Tingles of power surfaced all over his skin.

"Isn't that a little too advanced?" Corvus asked.

"These branches are hollow and brittle," Lothaire replied. "They're not like Earth trees. With the proper application of strength, I'm sure Billy will be able to—"

SNAP!

The branch cracked in two, the pieces flying in opposite directions. One end embedded itself in a tree trunk, while the other disappeared amidst the leaf litter. Billy blinked in surprise. *What happened?* He looked down at his hands. The purple glow of magic faded from his skin, but energy kept surging through him, bouncing off his bones like a pinball.

"That..." Lothaire coughed. "That was quite impressive. Do you think you could put the branch back together again?"

"I'll try."

Lothaire summoned the pieces of the broken branch with a spell and held them out. The edges frayed and crumbled, dropping flakes of decaying wood to the forest floor. Where they had once joined was anyone's guess. Hiding his skepticism, Billy let the magic seep through his palms and saturate the branch. His skin grew hot as the pieces fused into an imperfect whole. Knobbly bits of wood jutted from the seam, but Billy resisted the urge to lop them off. Rubbing the itch out of his palms, he stepped back and let the others admire his work.

"Well, Billy, it seems your abilities are rather advanced for a beginner," Lothaire said. "They're not particularly elegant, but you can already do a lot more than most newbies."

"Rem tried to teach me magic a few years ago," Billy said. "Maybe my body remembers the training."

"Maybe," Lothaire agreed. "I know this is very exciting for you, but you need to be careful. One extra mage is not going to be enough to defeat Grigoth. I also suspect the trickster got more out of the deal than you think."

Billy opened his mouth to respond, but Darthan jogged through the forest toward them.

"Sorry to interrupt, but the others are keen to move on," Darthan said, dipping his head in a bow. Curiosity burned in his eyes, but he refrained from asking about their discussion.

"All right," Lothaire said, disposing of the branch. "Lead the way, Darthan."

Exchanging anxious glances, Billy, Corvus, and Rem trudged after the adults.

Chapter Fifty-Seven

THEY ARRIVED AT the Academy shortly after midday. Dead forests gave way to open, dusty plains, where three cinder-block towers spiraled into the sky. A twelve-foot stone wall surrounded the buildings, its crenellations laced with barbed wire.

This place is more like a prison than the labor camp was, Billy thought, straining to see through the gates.

Unlike the labor camp, however, the grounds at the Academy were in pristine condition. A long, windowless building connected the three towers, its gray facade lined with garden boxes. Each box boasted deadwood carvings of flowers in various stages of bloom. The front yard was raked smooth and inhabited by fifteen students in dark robes. The students stood in regimented lines, swords in hand, while a wraith in leather armor barked instructions.

"Were there any soldiers on-site when you studied here, Volner?" Lothaire asked.

"Not that I know of," Volner replied. "The professors are all armed, but they'll be busy teaching classes. As long as we stay out of their way, we should be fine."

"Easier said than done," Corvus said, staring at the wraiths in the yard. "Do we have to wait for them to finish, or is there another way in?"

"I thought we could go around the side and scale the wall with magic," Volner said. "Does that work for you?"

The other two nodded their agreement, prompting Lothaire to step forward. "Whatever you decide to do, be careful. Don't take unnecessary risks. I want every single one of you to come out of there alive and unharmed."

"We understand," Rem said.

The older wraith released a pent-up breath. "Good. And good luck with your mission."

"Good luck," Billy echoed, his gaze downcast. *I sold my soul to get magical powers, and they're still leaving me on the sidelines.*

Deep down, he understood why. Corvus needed someone who knew the layout of the Academy, and Volner fit the bill. It was logical to choose him over Billy. Besides, despite his apparent aptitude for magic, Billy was only a beginner. His powers had been granted by a trickster with unknown motives. Both factors made him a liability at best and a direct threat at worst. *It's a miracle Rem and Corvus still want me around.* No sooner had the thought crossed his mind than Rem's arms wrapped him in a hug. Mild surprise trickled through him when Corvus followed suit.

"You're our only backup," the wraith boy murmured. "If we're not back in an hour, storm the place with your crazy new powers, okay?"

The knot constricting Billy's heart loosened. "You got it."

The three wraiths walked toward the Academy with their heads held high. Then they scrambled through the blighted brush and disappeared from view.

Breaking into the Academy proved easier than Rem dared to imagine. Finding their way around was a different story. The corridors spiraled in odd directions, with loops and dead-ends at regular intervals. Staircases went to nonexistent floors, and doors opened to brick walls. Even with Volner's help, they took a dozen wrong turns before they found the right path.

Heavy oak doors—all pilfered from Earth—lined the hall around them. Most of them led to classrooms, while others led to supply closets. Volner stopped outside a door at the end of the hall, his ear pressed against the wood. After a short pause, he nodded. Rem delved into the flow of magic and manipulated the lock until it clicked. They all hurried into the room.

"Keep watch," Rem mouthed to Volner. The skinny wraith retreated to the threshold without a word.

"This place is insane," Corvus muttered.

Looking around, Rem had to agree with him. Over a hundred swords gleamed from wall-mounted racks, accompanied by battle-axes, daggers, spears, and an assortment of other weapons she didn't recognize. A suit of armor stood in the corner, its lustrous finish indicating it was for decorative rather than practical purposes.

In the center of the room, wooden racks bore rows upon rows of traditional wraith armor. Rem reached for the nearest garment and let the supple leather spill over her fingers. Similar armor had saved her life many times during the battle for the labor camp. It would serve their allies well.

Too bad we didn't have access to this stuff sooner, Rem thought. She eased the armor off the rack, shrank it down, and dropped it into her backpack. *One down, ninety-nine to go.* From a practical standpoint, they didn't need to empty the entire armory. Only fifty laborers had survived the previous battle. But with the Academy so close to the castle, Grigoth might call on the students for reinforcements. Removing their weapons would cripple any such attempts.

Rem crept between the racks, casting spells left and right and dropping the shrunken armor into her bag. The odor of magic hung heavy in the air, all the more pungent for being in an enclosed space. She glanced at Corvus, who had worked his way through an entire wall of swords. He met her eyes for a brief moment, then returned to work. Rem shifted her gaze to Volner. The sparse lighting accentuated the skeletal build of his limbs, and her heart twinged in sympathy. Plumping him up with ration cubes would take several months at best.

At least we were able to help him, Rem thought.

Despite his gaunt appearance, several positive changes had transformed Volner since their fateful meeting at the labor camp. Squared shoulders replaced drooping ones, and his eyes were bright and alert. Trusting him with the coveted third spot on their mission had given him a sense of purpose. With his nose pressed into the crack between the door and the jamb, nothing could escape his hawk-like gaze. Satisfied, Rem returned her attention to the armor.

It took thirty minutes to strip the room clean. Volner ushered them into the corridor, and Rem paused to lock the door behind them. The air tasted more wholesome in the lavish passageways. Less acerbic. Their footsteps echoed across the marble floor, deafening after their work in the armory.

A metallic crash joined the din, and Rem's head snapped toward it. Corvus stumbled to the right. A tin pail lay on its side next to him, its sudsy contents spreading across the floor. Inundated by the resulting flood, a wall-leaning mop fainted sideways, the handle clattering against the bucket.

Where did that stuff come from? Rem wondered, a spike of fear coursing through her.

Around the corner, a door swung open with enough force to hit the wall. The excursionary group shied away, pressing against each other. Rem flung a hasty cloaking spell, bending the surrounding light to render them invisible. Volner's heartbeat thudded against her back.

"Don't move," she murmured.

A tall wraith stomped into view, his too-small boots splitting at the seams. A sable cloak hung from his shoulders, bearing the insignia of a professor, but his scarred face suggested he taught something more active than English or Geometry.

"I know you brats are out here," he spat, nostrils flaring.

With a flick of his wrist, the wraith threw a spell at Rem. Purple light splashed across her chest, soaking her to the bone. The protective enchantments fell away.

"Run!" Corvus yelled.

But it was too late. A second spell sent all three of them sprawling to the ground, their limbs bound in place.

"Well, well, well," the man sneered. "Not one, but *three* troublemakers. Absent from lessons, using magic in the corridors… both expellable offenses. I'm honor-bound to take you to the principal."

The magic holding Rem in place loosened enough for her to adopt a kneeling position, which she did. Corvus and Volner followed suit, the latter dipping his head in a contrite bow.

"Yes, sir, Master Kereon, sir."

The wraith—Kereon—squinted at Volner. "Do I know you?"

"No, sir."

"You look like someone I hate."

Volner remained silent.

"What are you three doing here? What class are you supposed to be in?"

"Therapeutic Potions," Volner lied.

"Therapeutic Potions, eh?" The malice in Kereon's voice solidified. "That class was dropped from the syllabus five *months* ago!"

Icy water trickled down Rem's spine. *There's no way out of this one.* In one swift motion, Kereon curled his forearm upright, his palm facing the sky. All three teenagers lurched into the air, their legs dangling several inches above the ground.

"The principal is going to have a field day with you."

Panic flooded Rem's weightless body, and every iota of her being fought against the spell. Energy, wild and uncontrolled, seeped into her fingers. Reaching. *Straining* for the pail Corvus tripped over. The metal handle twitched. Then the whole vessel flew from its watery grave, smashing into Kereon's temple. The professor's head snapped back, his skull crunching against the wall behind him. He crumpled to the floor, leaving a smear of purple in his wake.

Rem collapsed on her stomach, the impact driving the air out of her lungs. Volner's slight weight landed on top of her, his bony elbow jabbing her in the ribs before he managed to roll free.

"Is he dead?" Corvus asked.

"Who cares?" Volner retorted. "We need to get out of here."

Rem rolled to her feet and rounded the corner. "We will. As soon as we've talked to some of the students."

Only one door in the corridor was open—the one Kereon had flung open in a fit of rage. Rem paused on the threshold, surveying the wraiths inside. *It's our classmates from Morton.* Age lined their faces, and their eyes lacked the carefree sparkle of youth, but she recognized them anyway. Chardein sat in the corner, his chiseled face handsome in the absence of its usual scowl. Almwin slumped over the wooden desk next to him.

Tearing her gaze away from them, Rem appraised the rest of the room. A blackboard hung on the wall to her left, depicting a series of advanced battle formations. A chest-high lectern stood in front of it, illuminated by a cluster of werelights. Corvus slipped past her and beelined for the lectern. *He might not have convinced them four years ago, but he'll do it this time. I know he will. This is his moment. His second chance. He's got this.*

"All right, class, listen up," Corvus barked. Every wraith in the room jerked pin-straight, their eyes wide. "Your dear Master Kereon is out of commission, so you're stuck with me. Resident troublemaker. Son of an oathbreaker. Gutless rebel. I'm sure you'll remind me of any other names I've missed."

"*Corvus?*" someone gasped. "Is that you? What are you doing here?"

At once, excited murmurings filled the room.

"I think you already know the answer to that question," Corvus replied, unfazed. "I'm here for the same reason I visited you at the homestead four years ago. To show you a better way of living. Are you happy here? Really? Is the Gloaming everything you hoped it would be?"

Silence reigned for a short time before Chardein cleared his throat. "We're fed well enough."

Corvus snorted. "Yeah right. Have you looked in a mirror lately, Chardein? Your cheekbones could slice a loaf of bread." Titters of laughter erupted from the audience. "In all seriousness, though, you need to have a good, hard think about your lives and what's important to you. At the moment, the only thing that awaits you is servitude and death. Even graduating at the top of the class won't save you now. All of Grigoth's agents on Earth are rotting in jail."

"The suffering is worth it if we destroy the humans," Chardein said.

All around him, wraiths nodded in agreement. Rem's heart sank, but Corvus seemed undaunted.

"And what would that accomplish?" he retorted. "Humans aren't the ones starving you or destroying magic. They aren't the ones who triggered the Oncoming Abyss. You think you're fighting for your homeland and for wraithkind by staying here, but you're not. You're fighting for a despot who is actively destroying both. Where does your loyalty lie? With a psychopath who's using you to gain power? Or with the people you love?

"Everyone's future is on the line here. My friends and I are going to take this fight to the castle, and we're going to stop ol' Griggles if it's the last thing we ever do. If you're willing to join us, we will give you all the food, weapons, and armor you need. If not, that's your funeral. Either way, we're leaving now. Stay or go. The choice is yours."

When Corvus stepped back from the platform, Almwin rose to his feet and marched over to join them. "For old time's sake?"

Memories of their time at Morton Elementary flashed through Rem's mind. "For old time's sake."

Corvus clapped Almwin on the back and turned to the others. "Last chance for food and freedom."

A handful of wraiths stood and made their way to the door. Not as many as Rem would have liked, but at least the others weren't shouting accusations of treachery.

"Let's go," she said, pacing into the corridor. "Which way, Volner?"

Volner took the lead, wending his way through the maze of marble.

They made it twenty feet before a bloodcurdling scream rent the air. Rem spun around, her heart stopping at the sight in front of her. *Kereon?* The professor's eyes were wide, wild with rage. Then, almost as soon as it started, the scream died in his throat. He pitched forward and lay still, a fountain of blood spurting from his back. Chardein stood over him, his posture rigid as though the shock of his own actions had frozen him in place. His eyes flickered up to meet Corvus's.

"I thought about what you said," he mumbled, prodding Kereon's lifeless form with a grimy boot. "For what it's worth, I think I just signed my own death warrant. Do you have room for another ally?"

The waiting was the worst part, Billy decided. He strained on his tiptoes, hoping to spy a flash of purple. To hear the dead leaves rustling against the stonework. Anything that might hint at his friends' return. He glanced at his watch. Fifty-eight minutes had elapsed since they disappeared into the brush. He looked at the wall. Bounced on his toes. Looked back at his watch. The glowing hands refused to move. *Where are they?*

Lothaire crouched in the dust, worrying the end of a stick between his teeth. During the first twenty minutes, he'd been in good spirits. He'd chatted with Darthan and insisted Billy sit down and relax. When Darthan returned to the forest, Lothaire fell silent and took to staring at the gates. He looked like he wanted to charge inside and rescue the teenagers from whatever terrible fate he'd imagined.

Billy's gaze dropped to his watch again. *Fifty-nine minutes.* Something moved in the brittle foliage, drawing his attention back to the wall. Moments later, Corvus scrambled into the open with Rem and Volner close behind. Relief loosened the chains around Billy's heart. They were alive.

Lothaire leapt to his feet and sprinted over to them, sweeping all three teenagers into a hug. "Did you get everything?"

"Cleaned out the whole armory," Rem answered. She turned and jerked a thumb over her shoulder. "We found some old friends too."

One by one, seven wraiths fought their way out of the dead scrub and lined up in front of Lothaire. They wore modest black robes, one set of which was flecked with purple.

"Chardein!" Lothaire greeted the odd one out with a bear hug. "I hope that isn't *your* blood."

"It's not. It's Master Kereon's."

"Kereon? Now that's a name I haven't heard in a good long while. He taught here when I was your age. Nasty temper on him. Killed three students in my class."

"Four in ours."

"Already?"

"Yup. But thanks to me, he won't be killing anyone else."

"Good. The world is a better place without him." Lothaire turned to the next wraith. "Almwin! Good to see you again. And Astrid! It's been a few years..."

Seeing Lothaire was preoccupied with the newcomers, Billy strolled over to greet his friends. Their faces lit up when they saw him.

"You cut it a bit close," Billy teased.

"That's all you have to say?" Corvus said, raising an eyebrow. "No congratulations? No 'good job' or 'way to go'?"

"You did do a great job," Billy reassured him. "How did you convince Chardein to come? The others I can understand, but him?"

"A few years in the Academy changed him for the better," Rem said, leading them away. "He was brilliant in there. He saved our lives."

Billy digested the information, unsure what to make of it.

"So what happens now?" he asked as they passed through the outer rim of the forest. The trees there grew in sparse rows, too scattered to provide cover from prying eyes. Even so, Billy immediately felt safer—less exposed than he'd been on the barren plains.

"Now we hand out the equipment," Rem said. She made a beeline for Darthan, who stood next to one of the laborers, chatting. "Or rather, we ask Darthan nicely if he wants to do it for us."

Darthan looked up, his eyes narrowing. "What are you kids trying to rope me into?"

"Handing out the swords and armor," Rem repeated. She shrugged off her backpack and handed it to him.

Darthan's eyebrows shot up. "You actually got them?"

"Obviously," Corvus said, handing over his backpack as well. "We wouldn't be here otherwise, would we?"

"You could have gotten chased off before you reached the armory," Darthan reasoned. He passed Corvus's backpack to his conversation partner, who strapped it across his chest. "Anyway, I'm glad you got out safe. Don't worry about the swords. We'll make sure the laborers get them."

The adults walked away, leaving the teenagers alone.

"The nerve of that guy," Corvus groused when they were out of earshot. "I can't believe—actually, you know what? Forget him." Pressing a hand to his stomach, he dropped his gaze to the ground. "If this is our last night together, I want us to be happy."

"Why would this be our last night together?" Billy asked. "We're going to make it through this battle. I know we are." When Corvus didn't respond, he turned to Rem. "What do you think?"

Rem hesitated, pulling ration cubes from her pocket and passing them out. Billy accepted his with a grimace, the dry taste of cardboard not quite forgotten.

"I don't know," she said. "Dad's got a good plan. We've got a good number of laborers on our side, not to mention seven new mages. Eight, including you. But Grigoth's powerful. I don't know if it'll be enough to defeat him."

"Why don't we recruit more people, then?" Billy suggested. "There are other labor camps, right? We could—"

"It's too late for that. The full moon is tonight, so we have to strike now."

The news silenced Billy. *We should have started recruiting earlier.* Even as the thought crossed his mind, he knew it wasn't a fair assessment of the situation. Their whole plan relied on speed and the element of surprise.

They didn't have the supplies or the manpower for a prolonged campaign. Given the fluctuating time differences between Earth and the Gloaming, they couldn't have controlled the date they arrived either.

"We can still win," Billy said, but his voice shook. "We *will* win."

Corvus met his gaze. "I've always admired your optimism. I just wish I shared it."

"So what happens after Grigoth gets killed?" Billy asked. "Do you have to vote on the next monarch or is it hereditary?"

"Neither. Whoever kills the previous ruler automatically inherits the throne and all the benefits that go with it. They can stop the Oncoming Abyss, restore magic, end the famine, fix my blood oath scar… whatever they want. Everything will go back to the way it was."

"What happens if *I* kill him? I mean, I know it's not likely to happen. But I'm not exactly…" Billy trailed off, gesturing up and down at his body. "You know. A wraith."

"We wouldn't have to kill you, if that's what you're worried about. You can abdicate and choose a successor."

"Yeah, but who would I choose? You?"

"Me?" Corvus choked out a surprised laugh and shook his head. "No. If it comes down to it, I think Lothaire should be king. He's the one who put this whole plan together. He's got the right temperament for it too. Calm. Always looking out for people. Listens to advice. Plus, he knows a lot about magic. If anyone can fix the Gloaming, it's him."

Billy glanced over his shoulder and caught a glimpse of Lothaire strolling toward them, his arm draped around one of the new mages.

"He would make a good king," Billy agreed. The full weight of what they were about to do hit him, and unexpected tears pricked his eyes. "Listen… whatever happens in the next twenty-four hours, I want you to know that I don't regret any of this. I'm glad we stuck together over the years. It hasn't always been easy, but—"

"Oh gag, save me the melodramatic speeches," Corvus interrupted. "We're going to make it through this, remember? You promised."

Billy grinned despite himself. *Let's hope it's a promise I can keep.*

Chapter Fifty-Eight

A HALF-DAY OF travel led them to the outskirts of Grigoth's castle. Soot-gray turrets punched holes in the sky, blotting out the sun and promising an eternity of trouble. From the safety of the forest, Billy scanned the parapets for any sign of movement. While most wraiths considered ranged weapons dishonorable, all bets were off when it came to Grigoth. The projectiles Billy carved at the labor camp proved that.

I didn't come all this way to die two hundred feet from the moat, Billy thought, tugging at the collar of his leather cuirass.

No danger lurked in the parapets, so he returned his attention to Lothaire, who ran around like a headless chicken. He'd divided their army into three groups—two large, containing twenty laborers and three mages apiece, and one small, which comprised everyone else. Weapons, armor, and magic radios had been distributed hours earlier, but that didn't stop the older wraith from checking and re-checking everything a hundred times.

Lothaire muttered an order to Chardein, and the mages raised their palms to the sky. Bleached-gold light spread from their fingertips, forming domes around the laborers. The domes grew steadily brighter until they burst, drenching the laborers in a glossy sheen.

"What was that?" Billy asked, intrigued.

"The mages are putting up energy shields," Rem explained. "The shields draw energy from the spellcaster's body to deflect magical attacks. We should make some too."

"How?"

"The same way you cast any spell. Immerse yourself in the flow of magic and focus on the end goal. In this case, protecting yourself from negative energy. Can you do that?"

"I can try."

Frowning, Billy opened himself to the electrical currents zipping beneath his skin. He strove to catch them, to harness them and bind them to his will. Pale yellow light filled his mind's eye. He imagined it enveloping him, lapping his skin like gentle ocean waves. An invisible force tugged at his chest, pulling him toward purity and safety and repelling all things detrimental. He focused on the sensation, letting it fill him up and overflow into the forest with garish brilliance. After a few seconds, the light dissipated.

"Did I do it right?" Billy asked.

"You did great," Corvus assured him. Judging by the oily quality of his skin, he hadn't wasted any time in casting his own energy shields. "Hey, look. Lothaire's getting ready to give a speech."

Billy glanced in Lothaire's direction. The older wraith stood on a tree stump, wringing his hands in front of his torso. One by one, the laborers noticed, and their idle chatter lapsed into silence.

"This is it, friends," Lothaire said. His voice was softer than usual, but a resolute energy burned beneath it. "D-day. Our final stand against Grigoth. I'm not much of a speechmaker, but I'm a strong believer in the Earth saying that actions speak louder than words. There is nothing I can say that would motivate you more than the sadistic actions Grigoth has already taken against you."

Around him, laborers bobbed their heads in agreement.

"If we win today, you will be free from his tyranny once and for all. Peace and prosperity will return to the Gloaming. If we fail, at least we will have gone down fighting. But men, women… I do not believe we will fail. I believe we will succeed. All tyrants must fall eventually, and Grigoth's time has come. One hundred and seven years of suffering, but no more. No more."

Newfound zeal bubbled up inside Billy, bursting from his lips like a cork from a bottle. He thrust his fist into the air. "No more!"

A few wraiths watched his outburst with grave eyes, but no one carried the chant. Heat suffused Billy's cheeks. *Why is everyone so solemn? If someone gave that speech in a movie, people would be cheering and amping themselves up for battle. Our army has all the energy of a funeral procession.*

"Thank you, William," Lothaire said, the smile audible in his voice. "Now, before we get stuck into Grigoth, I want to go over the battle plan one more time. I'm sure you're tired of me explaining it, but listen up anyway. Knowing what to do could save your life."

He steepled his fingers in front of his chest. "Squad Three, you will enter the castle first, through an underwater grate. You'll loop around to the portcullis and open it for the rest of us. Squad One, you will filter through the portcullis and vanquish any enemy soldiers you encounter. Once you're done with that, you'll take up a defensive position in the left-hand corridor. Squad Two, you will follow Squad One and assist them as necessary. When you reach the corridor, you'll take up a defensive position on the right-hand side."

Lothaire paused, scanning the crowd for nods of understanding. "Squad Three, as soon as you've granted us entry to the castle, you'll be merging with Squad Four—that's me, Darthan, Corvus, Rem, and William. Recent intelligence suggests the ceremonial basin is being stored in the East tower, so that's where we'll be going. We need to find the basin and use it to free as many wraiths as possible from the blood oath.

"The good news—well, bad news for us, I suppose—is that Grigoth will almost certainly notice that we're tampering with it. If he does, there's a good chance he'll attack us directly. Squads One and Two, if you happen to see Grigoth, don't engage. Withdraw to safety and alert us through the radios. No matter how brave you feel, your oaths will prevent you from winning that duel. Does everyone understand?"

A smattering of "yeses" met his question.

"Good," Lothaire said. "Squad Three? Time to roll out."

Eleven wraiths shuffled past Billy, their footsteps silent. He watched them pick their way across the banks and splash into the water, heading for the drain hole. The sight brought back memories of Seisan, and he looked away.

"All right, Billy?" Rem asked.

"I'm fine. Maybe a little nervous."

Rem lowered herself cross-legged to the ground and patted the dust next to her. "You should sit down. Conserve your energy."

"I can't. We'll have to go in soon."

"You know how long the secret passage is. We won't be needed for at least fifteen minutes."

She patted the ground again, and this time, Billy joined her.

Shouts pierced the air, drawing Billy's attention to the portcullis. Grigoth's soldiers swarmed behind it, clashing with a hidden enemy. Clashing with Squad Three. Purple light flashed through the room, turning their panicked shouts into wordless screams. The drawbridge jerked six feet into the air, its rusted chains groaning under the immense weight.

That wasn't part of the plan, Billy thought. *At this rate, the battle will be over before it starts.*

He snuck a glance at Lothaire. Their fearless leader stood motionless, his eyes riveted to the drawbridge. Billy followed his gaze. He might not be able to see through it, but judging by the clanging metal, both sides were alive to continue their deadly dance. After several minutes, the intensity of their screams dwindled, and silence descended over the castle.

Billy held his breath, praying for a miracle. Grigoth's soldiers weren't supposed to be in the courtyard at all, much less in numbers similar to their own. *I don't know what else we could have done. Sent more people in? The passage is big enough, but more people means more noise. The soldiers would have heard them for sure. Our people would have been slaughtered before they could leave the sewer, and then where would we be?*

A full minute passed, feeling more like an hour. The drawbridge creaked an inch higher. Then it plummeted toward their side of the moat, hitting the bank with an almighty crash. Jets of water sprayed in every direction. Almwin stood behind the portcullis, his sword painted purple.

All the air whooshed out of Billy's lungs. *They did it. They actually did it.* Almwin gave them a thumbs-up with his free hand and signaled to someone out of sight. The enormous gate heaved free of the ground, scraping the grooves designed to guide its path. When it reached the halfway point, Lothaire waved the rest of his army forward.

"Let's go," Corvus murmured, tugging his sword free from its sheath.

Flanked by his friends, Billy jogged over the rickety drawbridge and into the courtyard. Mutilated bodies littered the ground, the gray stone slick with blood. Some bore the royal insignia across their breastplates. Others had to be identified by the tattered sackcloth fabric poking out of their armor. Bile rose in Billy's throat.

Aside from Almwin, only one wraith in Squad Three had survived the attack. Billy looked away, choking down the metallic scent of blood and magic. A large wooden object caught his eye. Decrepit though it was, he recognized it straight away. *That's Seisan's sleigh. Of all the places to find it…*

He nudged Rem, who nodded, indicating she'd seen it too. "At least we have a quick way out if we need it."

Corvus scowled. "We're not going anywhere until Grigoth is dead."

The first two squads split off to guard their respective corridors, leaving Billy's group free to storm the East tower. More screams erupted behind them, lending wings to their feet. They arrived at the tower staircase in minutes. Lothaire threw open the door and took the steps two at a time. The rest of the squad were hot on his heels. Seven sets of lungs panted in the musty air.

"How much farther?" the surviving laborer gasped. Deep gashes marred his armor, severe enough to deform the surrounding leather. The dent pressed two inches into his solar plexus, restricting his ability to breathe.

"A couple more floors," Darthan said.

"And… you're sure… he'll come… to us?"

"Maybe not straight away," Lothaire answered, "but he will."

If we tamper with the basin, he'll be forced to, Billy thought.

A cry of alarm rang out from the front of the procession, startling him back to reality. The hairs on the back of his neck stood at attention, his every sense alert. The acetic odor of magic invaded his nostrils, and then an unarmed enemy soldier tumbled down the stairs, her face frozen in a mask of terror.

"Move on!" Lothaire barked. "We're almost there!"

Billy turned away from the unmoving soldier. *I'm sorry.* A small part of him wondered what her name was. How long she'd worked for Grigoth. If she supported him or if she stayed because her oath compelled her to. *The sooner we kill him, the sooner we can resolve this mess.*

Billy bounded up the stairs and squeezed through the tapered doorway. The room at the top boasted vaulted ceilings, white marble surfaces, and floor-to-ceiling windows. Flecks of variegated color twirled and leapt through the air, never staying in one place for more than a second.

In the center of the room, an oversized plinth held the very object they'd hoped to find. Dark and imposing, the ceremonial basin absorbed any light foolish enough to touch it. Intricate designs adorned each side, tempting Billy to take a closer look. Rem and Lothaire joined him, but the four oath-bound wraiths shrank into the corner.

"This is the basin, all right," Lothaire reported. He tapped it with a fingernail, and a harsh peal echoed through the enormous room. Everyone flinched.

The basin was a vessel of evil—of that, Billy had no doubt. *Every wraith here put their blood into this thing at some point, and it turned them into slaves.*

"What are you going to do?" Darthan asked. "Destroy it?"

Lothaire brushed the lip of the basin with glowing hands. "I'm not sure I can. If I know Grigoth at all, there'll be a whole lot of safeguards in place to protect it. When Seisan and I broke our oaths, all we had to do was extract our blood from the basin. I want to try the same thing with Corvus's blood. If that works, I'll try to extrapolate the process. With a bit of luck, I'll be able to get it working on a wider scale."

A dry, husky laugh filled the air. "Oh, but I wouldn't *dream* of giving up my little pets."

Billy spun around, fright squeezing the air out of his lungs. Grigoth strolled into the room, flicking his wrist in the laborer's direction. The man collapsed, clutching his chest. Almwin went down moments later, his face contorted in agony. Neither wraith moved again.

"You killed them!" Darthan shouted. He wrenched his sword from its sheath, muscles twitching in preparation for a charge.

"Such a pity," Grigoth replied in an airy tone. "But at the end of the day, they chose to betray me, and like any traitor, they got what they deserved. I'm sure you understand—or at least you will very soon."

Four spells whistled toward Grigoth, only to vanish several inches away from him. The king loosed a humorless chuckle, his eyes flinty. An immense weight settled over Billy's legs, locking them in place. The sensation snaked up his body, turning him into a living statue. Judging by his friends' feeble attempts to move, they were affected by the spell too.

"That's better," Grigoth said. He strolled between them, pausing in front of Lothaire. Hatred rolled off him in palpable waves. "*You.*"

"Let me go, Grigoth," Lothaire demanded. "I'm not your slave anymore."

"Once a slave, always a slave," Grigoth retorted. "You removed your blood from the basin, but not from me. Your servitude will never end as long as you live. Shall I be a merciful king and hasten your journey from this mortal realm?"

Lothaire remained silent, his chin jutting out in a gesture of defiance. Smirking, Grigoth moved on to Corvus, turning his back to the group standing by the basin. Billy strained against the binding spell, desperate to regain control. His legs and torso refused to move, but his index finger twitched. A twitch might not be enough to free him, but he'd take whatever leverage he could get.

"How's life, Griggleboy?" Corvus taunted.

A slap echoed through the chamber like a shotgun blast. "Mind your manners, Corvus. Didn't your father teach you any better?"

Enraged by the act of violence, Billy forced his finger to point in Grigoth's direction. Energy flooded his body, feathering his vision and drowning out Corvus's tirade. Sweat trickled down his forehead. His neck. The small of his back. *I want Grigoth dead. I want him dead now. The trickster told me I'd be powerful enough to do it, and I am. Die, Grigoth! Your time is up!*

Thrumming with electricity, he shot a lightning bolt at the king's head.

The shaft of white light arced through the air in slow motion, so bright it appeared solid. Billy's eyes watered, both from the spell's brilliance and its pungent aftermath, but he dared not blink. Halfway to its target, the bolt fizzled out of existence. Grigoth turned to face him, eyes blazing.

Billy's heart thundered in his chest like a stampede of wild elephants. Every fiber of his being wanted to flee the vengeful king, but his legs refused to move. Frantic, he tried to dive into the river of energy—to cast the spell that might save him—but it was frozen solid.

"We meet again, Billy," Grigoth intoned, standing nose-to-nose with him. With a wave of his hand, Billy's glamour fell to the ground in shreds. Darthan gasped in disbelief.

"For someone so full of surprises, you're extremely stupid, aren't you?" Grigoth asked. His upper lip curled into a snarl, exposing a handful of rotten teeth. The rancid stench of expired milk wafted toward Billy, and his stomach lurched.

"He's not stupid," Corvus spat.

The king turned on him, eyes flashing. "Only a fool sells his soul to a stranger for a cheap magic trick."

Billy's eyes widened in horror. Grigoth's skin bubbled like a tar pit, stretching and popping as his muscles lengthened and his joints found new homes. He seemed to inflate like a giant, hideous balloon—no longer Grigoth, but a dragon.

"Thoggri," Billy breathed.

"You lapped up my story like a hatchling," the beast gloated. "Thoggri is merely an anagram for Grigoth, and an obvious one at that. Your naiveté and lack of critical thinking have been a grave disappointment over the past few days. But don't feel bad, Billy. Such character flaws define your species."

Shock flushed out any anger Billy might have felt at the insult. *He played me. He got my memories, and I'll never get them back. I think he blocked my magic too. The energy's still there, but I can't use it.*

"You branded me in the cave," Billy croaked. "The scar from the blood oath."

"A crude replica without the basin, but an effective one," Grigoth sneered. "As ruler of this land, I have absolute control over magic. I can give and take it as I see fit. I can manipulate mages as I see fit. And you know what? I'm going to give you a little demonstration right now."

A presence invaded Billy's mind, scraping across his nerve endings like an ice-cold blade across blistered skin. He tried to jerk away, but to no avail. His body remained stock-still, a mere plaything for the dragon's desires.

"Stop!" Rem screamed. Her voice sounded muffled, distant. "Why are you doing this?"

You were arrogant enough to believe you could beat me, Grigoth said. His mind-voice tore through Billy's brain like a thousand tiny splinters. *Pathetic weakling. You couldn't hold a candle to my power.*

Billy's left leg trembled, and his foot shot forward against his will, landing at a clumsy angle. Pain lanced up his shin. The foot righted itself and dragged his other leg forward. One arm reached for his sword. *He's going to use me to kill my friends. They can't move. There's nothing I can do!*

That's right, Grigoth commented in a sing-song voice. *Kill them all!*

The sword was in his hand now, impossibly light with Grigoth's assistance. He shambled toward Darthan, his fear mounting when Corvus appeared in front of him. The wraith boy's movements were as mechanical as his own, but his eyes rolled back in his skull.

"Grigoth's possessing them!" Darthan shouted, struggling against his invisible bonds.

A blinding light exploded through the room, chasing the king from Billy's mind. Rem stood off to the side, panting heavily. A purple glow emanated from the edges of her palms, the wet sheen of her energy shield making it look more like blood than magic. Grigoth turned on her, jaws gaping. *Rem!*

In this form, Billy had no doubt the king would eat her. The ice in his mind shattered, and he fell into the river of magic. Another lightning bolt, stronger than the first, shot out of his hand. Like the first, it disappeared long before it reached its target. Grigoth knocked Rem off her feet in his haste to confront Billy.

"How *dare* you."

Panic set in. None of his attacks had worked, and yet he'd baited the king into another fight. *Think, think, think! He's shielded, but there must be something I can do.* Grigoth advanced on him, shaking the ground with every step. The heat of his maw washed over Billy, too close for comfort. In desperation, Billy used magic to boost the lights like Rem did. Reflexes snapped his eyes shut, and he fell to the ground, jarring his knees on the marble.

The light was brighter than Rem's. So bright he could see the world through his eyelids. Grigoth's shadow loomed over him, and he ducked his head, waiting for the end. His whole body shook with exhaustion. The spell's energy came from the Gloaming itself, but his body wasn't strong enough to be the conduit.

He let it burn through him anyway. Felt his palms blister and bleed down his wrists. Then, as if the plug had been pulled, the light and the energy sustaining it vanished into the ether. Bile rocketed up his throat, and he dry-retched several times. His eyes cracked open, squinting into the darkened room.

Grigoth was gone.

"What did you do?" Darthan rasped. "Where's Grigoth?"

Lothaire dashed to the window. "There!"

Sure enough, a void-black dragon beat its wings against the horizon. Angling away from the sun, it dive-bombed the trees and dipped out of sight.

"How did he get out without breaking the window?" Darthan asked.

"It's not real glass," Lothaire replied, pushing his hand through one of the panels. The window warped around his wrist like gelatin. "It's an illusion created by magic. Much like what Rem and Billy did, if I'm not mistaken."

Rem blushed lilac. "In a manner of speaking. I boosted all of the lights in the room to shine a prism directly into his eyes. The light from Billy's first attack seemed to affect his pupillary response, so I figured he didn't have magical defenses against that. Turns out I was right."

"Only you would find a way to defeat someone by gazing into their eyes," Corvus teased.

A smile flitted across her face. "You're lucky I did. I think Billy deserves some credit too, though. He's the one who made it work." She turned to Billy, her smile dissolving into concern. "Hey, are you okay? Your hands are bleeding."

Dazed, Billy lifted his palms to inspect them. Scarlet ribbons twisted around his fingers and dripped to the floor. "Oh yeah. I forgot about that."

"Your spell must have been insanely powerful for that to happen," Rem commented. She pulled out a potion flask, unstoppered it, and pressed it to his lips. "Here, this will fix you up."

The salty smell made him wrinkle his nose, but he swallowed it without complaint. At once, the blood flow tapered off.

"Better?" she asked.

"I… I don't know." He reached for the flow of energy, but it eluded him. "I think I'm okay, but I can't feel my powers anymore."

"At all?"

Billy shook his head. "Grigoth blocked me from using them when we were possessed, but I could still feel the energy. Now… it's gone."

Corvus took his hands and dabbed them clean with a rag. "Grigoth must have stripped them before he left. I'm sorry, Billy. I know how much they meant to you."

"Wait a minute," Darthan interrupted. "How did he have magic in the first place? He's a human!"

"It's a long story," Lothaire said. "He traded some of his memories to Grigoth in exchange for the ability to use magic."

"That sounds a bit fishy to me. No surprise that Ol' Griggles voided his side of the deal, though." Darthan turned to Billy. "Did you at least get your memories back?"

Billy's heart sank further. "I don't think so."

I should have known he'd double-cross me like that. My magic was useless. All I did was scare him away, and I have no idea what he got in return.

Rem and Corvus hugged him, but the pressure in his chest didn't go away.

"There's something else I don't get," Darthan said. "How did Rem break through Grigoth's mind control so easily? I couldn't fight him off no matter how hard I tried."

"I had a pretty big advantage," Rem said, showing him her unblemished palms. "It's a lot easier to break free if you're not blood-bound to him."

Darthan's face paled, and he lowered himself to the floor. "Well, I'll be. A human child and a second unbound wraith in the Gloaming. What is the world coming to?"

"Destruction, unless we hurry," Lothaire deadpanned. "Grigoth will be on his way to the portal as we speak. I'd bet my life savings he's using magic to speed up his journey too."

"He has Seisan's sleigh," Rem reminded him. "I saw it on the way in."

"A trophy more than a tool, I'm sure," Lothaire said. "He's the king. He can teleport anywhere he wants within the Gloaming."

"Do you think we can take the sleigh, then?"

"We can, and we should. If it's unusable, we'll have to build one from scratch. It'll take too long to reach the portal on foot, even if the time discrepancy is in our favor this time." He grabbed Corvus by the shoulder and guided him to the basin. "All of you should go downstairs and try to secure the sleigh. I'll get to work on the blood oaths."

"Forget that," Corvus said, gripping the basin with both hands. Purple energy exploded from his palms, cracking the granite clean in half.

"What did you do that for?" Lothaire exclaimed. He pawed at the crumbling seam, tears welling up in his eyes. "I could have freed everyone from the oath. Now they'll be bound to Grigoth forever. *You'll* be bound to Grigoth forever. There are too many ancient enchantments on this basin. I can't fix it. There's nothing I can do."

"You worry too much," Corvus said. The set of his jaw softened, losing the wince he'd worn for the past four years. "Breaking the basin was enough to free everyone from the oath. The pain from my scar is gone, so I think it's safe to say the blood oath is history."

Lothaire gaped at him. "Why would you risk people's lives on a *hunch*?"

"It wasn't a hunch. I knew it would work."

"How?"

"I read it in Grigoth's mind when he possessed my body. Telepathy goes two ways, you know."

"He could have been lying."

"With words? Yes. But I looked into his heart. He was terrified we'd break the basin and free all his subjects."

"Insanity," Darthan muttered. "Absolute insanity."

"None of this matters," Rem said. "We need to leave. Now."

Lothaire glanced at their fallen allies, then inclined his head in a jerky nod. "All right, everyone. Down to the sleigh."

Chapter Fifty-Nine

THE WEREFOREST BOWED before its king, every branch bending low to conceal his flight from the castle. Large, ungainly shadows flitted beneath him as he pushed his atrophied wings to their limits. His dragon form had been graceful once. Lithe. Perhaps even beautiful.

Now, corrupted magic seeped through his bloodstream like a spilled inkwell, blotting out the wraith he used to be. But tainted or not, this was far from the end. The Gloaming demanded a monarch, and with no natural heirs to succeed him, Grigoth was all but immortal. As long as he didn't fall victim to the Oncoming Abyss, nothing short of murder could end his life.

According to the human child, that was why the pathetic band of malcontents stormed his castle in the first place. He should have felt affronted by the act of rebellion. Outraged, even. Instead, a wave of lukewarm disappointment rolled through his veins. Their spells hit his invisible energy shield like errant flies on a summer's day—vexing, yes, but feeble and ultimately futile. Removing the human child's magic was the only highlight of the encounter.

Even that failed to entertain him for long, though, hence why he'd chosen to leave. Not because they hurt him, or because of the trick with the lights, but because he was bored and had better things to do. The weaklings wouldn't believe that, of course. They were probably stumbling after him already, looking for another fight. They might even believe they could win.

Let them come, Grigoth thought, his lower lip curling into a snarl. *Let them bear witness to the full extent of my wrath. Let them see what happens to those who cross me and feel the full weight of regret before they die.*

He opened himself to the flow of magic. Let it crawl under his skin like a colony of fire ants. With a single thought, the Gloaming's energy bent to his will. The world around him warped like a Salvador Dali painting, teleporting him to Oilskin Lake.

In his mind's eye, the Oncoming Abyss advanced two square miles, snuffing out sixteen lives. Unfortunate, perhaps, but a necessary sacrifice. The Gloaming was doomed anyway. The fabric of reality had frayed and split down the middle, and for all his power, he couldn't stitch it back together. An uncorrupted mage might be able to, but Grigoth would have to die or abdicate first.

He intended to do neither.

Abdicating would nullify the oath protecting him, and the people would kill him without a second thought. He had no intentions of making their job easy. Besides, the throne was rightfully his. King Vaeril obviously hadn't wanted it, or he would have done a better job of defending himself. There was no reason for people to get up in arms about it.

The doddering old fool had been on his last legs anyway. Complacent, dependent, gullible—everything Grigoth hated. The day he decapitated his predecessor, he'd vowed to be the strongest king the Gloaming had ever known. If that meant he had to do everything himself, then so be it.

The same mindset gave birth to his current plan. With civil satisfaction at an all-time low, infiltrating Earth had been a risky move. The farther his agents traveled from the portals, the weaker his grip on them became. It was no great surprise when he lost contact with them altogether. Fortunately, he'd implemented a backup plan, one that dated back to 2001.

The Halloween Massacre.

As much as he enjoyed slaughtering humans, his actions that night were a means to an end and nothing more. In the abandoned town center—in the silent, blood-soaked aftermath—he'd buried a Genesis Kernel. A blueprint for the Gloaming in its original form.

If allowed to germinate, it would terraform the planet to replicate his homeland in perfect detail, minus the Oncoming Abyss. Magic would go back to normal. All blood oaths would remain intact. In theory, he could have planted it in the Gloaming instead, but the Kernel took fifteen years to germinate. The chances of losing it to the Abyss were too high. Subjugating Earth was the safer, more logical option.

Soldiers garbed in leather armor emerged from the trees, their swords drawn. Unable to suppress a sneer of contempt, Grigoth pushed his mind toward theirs. Thousands of bodies went rigid as he scoured their thoughts for any hint of rebellion. Their minds felt strange to him—stranger than usual. Something had changed. He eased up on the assault but kept their free will smothered, relishing their discomfort.

Even if nothing were amiss, they deserved to suffer. After all, it was their fault he hadn't been able to return to the Kernel when it first reached maturity. They were too weak to cross the portal unaided, and his tainted magic prevented him from helping. The energy needed to teleport them would have brought the dimension to the brink of collapse. While he could escape unscathed, his subjects couldn't, and ruling the world wasn't any fun if he had no one to boss around.

And so he'd waited. Patiently at first, and then less so as the Kernel called out to him across time and space. Four years passed, but finally— *finally*—the full moon aligned with Halloween and weakened the barrier between worlds. His time was now. The traitorous scum would die alongside the humans they loved so much. And when every last drop of their blood was spent, he would activate the Kernel. Earth would become the Gloaming two-point-oh.

A new planet.

A new dimension.

A new universe, ripe with possibilities.

Smiling, Grigoth passed through the portal.

Chapter Sixty

"We shouldn't be here."

Hamish sat motionless on the post-and-chain fence that separated Oilskin Lake from the rest of Morton. Snapping out of his thoughts, he shot his brother a dirty look. "We have to be here, whether we like it or not. The bad wraiths might jump out of the lake soon, and we're the last line of defense."

"It's still stupid," James retorted, crossing his arms. "Do you really think we can take those things down with a *song*? I almost believed it when we were in Wraithland, but this is insane. It's not even going to work."

"How would you know?"

"This isn't helping," Jarsha cut in, holding up his hands for calm. "We should be focusing on our real enemies, not attacking each other." He took a deep breath and fished the versailliad from his pocket. The bronzed metal glimmered in the moonlight. "I've been practicing a lot since we got back from Wraithland. I've got the Song of Death down perfectly. Hamish has his mini keyboard, and he's memorized the Song of Fear. We've got everything we need to defeat Grigoth. We can do it for sure."

James scowled. "In case you've forgotten, Wolpeth didn't think this would work and neither did the nurse. Forgive me for not wanting to stand around and wait for my own death." He spun on his heel and paced away. After a few steps, he turned back to Hamish, running an agitated hand through his hair. "Mom and Dad would have a fit if they knew we were here. You saw how worked up they got about Billy leaving."

"Yeah, but they *don't* know we're here," Hamish pointed out. "I'm staying no matter what, so don't bother trying to tell me I shouldn't. If *you* want to go, then go. Me and Jarsha can do this without you."

The whites of James's eyes grew wider, reflecting the full moon. He hesitated, then lowered himself onto the fence, a few feet away from Hamish. The chain swayed beneath them.

"Fat chance," he said. "You're stuck with me."

Hamish couldn't stop a smile from hijacking his lips. *He might complain a lot, but I'm glad he's got my back.* Patting down his coat pocket, he retrieved the earplugs Jarsha had given him and wedged them in his ears. James did the same with a pair of earplugs he'd found in the garden shed. Bending down, Hamish scooped his mini keyboard off the dew-soaked grass and balanced it across his lap. It was a toy, not a real instrument—a colorful hunk of plastic with delusions of grandeur. But with the aid of a 100-watt amplifier, it would get the job done.

Jarsha glanced at his watch. "Two minutes to midnight."

Hamish reached for the cable connecting his keyboard to the amp, feeding it through his fingers until he found the plug. He gave it a judicious shove, making sure it fit snugly in its socket. Satisfied, he hovered his cold-stiffened finger over the power button.

"We've got this," he murmured, more to convince himself than anyone else.

Playing on stage for the first time had been one of the most terrifying experiences of his life, but the next few minutes would surpass that. The stakes were higher, he'd practiced less, and while their rehearsal had sent Fluffy into hiding, victory over Grigoth was far from assured.

"One minute."

Nerves burned a hole in Hamish's stomach. Best case scenario, Billy had succeeded in his mission, and the wraiths wouldn't come.

Midnight would be a time of celebration and reunions. He'd cast his earplugs aside and frolic across the grass. Jarsha would play the Song of Life in all its glory. But what if Billy *hadn't* stopped the bad wraiths? What would that mean for his brother? For his family? For him?

"Three, two, one…"

Energy cracked through the air like a whip, searing angular wounds into the sky. Thick, acrid smoke billowed up from the lake, swarming into Hamish's eyes, nose, and lungs. He buried his mouth in the crook of his arm, suppressing reflexive coughs. A multitude of large, dark masses emerged from the lake, their forms blurred by his welled-up tears. In the center, a larger, darker mass rose, flitting between the new arrivals like a shadow.

The hair on Hamish's neck stood on end. *That can't be a shadow.*

And he was right. A shadow needed light to exist, but all sources of illumination, including the moon, had been occluded by smoke. What he saw wasn't a shadow, then, but something else. Something that violated natural laws and craved destruction.

A reedy tone floated through the air, quiet but steady, and Hamish jolted back to reality. *I've got to play!*

He punched the power button, bringing the keyboard to life. Tiny green lights flickered on the control panel, not bright enough to show him where the keys were, but bright enough to hint where they should be. He splayed his trembling fingers, feeling for middle C like Mrs. Price taught him. Relief flooded his body when the expected note rang out.

Synching the Song of Fear with the Song of Death was a lot more difficult here than in practice. A few fumbling seconds passed before he managed it. Even then, his efforts sounded choppy and heavy-handed, like a cat was running across the keys. Despite his haphazard playing, the wraith warriors fell to their knees. A curious mixture of terror and sheer exhaustion lined their faces.

The largest of the dark shapes reared up, parting the smoke like a twisted version of Moses and the Red Sea. Moonlight pierced the clouds, revealing the shadow monster's form for the first time. Black, leathery wings extended twelve feet from its draconic body. Iridescent threads rippled through them, pulsing in time with the dragon-wraith's footsteps. The monster—*Grigoth*—lumbered closer despite their musical onslaught. A low rumble emanated from the king's throat.

It's not working on him, Hamish thought. His hands froze on the keyboard, silencing his part of the song. *He's going to kill us if we don't run.*

Something orange-gold glinted between Grigoth's teeth. James, apparently realizing the danger, leapt to his feet and sprinted away from the lake. His lean figure vanished into the night. Hamish jumped up too.

"Jarsha, we've got to run!" he yelled. "He's—"

Yellow fire spewed from the dragon's maw, hitting Jarsha square in the chest. The versailliad let out a strange, tuneless wheeze, and Jarsha fell flat on his back, unmoving.

The air seized in Hamish's lungs. Grigoth sneered, his scaly upper lip lifting to reveal rows upon rows of pointed teeth. The dragon stared at Jarsha's fallen body, then turned back to the warriors. They struggled to their feet, shaking off their music-induced stupors. Without a word, Grigoth led them in the direction James had fled.

A few warriors glanced at Hamish as they left, but no one tried to hurt him. Their eyes were dull and listless, like their souls had died years ago and the rest of their bodies were only just catching up. Even so, Hamish didn't dare to move until they, too, dissolved into the night.

"Jarsha?"

Getting no response, he tottered over to the young wraith. Jarsha looked so still in the moonlight, his eyes open and glassy. Soot marred the center of his jacket. Hamish looked for the frosty puff of air that would confirm if his friend was breathing, but it didn't come. Tears pricked his eyes. *I can't let him die! I've got to try something.*

Lacing his fingers together like he'd been taught in health class, he drove his palm into Jarsha's chest. Instead of meeting a solid body, his hands passed through the blackened spot and collided with the grass below. Sick to his stomach, Hamish pulled apart what was left of his friend's jacket. A giant cavity replaced the skin, bones, and organs that once resided beneath it.

There's no coming back from this, Hamish thought, tears spilling down his cheeks. He leaned over his friend's body, embracing what remained of his torso. Grief racked his slender frame, his hitched sobs filling the air. *The bad wraiths must have killed Billy as well. They wouldn't have been here to kill Jarsha otherwise. There's nothing I can do. They're going to kill everyone!*

He didn't know how long he lay there, draped over his best friend's body as it succumbed to the cold. Their best efforts had failed. Jarsha was dead. Soon, James would be too. In the distance, an explosion roared, followed by scattered screams. No one in Morton was safe. Not his parents. Not his neighbors. Not his friends. Not even Mrs. Price.

Shaking, Hamish withdrew from Jarsha. The world spun in dizzy circles, disorienting him. A shiny lump of metal caught his eye, and he forced himself to focus on it. *The versailliad.* It had bounced a few feet away from the spot where Jarsha fell, its transparent gems producing a faint glow. Hamish strained for it, pulling it toward him with his fingertips.

Despite the frigid evening, the metal warmed to his touch. Purple lights leapt across the gems, their dance telling a story he couldn't understand. *They've never lit up for me before.* Without thinking, he brought the instrument to his lips and blew. A beautiful, lilting melody soared up to the heavens, so familiar and unexpected that he pulled back in shock. *The Song of Life?*

He glanced at his friend's corpse. "J-Jarsha?"

The versailliad's lights spasmed in a dizzying pattern, bright and urgent.

"Are... are you doing this?"

The lights guttered like dying candles, then resumed their frantic activity.

"One blink for yes, two blinks for no, okay?" Hamish said. His hands shook so hard he nearly dropped the instrument. "Are you there, Jarsha?"

One blink.

Hope rose in Hamish's chest. "Are you helping me to use the versailliad?"

Another blink.

"Would playing the Song of Life bring you back? Is that what I'm supposed to do?"

Two blinks.

"Okay, not the Song of Life, then," Hamish murmured, his brain kicking into overdrive. "Do you want me to use the versailliad for something?"

A single blink.

"Do you want me to go after Grigoth?"

Another blink.

Hamish took a deep breath, clutching the versailliad with both hands. "All right. I'll do it. I'll do everything I can to avenge you, Jarsha. I swear it."

The gems burst into another light show, lending him the courage he needed to enter the chaos. The asphalt vibrated beneath his feet as he ran. Explosions ripped through a distant house, bringing the structure to its knees. People, both human and wraith, clashed next to its burning remains. Hamish darted into a side street to avoid them.

"I hope you've got a plan," Hamish murmured, eyeing the versailliad. "Jarsha, are you going to use me to play the Song of Death?"

Two blinks. *No.*

"The Song of Fear?"

No.

"You do have a plan, though, right?"

Yes.

Hamish breathed a sigh of relief. "Okay, good. I trust you."

He trotted down the empty sidewalk, praying no one would spot him.

Dark buildings surrounded him on all sides, almost unrecognizable at this hour. Shops, restaurants, offices, an old church...

The versailliad burst into a flurry of light, stopping Hamish in his tracks. "What is it, Jarsha? Am I in danger?"

No.

"Do you want me to do something?"

Yes.

Hamish gazed up at the church. "Is Grigoth in there?"

No.

"Do you want me to go in?"

Yes.

"Why?" The lights remained dim. "Well... I suppose there are a lot of microphones and amps in there for the church band. Is that it? Do you want me to play the versailliad through the speakers?"

A brief pause met his words, followed by a single blink. *Yes.*

"Okay. Good idea."

Anything to avoid facing Grigoth head-on.

He scurried up to the door and jiggled the handle, surprised to find it unlocked. The heavy oak swung inward, revealing a narrow foyer lined with faux-granite vinyl. He'd only been to this church a few times—his family attended the one on the other side of town—but he knew it well enough to locate the nave where the congregation sat.

He groped the plastered wall for a light switch and flipped it on. Nothing happened. Blowing out a frustrated breath, Hamish made his way down the aisle. His fingertips brushed over the backs of the ancient pews. *Of all the times to have a power cut...*

"Now what do we do, Jarsha?" he asked. "The amps aren't going to work without electricity."

He climbed onto the stage and flipped the on-switch for every piece of electronic equipment he could find. Nothing worked. Hamish tilted his head back and groaned. The sound bounced back at him, far louder than expected. Disconcerted, he glanced up. Empty blackness filled the space where the ceiling ought to be. *Is that a bell tower?*

He couldn't remember seeing a bell on his way in, but that didn't mean the church didn't have one. Judging by the acoustics at this lower level, the versailliad's song would carry for miles at the top of the tower. Grigoth wouldn't be able to escape it.

"That's what you want me to do, isn't it?" Hamish asked. "Use the tower to amplify the versailliad."

The response was immediate. *Yes.*

Emboldened by Jarsha's support, Hamish shuffled to the back wall and felt his way to the staircase. The wooden steps creaked as he spiraled into the cobwebbed heights of the tower. A holey platform greeted him at the top, containing more air than wood. Hamish straddled one of the support beams, not daring to get close to the center.

"I'm ready, but I don't know what to do," he told the versailliad. "Help me like you did at the lake. *Please.* We need to stop Grigoth."

A calming presence enveloped his mind, steadying his hands and warming his heart. *Jarsha.* Emotions swirled through him, too fleeting to grasp. Fear and sadness came first, only to be swept away by determination. Something else lingered in the back of his mind too. Something he didn't recognize. A desire for revenge. A desire to rid the world of Grigoth's poisonous presence once and for all.

Hamish touched the versailliad to his lips and began to play.

Chapter Sixty-One

JAMES HAD NEVER run so fast in his life. Adrenaline turned his body into a puppet, snapping his legs up and down in jerky movements beyond his control. His feet hit the sidewalk like jackhammers, each step making his vision go blurry. Deep, booming sounds followed him, each one threatening to surround and engulf him. The sounds flew through the air, burrowed under his feet, vibrated inside his skull…

An explosion ripped through the night behind him, and he rode the shock wave face-first into the concrete. He pushed himself upright, hot blood dripping down his cheek. Orange firelight illuminated a series of hairline cracks in the ground in front of him. Would Grigoth split them farther open? Fracture the earth until the marrow bubbled up and sucked him down into its fiery core?

James scrambled to his feet and resumed his headlong sprint. A sharp pain shot up his right leg, but he did his best to ignore it. If the monstrosity behind him caught up, he could lose his legs altogether.

With every step, the detonations grew quieter, farther away. The streetlamps around him went dark, but the glow of distant fires lit his path. James's vision blinked back into focus. Somehow, he'd made it to his home street. Unlike other parts of Morton, it had yet to be touched by Grigoth's wrath. Yellow candlelight spilled from his neighbor's windows, soft and welcoming after his ordeal. Mr. Roger peered from the bay window overlooking the street, the curtains pulled tight around his cheeks.

James sprinted up the driveway to his own house and pounded on the door. Mr. Porter opened it, his wary expression dissolving into shock.

"*James?* Why aren't you in bed? Where've you been?"

Mrs. Porter appeared behind her husband, clad in a pink dressing gown. Dark circles underlined her eyes, and concern etched deep wrinkles in her forehead. Her gaze fixated on his bloodied cheek.

"Are you all right, James?" she asked, her voice thick. She sounded like she'd been crying. "Where's Hamish? Is he with you?"

"I… I don't know," James said. "I just ran as fast as I could. There was a huge monster. A wraith thing. I didn't know what to do."

I could have warned people!

Another explosion rocked the ground, this time much closer. A cacophony of screams pierced the air, followed by the agonizing sound of houses being ripped apart. Mr. Roger burst out of the neighboring house, his adult daughter holding the crook of his elbow. Dressed in pajamas, they hobbled to their beat-up Toyota.

"Hey!" Mr. Porter yelled. He grabbed James by the wrist and dragged him over. "Sir! Wait!"

"We're evacuating," Mr. Roger rasped, slipping into the driver's seat.

"Take my son with you. My other boys are out there somewhere, and I have to go and find them. James, get in the car."

The grip around his wrist loosened, and someone shunted him into the back seat. The door slammed shut behind him. At once, the car surged forward, cutting through the haze of smoke and early morning fog. He wrenched his body around, desperate to catch another glimpse of his parents, but they'd been reduced to a pair of dots on the horizon.

Sodium arc lamps formed an honor guard on either side of the road as they escaped the doomed town. Their glass bulbs hovered against the sky like UFOs, beaming shafts of amber light at the tarmac below. One by one, the lights shuddered and went out, dying like dominoes alongside the car. Behind them, crimson flames leapt into the sky in sinister triumph.

No one could survive that. James pressed his forehead against the cool glass, fighting back tears. *If I'd looked after Hamish like I was supposed to, Mom and Dad wouldn't have stayed back to look for him. We could have left together.*

"It's all my fault."

He didn't realize he'd spoken the words aloud until Mr. Roger gave him a sharp look in the rearview mirror. "You're just a kid. Of course it's not your fault."

The hoarse reassurances continued, but James tuned them out. He *wasn't* just a kid. He was nearly sixteen, for crying out loud. Practically a man in his own right. He should have been able to handle it. How many hours had he spent at the gym, bulking up for basketball? He'd pushed himself to the limit. Gained muscle and speed. He should have been able to use that to his advantage today, but he ran away instead. Like a coward. He could have helped Hamish. And now, his brother was almost certainly dead.

It *was* all his fault.

If by some miracle his parents were alive, they would never forgive him.

If Billy was alive, he'd never forgive him either.

First Heather and now Hamish.

A tsunami of grief knocked the wind out of him and he doubled over, tears streaming down his cheeks in earnest.

Chapter Sixty-Two

BILLY DOVE HEADFIRST into the portal, submerging his body in the brackish water. Icy currents of magic swirled around him, shriveling his lungs as they tugged him back to Earth. For a moment, he almost forgot to keep holding his breath. The base of his skull vibrated, and he rocketed to the surface, flailing to regain his footing in the muddy shallows. Sheer desperation hadn't gotten him home any faster than Lothaire's magic alone, but he didn't regret trying.

Slicking back his hair, Billy surveyed the grassy clearing. Grigoth was nowhere to be seen, but the trail of destruction proved he'd come through the portal. Distant explosions rent the air, accompanied by bloodcurdling screams. The sky glowed orange like molten lava, reflecting the fires below. Billy scrambled up the banks to join his friends, who gathered around the broken body of a young wraith. The lifeless face stared up at him, hauntingly familiar.

"It's Jarsha," Billy said, averting his gaze. "Grigoth's stooped to killing kids."

Lothaire stalked over to the fence separating Morton Park from the rest of the town. His indigo eyes burned orange as he observed the waiting inferno.

"What do you think?" Darthan asked, joining his friend.

Lothaire exhaled. "It doesn't look good, but I think the humans are starting to fight back. If you listen…" A cacophony of pops and rifle cracks echoed through the night. "Gunshots."

"It's a dangerous game, doing that," Corvus said. "The portal will be fully open any minute now, thanks to the moon. When that happens, guns will stop working, just like in the Gloaming. They're going to get slaughtered."

"That's why we've got to move quickly and quietly," Lothaire said. He launched into a brisk walk and beckoned for the others to follow. "We should stay away from the center of town too. We don't have any human glamours with us, and I'd rather not get shot today."

"We could get some from the house," Rem suggested, but Lothaire shook his head.

"I think it's safe to say our house has been destroyed. Billy, you're a human. Do you want to go and talk to whoever's shooting?"

Billy blinked. "Why on earth would I want to do that?"

"Someone needs to warn them of the danger. Of all of us, you're the least likely to be shot on sight."

A bitter taste formed in Billy's mouth. *Walking into gunfire. Why not?*

"All right, I'll do it," he said. "What about you guys? What are you going to do?"

"We"—Corvus's face darkened—"are going to fight Grigoth and kill him dead."

The intensity of his expression sent shivers down Billy's spine. Something dangerous lurked behind his friend's eyes. Something primal and unyielding. Corvus wouldn't stop fighting until Grigoth had been blown to smithereens. Rem, Lothaire, and Darthan sported similar expressions.

"Good luck," Billy murmured. *I wish I had their confidence.*

"You too," Corvus said. "Try to keep those gun nuts from killing us."

"I will."

Knowing his courage would desert him if he hesitated, Billy jogged away from his friends. Fear and exhilaration danced a tango in his heart to the beat of a thousand gunshots. Of all the stupid things he'd done in his life, traipsing into the middle of a firefight ranked among the worst.

Bullets whizzed overhead, glancing off ruined houses. Wraiths swarmed in the distance, swinging their swords at anyone who came close. People on both sides collapsed, some torn up by bullets, others by swords. Billy ducked into a side street, hands raised to prove he didn't have a weapon.

A man in combat fatigues jumped at his sudden appearance, and the barrel of his rifle jabbed Billy in the chest. Uncertainty flashed through the man's eyes, and he lowered the gun.

"You scared the living daylights out of me," he complained. "What are you doing out here?"

Billy raised an eyebrow. "All this destruction and you really have to ask?"

With the gun out of the picture, his senses tuned back in to the present. Pale and baby-faced, the man couldn't be much older than Billy himself. The name and insignia on his chest identified him as Private Fischer of the US army. Farther down the street, a second soldier ducked behind a stucco fence for cover.

"What's wrong with you people?" Fischer demanded. "You're the fifth person I've caught wandering around tonight. You were told to either stay in your home or evacuate. It's not safe out here. Why does no one ever listen to the red alerts?"

"I've been out of town. I didn't know there was a red alert."

"You expect me to believe that? I bet you heard the invasion announcement on the news and thought you'd get up close and personal with some wraiths."

"You knew the invasion was coming?"

Fischer gave him a look. "Of course we knew. Everyone knew. Don't you watch TV?"

"Not recently."

"It was all over the evening news. The wraiths in Paris made a video threatening Morton. It wasn't a direct threat, but the brass saw through it. Not too smart of them to give away their plan, was it?"

"I guess not," Billy said, his mind racing a mile a minute. *The only way they could let something like that slip is if they were deliberately trying to circumvent their blood oaths. But if they're doing that, maybe they got caught on purpose too.* "Did they tell you that guns wouldn't work against them?"

"Sure they did, but they were wrong. I've taken down eight wraiths tonight, and they bleed pretty good." Fischer smirked, then sobered. "Why are you still here? I told you that civilians need to stay off the streets."

"I know you're just doing your job, but I'm not an ordinary civilian," Billy said. "I know a lot more about this situation than most people. Very soon, your guns are going to stop working, and the wraiths are going to wipe you out. My friends are hunting down their leader as we speak. You need to get out of Morton while you still can."

"No, *you* need to get out," Fischer retorted. "We know what we're doing, and our firepower is more than sufficient. See this baby here?" He patted the stock of his rifle. "It's going to knock the wraiths dead. Every last one."

"You don't understand," Billy ground out. "It's not a question of firepower. The wraiths that came here aren't some random disgruntled citizens. They have powers. Real, genuine magic."

"I'm sure it seems that way to you, but we have it under control," Fischer said. "Now if you don't mind, I've got a job to do. Get out of town, kid. We'll have things wrapped up by the morning."

The soldier shouldered his gun and walked off. Billy watched him go, anxiety gnawing at his gut. Behind him, a gust of wind swept broken weatherboards into the air and juggled them in a haphazard fashion. At the same time, the rattle of gunshots petered into silence. The wind died down as quickly as it had risen, and the debris fell with a mighty crash. The gunshots did not resume.

This is it, Billy thought, his stomach roiling. *Guns and technology are being wiped out. The soldiers are doomed.*

Judging by Fischer's confident gait, he didn't realize the danger of the situation. He probably thought the lack of gunfire meant they'd won the battle. *He's going to get himself killed.* Another explosion ricocheted off the surrounding buildings, kicking Billy's weary legs into action. He sprinted in a random direction, striving to escape the chaos he'd found himself in.

Where are you, Grigoth? I know you can read my mind. Come and find me. We haven't finished our conversation.

Corvus hobbled along the road, teeth gritted to keep from wincing. A piece of wooden shrapnel had embedded itself in his knee, burrowing deeper with every step. In the wider scheme of things, a splinter was more of an annoyance than anything else. But today, after coming so close to defeating Grigoth, his annoyance festered into anger and then bubbled into an all-encompassing rage. He would explode if he didn't blast the tyrant into next century, and soon.

"Corey!" a woman's voice shouted.

Corvus ignored her—or at least he tried to. A pair of slim arms wrapped around his shoulders, squeezing hard enough to leave bruises. He wrenched himself free, violet energy spilling out of his pores.

Mrs. Porter.

Four years had passed since she threw him out into the streets, and the interim hadn't been kind to her. Sunken, red-rimmed eyes peered at him from a bed of deep-set wrinkles, and her once-immaculate hair flew in all directions. Deep down, Corvus no longer bore her any ill will. But right now, every fiber of his being—every single cell and dendrite—was geared toward the destruction of his greatest enemy. Nothing else mattered. Blocking out her sobs, he pushed past her.

"Billy!" she shouted. "Where's Billy?"

"He's fine," Lothaire said. "I sent him somewhere safe. Somewhere with guns."

"Fat lot of good that'll do," Mr. Porter groused. His voice was a few pitches higher than Corvus remembered. "All my guns are jammed and so are everyone else's. I don't understand what's going on."

"Well, *Dad*, this is the wraith invasion you've been waiting for," Corvus snarked. "I hope it's living up to your expectations."

"But there was a dragon thing," Mr. Porter said. His wild gesticulations unsettled the AR-15 strapped to his back, and the stock careened into his neck. "Is that a wraith too? Is it like the Monster of Morton?" He collapsed to his knees, burying his face in his hands. "It's happening again, ain't it? It's over. There's nothing we can do."

If he'd been anyone else, Corvus would have felt sorry for him. Given their history, he couldn't bring himself to care. Unlike his wife, Mr. Porter wouldn't hesitate to pump him full of lead if his guns still worked.

"Mr. Porter, I need you to calm down and get your wife and kids out of Morton," Lothaire said. "I understand that you lost your daughter during the last massacre, but there's no reason for you to lose the rest of your family too. Let us take care of this."

"How can we leave when we don't know where Hamish and Billy are?" Mrs. Porter wailed.

Rem's brow crinkled. "Hamish is missing?"

Mrs. Porter nodded, sniffling. "James came home so scared he could hardly speak. We sent him out of town with our next-door neighbor, but Hamish is still out there. And you haven't told us where Billy is either."

"Don't worry about Billy," Corvus said. "He's working with us. He can handle himself."

"And Hamish?" Mrs. Porter demanded. "He's only twelve!"

"We didn't see Hamish," Rem cut in, shooting Corvus a meaningful glance. "I don't know where he is, but I remember Billy saying he was friends with Jarsha. He might have… gone to help him?"

A low moan escaped Lothaire's throat. "Oh no."

"What is it?" Mr. Porter asked. "Who's Jarsha? That sounds like a wraith name to me."

"It is a wraith name," Lothaire said.

Mr. Porter's face contorted into a rictus of disgust. "I don't believe it. Not Hamish. I didn't raise my children to be like this. To get involved with… with demon spawn like you. Now look what's happened."

"This would have happened whether they got involved or not," Corvus retorted. "Grigoth's invasion was inevitable. You should be proud that your sons care enough to do something to stop him. I don't see you doing anything to help."

Mr. Porter rose to his feet, gaping like a fish. Unspoken words swam through his eyes, dissolving before they reached his tongue.

"I can't," he choked out at last. "I don't know what to do."

Lothaire placed a hand on Corvus's shoulder, stopping him from shaking some sense into the man.

"There's nothing you can do," the older wraith told Mr. Porter. "We'll keep an eye out for Hamish, but you need to get out of here while you still can. Morton's not going to survive the night."

"I ain't going nowhere!" Mr. Porter snapped. He turned and cupped his wife's cheek. "Take the truck and get as far away from Morton as you can. I'm gonna stay and get our boys out safe."

"I'm not going anywhere either," Mrs. Porter retorted. "There is no power on this Earth that can keep me from my children."

I hope that extends to powers beyond this Earth, because you're doomed otherwise. Shaking the thought from his mind, Corvus plunged into the broiling pit of rage that had become a second home to him over the past hour. *Why are we standing around chatting when we should be blasting Grigoth to smithereens?* He focused in on his anger. Delved into it until the emotion consumed his body, emulating the Vikings of old. Another voice broke through his concentration, its familiar nature turning his fury into calm relief.

"Hey, guys, what's the situation?"

Standing behind him, thumbs looped through his sword belt, was Billy.

Two strange adults—a man and a woman—stood next to the group of wraiths when Billy showed up. Plaster chips dusted their hair, and they trembled like candles in the wind.

This is what Grigoth does to innocent people, he thought.

The more he looked at them, though, the more he realized something wasn't right. The woman ran to him and swept him into her arms, mumbling something unintelligible through a fit of tears. Billy stiffened at the unexpected contact, but he didn't pull away.

"There, there," he said, awkwardly patting her on the back. *Who is this woman?*

He recognized her from somewhere, but he couldn't place it. Nevertheless, their embrace soothed the ache in his heart—the ache that developed after he first met Thoggri.

"Your mother and I have been worried sick," the man said, a single tear rolling down his cheek. "Do you have any idea how it made us feel to find your note? What were you thinking?"

In spite of the accusations, Billy fixated on a single word. *Mother? But she can't be! I would have recognized her.* He closed his eyes, trying to call up an image of his parents. His mind remained blank. *Why can't I remember them? This doesn't make any sense.* A possible explanation presented itself, and his eyes flew open.

Heart thumping, he studied the woman in front of him. Pale cheeks. Liquid brown eyes. Button nose. All were features they shared. In the man, he saw his crooked teeth and wide-set jaw. Billy's stomach dropped out from under him, evoking the same heady nausea as riding a rollercoaster for the first time.

"You're my mom?"

"Of course I'm your mom." Tears sprang to the woman's eyes, and she looked to the wraiths for answers. "What's wrong with him? Why doesn't he know who I am?"

"Your son was forced to make a hard choice," Lothaire said, placing a hand on Billy's shoulder.

Before the wraith could explain, Billy jumped in. "I was offered magical powers strong enough to stop Grigoth, but I had to give up some of my memories in exchange. Up until now, I didn't know which memories I lost, but judging by your reactions, it was my memories of you."

"Why would you do that?" the man croaked. A second tear rolled down his cheek to join the first. "We raised you better than this. You know not to meddle in witchcraft." He turned to the wraiths, eyes blazing. "You put him up to this, didn't you? You're trying to take my boys away from me."

"I made my own decisions," Billy interjected, his voice firm. "I was separated from my friends and couldn't ask them for advice. They told me it was a stupid idea afterward, but by then it was too late."

"Your witchcraft didn't even work, did it?" the man retorted. "This Grigoth or whatever you call it still came. You defiled your soul for no reason."

"Not for no reason," Billy said, looking him square in the eye. "I did it because I would do anything to protect the people I care about. I might not remember you, but I must have loved you a lot to risk making the deal."

The man held his gaze, then heaved a sigh, his eyes flickering to the ground. Whether he was ashamed of the things he'd said or of his son's actions, Billy couldn't tell.

"If we survive this, I guarantee I can restore your son's memories," Lothaire said. "But for now, we have to focus on the present. We need a secure spot to—"

A lightning bolt struck him square in the chest, and he collapsed, stone dead.

Billy scrambled for cover behind a fence. A fireball crashed into the house behind him, mere inches away from singeing his hair. The moment it dissipated, Billy performed a quick headcount. Both of his parents cowered in the dirt next to him, their bodies pressed against the fence. Darthan stood behind a gatepost, peeking out into the street. Corvus staggered through the open gate, pulling Rem after him. She fought against his grip, yanking her wrist free and running back to her fallen father.

"Rem, no!" Corvus shouted.

He moved to chase her, but Darthan grabbed his shoulders and threw him behind the fence. Without missing a beat, the older wraith dashed into the open and scooped Rem off the ground. He made it within two steps of cover when a bolt of lightning carved open his spine. Rem stared at his smoking corpse as if in a daze.

"Come on, Rem!" Corvus shouted.

Cursing, he sprinted over, grabbed her around the waist, and pulled her to safety. A second bolt blew a hole in the ground she'd been standing on. Dirt and concrete dust rained on their heads.

"Come out and play, Rem." Grigoth's cocky voice boomed over the wasteland. "Bring your little friends with you!"

Rem leapt forward, but Corvus and Billy tackled her to the ground. Whatever he might say, the hard edge in Grigoth's voice told Billy he wasn't playing around anymore. He would kill them on sight.

"It's over, Grigoth!" Billy shouted. "We broke the ceremonial basin. All of your people are free from the blood oath. It won't be long before they realize that and turn on you. Abdicate now and set things right."

A low chuckle rumbled through the air. "Why should I do that when I'm having so much fun?"

"Don't *talk* to that thing!" Mrs. Porter shrieked. "We need to get out of here!"

"Leaving won't stop him," Corvus told her. "The only way out is to kill him."

Music dipped and swelled within the confines of the bell tower, spilling out into the street. Hamish strained to hold the wavering note as long as possible. On the verge of passing out, he pulled back from the versailliad, gasped stale air into his lungs, and resumed blowing. True to Jarsha's word, the melody sounded nothing like the Song of Death. It shared the same tonal quality, but the tempo was faster, the time signature livelier. It wasn't a song of heavy-hearted peace and closure, but of endings and hope for a brighter future.

The music writhed through his veins, flinging stars across his vision and sending his heart aflutter. Although it was his friend's disembodied spirit who created the song, its aching melody resonated within the deepest parts of his own soul.

This was real music.

This was real magic.

Not copying Elin's work note for note, but making something beautiful from their own suffering. The soaring highs and searing lows poured out on a single breath, moving the whole world—no, the whole *universe*—to take a stand against the tyrant king.

The ceiling struts groaned when he paused to take a breath. Something purple flashed past the stained-glass window, and Hamish froze. A small army of wraiths congregated outside.

"Please, Jarsha," he whispered. "I thought we were stopping the wraiths, not calling them over."

Jarsha's mind brushed his, sending him a series of images. Oilskin Lake. A closing door, stopped and held ajar. A dripping tap. A candle being blown out.

"We're using the song to close the portal, but not all the way," Hamish guessed. "Just enough to limit their access to magic."

The lights on the versailliad blinked once. *Yes.*

The sign strengthened Hamish's resolve. Keeping an eye on the soldiers, he lifted the instrument to his lips and blew. A ball of violet energy struck the tower, accompanied by the sound of splintering wood. Blistering heat soaked his skin, and his muscles convulsed to escape it. The music stopped as he fought to regain control of his lungs. Pressing his lips to the mouthpiece, Hamish blew into the versailliad again.

This is it. Our final song.

The ceiling struts collapsed around him.

Billy marched into the street on wobbly legs, flanked by Corvus and Rem. The former looked furious enough to kill someone with a single glance. The latter bore a vacant expression bordering on unhinged. Billy didn't know which one scared him more. Averting his eyes from the bodies littering the street, he zeroed in on Grigoth. The wraith—*dragon, really, let's call it what it is*—prowled toward them.

A self-satisfied smirk spread across Grigoth's features. Twelve-inch claws clacked against the asphalt, stained with the blood of his enemies. He swiped at Billy's chest, missing by a hairsbreadth. Billy yelped and stumbled back. Behind him, his mother wailed.

Corvus sprang forward, sword whistling through the air, but Grigoth batted him aside like a cat playing with a mouse. The wraith boy crashed to the ground, face contorted in pain. Grigoth loomed over him, ready to crush him with his massive forearm. Faster than the eye could see, Rem slashed at the offending limb. Grigoth bellowed, a horrible grating noise that drowned out everything else.

Billy dropped his sword and clamped his hands to his ears, desperate to escape the aural assault. It felt like a pickaxe had been driven through his eardrums. Something wet and sticky spilled from his ear canal to his neck. He touched it and pulled his fingers away to examine them. *Blood.*

The savage roar trailed off, leaving him dazed. Nestled in the ghostly aftersound, strains of a foreign melody stirred his soul. The more he focused on it, the more powerful it became. One look at his friends told him they heard it too. *Not a hallucination, then.* The juxtaposition of wholesome music against a violent backdrop should have been too jarring to reconcile, but something about it felt right. Invigorated, Billy retrieved his sword, keeping a wary eye on his enemy. The dragon king stood with his body low to the ground, teeth bared.

Corvus scrambled upright, sword raised. "Take this!"

The blade buried itself in Grigoth's hide, halfway to the hilt. The dragon whirled around, throwing Corvus ten feet through the air. Billy darted forward, swinging his own sword. Several feet before his target, he tripped over a rogue brick and fell. Stars exploded across his vision as his chin hit the asphalt.

A flash of silver skittered past him. *My sword!* The weapon grazed the tip of Grigoth's talon, leaving a paper-thin cut in its wake. Billy scrambled to grab it, but the dragon kicked it aside and slammed him into the ground. Through the haze of pain, he was vaguely aware of Corvus dragging him out of harm's way.

"Rem!" Corvus yelled, scurrying back into the action.

Pure white light surrounded Rem, lifting her high into the air. Her eyes bulged, and she scrabbled at her throat with glowing hands, as though attempting to override the spell. Corvus thrust his sword into Grigoth's belly, all the way to the hilt this time. The dragon's maw snapped open, emitting a wet, gurgling sound instead of his once-mighty roar.

Despite the ferocity of the attack, the spell holding Rem remained. Before Corvus could withdraw his sword, a prison of white light descended over him too. As with Rem, it shot him several feet into the air. When the boy reached the zenith of his flight, Grigoth released the spell and slammed both wraiths into the asphalt, where they writhed in agony.

A bright orange light bloomed in the sky, making Billy flinch. Every fiber of his being screamed at him to find cover. *Grigoth's going to rain fire down on us!* He lurched forward, desperate to save his friends, when the reality of the situation caught up with his imagination. The orange light wasn't fire at all. It was a streetlamp.

A streetlamp!

Billy's heart raced out of control. If the light was on, technology was working again, and if that was the case…

"Give me your gun!" Billy shouted, sprinting back to his parents.

He wrested the rifle from his father, relieved when the man didn't try to stop him. Shoving a new magazine into the well, he jogged back into the open, flicked the safety off, and rested the stock on his shoulder. Grigoth turned to him, eyes blazing with malevolent energy.

Billy squeezed the trigger.

Bullets tore through the dragon's scales, ripping free chunks of flesh and flinging them into the night. Grigoth reeled back, streaks of blood giving definition to his shadowed curves.

I don't need to know where your heart is with a gun like this, Billy thought, gritting his teeth.

Bullet after bullet cracked out of the rifle for what felt like minutes but was closer to ten seconds. The hollow clack of an empty chamber replaced the loud report of gunshots, prompting Billy to release the trigger. A tense silence descended over Morton, broken only by the pulse throbbing in his temple.

For a moment, Grigoth remained upright, his lips parted in a snarl. Then he fell in slow motion, smashing into the ground with enough force to bring down the one surviving house in the street. Blood pooled beneath the fallen dragon, spreading out like a disease. At the same time, a powder trail of excess energy burned through Billy's arteries, igniting something deep within his brain. A thousand images flashed in front of his eyes, once lost to Grigoth's meddling but restored to their former glory. His parents. His brothers. His grandparents. Everything.

He fell to his knees, overwhelmed by the torrent of memories. The gun clattered to the ground.

I… I remember. Does that mean Grigoth's dead?

He glanced around anxiously. The dragon didn't move. Farther down the street, wraiths dropped their swords and started tending to their victims' wounds. A flash of movement caught his eye, and he turned to see Corvus and Rem hobbling toward him. Guilt twisted his gut when he realized he hadn't bothered to check on their well-being.

"Are you two all right?" Billy asked. Anxious energy seeped from his body, wrapping his friends in a lavender glow.

Corvus prodded his ribs. "We are now. Thanks for healing us."

"I…" Billy blinked, unable to process what had happened. "You're welcome. I wasn't even trying to heal you, though. I mean, I thought my magic was gone forever."

Rem nudged Grigoth's tail with her shoe as if to confirm he was dead. "Normally it would be, but you're the one who landed the killing blow. You're the reigning monarch of the Gloaming now, and that means you've got unlimited power."

Billy grimaced. "I don't think I want unlimited power. You said I could transfer the kingship, right?"

"You can, but we'll have to go back to the Gloaming to do it," Rem said.

Billy glanced at his parents. "All right. We can go in a minute."

He picked up the rifle and returned to the fence, a twinge forming in his chest. Mr. Porter clung to his wife, trying to suppress the sobs racking her slight frame. As much as Billy hated his father's attitude, he couldn't find it in his heart to hold a grudge any longer. The weapon that would have killed his friends had saved them instead. For today, at least, that was good enough.

"You're safe now," he said, offering the gun to Mr. Porter. When the man didn't take it, Billy laid it on the ground next to him. "I'm going away with my friends, but I'll be back soon."

"What about your brother?" Mrs. Porter asked, her voice hoarse from crying. "Hamish isn't safe yet. We don't know where he is."

Billy froze. "What?"

No, no, no. Not Hamish. He was fine when I left. He promised he wouldn't get involved. He knew what was going to happen. He must have left town. That's it. It's got to be.

But when his mother choked out a story about James crying on the doorstep, he knew in his heart that something had gone terribly wrong.

"Billy?" Corvus said, placing a tentative hand on his shoulder. "We need to leave."

"No!" Mrs. Porter cried. "Please, Billy. We need you to stay here. What about Hamish?"

Conflicting emotions warred in Billy's chest. He wanted to stay, to find his brother, but what good would that do? If his brother survived, rescuers would find him soon enough. If he didn't... well, that didn't bear thinking about. Returning to the Gloaming was another matter. Thousands of wraith lives depended on him. Whoever held the throne could end the famine with a click of their fingers. Restore the natural order of magic. Stop the Oncoming Abyss once and for all.

"I'm sorry," Billy croaked.

Turning his back on the burning town, he followed Corvus and Rem into the dark.

Chapter Sixty-Three

A THOUSAND GALAXIES surrounded Billy as he returned to the Gloaming. Magical currents buffeted his body, leaving vibrant energy trails in their wake. When he landed on the lake bank, he felt as light as a feather—happy, relaxed, and without any trace of the dizziness that plagued his earlier crossings.

Morning had risen over the Gloaming in their absence, the purple sun casting lukewarm rays across the land. Billy inhaled deeply, savoring the crisp scent of dawn. With Grigoth gone, everything from the dirt beneath his feet to the magic spinning inside his chest had been disinfected. Soon, the Gloaming would be ready to bear new fruit.

"We should place a temporary seal on the portal," Corvus said, gesturing at the lake. "If we don't, people are going to wander in and out as they please, and I don't want anyone else to die today."

"Good idea," Billy said. He directed his will toward the lake, severing the connection to Earth. "Done. Have you thought about who's going to take the throne since Lothaire can't?"

Rem and Corvus exchanged glances.

"You should take it," Corvus told her, lowering his gaze. "You're kind. Understanding. Wise. Everyone would love you. They wouldn't love me. I don't have the right personality to be king."

"They'd learn to love you," Rem said. "After all the sacrifices you've made for their sake, how could they not? I couldn't have done half the things you did."

"But I don't *want* the throne," Corvus protested. "I don't want to be responsible for thousands of people. You know how bad I am at dealing with stress."

"There's only one solution, then," Billy said, patting his shoulder. "You'll have to rule together."

Corvus turned to Rem. "Can we do that?"

"I don't see why not."

"It's never been done in the history of wraithkind."

"Wraithkind has never had a human ruler before either, but here we are," Rem pointed out. "Billy? We're ready to accept the transfer of power."

"What do I need to do?" Billy asked. "Point and think?"

"Not this time," Rem said, taking his hand. "You'll need to keep physical contact with both of us and say the words aloud."

Corvus grabbed their free hands, completing the triangle.

"Repeat after me," Rem instructed. "'I hereby relinquish my position as ruler of the Gloaming and bestow my sovereignty upon Corvus Seisansson and Rem Lothairesdaughter.'"

Billy rehearsed the sentence in his head, mouthing the words to make sure he wouldn't trip over them. Satisfied, he repeated the phrase aloud. As the final syllable passed his lips, a strong electric current shot down his arms. It flowed into his friends, cauterizing the hole in reality from which his own magic stemmed. Exhaustion overwhelmed him, and he sank to his knees.

I'm just Billy again, he thought, his eyelids drifting closed. *Normal, human, non-magical Billy.*

Rem shook her hand free from his and cupped his cheek. Warmth spread through his skin, buoying his spirits and lending strength to his limbs. His eyes flickered open, and he pushed himself back to his feet.

"Did it work?" he asked.

"Feels like it," Corvus said, rolling his shoulders. "The easiest way to find out for sure is to try and teleport. Anyone up for a trip to the Oncoming Abyss?"

"Not really, but let's do it anyway," Rem said. "The sooner we stop that thing, the better. Are you okay to come with us, Billy?"

"Sure, why not?"

At once, darkness swirled around them. When Billy came to, they stood at the edge of a forest. A thick wall of smog towered over them, stretching so high he couldn't tell where it ended and the sky began. It moved so slowly it appeared stationary, but the immensity of its presence sent jolts of cosmic terror up and down his spine.

His brain vibrated within the confines of his skull, and he averted his gaze. *Just looking at that thing would be enough to drive anyone mad. It's not some kind of souped-up natural phenomenon. It's alive. Hungry. Waiting to feast.* He edged away from it, shivering.

"I kinda hoped the Abyss would vanish when we killed Grigoth," Corvus said. He stared up at it, his mouth parted in a small O.

"Unfortunately, it doesn't work that way," Rem said. "Come on, we need to focus. If we do this right, we might be able to make it disappear instead of just stopping it."

"You think so?"

"It's worth a shot."

"All right. Let's do this."

Heartened by their confidence, Billy watched as his friends delved into the flow of royal magic. At first, it seemed futile. The Abyss didn't respond to their attacks any more than an elephant would react to an ant. Then pinpricks of light formed amidst the blackness—tiny stars of hope that urged them to keep going. More holes filled the wall, growing larger and larger until they showed Billy a view of the other side.

There's land over there, he thought, excitement welling up inside him. *Maybe Grigoth didn't damage the Gloaming as badly as they thought.*

But as the Abyss melted into nothingness, his stomach sank. An ocean of ashes greeted them, stretching as far as the eye could see. Corvus dipped his sword into the chalky-gray flakes, burying it to the hilt. Frowning, he pulled back and wiped the blade clean on his greaves.

"It's at least four feet deep," he reported, re-sheathing his weapon.

"Probably a lot deeper, but we don't have a reliable way of measuring it."

"Can we fix it?" Rem asked. She raised a glowing hand, trying to lift the ashes into the air. Nothing happened.

"I guess not," Corvus said. "We might be able to clean it up with old-fashioned Earth tools, but I'm not sure it would be worth it. This is a dead space. There's no magic running through the soil anymore."

The news soured Billy's mouth, but he tried to look at the positives. *The Gloaming's safe now. No one's in danger of being wiped out by a giant shadow. And the wraiths still have miles and miles of usable land. They can rebuild. They can find a new normal.*

"Our parents wouldn't have given up so easily," Rem said. "They told us the Gloaming could be restored if an uncorrupted mage was on the throne. There must be a spell or something we can use. We just have to find it."

Corvus looked unconvinced, but he nodded. "Yeah, maybe you're right. We should look into it later. For now, though, I think we should head back to the castle. Our allies might need some help."

"That's fair," Rem conceded. "Ready, Billy?"

Billy gritted his teeth in anticipation. "Ready."

He felt a sharp tug behind his belly button, and the next thing he knew, he was standing in the middle of a cavernous room. Dark gray stone lined the walls and floor, and an obsidian throne with harsh edges rested in the far corner. In the center of the room, an enormous tarpaulin covered the floor. A lone wraith huddled beside it, his eyes despondent.

"Volner!" Corvus called out, raising his hand in greeting. "Is everything under control here?"

Volner's eyes widened. "Where did *you* come from?"

"Grigoth is dead. Rem and I inherited his power. We decided to teleport in," Corvus explained. "What's going on with Grigoth's soldiers? Have they stopped fighting?"

"You killed him?" Volner's voice rose a couple of pitches. Corvus gave him a pointed look, and he swallowed. "Right. Of course. I knew you could do it all along."

"So about those soldiers," Rem said, steering the conversation back on track. "Do you know if they've laid down their weapons yet?"

"They have. They surrendered right after you left. It was the strangest thing too. There were only six of us left—me, Chardein, and four laborers—and close to fifty of them. One minute they were charging at us, and the next they were kneeling on the ground, sliding their weapons to the front of the room. I've never seen anything like it. Why would they give up when they have the advantage?"

"They didn't want to fight you in the first place," Corvus said. "As soon as Grigoth left, they wouldn't have felt obligated to continue. The same thing happened on Earth when Grigoth died."

"Where's Chardein?" Rem asked.

"I don't know," Volner said. "He and the laborers have been wandering the halls for the past few hours, healing everyone who needs it and fetching the bodies of our fallen allies." He glanced at the tarpaulin. "I wanted to go with them, but he told me to stay here and guard the dead."

"That's an important job too," Corvus said, following the boy's gaze. "All of these men and women are heroes, and we should honor their sacrifice. I'll send a message to the undertaker and see if we can hold the funerals before sundown."

"Here at the castle?" Rem asked.

"I think that would be for the best," Corvus said. "Blackbriar Cemetery is all but abandoned because of how remote it is, and they deserve better than that. We've got more land than we need, and their headstones will serve as a constant reminder of what we sacrificed to get here."

"All right. I'll mark out an area for it," Rem said.

She hurried away with long, loping strides, eager to get started. Seeing the wraiths so solemn and pragmatic made Billy acutely aware of his status as the third wheel. This wasn't his home. He didn't have a say in what happened. But all the talk of funeral arrangements pushed his thoughts in a dangerous direction. *What if Mom and Dad are busy planning Hamish's funeral while I'm stuck here?*

"I want to go home," he blurted out, interrupting whatever Volner was saying. The boy's mouth snapped shut, and he looked to Corvus for support.

"I know you do, Billy, but it's not a good idea at the moment," Corvus said. "The portal is sealed—"

"So unseal it. You're the king. You can do whatever you want."

"Not today. You're tired. We're tired. The castle's a mess. The whole dimension's a mess. There are funerals that need to take place. Morton is all but burned to the ground. You don't have a home to go to anymore."

"But my family—"

"They'll be fine. I know you want to be with them, but you're better off staying here for now. We'll take you back to the portal tomorrow, after you've had some rest. Okay?"

Billy sighed, defeated. "Okay. Where am I supposed to sleep?"

"I'll show you to one of the guest rooms," Corvus said. He turned to Volner. "Will you be all right here?"

"Yeah. No problem."

"Good man. I'll be back in a minute."

Eyelids drooping, Billy let Corvus guide him into the corridor. The temperature dropped several degrees, drawing goosebumps to his skin. They traversed two flights of stairs and stopped outside a wooden door. The door swung open of its own accord, revealing a sumptuous bedroom suite.

"Well, this is it," Corvus said, maneuvering Billy over the threshold. "There's a charmed bell in the corner if you want someone to come and get you when you're done sleeping."

"Thanks," Billy said. He dumped his backpack on the ground and collapsed onto the four-poster bed. The mattress molded to his body, cushioning his aching muscles. "I'm going to lie here and not move for at least eight hours. See you in the morning, Corvus."

"It's already morning," Corvus pointed out in a bemused tone. "Sleep well, buddy."

Billy dozed off before the door clicked shut.

A faint *pop* drew Rem's gaze from the DIY graveyard to the courtyard entrance. Corvus staggered between the stone arches, his knees buckling under the weight of an elderly man.

"It's all right. We're here," Corvus said, trying and failing to extricate himself from the man's grip.

Rem hurried over to help. "Is that him?"

"Yup," Corvus said. The man regained his footing, tipping Corvus off-balance in the process. "Rem, this is Wolpeth, the undertaker. Wolpeth, this is Rem, my co-regent."

Wolpeth bowed low. "A great pleasure to meet you, Your Majesty."

"Please, call me Rem."

"If you insist, Rem."

"Wolpeth nearly got caught in the Oncoming Abyss," Corvus explained, shaking out his mussed jacket. "He was down in the catacombs when the fog closed in."

"It swallowed an entire section of the main passageway," Wolpeth rasped, his eyes wide. "Another couple of seconds and I would have been trapped down there for all eternity. I've never seen it move that fast before, and I've been monitoring it since it first appeared."

"That sounds terrifying," Rem sympathized. "It's a good thing we were able to stop it in time."

"You're telling me. Now all you have to do is fix the food shortage and every wraith in the Gloaming will be singing your praises."

"I know. That's our next priority," Corvus said. "We're heading out to the supply depot soon to get ration cubes for the laborers. We can get some for you as well if you want."

"That would be wonderful. I ate yesterday, but the trip here made me a bit lightheaded. I don't want to pass out in the middle of giving someone their last rites."

"We don't want that to happen either. The funeral ceremonies won't be for a few more hours, so you can relax in the meantime. Feel free to make yourself at home in the castle."

"Thank you, Your Majesty."

"Just Corvus is fine."

"As you wish." Wolpeth gave another swooping bow and hobbled up the stairs to the foyer.

What a strange man, Rem thought.

"It took me an hour to convince him to teleport with me," Corvus said, as if reading her mind. "He thought it was some kind of dark magic and that I was trying to curse him."

"Ah. That explains a lot."

"Does it?"

"The only wraiths who can teleport are Enforcers and the reigning monarch. He probably thought you were working for Grigoth."

"I told him Grigoth was dead."

"Yeah, but that's exactly what a Grigoth-loving Enforcer *would* say to lure someone in."

Corvus's forehead creased, drawing his eyebrows into adorable peaks. "You've been watching conspiracy videos on YouTube, haven't you?"

"Not in the past week."

"Yeah, well."

He moved closer, wrapping his arms around her waist. Rem nuzzled against his chest and closed her eyes, inhaling his scent. Sandalwood mingled with the subtle musk of sweat and cheap deodorant—not the most enticing smell in the world, but in that moment, she loved it anyway. It reminded her they were still alive.

"How's the graveyard coming along?" Corvus asked, his chest rumbling against her ear.

"It's pretty much done. I excavated some space for the memorial stones along the edges of the courtyard, and I made some fake flowers from the rubble. They're just like those wooden flowers we saw at the Academy. Oh, and I've got a team of volunteers carving the memorial stones as we speak."

"That's great. So you're ready to go?"

"Go where?"

"To the supply depot. We have to hand out rations, remember?"

"Right. Of course." Rem shook the mental fuzz from her head. "Sorry. I was thinking about the funeral."

"Oh." Corvus traced small circles on her back with his fingertips. A few seconds passed before he spoke. "Are you worried about it?"

Concern laced his voice, tugging at her heartstrings.

"A little," she admitted. "I've never been to a traditional wraith funeral before, but I've heard what happens at them. I don't want to watch our friends burn. Not after what Grigoth did."

"It won't be anything like Grigoth's fire," Corvus reassured her. "Wolpeth can vaporize their bodies in milliseconds. Turn them back to stardust and scatter their atoms across the universe. Much nicer than leaving a rotting corpse for some poor farmer to find, if you ask me."

"Yeah, I suppose you're right," Rem mused. Catching herself, she pulled back from Corvus and gave him a disapproving look. "You should be more careful about the way you phrase things. Irreverence isn't a very kingly trait."

"No, but it's the trait you love me for," Corvus said, batting his eyelashes at her. "Shall we go? I want to get the food situation squared away as quickly as possible."

"I'm ready when you are."

Animated chatter roused Billy from his slumber. He rolled over, a soft groan issuing from his throat. The glow of werelights wormed behind his eyelids. *What time is it?* In the windowless bedchamber, it was impossible to tell, but his watch suggested it had been a few hours since

Corvus left. The voices outside his door grew fainter as the wraiths walked away, but Billy couldn't go back to sleep. With a yawn, he heaved himself into a sitting position.

A mahogany wardrobe lined the back wall of the room, braced by two small end tables. The one on the left bore a transparent washbasin half-filled with steaming water. A fluffy white towel rested beside it. The table on the right held nothing but an ornate handbell. Billy shambled over to the basin first, trying to scrub some warmth into his sleep-chilled limbs.

Once he'd shed the dirt of battle, he rifled through his bag for some fresh clothes. Most of the garments he'd brought with him were damp and musty, but he managed to salvage a pair of track pants. Dressing his top half proved more difficult, so he abandoned his bag and threw open the wardrobe.

Robes, tunics, hoodies, and jeans of all sizes hung side by side, blending modern and traditional styles. Billy grabbed the smallest hoodie—a plain black number—and pulled it over his head. It was baggier than he liked but thick enough to stave off the cold.

Stomach growling, Billy shouldered his backpack and headed out the door. Corvus said the bell would summon someone to help him find his way around the castle, but he didn't need help. The only place he wanted to go was the kitchens, and he knew how to get there by himself.

No wraiths walked the corridors during his descent, but wherever they were, they'd done an exceptional job of cleaning up after the battle. Devoid of blood and debris, the gray floors shone like silver, and the windows sparkled like diamonds.

Voices emanated from the kitchen when he arrived, both familiar and unfamiliar. He knocked twice and went in. Corvus and Rem perched on the countertop, nursing mugs of something that smelled like honeyed tea. The oldest wraith Billy had ever seen reclined in a leather armchair opposite them.

"You're awake," Corvus said.

"Surprisingly." Billy closed the door behind him. "How long was I out?"

"Close to sixteen hours."

"Did I miss the funeral?"

"By a few hours, yeah. We tried to wake you, but you were really out of it."

"I'm sorry."

"No need to apologize. It's been a long time since you've gotten any real sleep." Corvus gestured to the elderly wraith with his free hand. "This is Wolpeth, the undertaker. He's going to be staying with us until we get Lothaire and Darthan's bodies back for burial. Wolpeth, this is my friend, Billy."

"Another human?" Wolpeth rasped. His gaze roved the air, never settling in one place for more than a second. "Thank you for your service, Billy."

"Uh, you're welcome," Billy said, blinking off his surprise. "Did you say there are other humans here?"

"Not here, no," Wolpeth corrected. "Three younglings came to visit me a few days ago at Blackbriar Cemetery. Two human lads and a wraith. Determined young fellows. Wanted to know all about music-based magic and wouldn't take no for an answer."

Billy's heart sank. "Do you remember their names?"

"I'm afraid not. Names are one of the first things to go when you get to my age."

"Was Hamish one of them?"

"I really couldn't say."

Billy's throat tightened. "I told him to stay out of it."

"It could have been anyone," Corvus said, but his words held no weight. "Even if it *was* Hamish, that doesn't mean anything. Your parents said James was with him when Grigoth attacked, and James survived. Hamish probably did too."

Billy folded his arms to hide the way they trembled. "Jarsha didn't."

Rem hopped down from the countertop, set her mug aside, and

embraced Billy. A wild surge of emotions flooded through him, pushing a few tears from his eyes before he managed to rein them in. He wiped the evidence away with his sleeve.

"Come on," she murmured. "I'll take you to the portal."

Electricity enveloped his skin before he could protest, forcing his eyes shut. Tingles raced up and down his spine, and then he was blinking and gasping for air in a leafless forest. The portal lay in wait, dark as ever but emitting a scent as clean and crisp as the first snowfall of winter. He tried to step into the lake, but Rem held fast to his sleeve.

"Billy... I know this isn't the best time, but I need to tell you something."

"What is it?"

Rem released him and wrapped her arms around herself. "Corvus and I were talking while you were asleep. It's going to take a few weeks for everything to settle down here, but now that we're king and queen, there's nothing to stop us from reinstating our Promising spell." Lilac suffused her cheeks, her lips parting in a radiant smile. "Corvus and I are getting married."

Of all the things Rem could have said, this was the least expected.

"Oh, wow. Congratulations!" Billy tried to inject some enthusiasm into his voice. "You always said you would do that if we defeated Grigoth, and now we have."

"Yup. Formal wedding ceremonies are unheard of in the Gloaming, but I think it's important we have one, especially in light of recent events. We'd be honored if you could step in as Corvus's best man."

"I... yeah, of course."

"Your family would be welcome too. Even your dad."

"Are you sure that's a good idea? What would Corvus say?"

"It was his idea, believe it or not. He's been a lot more reflective since the battle ended than he usually is. Both of our parents are dead now, but you guys shared a family for three years. As much as he hated hiding who he was, he enjoyed spending time with your mom and dad, just being a normal kid. He still thinks of them as family, and he wants to make things right with them.

"So many people have died in the past few days, both human and wraith. Life's too short to hold grudges. And considering we saved your dad's life in battle, we thought he might be willing to at least try."

"I don't know…"

"It's not like I'm asking him to walk me down the aisle," Rem persisted. "All I'm asking you to do is talk to him."

Billy wrinkled his nose. "Yeah, the aisle thing might be pushing it a bit far. I'll talk to him, but I can't promise anything."

"Thank you," Rem said, crushing him in a brief hug. "I'm sorry to spring this on you when you've already got a lot on your plate, but we might not see each other for a few weeks. I thought it was better to tell you in person rather than through the notebook."

"I understand," Billy said. He backed into the water, wincing as it soaked into his socks.

"Let me know as soon as you hear anything about Hamish, okay?"

"Yeah. I will."

Rem raised her arms in the air, a sad smile playing across her lips. Her face was the last thing he saw before the world faded and a tidal wave of magic carried him back to Earth.

Chapter Sixty-Four

THE NOONDAY SUN shone on Morton Park, gilding the dew-soaked grass and bathing Billy's skin in warmth. Miry water sucked at his ankles, cold and slimy against the sliver of exposed skin. Grimacing, he trudged up the banks to freedom. The fence around Oilskin Lake lay in pieces, the posts shattered and the chain coiled up like a snake.

A large black box sat two feet away from the post nearest Billy, tempting him to investigate. *That wasn't there last night, was it?* His memory banks were too scrambled to remember, but he approached the box anyway. *What is that? A guitar amp? What's it doing here?* Behind the amplifier, he spied a rainbow-colored rectangle. Hardly daring to breathe, Billy picked it up. It was Hamish's toy keyboard.

He jerked upright, dropping the instrument. *Why would he bring this here? And why did he leave it behind? Because he had to run away in a hurry? Or because Grigoth ate him?* Something else nagged at the back of his mind, something important, but he couldn't put his finger on it. Then it dawned on him. *Jarsha's body is gone. They couldn't have buried him already, could they?*

Billy's feet hit the tarmac before he realized he was running. Burnt-down houses lined the streets, their gaping wounds all the more horrifying in the cold light of day. As far as he could tell, no bodies lay amongst the wreckage. He slowed to a walk as he entered his home street, his lungs frozen in anticipation. In the absence of his thundering footsteps, an eerie silence smothered the town, making it easy to imagine himself as the last person on Earth. His heart beat in his ears as the tin roof of his house came into view. The center dipped, but it hadn't caved in.

The weatherboard facade had been stripped down to the insulation, the front door blown off its hinges. Red and yellow tape formed an X over the empty frame, warning him of the danger inside. He ignored it and ducked under the flimsy barrier. Exposed beams jutted from the ceiling like broken bones. Keeping his head down, he picked his way through the rubble to his room. Something heavy blocked him from opening the door more than an inch, but a swift shoulder-charge soon changed that. *What's another dented door when the whole house is on the verge of collapse?*

Having gained access, he knelt next to the fractured remains of his dresser. He pushed aside shards of wood and scraps of burnt clothing to retrieve his cell phone. The plastic case was scuffed and half-melted, but he pressed the power button anyway. Colors swirled across the screen, accompanied by a welcoming chirp. Billy breathed a sigh of relief. More than three hundred missed call notifications lit up his phone, all from his parents. Chewing his lip, he speed-dialed his mother. She picked up on the second ring, her voice tremulous.

"Billy? Is that you? Where are you?"

"Yeah, it's me. I'm at the house. Where's Hamish? Have you found him?"

"We'll be right there, honey. Stay where you are, and don't go inside. It's not safe."

Too late for that, Billy thought. "Is Hamish with you?"

"H—"

The connection fizzled into static and cut out altogether with three distorted beeps. A frustrated scream tore from his throat, and he hurled his phone at the wall. The screen shattered and went black. People always said no news was good news, but in this case, he didn't believe it.

He left the phone where it fell and retreated to the lounge. The cloying stench of rotting fruit wafted toward him, weaving its way through base notes of smoke and burning wood. Photo frames littered the floor, each holding precious memories of his family. He picked up the nearest one, a lump forming in his throat.

Hundreds of cracks spidered across the glass, but he knew the picture well enough to make it out. James, Hamish, and a younger version of himself sat on a Texan beach, next to a three-foot-high sandcastle. Grins lit up their expressions, bright enough to give their fluorescent board shorts a run for their money. It had been a simpler time then. The tide had swept their creation out to sea while they slept, but an hour was all it took to rebuild it, bigger and better than ever.

If only it were that easy to rebuild our lives, Billy thought, placing the picture back amongst the rubble.

Sniffling, he stumbled to the front door, swooped under the tape, and trudged across the dead lawn. When he reached the curb, he plunked himself down and hugged his knees. *Please let them show up soon. Please let Hamish be safe.*

He heard the rumble of the pickup before he saw it. When the rusted vehicle came within twenty feet of him, it screeched to a halt and the doors flew open. Mr. and Mrs. Porter jumped out of the front, James from the back. All three collided with him at once, knocking the air out of his lungs. The embrace brought tears to his eyes, but he refused to indulge in it for long.

"Where's Hamish?" Billy demanded.

Mr. Porter stepped back, his gray eyes stormy. He shook his head, the gesture so small it was almost imperceptible, and his wife burst into sobs. Billy's stomach dropped to his feet.

"We buried him yesterday," Mr. Porter said. "We wanted to wait 'til you got back, but we didn't know how long you'd be gone. Your phone was off."

Grief choked Billy's voice. "I was only gone for a day."

"You were gone a whole week!" Mrs. Porter cried. "We thought you were never coming back."

"It was only a day from my perspective," Billy repeated. His throat felt raw, hoarse. *The time fluctuations have never been that extreme for short trips before.* "I absorbed Grigoth's power when he died. I had to go back to the Gloaming to get rid of it."

For a long moment, no one said anything. Then Mr. Porter cleared his throat. "Are you… all right now?"

"I don't have any wraith powers, if that's what you mean."

"No, I…" Mr. Porter paused and shook his head. "Never mind. Do you want to see Hamish's grave?"

"Yes, please."

They all bundled into the car, James scrubbing at his face to hide the onslaught of tears. Guilt tugged at Billy. *I was so busy worrying about Hamish I didn't even think about him. He probably thought I was dead this whole time too.* The road unfurled before them like a gray ribbon, twisting and winding its way through the countryside. No one spoke for the duration of the journey, too wrapped up in their own thoughts to compete with the engine noise.

After twenty minutes, Mr. Porter pulled over, and they clambered out. As a group, they passed through the brick gates of Richfield Cemetery. Mr. Porter led the way across the stubbled grass and stopped in front of a small, cambered headstone.

Musical notes decorated the granite, surrounding Hamish's name and photo. A fresh bouquet of forget-me-nots rested at the base. Billy knelt in front of it, unmoving. The rest of his family stood a few paces back, locked in a three-way embrace. It unnerved him to think Hamish's body was six feet beneath him—so close, yet so far away. He wondered what his youngest brother looked like at the funeral. Calm and peaceful? Or burnt badly enough to warrant a closed casket?

"I'm sorry, Hamish," Billy murmured.

He rose to his feet and shook the pins and needles from his legs. The mere thought of leaving disgusted him, but he couldn't ignore the windchill gnawing at his bones.

"Rescuers found him in a church," Mrs. Porter said when Billy rejoined them. Sniffles punctuated her speech. "The ceiling collapsed on top of him. Crushed his chest. The coroner said it would have been very quick. He didn't suffer before the end."

Billy nodded, unsure of how to comfort her. "I'm glad he didn't suffer."

They lingered a few more minutes, then trudged back to the car, their cheeks flushed with cold. Mr. Porter punched the heater on and pulled a strange conch-shaped object from the glove box.

"They found Hamish holding this," he said, handing it to Billy. "Does it mean anything to you?"

Billy turned it over in his hands, studying the transparent cabochons. "I've never seen it before. Did he take it from the church?"

James glared at him with bloodshot eyes. "He didn't steal it. Jarsha gave it to him."

Stunned by his brother's renewed capacity for speech, it took Billy a few seconds to respond. "What is it?"

A choked sob escaped James's lips and he turned away, leaning his forehead against the window.

"He's been too upset to tell us what Hamish was doing with it," Mrs. Porter explained. "The only thing we've been able to get out of him is that it belongs to a wraith called Wolbeth."

"Wol*peth*," James corrected, his voice stuffy with mucus.

"The undertaker? I met him at the castle this morning," Billy said.

"Can you get it back to him?" James asked.

"Yeah, I'll do that," Billy promised. He tucked the object into his bag as Mr. Porter started the engine. A myriad of questions buzzed through his mind, but he settled on the easiest one. "Where are we going now?"

"Back to Richfield Motor Inn," Mrs. Porter said. "We'll be living there until we find a suitable place to rent."

"We're not going back to Morton?"

"I don't think so, honey. The whole town is wrecked. It could be years before it's habitable again."

"But I need to be close to the lake," Billy protested. *The magic notebook won't work in Richfield. It's too far away.*

"Well, I'm sure you can visit it from time to time," Mrs. Porter said. "We've all been through a very stressful experience, and the best thing we can do right now is settle down. Bring some stability to our lives. Richfield ticks all the boxes."

"I suppose," Billy mumbled. *I'll find a way to contact Corvus and Rem, no matter what. In the meantime, I need to stay positive.* "Zane lives in Richfield. Maybe I can hang out with him again."

A heavy silence fell between them.

"I'm sorry, Billy. His name was on the list of the dead."

Billy froze. "That's impossible. He wasn't in Morton."

"Apparently, he was." Mrs. Porter rummaged through her handbag and gave him a rolled-up newspaper. "You can check it for yourself if you want to."

He unrolled the paper—a community rag that smeared ink all over his hands—and opened it to the first page. Every name hit him like a punch to the gut. Zane Williams. Murdock Smith. Shauna Davies. Jeffrey Bancroft. Hamish's piano teacher, Lynne Price. More and more names he recognized, both from Morton High School and the broader community. He might not have gotten along with all of them, but that didn't mean they deserved to die.

"Did *anyone* survive?" Billy asked.

"The people who obeyed the evacuation order did," Mrs. Porter replied. "As for everyone else… I'm not sure. The *Richfield Chatter* said that seventy survivors were pulled out of the rubble, but not all of them made it to the hospital alive."

Numb, Billy flipped to the next page. The headline stared up at him in bold, defiant print. *Dragon Hoax Goes Too Far, Kills Hundreds.*

"What is *wrong* with people these days?" he exclaimed, unable to stop himself. "They think what happened in Morton was a *hoax?*"

"Disgusting, ain't it?" Mr. Porter said. "The TV coverage is even worse. They keep saying Grigoth's corpse was an art installment and that we're a bunch of crazy people who lit our own town on fire."

Billy shook his head in disbelief. "Journalists shouldn't report on things they don't know anything about."

"Exactly!" Mrs. Porter joined in. "The news is a bunch of lies these days. All of it. What happens if another dragon-wraith comes rampaging across the planet? If people think it's a hoax, they won't run when they need to. We'll have a repeat of Morton."

"True, but I don't think that will happen," Billy said. "Rem and Corvus sealed the portal. They won't let anyone or anything cross it. Not without setting up safeguards first."

"When you say Corvus, you mean our Corey, don't you?" Mrs. Porter asked.

"Yup. He and Rem have taken over from Grigoth as co-regents. He's *king* of the Gloaming now. I've been telling you from the start that not all wraiths are the same. Corvus… Corey is a great wraith. One of the best."

"That's directed at me, ain't it?" Mr. Porter asked, his tone glum. When Billy didn't answer, the man eyed him in the rearview mirror. "Don't spare my feelings. I wasn't… I wasn't the father he needed. I should've stuck by him. I should've *listened* when you said he was a good person. If I hadn't brushed you off, if I hadn't said all those horrible things, maybe you boys would have trusted me. Maybe you would have told me what was going on instead of trying to fight Grigoth by yourselves. Maybe Hamish would still be alive."

"Don't blame yourself, dear," Mrs. Porter said.

"He *should* blame himself," Billy interrupted, stunning his mother into silence. "How else is he going to learn if he doesn't remember what this moment feels like?" He paused, shaking with grief. "If you hadn't talked about killing our friends all the time, we wouldn't have had to sneak around behind your back. Hamish wouldn't have fought."

"I know," Mr. Porter said quietly. "I'm a failure of a father."

His candidness shocked Billy back to his senses. "No, no. I went too far. I'm sorry. You're not a failure. I shouldn't have blamed you. You made mistakes, but you didn't kill Hamish. That was all on Grigoth."

Mr. Porter's jaw clenched. "No. You were right to criticize me. After Heather died, I shut down, and you suffered for it. I'm sorry for that, Billy. James, I'm sorry to you too. I'd apologize to Hamish and Corey if I could, but it's too late now. I can't say it to their faces."

"It might be too late for Hamish, but it's not too late for Corvus. You can still tell him."

"How? I thought he went back to his own world."

"He did, but he can visit Earth whenever he wants. Also, he, uh… invited you to his wedding."

"He… what?" The pickup swerved, and Mr. Porter fought to bring it under control. "Why would he do that?"

"You can ask him yourself once you've apologized."

Thoughtful silence stretched between them. After a while, Mr. Porter coughed and loosened his collar. Hope softened his steel-gray eyes.

"I don't deserve another chance after the things I said to him. But if there's anything I can do to make up for it, I'll do it. Anything at all."

Chapter Sixty-Five

CHRISTMAS CAME EARLY for the Porters that year. After three weeks of intense negotiation, their insurance company buckled to media pressure. The family was reimbursed for the full market value of their house, along with some extra money to replace the things they lost.

James spent his portion on clothes and furniture for his new room. Billy—having grown used to his limited wardrobe and lumpy mattress—bought a moped. Mrs. Porter begged him to return it, denouncing it as a "death trap on wheels," but Billy turned a deaf ear. Riding through the countryside filled him with a profound sense of peace, and the practical benefits outweighed any dangers.

He visited Hamish's grave several times a week, sitting in silence while the wind blustered through the trees. Twice, he picked wildflowers and placed them next to the wilting forget-me-nots. Most of his trips, though, were to Oilskin Lake.

As expected, the distance between Morton and Richfield was too great for the magic notebook to overcome, so he returned every afternoon to chat with Corvus and Rem. He talked to them about Hamish, his surviving family, and coming to terms with life in Richfield. In return, they kept him up to date on their exploits in the Gloaming.

They'd abolished every trace of blood oath magic since Billy left, choosing to rely on their energy shields for safety instead. It was a risky move, but they couldn't justify taking away their subjects' agency like Grigoth did. So far, no one had tried to attack them or cause mischief.

The food situation had also improved somewhat. While not plentiful, ration cubes were handed out as needed, and the fields were prepared for new crops. Rem and Corvus strove to heal the Abyss-damaged areas of the Gloaming too, hoping to create extra space for planting, but to no avail. Every time Billy asked them about it, their replies grew terser, and he soon stopped mentioning it altogether.

Instead, he cheered them up with news of his father's change of heart. Exclamation marks littered an entire page of the notebook in response, written by both Rem and Corvus. Despite her earlier joking, Rem asked him if Mr. Porter would be willing to walk her down the aisle since her own father couldn't. Much to Billy's surprise, the man had agreed.

From that moment on, their wedding plans became a frequent topic of conversation, ranging from the decorations (tinsel and indoor fireworks) to the food (ration cubes disguised as red velvet cake) to the guest list (every wraith in the Gloaming).

Billy stood by the portal now, with his parents hanging back next to the road. Corvus had promised to pick them up at ten-thirty, but whether he would arrive on time was anyone's guess. Billy glanced at his watch. *Two minutes to go.*

According to Rem, time fluctuations shouldn't be a problem anymore. They'd been caused by massive energy surges, both from Grigoth's corruption and the repeated transfers of power. The energy surges had rebounded between the two worlds, shorting out the connection between them. With the Gloaming stabilized, its timestream should synch up with Earth's for the first time in a century.

Electricity whined through the air, bringing goosebumps to Billy's skin. Moments later, Corvus materialized in the shallows of the lake. He scrambled up the banks, careful not to get mud on his tuxedo. Although the ends of his trousers had been underwater, they didn't look wet.

"You made it!" Billy exclaimed.

Corvus's lips parted in a timorous smile. "Of course I made it."

They collided in a crushing embrace, and six weeks of tension melted from Billy's body. His friend was back. He wasn't alone anymore.

"How are you doing?" Corvus asked, pulling away to examine him. Concern swam through his liquid purple eyes. "I know we've talked through the notebook, but it's not the same."

"I'm all right," Billy told him honestly. "Things have been difficult, but I'm coping."

"I'm glad."

Billy inclined his head toward the portal. "Where's your bride-to-be on this fine morning?"

"Busy holding court."

"On her wedding day?"

"No rest for the wicked." Corvus glanced at Billy's parents. "Shall we go and fetch the rest of your family?"

"Sure," Billy agreed. "James isn't here, by the way. I tried to convince him to come, but he flat-out refused. He said he'd never set foot in Morton again as long as he lives."

Corvus bit his lip. "Ah. Yeah. That's understandable. Maybe we'll see him another time?"

"I hope so."

Mrs. Porter rushed to greet them, her arms spread wide. Corvus slowed but couldn't avoid being smothered in a maternal hug. "Corey, sweetheart. How are you?"

"I'm fine, thanks. How are you?"

"Good, good." Mrs. Porter pulled back and beamed at him. "Look at you. You've really grown up."

"Yup. That's what teenagers do," Corvus joked, stifling a nervous laugh. When her husband entered his field of vision, his mirth vanished. "Hello, sir."

"How many times," Mr. Porter said, "do I have to tell you to call me Jerry?"

Surprise flitted across Corvus's face as his former foster father wrapped him in a hug. After some tentative backslapping from both parties, the man stepped back to give him space.

"I, uh…" Corvus paused and cleared his throat. "I heard you'll be walking Rem down the aisle today."

"If that's what you want, then I'd be honored to," Mr. Porter said, bowing his head. "But before we do anything else, I owe you an apology." He met Corvus's eyes, shifting his weight from foot to foot before locking his legs straight. "From the bottom of my heart, I am so, so sorry for the way I treated you, Corey. What I said and did to you was inexcusable. I know there ain't nothing I can say to make up for it, but I promise I'll do everything in my power to earn your forgiveness."

Relief flashed across Corvus's face, so palpable it looked like he might fall over. "All right. I accept your apology."

"Just like that?"

"Life's too short to hold grudges. After what happened with Hamish, I'm sure you feel the same."

Mr. Porter nodded, tears filling his eyes. His voice was soft when he spoke again. "If I hadn't been so bullheaded about wraiths, a lot of things would be different. Hamish might still be alive, and we'd be celebrating the seven-year anniversary of you joining our family. I've lost two of my children in the past twenty years, and there ain't nothing I can do to bring them back. But so long as there's breath in my lungs, I won't lose another. I won't lose you."

White satin sheets hung from the ballroom ceiling, softening the castle's stone walls. Multi-colored orbs danced amongst the well-wishers, reflecting off people's jewelry and the tinsel overhead. Billy stood at the front of the room, one step behind Corvus's right shoulder. Curious eyes bored into his skull, but his discomfort didn't last long. The acapella choir rose to their feet, their voices blending in a unique rendition of the wedding march. Every person in the building twisted in their seats to catch a glimpse of the bride.

Rem walked down the aisle in measured steps, resplendent in her cream-white gown. Pride welled up inside Billy. She'd been like a sister to him through the years. Not the sister fate stole from him, but every bit as important. Mr. Porter guided her forward in time with the music, careful not to bump her bouquet. Although she'd been unable to import flowers in time for the ceremony, Rem had charmed some ribbons into the shape of roses. No matter how long Billy stared at them, he couldn't tell them apart from the real thing.

He snuck a glance at Corvus. A grin stretched across his friend's face, so wide it verged on cheesy.

Good for you, buddy, Billy thought. *After everything you've been through, you deserve to be happy. You both do.*

Rem reached the end of the aisle and slipped her hand into Corvus's. A waist-high altar lay before them, draped with a sleek white tablecloth. In the center, a gold filigree stand boasted a pair of crystal flasks.

Volner emerged from a side room in sumptuous purple robes. The wraith stood tall and regal, his walk purposeful. He looked like he'd been a marriage celebrant for years rather than a few short days. Having fulfilled his duty, Mr. Porter took a seat in the front row, leaning forward to make sure he didn't miss anything.

"Welcome, ladies and gentlemen," Volner intoned. "We have gathered here today to witness the bonding of Corvus Seisansson and Rem Lothairesdaughter. Although ceremonies of this ilk are highly irregular in the Gloaming, the beloved couple hope you will accept theirs in the spirit with which it is conducted. They do not aim to emulate human traditions for tradition's sake, but rather to publicize the vows that most choose to keep private.

"They offer this freely so that all might know they share a unified stance, both as bondmates and as co-regents. Does anyone present object to this?"

No one spoke, their eyes riveted on Volner.

"Very well," Volner said. "Corvus Seisansson, do you take Rem Lothairesdaughter to be your lawful bondmate? Do you promise to love, serve, and protect her to the best of your ability, both in life and in death? Furthermore, do you promise to help her to make wise decisions and assist her as she rules over the Gloaming?"

Corvus squared his shoulders, radiating pride. "I do."

"And do you, Rem Lothairesdaughter, take Corvus Seisansson to be your lawful bondmate? Do you promise to love, serve, and protect him to the best of your ability, both in life and in death? Furthermore, do you promise to help him to make wise decisions and assist him as he rules over the Gloaming?"

Rem's eyes shone. "I do."

"Please step forward to the altar."

Corvus and Rem obeyed, their backs to the congregation. Volner presented a ceremonial dagger to Corvus, who made a small incision at the base of his thumb. Corvus held his hand above one of the flasks and allowed a single drop of blood to spill into it. Rem mirrored his actions with the other flask. Once they were done, Volner cleansed the blade with a quick spell and secreted it into the folds of his robe.

"Please join hands," he instructed.

Corvus and Rem pressed their injured palms together. A purple glow enveloped them as they healed each other's wounds.

"By the power vested in me by the kingdom, I now pronounce you lawful bondmates."

Rem and Corvus leaned in without being told, their lips meeting in a soft kiss. The orbs illuminating the room burst into thousands of luminous sparks.

Those must be the indoor fireworks Rem was talking about, Billy thought, watching them with awe.

Although the kiss had ended, the fireworks showed no signs of slowing down. They twirled across the ceiling, showering guests in all the colors of the rainbow. The choir launched into another dreamy melody, their voices echoing off the walls. Volner bowed to the new bondmates and ferried their precious blood-flasks into one of the side rooms.

"Let this be the last time Rem and I spill blood for any purpose,"

Corvus said, holding up his palm for the audience to see. "From now on, let there be peace and freedom for all."

The purple sun sank in the sky, ever closer to touching the horizon. Billy stood on the parapets of the castle, gazing out over the Gloaming. Corvus and Rem leaned on the stone railing to his left, still garbed in their wedding attire.

"So you're married now," Billy said. He shook his head, trying to process the enormity of the thought. "What's next? Kids?"

"Not for a while," Corvus said. "Ruling an entire kingdom is hard work, and things are going to be hectic for years to come. We could get the Hatchery to take care of our kids, but…" He shrugged. "We want to be there for them the same way our fathers were there for us."

"Exactly," Rem said. "Even in the future, we'll always be rulers first and parents second. Every wraith in the Gloaming is our responsibility, and we can't afford to take that lightly."

"That makes sense," Billy said. "Maybe by the time you do have a kid, the school exchange between Earth and the Gloaming will be up and running again. I could keep an eye on them for you."

Rem smiled. "I'm sure our future kids will be very excited to meet their Uncle Billy. I don't think we'll be letting *any* wraith cross the portal any time soon, though. I like the school system on Earth, and I think there's a lot our hatchlings could learn there, but it's too dangerous right now. I don't want anyone to be killed for their species."

Images from the TV news crossed Billy's mind, and he shivered. "That reminds me. Did you ever find out what was going on with the wraiths posing as humans? Were they killing people and taking their identities? Or did they develop a random glamour and work their way to the top like everyone else?"

"We don't know, and we probably never will," Rem said. "All of them are dead, even the ones who tipped off the media. For the sake of our sanity, I think it's best not to dwell on it."

"Yeah. Maybe you're right."

"Of course, that doesn't change the fact we need to deal with the fallout," Corvus said. "Billy… I have a favor to ask."

"What is it?"

"Will you help us by acting as an ambassador between our worlds?"

Billy blinked. "Me? But I barely know anything about what an ambassador does."

"You'll learn over time," Corvus reassured him. "In all honesty, there's no human I would trust more for the position."

"Well, duh." Billy rolled his eyes and gave him a friendly punch. "I'm the *only* human you trust."

"Ow!" Corvus rubbed his arm. "Assault on the king!"

Both boys dissolved into laughter, and Rem shook her head disapprovingly.

"The main issue we're facing at the moment is the food shortage," Corvus explained when they sobered. "We've been giving people as many ration cubes as they want, but our supplies are disappearing faster than we expected. Some of the laborers have volunteered to plant crops, but it's going to be a few months before we'll be able to harvest them. We'll need to import food from Earth in the meantime. Do you think you can help with that?"

"Won't it disintegrate, though?"

"Not anymore. Grigoth's rules lost their power when he died."

Billy rubbed his chin. "All right. I'll see what I can do. How much food are we talking about, by the way? Because it could get super expensive, super fast."

"Don't worry about the cost," Rem replied. "We sold the house before we left. Seisan's too. Dad's savings account is loaded from that, and we've got a fair amount of gold in the treasury. We'll make sure you have access to it."

"You expect me to walk into a supermarket and pay with gold?"

Corvus's eyes narrowed. "I can't tell if you're being serious or just messing with us."

"I'm messing with you. I'll sell the gold to a merchant and use the money to buy the food. My grandpa used to work with a gold merchant in Texas, so I'm sure I can get a good price for whatever you give me."

"And you'll order food from wholesalers, not from a supermarket, right?" Rem prompted.

"I'll have to do some research into which company is the best. But yeah, of course I will."

"That's what I like to hear," Corvus said. "See? You're doing a great job already. I'll have to give you a raise."

Billy squinted at him. "You mean you're actually going to pay me?"

"Of course I am. How else am I going to retain top talent?" Corvus winked.

"Now *I* can't tell if you're messing with *me*."

"I'm not. Being an ambassador is hard work, and it's going to take time away from other things you might want to do. Things like finishing school, working a normal human job, pursuing hobbies…"

"Rebuilding the town," Billy muttered.

"Exactly! We don't expect you to give up your time without compensation."

"Wow, okay. I didn't expect that, but I'll never say no to a bit of extra money," Billy said. They stood in comfortable silence while he mulled over his new position. "You've told me about the food situation, but what else do you want me to do? I know ambassadors try to negotiate peace, but I have no idea how to do that."

"Don't worry about anything but the food for now," Rem said. "It's going to be a long road to true peace, and I doubt it will happen within our lifetimes."

"There must be something extra you want help with."

Rem tucked a strand of hair behind her ear. "Not yet, but maybe in the future. You know how we were talking about the Abyss and how to deal with the aftermath? Well, it turns out I was right about there being a way to fix it. It's not a spell, though. It's a charmed object called a Genesis Kernel."

Billy blinked. "You want my help to use a charmed object?"

"No, that's not the issue," Corvus said. "We've found plenty of books in the castle library explaining how to use one, but we can't use what we don't have. Turns out, Grigoth planted one somewhere in Morton. We might need your help to find it."

"What does it look like?" Billy asked.

"Like Rem said, we're not looking for it at the moment. Our only priority is the food situation."

"I'm not going to spend all of my waking hours getting food for you, though. I could help you look for it in my spare time."

Rem smiled. "We appreciate your willingness to help, but that isn't going to work. It's only detectable with magic."

"You could always grant me magic powers again," Billy said, nudging her with his elbow.

"Do you really want them?" Corvus asked, his expression turning serious. "Because I'll give them to you if you do."

"Wait, really?"

"Sure. I don't think you'll be able to find the Kernel on your own, considering how big the town is, but maybe having magic will help you with household chores or something. That's why you originally wanted powers, isn't it?"

Excitement rose within Billy, but common sense kicked it back down. "Will it trigger another Oncoming Abyss?"

Corvus frowned. "I don't think so. Why would it?"

"Because I'm not supposed to have powers like that. You'd have to change the rules of magic to give them to me, wouldn't you?"

"I didn't think of it that way. If it did happen, it wouldn't be that much of an issue. As long as we reverse the spell straight away, the Abyss would disappear again."

Billy thought about it. As much as he loved magic, it had never helped him as much as he needed it to. And although it might save him time when cleaning his room, he didn't want to put the Gloaming back in danger.

"I really appreciate the offer, but I'll pass," Billy said. "Great power, great responsibility and all that. I can't abuse my ambassador privileges when I only just got the job."

"The original Spider-Man," Corvus quipped.

"What?"

"You were quoting Uncle Ben."

"I… yeah, I was. I can't believe you recognized it, Mr. I-Don't-Watch-Movies."

"What can I say? I'm full of surprises." Corvus rose to his feet. "Come on. We'd better head back down to your parents. It's getting late."

Billy and Rem followed him through the winding staircases back to the ballroom. The fireworks were still going strong, sending explosions of color across the white draperies. Most of the guests had left hours ago, but Mr. and Mrs. Porter remained in their seats, nibbling slices of cake.

"Ready to go?" Billy asked them.

"We're ready," Mrs. Porter answered, dusting the crumbs from her fingers. She turned to the wraiths. "Thanks for inviting us. We had a great time."

Rem inclined her head. "You're very welcome."

Corvus placed his hands on the adults' shoulders, and the three of them winked out of sight. Rem's teleporting spell caught Billy a second later, sweeping him through the weightless dark. They landed next to Corvus and the others at the portal.

Rem nudged Billy's arm. "Hey, soldier. Are *you* ready to go home?"

"I guess I'll have to be," Billy replied. "Are you ready to stay here in the Gloaming?"

"Not really, but I'll manage," Rem said. "It's been great spending time with you again, you know. I'm going to miss you."

"I'm going to miss you too. Both of you." He pulled the strange conch-shaped object from his pocket and handed it to her. "My parents said Hamish was found with this. I was supposed to return it to Wolpeth, but I didn't get the chance. Do you think you could bring it back to him for me?"

"I'll do that," Rem promised. As soon as she took it from him, the transparent gems turned purple. "What is this, anyway?"

"I wish I knew."

"It looks like a traditional wraith instrument," Corvus said, leaning forward to inspect it. "I read about a few different ones in the castle library. This one's called a versailliad. Apparently, if you touch the gems, it'll make noise." He brushed his fingers over the closest one, evoking a shrill squeal. "Sorry. I thought it would sound better than that."

"You probably just need to practice," Rem said. She touched the same gem, and a gentle burbling came out. "You know, it's weird. I've never seen something like this before, but it feels familiar somehow."

"It sounds familiar too," Billy said. "I'm sure I've heard it before. Remember that weird music during the battle?"

"Oh yeah!" Rem exclaimed, her eyes widening. "It does sound like that. I was wondering where I recognized it from."

"So Hamish was playing music instead of hiding. Why would he do that?"

"From what I've read, a versailliad can produce powerful magic if you play the right notes," Corvus said. "Wolpeth told us three boys came and asked him about music magic. Since you said this belongs to him, I'd say Hamish was trying to cast a spell of some kind."

"To defend himself?"

"Defend himself. Fight back. Something like that."

"But it didn't work."

"I wouldn't be so sure about that." Corvus took the versailliad and pressed it to his forehead. After half a minute, he lowered it and met Billy's gaze. "Think about it. When did the music stop? Right around the time electricity started working again. Maybe Hamish used the versailliad to fight the portal instead of the soldiers. If he did…"

"Then he's the reason we won," Rem finished. "Limiting Grigoth's power limited his shields. If Hamish hadn't used the versailliad, there's no way we could have killed Grigoth. Hamish was a hero."

Tears pricked Billy's eyes. "Of course he was. He was my brother."

"And our son," Mr. Porter added, wrapping an arm around his wife.

The five of them stood huddled together for a long time, mumbling reassurances. Corvus broke away first and tucked the instrument into his pocket.

"I'm sorry we have to leave each other on such a miserable note," Rem said.

"You have nothing to be sorry for," Billy told her. "It's a horrible situation, but I'm glad we could figure out what happened. At least now we have some closure."

"That's true. I'm glad Corvus and I could help in some small way."

Mr. and Mrs. Porter retreated to the edge of the lake, arm in arm, but Billy hesitated. "This is really it, huh?"

"For now, at least," Rem said. Without preamble, she and Corvus engulfed him in another hug. "We'll be working together, but I doubt we'll see each other as much as we did in school. We'll have to make the most of the times we can."

A lump rose in his throat. "Yeah. I guess you're right."

Corvus mumbled something, his words almost lost in the wool of Billy's blazer. "We'll be okay, won't we?"

"Yeah, we'll be okay," Billy said, looking over the landscape a final time. A slight breeze ruffled his hair, and he pulled his jacket tighter around himself. "We'll always be okay."

The wraiths released him, and he trudged into the lake, watching the midnight-purple water swallow his shoes. Electricity hummed through the air, dancing across his skin. In its power, he felt the truth of their parting words.

It really would be okay.

Maybe not today or tomorrow, but eventually, things would work out. In the meantime, their friendship would tide them over.

With a smile, Billy stepped through the portal and returned to Earth.

Note from the Author

Thank you for taking the time to read The Gloaming. If you liked it, please take a few minutes to write a short review. Even a couple of sentences can make a HUGE difference to authors who are trying to build their readership.

If you're interested in my other books, you can read them here: https://www.amazon.com/J.R.-Schuyler/e/B06WD7YZSC

You can also follow me on Twitter @jrschuyler1 to stay up to date with my latest projects.